7/19

LIKE
NEVER
AND
ALWAYS

LIKE NEVER AND ALWAYS

Ann Aguirre

TOR
TEEN

A TOM DOHERTY ASSOCIATES BOOK

New York

LIKE NEVER AND ALWAYS

Copyright © 2018 by Ann Aguirre

A Tor Teen Book
Published by Tom Doherty Associates
175 Fifth Avenue
New York, NY 10010

www.tor-forge.com

Tor® is a registered trademark of
Macmillan Publishing Group, LLC.

The Library of Congress Cataloging-in-Publication Data
is available upon request.

ISBN 978-0-7653-9758-4 (hardcover)
ISBN 978-0-7653-9761-4 (ebook)

Our books may be purchased in bulk for promotional,
educational, or business use. Please contact your local bookseller
or the Macmillan Corporate and Premium Sales Department
at 1-800-221-7945, extension 5442, or by email at
MacmillanSpecialMarkets@macmillan.com.

First Edition: July 2018

ıted in the United States of America

) 9 8 7 6 5 4 3 2 1

For Karen and Fedora.
Without your encouragement,
the stories might cease forever.

That time was like never, and like always.

—Pablo Neruda, from "You Will Remember"

LIKE
NEVER
AND
ALWAYS

I'm in the front with Nathan, and the radio's on. We're arguing about the name of the band like the fate of the world hangs in the balance. There's only silence from the back, but Clay and Morgan don't talk much when they're together. I may be an asshole for thinking so, but Clay's primary attraction probably isn't his beautiful mind. Though I don't completely support their hook-up, I admit it's fun—best friends dating brothers.

The wind whips my hair like angry fingers, but it feels good with the top down. Normally Clay wouldn't let Nathan drive his baby, a Corvair convertible that he's restoring, but he gave up his keys before we left Emma's party. Maybe two beers aren't enough to matter. Whatever. I'm enjoying the chance to ride shotgun. If I squint, the stars blur into lines of light. It's so quiet, no other cars for miles. Nathan flashes me a grin and steps on the gas. The Corvair leaps forward, more wind, more freedom.

"You're beautiful," he says.

For this moment, I feel like I am.

This moment, it's a shimmer, a heartbeat, his smile imprinting on my heart. The sweetness tightens my chest. If only time could stop.

But it doesn't.

The world crumples inward, spins sideways. Pain explodes in petal fragments, blood bright, hot, and vicious. Pinpricks of light fill me, spreading in my head into a white field. I can't see for the dark and the bright. Hurts to breathe. *I won't die like this. I won't.*

I can't speak. I'm falling. Flying? The agony flowers, becomes unbearable. I cut loose.

"Morgan!" Clay shouts.

This sucks. His voice can't be the last one I hear.

1

Something is beeping, and there's a Darth Vader sound, too.

Everything hurts. This is encouraging since I thought I was dead. My eyelids are too heavy and they won't open, but I flex my fingers to reassure myself they still work. Nothing. I try again, though my body feels like lead. This time, I manage a flicker of movement and it prompts an intake of breath from whoever else is in the room.

"Are you in there? Can you hear me?" That's Clay, sounding hoarse.

Why is he in my room? Where's Nathan? Morgan? Anyone would make more sense than Clay. We were never close, though we silently agreed to a mutual armistice once I started going out with Nathan. Terror slithers in me like a coiled, tentacle-thing, twisting until I have only this thought: *What if they didn't make it? What if it's just Clay and me?* That would explain why he's sitting with me, a sort of grisly survivor's solidarity.

No, that can't be true.

Clay sighs, and then he takes my hand. His fingers are hard and callused, completely unlike his brother's. "Your dad will be back soon. I made him go to the cafeteria. He's been here non-stop, not eating or sleeping."

Where's my mom? But there's something in my throat and I can't ask. Then it hits me; I'm on a breathing machine, probably waking up from a coma. Well, trying anyway. My body hasn't caught up to my mind yet. What if I have . . . what's it called? Locked-in syndrome.

It's too much. I'd rather go back into the dark, so I let go and fall.

Clay's voice recedes.

The next time I wake, my eyes snap open. It takes me a while to focus. The room is dim, apart from the low beam near the door and the illumination from the medical equipment. I'm alone, but the call button is within reach, provided my arms work. It takes me three tries, but I smack the device successfully.

The nurse comes quickly, a round-faced older woman in a scrub top covered in pink hearts, and cheerful fuchsia pants. "You must be scared, huh?"

I nod. There are so many questions, but I can't ask them. My throat hurts and I feel like throwing up. This tube needs to come out ASAP.

"I'll call the doctor and the respiratory therapist first thing. We'll check you out and if you're ready, we'll wean you from the ventilator. Want me to notify your family?"

I nod again. That's when I realize she's only asking me yes or no questions. That makes things easier, but I guess I should expect her to be a pro at this. I raise trembling hands to my face and am surprised to find it bandaged. Why that startles me, I'm not sure, but my body awareness isn't great at the moment. Certain aspects are muffled while other parts blaze with raw agony. I don't feel right, like my skin is too big or something.

"You're loopy," the nurse guesses. "Try not to worry. You've had a rough few days, but you came out of surgery strong and your dad says you're a fighter."

Where are my friends? I ask in my head. *What happened to everyone else?* I know Clay made it, at least I *think* I know. A pervasive memory separates from the murk of my foggy mind.

He's beside me, and it's dark. Clay is crying, his head resting on the bed beside my fingers. The IV stings my wrist, but I can still feel the hot plip of his tears on the back of my hand, like the inexorable drip keeping me alive.

Modern medicine is amazing.

And invasive.

Mute, I can't protest as a squadron of professionals do all kinds of tests. But I'm pleased with their conclusion by the time the hospital is bustling with shift change; they've decided I'm ready to come off the artificial breathing apparatus. Apparently the one I've been using pushes back into my lungs so I don't lose capacity or something. I don't understand it all, and they talk about waiting for my dad. I'm a minor, and I don't know if they need permission, or if it's more of a courtesy, like he wouldn't want to miss the big un-tubing.

The door opens as the doctor, nurse, and respiratory specialist are confabbing. I recognize the man standing there, but he's *not* my dad. This is Mr. Frost, my best friend's dad. Horror crawls through me. Morgan and me, we don't look anything alike. How bad was the accident? Maybe . . . her face was too beat up for them to tell? And *mine, too*? But that hardly makes sense because she's six inches taller. The grisly thought occurs to me that maybe her body was damaged, dismembered, even, so—

Oh my God, no. I can't let myself think about it.

Even our names put us in different camps: Olivia Burnham and Morgan Frost. Clearly her parents took one look at her and thought, *This kid will be incredibly cool, might as well name her for it.* Any popularity I've enjoyed has come since we made friends when comic book nerd Ed Keller said we should because then we could form the crime-fighting duo of Frost and Burn. To quote an old movie with a sad ending, that was the start of a beautiful friendship. She's the trendsetter, the one who finds the coolest music before anyone else and decides when people should stop wearing things or adopt a new look, usually something fresh in Tokyo or Paris.

They don't know who I am.

There are no words for the horror washing over me like the sluggish lap of dark water against the lip of the quarry where we aren't supposed to swim. I get a little frantic, but they misinterpret my response and so I get a lecture about exactly what they're going to do to me. That's worse than if they just removed the tube right away. Morgan's dad is hovering, the circles beneath his eyes pronounced. He should know by *my* eyes. I'm looking right at him, trying to tell him with telepathy but he never flickers. Instead he mistakes my stare for fear so he murmurs reassuring nothings as the medical team gets to work.

When they finish, I'm breathing on my own. It feels weird and my throat hurts, but it's not as bad as I expected. From what I remember, strep was like knives whereas this is residual soreness and a dry, rough feeling. I swallow a couple of times experimentally and I show how awesome I am by not throwing up.

"You're doing great," the nurse says.

"What day is it?" Of the hundred questions teeming in my brain, that one pops out first in a voice so rough that it doesn't sound like mine. Or Morgan's, for that matter.

Nobody seems surprised.

Mr. Frost answers. "Thursday."

Almost a week. We were out Friday night, two weeks before school started. Well, for Nathan, Morgan, and me, anyway. Clay already lives like he's grown, doing shit that earned him the notoriety that made people steer clear even before he dropped out. In different ways, the Claymore boys both have reputations; teachers projected remarkable things for Nathan, "explosive success" even, whereas some asshole on the yearbook staff tagged Clay as most likely to be blown up in a meth lab before he's twenty-one.

"What happened?" I whisper.

It's the least of what I want to know, but the knowledge they possess and I don't might as well be grenades. If awareness goes off like I'm afraid it will, the impact will leave an imprint of me on the wall, nothing left but nuclear shadow. Cowering in the hospital bed, I'm a ghost at the top of the stairs, waiting to find out I was dead all along.

"There was a car accident," Mr. Frost says. He reaches out, then hesitates, like he isn't sure where to touch me. In the end, he pats my hand and I don't pull away. "A driver got lost and was wandering the back roads, fiddling with his GPS. He hit the passenger side head-on. . . ." He stops and glances at the doctor as if for approval.

To me the medical staff look uncomfortable, like they don't want to give personal advice. *Can bad news wait?* Mr. Frost wonders quietly. *Well, she just woke up from a coma,* the doc is probably thinking. But the parent is king in these matters, especially if it doesn't threaten my immediate survival.

Finally, Nurse Pink Pants says, "Why don't I go get a Popsicle? Your throat must be dry. We can give you five minutes before we do the swallow test."

That sounds pornographic.

I'm thinking this as everyone else files out, so Mr. Frost can have a Serious Talk with me. I have pterodactyls in my stomach because once he speaks his piece, I have to convince him I'm not his daughter.

"This will be hard to hear," he says softly. "But I feel like it's best not to hide the truth. Liv didn't make it. I'm sorry."

2

That means Morgan *is dead, and they don't know.*

Not Morgan. I can't breathe.

Maybe the doctor was right to withhold judgment on whether I was strong enough for shocking news. If I'd known that night at Emma Lin's party was the last time I'd ever talk to Morgan, I'd have said something more meaningful. I can't even remember exactly what we rambled about, stupid stuff on the Internet, what the hell was Amanda Olsen wearing and whether Eric Mitchell would ever get up the courage to speak to Kendra Sanchez. A thousand moments like that, a million, but they couldn't encompass the magic that was Morgan Frost.

I close my eyes. Take a choking breath.

"I'm sorry," Mr. Frost says again.

He's trying his best to comfort me and I *have* lost my best friend. That's when it hits me. *My parents think I'm gone.* I imagine their numbness and grief, making arrangements, notifying other relatives. My whole body shrinks. More and more awful, piled like bricks until it's Empire State Awful, a hundred and two stories tall.

I can't process or fathom how the hospital could've made this mistake. Even if we were both *really* hurt, they should be able to run tests, right? Dental records are always used in TV shows. With every fiber of my being, I want my parents; they need to fix this.

Everyone thinks I'm dead—my family, friends at school, and Nathan. *Oh my God, Nathan.* How am I supposed to break the news to Mr. Frost? I'm so cold my teeth are clacking. "What . . ." My words trickle off.

Is it grisly to want details? But I need them. I can't remember anything except that damn song on the radio. *Hope I never hear it again.*

"Olivia didn't have on her seat belt. She was thrown from the car and they found her body in a field nearby. The police . . . they said it was quick."

It's so strange, hearing about my own death, knowing it's my best friend they're talking about, not me. Morgan had only been home a week when we went to Emma's party. *One last summer blowout before we buckle down*, she'd messaged.

I'm still unable to believe any of this, processing slow like an outdated computer. My brain keeps skipping; it won't stick on the idea that Morgan is really gone. This must be a morphine dream. Any minute, I'll wake up, and my family will be here. They'll tell me that Morgan is just down the hall, right?

I try pinching myself and then squeezing my eyes shut, but it only makes Mr. Frost ask, "Are your eyes bothering you?"

Damn. This is reality.

I should just tell him. Then he can call my parents; I need them here. This situation is too much for me to handle on my own. He's waiting for an answer so I shake my head, working up the courage to drop this massive bomb.

"What about Nathan and Clay?" Shock has me asking random questions. I can't make myself tell the truth yet—*I'm Liv. Morgan is the one who died.* Not right to her father's face.

"Nathan spent one night in the hospital. Clay walked away with cuts and bruises, probably because he was drinking." Mr. Frost's tone says he disapproves, but if he argues with his daughter about dating the town bad boy, she'll dig her heels in even more.

And he's not wrong. She enjoys the risks associated with Clay. He's not like the guys at school; he has an edge. With Clay, you never know if you'll get the carrot or the stick, though I admit he treats Morgan better than I anticipated. When they first hooked up, I expected a hump and dump, then a night of tears punctuated by too much ice cream.

It never happened.

Mr. Frost is rambling about how alcohol loosens you up, so that's probably why Clay isn't hurt as bad. But part of what he's saying is true; I mean, I remember that I didn't put on my seat belt that night. *No big deal. We're only driving five miles to Morgan's place, and there's no traffic.* I didn't consciously think that or anything, but Clay's Corvair doesn't exactly encourage thoughts of modern safety. There's a timeless air to that car— or there was. It's probably totaled.

But . . . I can't wrap my head around an error of this magnitude. A slow throb starts in my temples as I try to put it together, and it physically hurts to imagine how damaged Morgan's body must be. Was she not wearing her seat belt either, so we were both launched while the boys held on . . . ? *Clay wouldn't let Morgan get hurt,* I think, *so she can't be dead. She can't be.*

This is a mistake.

But the other explanation is that *I'm* dead. Which makes no sense. They found a body in the field; that's a fact. Before I can decide how to bridge the subject of mistaken identity, the medical crew traipses back in with a frozen treat and the promise of another test. Mr. Frost takes off like he was waiting for this chance while I swallow a cowardly wave of relief and suck on the Popsicle. The cherry is too sweet, cough syrup instead of juice, and it's like I can taste the red dye number 40 in actual chemical tang. That's something Morgan would've said, though I always thought she was being dramatic.

I should've just blurted it out before. I force the Popsicle down.

The doctor talks a little more about my care and recovery plan, detailing my injuries, but I'm distracted by how he constantly calls me Morgan, like I need anchoring. This is probably some bedside manner thing, but in my case it's a jolt, a needle-sharp poke. Each time, I take the bait, chasing the rabbit down the hole, and I drink the bottle marked *I'm not Morgan.* It feels like hours later when the specialist finally leaves.

Then it's just me and Nurse Pink Pants, wearing a sympathetic look. "We're moving you to a regular room now. That means you're doing great."

"Moving?"

"We'll do all the work."

They do. I stay in bed, while it gets wheeled to my new digs, a private room that my parents never could afford. *They should be here.* How can they not know . . . ? The numbness and shock are wearing off, and I want my mom so much it hurts. She would hug me and my dad would bring a thermos of my favorite tea. Hell, I'd even settle for my little brother, Jason, who spends more time with his handheld games than me. I'd trade all this hospital luxury for a minute with my actual family.

I get isolation instead.

Morgan's dad is the CEO of a small IT company, Frost Tech, and he employs a lot of locals. Morgan tells the most hilarious stories about how all the MILFs about town hunt her dad like big game. The truth will wreck him; Morgan is the only family he has left.

The TV is on, running a special bulletin about missing girls in Monroe County. That's too depressing, and I already have enough darkness in my brain. I turn it off as the pictures of the lost flash on-screen.

A bit later, Nurse Pink Pants bustles back in with some gear on a tray. "Let's get those bandages off. I'm sure you're probably worried about your face, a pretty girl like you."

That's the last thing on my mind, but it occurs to me that once I'm unbundled, that should clear everything up. No more worries about how to explain—my features, however distorted, will be all the clarification they need. Then someone can call my parents and . . . Morgan will be dead; it'll be official. I swallow hard. There's no way I can be relieved . . . or anything but empty. There's no bright side here.

She gets to work when I don't reply and is snipping away when the door cracks open. Clay comes in first, shadowed by Nathan, who looks like deep-fried shit. My gaze lingers on his face. He hasn't shaved since the accident, it looks like. Normally, Nathan and Clay are like night and day, but right now, I see the family resemblance.

"We're just in time for the unveiling, huh?" Clay smiles at me.

"Hey, Morgan." Nathan doesn't look at me, and it's hard to see him so heartbroken, but he'll cheer up soon enough.

I imagine him running to me when the gauze comes off. We've been dating for a while now, and I don't doubt Nathan loves me. Thinking that I died because of him, while he was driving—it must be eating him alive. I'm unsure how Clay will cope with learning that Morgan died on that dark country road, but the truth has to come out.

"There," she murmurs at last, offering a hand mirror. "Don't focus on the stitches or the swelling. Try to believe that it's not as bad as it looks, okay?"

I steel myself . . . and stare.

It's not bad. It's worse, a thousand times worse. Because despite the damage the nurse mentioned, I'm definitely registering Morgan's face: her nose, her mouth, her chin, her black hair and blue eyes.

But I'm not Morgan Frost. For the last sixteen years, I've been Liv Burnham . . . and apparently, *I* am dead.

3

Once Nurse Pink Pants leaves, it's just Nathan, Clay, and me. I can't remember the last time I saw Nathan in a hoodie, but right now he's an echo of his older brother. There's no question they're both hot, but usually Nathan is clean-cut and polished, none of Clay's shadow.

I want to hug Nathan and tell him I'm right here, but now that I've seen the mirror, I understand how crazy it will sound. With an aching heart, I let him mumble without making eye contact, and then he slips out to give me some privacy. With *Clay*. Before this moment, I never wondered what he talked about with Morgan when they were alone. Maybe in some snarky part of me, I figured it was all heavy petting because Clay strikes me as teaspoon deep, but that's certainly not on—for so many reasons.

What am I supposed to do? I can't be Morgan. This can't be happening.

"I wish I was better with words." Clay's voice is husky, and his eyes are soft.

This is how he looks at Morgan when nobody else is around. And I shouldn't be seeing it.

He perches on the edge of the bed, taking my hand with a tenderness I can't believe. "But you already know that's not me. So you don't expect me to know how to make it better, huh?"

"No," I say.

That much is true.

I stare at his hand, wrapped around mine. While I'm looking down, he cups my cheek in one large hand. But he doesn't lean in, thank God, or I'd have to make some excuse. It's unnerving being this close to Clay, and I want to scream because I'm worried about Nathan. He thinks I'm dead, just like my parents do. He's in the hallway alone, chewing himself up about the accident if I know him at all, and I can't stand it because I'm holding hands with his brother.

Maybe this is hell. Maybe I *am* dead and the afterlife is way more FUBAR than I could've possibly imagined. I never pictured Clay touching me like this, though I'd have said hell would freeze before this would happen. I was wrong about him, too; right now, I can see he cares for Morgan.

"I'm real sorry about Liv," he says. "And I don't know what to do here. I get that you're not a talker, but you have to give me something, sweets."

I close my eyes then. Because it's not Liv who's gone; it's Morgan. And nobody in the world knows except me. In this moment, I feel completely alone. I want my mom. My dad. Nathan. My old life. Bewilderment and sorrow are duking it out, but I can't cry in front of Clay. I'm thirsty and my throat hurts, and the medication is making me feel weak and shaky. Despite my best efforts, a tear slips out. I feel it tracing down my cheek and then rough fingertips dust it away. Shocked, I open my eyes to find Clay's face right next to mine.

Morgan's.

At this distance I can see the green and gold flecks in his hazel eyes, dark stubble on his jaw, and the slightly chapped burn of his lips. His arms are gentle when they go around me; I'm shocked into stillness by the strength and heat of him. For two seconds, I lean. The situation is too big and I can't fix it.

Then I sit back and say, "It hurts."

Clay lets go as if galvanized with a cattle prod. "Sorry. God, I'm sorry. You look slagged. Should I . . ."

Say it. Offer to let me rest.

But he doesn't. I can tell he wants me to ask him to stay. And if circumstances were normal, I'm sure Morgan would. Maybe they wouldn't talk. Maybe they'd just hold hands and watch TV until the drugs took her away. But I can't leave Nathan alone, and I'm dying inside, imagining how my parents feel. My silence builds too long and hurt flashes in his eyes, making him drop his hand from my face.

"I'm worried about your brother," I say.

Which is true, but maybe Morgan wouldn't be. I feel so uncertain in her skin. *How* is this happening? There are no sensible answers to that question.

Before I woke up in this hospital bed, I'd have said that I understood her better than anyone else. Now I'm left to wonder how much I really knew, how much I assumed.

The hurt shifts, then Clay gives a wry smile. "Liar. You just know *I* am. He was nuts about Liv." Was, as in not anymore, because I have ceased to be. The past tense staggers me.

For everyone in the world, Liv Burnham is a memory. She's a deceased daughter, a lost love, or just the girl in homeroom that they didn't know too well, and that's kind of sad, right? To some people, this might seem like a miracle—that I'm still here—but I can't help thinking this is a mistake. Something went wrong, or Morgan would be, not me.

Why am I here?

If I could fix it, I would. But I don't *know* where Morgan went or why I was left in her place. Religious people would talk about God's plan and how I have work to do here on earth. The same thing could be said of anyone, though. How many people are good to go at the ripe old age of sixteen?

Seventeen. Morgan's seventeen.

Though she's only six months older, April to October, the difference in our birthdays means I'm a junior this year while she's graduating. Would have. Jesus Christ, the tenses will kill me. My eyes fill with tears, but Clay is *still here.*

While I silently freak out, Clay goes on, "A few weeks back, they were comparing notes on colleges, trying to figure out if there was any intersection of first picks that would give them a reasonable shot to see each other now and then."

I remember that convo. We mentioned Stanford and Berkeley as possibilities, though neither one of us was thrilled with the idea of the West Coast. Duke and Davidson came up, too, much closer to home. Nathan always joked about attending the same college, but it didn't seem likely we could find a university with great programs in both our respective interests. And after half an hour, we'd stopped thinking of the future and made out instead.

That's it. I can't take anymore. I break down.

Morgan would probably never do this because she's cool and strong. I can't remember ever seeing her cry, though I'm sure she did. Maybe she preferred to do it alone like a wild animal. Though she was my closest friend, there was always a wall between her and . . . everything. I know she valued me as a person, but damn, that sounds so detached. Morgan was Morgan. Bright, clever, a little bit wild. Other adjectives pile up like happy puppies.

Untouchable. Unknowable.

Gone.

The word cracks me open. I'm sobbing, loud, noisy gulps and streaming tears. It's too much, I'm alone, I can't deal, and Clay is watching it all happen with his mouth half open.

Then he springs into action, pulling me against him gently, and I don't have the strength to resist. I cry into his chest while he whispers into my hair, comforting bullshit. "That's good, let it go. Otherwise this will eat you alive, like everything else."

I don't have any clue what that means. And I *hate* that he knows her better than I do. I loved her, too, and I lost her and I'm the *only* one who knows. If I wasn't so sore, I'd probably hit him, the ultimate cliché. But I'm too wobbly, woozy, weepy. It takes ten minutes before I'm wrung out, but Clay seems lighter, like our relationship has deepened.

He thinks Morgan let him in. Poor bastard has no clue that I'm a stand-in.

"We'll get through this," he whispers.

I'm not your girlfriend. I'm not who I was or who you think I am. I'm . . . wrong, a thing that shouldn't exist.

"I miss her."

Morgan and me, both of us. I miss us both.

"They had a nice service."

"What was it like?" My voice is muffled in his shirt.

"Everyone from Liv's class came, half the seniors, too. They pretty much gave everybody the day off and most of the teachers showed up. Mrs. Caruso sang 'Defying Gravity.' There wasn't a dry eye in the place after the 'kiss me good-bye' line."

Oh God.

That's my favorite song—from my favorite musical. A few months ago, Nathan borrowed his brother's car and drove us to Atlanta, surprising me with tickets. I can picture everything so clearly. My parents would've used the Purcell Funeral Parlor downtown, and my mom probably ordered the flowers.

I can't breathe.

"There were a lot of wreaths and bouquets, too. Purple and yellow flowers everywhere."

Hyacinths and jonquils. Sorrow and sympathy. That subtlety would be my mother's doing. She loves the elegance of the Regency period and the language of flowers. It's probably just as well that I missed the funeral. Seeing my own face in the casket, hearing that song . . . I wouldn't have survived without a breakdown. Shit, maybe I'm having one now.

Listening to Clay's heart makes me feel a little better, and that's wrong, too. Everything about this situation is. How can I even leave the hospital? I'll have to go home with Morgan's dad, live in her room, go to school and be a senior, sitting in her classes. A shudder rolls over me as I ease back.

"I need to crash," I say around a jaw-cracking yawn that I don't have to fake. "Seriously, go take care of your brother."

"Someone has to." Clay kisses the top of my head. "Your dad will be back soon."

Please, no.

But he's right. I manage an hour of fitful sleep before the nurse is back to take my vitals and Mr. Frost is dozing in the chair. He rouses while she wraps the cuff around my arm, and gives me a sweet smile.

"You're already looking a lot better. It shouldn't be long before they'll let you go home. If necessary, I can hire a nurse, whatever she needs." The latter he adds for our silent audience's benefit, I suspect.

Nurse Pink Pants laughs. "Convince the doctor, not me."

If I had been listening, I'd know exactly what was wrong with this body. There's a low, burning pain in my abdomen, a sharper one in my shoulder. My face is sore, and my pelvis feels weird, though that might be the meds.

I close my eyes and pretend none of this is real.

4

Two days pass in a pain-fogged haze. Because I don't want to deal with any of this, I'm constantly maxing out my meds, and they leave me in a dreamy stupor. But the nurses are wise to this bullshit, and they fill my tubes with weaker doses until it's not enough to conk me out.

We make progress, medically speaking. Since they give me no choice, I get up and move around. For so many reasons, this is beyond bizarre. I'm too tall and my legs feel wrong. I used to be five feet two. Nathan's pet name for me was "pixie," and I didn't even mind when it came from him. Before, I had a sporty build leftover from when I did gymnastics, brown eyes, and auburn hair. I got lucky and escaped the freckle gene that left my mom looking like fairies had an orgy on her back at summer's end. All of that added up to cuteness, though Nathan always insisted I was beautiful.

My breath emerges in a sigh so strong it's almost a whimper. The nurse's gaze snaps up to mine in alarm because she's messing around down south. "You all right?"

"This isn't my best angle," I mumble.

She laughs. Then the catheter comes out—talk about a burning sensation—and I get praised a while later for making urine on my own. It's inspected for blood, but apparently I'm okay in that department. Clumsily managing my IV stand, I shuffle back to bed and fake-Morgan through visits from Clay and Mr. Frost. The whole time, I have one thought on loop: *I need to set everyone straight. I have to.*

But . . . I'm scared.

I'm so scared.

The rational part of my brain insists they won't believe me. Mr. Frost will call in the most expensive psychologist he can find and they'll call this shock or denial. I can hear it now—*It's understandable, your best friend is gone, and you're having trouble accepting reality.* If I persist in my claim that I'm Liv, not Morgan, they'll decide I'm delusional. Then I go into treatment with a patient, pipe-smoking, tweed jacket–wearing intellectual type. If I *stick* with this story, I'll end up in a posh facility populated with troubled rich girls.

At two in the morning, I stare at the clock, listening to the muffled sounds of the night crew doing their checks. Are my parents awake? Crying? At least they have my little brother, right? Jason has always been a good kid, and I hope he takes care of them while I figure out how to fix this. It'll be so hard if I meet them before I work out what to do. Picking up the phone, I trace the fingers over the numbers that make the landline ring at my house. What would I say?

Mom, it's me. Everything is so messed up, and I want to go home.

But she'd hear Morgan's voice, not mine. I've noticed that as my throat recovers from the tube, I sound more and more like her. There's no evidence apart from my word. Quietly I put the phone down without dialing. For two more days, I follow instructions and speak little. Surely emotional withdrawal is natural under these circumstances. I suspect that's how Morgan would grieve anyway. She never liked showing weakness or admitting when she needed help. I remember finding her surrounded by a two-foot wall of crumpled paper, eyes aflame with frustration because she couldn't get her self-portrait for art to turn out right.

I ended up drawing that picture for her. Funny, she was so good at faceless sketches of elegant figures wearing incredible outfits, but her own features stymied her.

Where'd you go, Morgan? Why did you leave?

That night, Nurse Pink Pants, though today she's in violet and turquoise, brings news as I'm rearranging the food that should be labeled Bland Diet. "I went over your chart with Dr. Jackson last night, and he's agreed to discharge you in the morning."

She seems to be waiting for a response.

"Cool," I mumble.

The nurse seems underwhelmed with my enthusiasm as she leaves.

I should be excited. Nobody wants to stay longer than absolutely necessary in a hospital, even if they're really ill or injured. This is why wealthy people pay for in-home care, something Mr. Frost has been pushing for since the beginning. I'm sure he thinks it's strange that I'm not begging to come home and recover in a more familiar and welcoming environment. The truth is, I'm only delaying the inevitable because I can't *ever* go home.

This is underlined and punctuated with an exclamation mark when Mr. Frost comes in, trailed by my wan-faced parents. *Oh, shit.* Pain flares in my temples as I stare at them. It's like looking directly into the sun when you already have a migraine. They look at me, so washed in sorrow that they can't even smile.

Because I'm a reminder of their loss. Mr. Frost's daughter made it while theirs didn't. Yet because they're good people, and they know Morgan was my best friend, they're here. They're making the effort.

"You're looking much better," my mom says. Her eyes are red-rimmed and her hair looks as if she put it up in a ponytail a week ago and hasn't taken it down since.

"We were here before you woke up," Dad adds.

"Thanks," I whisper.

My overwhelming instinct is to babble everything out, dump it at my parents' feet and let them fix it. There's nothing they can't set right because they're amazing, and they'll recognize their own daughter even in someone else's skin, like a weird changeling or whatever the hell I am. I know things only someone from our family could; I can tell the story about how Jason pooped in the cat box when he was two. *That's proof, sort of. Maybe they'll listen?* Words fill my throat like vomit but I swallow them down because this is beyond a rock and a hard place. It's incomprehensible. The cold voice of reason reminds me that a mental health professional will say, *Liv told you that story, Morgan, so you incorporated it into your delusion.* Staring at my parents, I waver.

What if hearing this hurts them more? It's more painful than a clean break . . . because I can't be Liv again. Her body is indisputably in the ground.

As I frame that thought, the shakes set in. It hurts so much that I can't breathe properly, and each inhalation smells like copper, as if I have blood in my nostrils. I imagine my flesh and bone in the casket, below layers of dirt. The macabre impulse sparks—I should dig it up to see for myself, only that won't solve this problem. It'll only convince my parents and Mr. Frost that there's something terribly wrong with Morgan.

Me.

I never thought I'd feel so grateful to Clay but when he strides in, my heart settles. This isn't the time. I can't confess with Morgan's boyfriend in the room, so he's taken the onus off me. Plus, Mr. Frost would definitely give my parents trouble, even if they believe me.

So whatever I decide to do, I have to plan it well, and the clock is ticking. Tomorrow I start truly living Morgan's life.

5

I'm in the front seat of Mr. Frost's Cadillac, buckled in safely, and he's driving ten miles below the speed limit, constant anxious glances at me as we go. It would be natural if I were terrified of cars, but I don't remember much about the accident. It's all jumbled in my head, and I only remember talking to Nathan moments before it happened.

"You can rest when we get home," Mr. Frost says. "Wanda will fix you a tray. She's been cooking all day."

For a minute, I have no idea who that is, then I figure out it must be their housekeeper, who I've always called Mrs. Rhodes. But I'm not sure if that's what Morgan says. Probably not, as the woman has been working for the Frost family for ten years. Morgan's mom died when she was seven, and Mr. Frost hired a lady to help with household management.

"Thanks."

"I know you're struggling. Do you want me to make you an appointment with—"

"No," I cut in. Therapy is the last thing I need. A smart, determined person poking around in my head? That's a recipe for disaster. "I just need . . . some time."

That sounds reasonable, right?

"Okay. But promise me you'll talk to Clay, at least."

Shit. I was planning to break up with him first chance I got, but it occurs to me that Mr. Frost will take this as erratic behavior. They've been together almost six months, Morgan's longest relationship to date, and if I dump Clay, it'll probably read as a danger sign.

I make an assenting noise, one Morgan used when she felt impatient. God, I hate that I'm copying her. The deeper into this life I sink, the harder it will be to extricate myself later. Presuming that's possible.

"Your phone was broken," he goes on. "I got you a new one and had the techs at work transfer all your content and contacts. Don't worry, I didn't read your messages."

"Where is it?" That seems like her; she always had her cell in hand.

"In your room. I can carry you if—"

"Pass. I can make it up the steps before collapsing. I won't tear my stitches." The sharpness slips out because I just can't handle his hovering.

Since that's probably how Morgan would feel too, Mr. Frost relaxes a little as he pulls into the drive. Next, he taps the button to open the massive black wrought-iron gates. Getting onto Frost property is an immense production. There are cameras mounted on the stone posts on either side and they swivel as we go past.

I wish with all my heart that I was going home to our cozy three-bedroom ranch house and that I could crawl under the covers in my own bed. Instead, an imposing stone villa comes into view as we round the curve. The variegated granite gives it a shimmer effect when the sun catches it right. As a kid, I thought of it as Morgan's princess castle, but as we got older, so much space for two people seemed sad.

It's a quarter mile from the gate to the mansion, lined on both sides with a lovely mix of black gum, crab apple, magnolia, and redbud trees. In the spring this drive is breathtaking, but it's late summer, and I'm watching the rearview mirror. Those closed gates make the whole place feel like a prison.

Mr. Frost parks the car. I always loved the fountain in the center of their circular drive. It's rigged with special lights, so when Morgan hosts a party, it glows red, green, blue, shifting through all the colors on a timer, while frothy streams shoot up in different patterns. Today the fountain is turned off, so the stone rim is dry, catching sparkles from the sun. Despite the sweltering heat I shiver as I step from the air-conditioned car. Mr. Frost takes my arm and I throttle the urge to pull away.

You're not my father. Don't touch me.

But this isn't his fault, either.

Just a little longer. Then I'll have some privacy.

Yet when I'd dismissed that flight of stairs I didn't realize how much it would hurt hauling myself up them. Mr. Frost hovers as I struggle but I wave him off. I rode in a wheelchair down to the car and haven't walked all that much. Each step pulls the incision holding my guts in, and my shoulder throbs like crazy. By the time I get to Morgan's room, I've broken out in a cold sweat and I fall onto her bed with a quiet groan. I put on sweats for my discharge, so I don't have to change clothes. In hindsight this seems like awesome planning.

I'm hurting bad enough that I don't even care about my situation at the moment. Sleep is all I need; it's everything. In ten seconds I'm out.

When I wake, the rich glow of twilight tints the room purple, which is an improvement. Morgan's room is all cool elegance, white plus white. Before, I was afraid to spend much time in here. One dropped slice of pizza or a broken ink pen would ruin everything. But Morgan said it made her feel peaceful . . . like a snowy field. We don't get much snow in Renton, maybe a sprinkle once a year. It definitely never sticks or stays.

There's a tray waiting beside the bed, which means Mrs.

Rhodes came in while I was crashed out. That probably wouldn't bother Morgan, but it's kind of freaky for *me*. My mom and dad never come into my room. If they need me, they knock. My mom isn't the snooping kind. She doesn't rifle through my belongings or poke at my computer. It's not that she's perfect, but when she loses her temper, she always apologizes afterward and explains why, so I know it wasn't me. I mean, sometimes it *is* my fault because I'm not flawless either. And sometimes we misunderstand each other. I think of all the times I shoveled down something she cooked and ran back to my room without saying more than ten words, and I choke up.

I'm sorry. I didn't know how fast it could all be taken away.

My dad is a little tougher. He's a college professor and he's always demanding to see my homework. I swear he scores my papers harder than my actual teachers, but his criticism gets me better grades. On weekends, he's all about cooking pancakes for brunch and then book shopping. His idea of family togetherness is a monthly book club, where we all discuss what we read. I pretend to hate it, but honestly, it's kind of cool.

Overall, I won the parent lottery, and I can't stand that they're only three miles away, three miles that might as well be three thousand. My brother used to text me when he wanted something, and I'd go down the hall to find him surrounded by video games and chip bags, no matter how often Mom yelled at him for eating in his room.

Jason Montgomery Burnham, we'll get roaches. Rats. Rats and roaches. Is that what you want? One day I'll come in here to find you covered in them.

The light flips on. Someone's in the room without knocking. I bite my lip against the instinctive complaint. "Yeah?"

"It's me." Mr. Frost steps into view. "Did I wake you?"

You just turned on the light in a dark room. Stupid question, your answer is yes. Except for two inescapable facts: one, I was already up, and two, that's bitchy, as Morgan seldom was. Only in this cool, vague way, so the person she insulted was never completely sure if she meant that how it sounded. But I don't have her command of verbal subtlety.

So I just shake my head.

"Have you eaten?"

"No, I just woke up." Again, duh. It's so awful that I think Mr. Frost is an idiot when he's trying so hard. But I can totally tell that technology is his forte, not people.

"Do you mind if Clay keeps you company?"

"It's fine." I never would've guessed he'd be so diligent about visiting a sick girlfriend.

Seems like Morgan was right in picking Clay, against popular opinion. I remember how shocked everyone was when she showed up with him at prom. He quit school two years before and was basically off the market, dating-wise. People said he preferred hooking up with older women. In Clay's own words: *Schoolgirls are a pain in the ass . . . and a waste of time.*

Morgan changed his mind. And now I'm reaping the benefit.

So damn wrong, on every level.

6

Never did I picture Clay hanging out at Morgan's house. In fact, I was never sure if her dad knew they were together. Morgan wasn't big on explaining herself, even to me. So it's awful, but I imagined him as a dirty little secret. See, the Claymore boys are what my Mamaw would've called white trash. Their dad died in a mine accident when Nathan was ten. As for their mom, well, her habits are . . . irregular at best.

None of that is Clay or Nathan's fault. Regardless, I *love* Nathan. His family situation never impacted our relationship, except that he spent a lot of time at my place.

But now I'm tangled up with his older brother.

Feeling guilty, I muster a smile as Clay steps in. He hovers by the door with enough awkwardness that I can tell he hasn't been here often, and he contrasts sharply with the décor. Everything in here but Clay is sleek, delicate, and feminine, like a room designed for a shoot at *Marie Claire*. But he's *not* a stealth boyfriend, that's for sure, even if he's not who Mr. Frost would pick for his pride and joy.

At this point I have no idea what she'd say or do. But this is uncharted territory for anyone. Their relationship hasn't been tested by tragedy, so it's not like I'll set off Clay's alarm bells, no matter how I act. *I'm so sorry, Morgan.*

"Looks like you came from work," I say.

Clay has on faded jeans and a black T-shirt imprinted with a logo. Before, I was nearsighted but now I can make out the words from here. The name of the shop is India Ink; the design's pretty cool, actually, red and bronze with a steampunk vibe: a skull wearing a top hat and goggles, with a cog to frame it. INDIA INK curves in a banner above, which looks like it has ink spattered on it.

"Yeah. I've been worried about you all day."

I have to remind myself he's talking to Morgan, not me. He'd want to pull my soul out through my nostrils if he knew the truth.

"I . . . hurt." This is bald, basic truth on every possible level.

"Do you have any meds you can take?" He crosses the room and as I'm watching, I realize he's taller than Nathan.

Because he's thicker, Clay doesn't register the same lankiness. I'm guessing he's six one to Nathan's five eleven, broader at the chest and shoulders. Nathan is lean like a swimmer, but nicely muscled. They both have hazel eyes, though Nathan's are greener while Clay's tilt heavier toward gold. Both have strong jaws. Nathan's face is narrower and his brows aren't as heavy. Clay usually looks sleepy, as if he's bored by life *and* you, whereas Nathan is sharp and focused, strong on eye contact and quick with a smile. When forced to talk, Clay deploys this annoying drawl, like each word costs him money, but Nathan never met a stranger.

I love that about him.

I never told him. Because I was worried how he'd take it, I was waiting for Nathan to say it first. Same reason I never had sex with him, though Morgan said I should get it over with. She'd laughed and said, *You're so cute, Liv. You think it'll ever be magical? Please. At best it won't suck and it'll be fast.* Now, I can never say it. I can't touch Nathan at all.

My chest hurts.

Belatedly I realize Clay is waiting for an answer. "Sorry, light-headed. I have to eat something before I can take any pills. Let's see what the housekeeper sent up."

"Must be nice," Clays mutters.

But he's smiling. Clearly, he doesn't hold Morgan's privilege against her. Perching on the edge of the bed, he sets the tray across my lap and I uncover it. There's fresh fruit, tofu-yogurt, homemade vegetable soup, and gluten-free rice crackers. *Shit. Morgan's a vegetarian.* She doesn't eat anything artificial and she's sugar-free, caffeine-free, gluten-free, meat-free, and dairy-free. I want to cry because I can't remember which restrictions stem from allergies and which from personal preference. From my earliest recollections, she was a picky eater and she went to the doctor a lot. When we went out, she never ordered much. Kids at school said she had an eating disorder or she must be stuck-up, but there are reasons she's so careful. One time she scared me to death when her face puffed up and she had a tough time breathing.

What did we have that day? I think for a few seconds. *Seafood. So now I'm taller and I have better vision but I can't eat anything with a shell.* A quiet sigh escapes me. *Dammit. I love shrimp étouffée.*

"Doesn't look good?"

I glance at Clay, who's stolen a rice cracker and is holding it to the light. Then he chomps it without prejudice. "Not bad."

The food is delicious, actually, filling and delicately flavored. Mrs. Rhodes knows her business. I eat everything because I owe it to Morgan to take care of her body. Which makes it sound like she's a car I borrowed. It's all I can do not to whimper. Clay doesn't say much until I move to shift the tray. He does it for me, then brings two pills and water.

I knock them back and swallow. "Thanks. How was work?"

Clay's eyes widen slightly. This is not something Morgan's

ever asked, apparently. But if I don't make conversation, he may want to make out. That train can *not* leave the station. Though it will be tricky—and I feel rotten—I have to put him off long enough that I can break up with him and not have Mr. Frost associate it with the accident.

"You really want to know?" he asks.

"Definitely."

So he tells me about his boss, a woman in her forties named India, though he's pretty sure that's not her birth name. Four other people work as artists there: Tank, Gail, Rodney, and Blue. He talks about these folks with unusual enthusiasm; he's lost his perpetually sleepy expression, so I'd call this his excited face.

"I have a long way to go before they'd even remotely consider me for an apprenticeship but it's beyond cool that I'm on site and learning. Not full-time." From his expression I can tell he wishes he got more hours.

"Walk me through an average day."

"I'm there Wednesday through Sunday. I pitch in as needed, clean up and close the place down." His tone is quiet. "But I'm curious why you're asking. I mean, you only cared about my days off before."

How the hell did these two hook up?

I was with Nathan first, and sometimes the three of us hung out, but it wasn't regular. Mostly it was Nathan and me or Morgan and me, but it wasn't like I forced Nathan to get his brother to round out a double date. When she hooked up with Clay, Morgan told me she had a new boyfriend. I bugged her for days, begging for details, but she was delightedly sly, savoring the surprise. A few weeks after that, he took her to prom. But like the dietary stuff, I can't ask Clay to remind me of "our" romantic past.

"I just wanted to know what you do. Is that weird?"

"Nah. It's cool." Clay's got a dimple in his left cheek.

Never noticed that before.

"You're being so nice. So . . . I'm trying too." *Harder than you know.*

"That's not really your wheelhouse, huh? We both know you only let me call you sweets because I do it ironically."

At this I laugh because that's *so* Morgan, locking onto a pet name that isn't one at all. The motion pulls my stitches, and it hurts. Reminds me that I'm here and she isn't. I shouldn't be in her bed, eating her food, talking to her boyfriend. But I can't dissolve in front of Clay again; he'll take it as a sign that Morgan trusts him when it's only that *I'm* a complete wreck.

I'm about to play the sick and fragile card when he leans in and kisses me with exquisite tenderness. My hands fly to his chest, but . . . his mouth, his mouth, his *mouth*, hot and rough and soft. I don't shove, because there's a glorious, wicked spark, low and sweet. As first kisses go, it's all gossamer, butterfly gentle, delicate as air. While it's happening, I don't consider Nathan. Memories of his brother, *my* boyfriend, crash in on me when Clay drags rough knuckles down my cheek. And I hate myself because I don't hate it; the path of least resistance beckons.

It'd be so easy to slide into this life and make everything of hers mine.

7

I spend a week convalescing.

At the end of that time, Mr. Frost takes me for a checkup, where Dr. Jackson compliments my healing prowess. Another three weeks and Morgan's body will be more or less recovered—with a few fresh scars to show for the experience. It's quiet on the way back from the clinic, mostly because I don't know what to say.

I'm still marshaling my strength and formulating my next move, but the problem is, there's no roadmap for a problem like mine. I can't even use Morgan's computer to search for similar cases; I don't know her password and all of my guesses resulted in an admin lock. I might have to "accidentally" drop it so Mr. Frost will get a new one. That bothers me but he can afford it. Plus, I'm sure he'll just bring home a spare Frost Tech model.

Using Morgan's phone feels weird, especially when Clay messages me. I've dialed way back since he kissed me. Like a chicken-shit, I asked for space via text, and he hasn't been over to the house since. It's possible that I can kill the relationship with neglect, though that route is circuitous and painful. In my real skin I'd never do that; with the guy I dated before Nathan, I made a clean break. But I have to walk a delicate line between sanity and survival.

"You don't have to go to school tomorrow," Mr. Frost says. "Nobody expects you to. I've already spoken to the principal. He said the teachers will be happy to e-mail your assignments until . . ."

Until when? I feel better? My best friend isn't dead? Or when some other tragedy has supplanted this one, so people don't stare and whisper as much? None of those responses is suitable, so I dredge up something else.

"What did the doctor say?"

"That it's up to you. You're still recovering, so if school takes more out of you than expected, you can always go home early."

For the first time, I don't try to guess what Morgan would've said. "It's better if I at least *try* to go. Get back into a normal routine. That's supposed to help, right?"

Mr. Frost smiles. "I agree. But don't push yourself. You'll be excused from PE for the next month, obviously. I've arranged to get you into study hall that period."

Most people opt out of PE as soon as they can, but Morgan likes it. She says it's her easiest grade and she gets a workout during the day, guaranteed. I'm the reason Morgan doesn't go to a pricey private school twenty miles away. When she finished sixth grade, she begged her dad not to make her attend Glen Forrest on her own. Since our school system is decent, he agreed. Otherwise, I'd be headed off to an academy where I don't know anyone.

Nathan. Tomorrow I get to see Nathan.

My old life is over, I get that. At least until I figure out how to prove I'm not crazy. But God, I miss him, almost as much as my family.

Almost as much as Morgan.

I haven't let myself think too much about how she'd feel about this. She could be hard to read, so it's possible she'd think the whole mess is hilarious and would make popcorn to watch me struggle. But she was also possessive, so she might be furious, too. And it's that side of her that I imagine watching me, judging, condemning.

Mr. Frost drops me off at the mansion before heading back to work. I let myself in; with gates like these, they leave the front doors unlocked during the day. Mrs. Rhodes comes out of the kitchen to greet me with an uncertain smile. She's wearing black pants and a white shirt with a patterned apron over the top, not quite a uniform, but a nod at one.

"Can I get you anything?" There's a subtle tension here, some history I'm not privy to.

The older woman stands quiet, eyes down, like she's expecting . . . something. Maybe she was temperamental with the housekeeper? But if Morgan used to throw fits in private over the wrong brand of rice cracker, I can't because I have no clue what the right one is.

"I'm fine. Thanks."

A little breath slips out of her as I turn for the stairs. Relief?

I go down the back stairs to the patio. There's a pool out here that I can't swim in right now, but I can sleep in the sun until I feel better. Before I can settle in, Mrs. Rhodes is beside me, wearing an alarmed look.

"Are you feeling all right?" She peers at me.

"Uh. Well. I thought I'd take a nap."

"Did you put on sunblock?"

Right. Shit. Morgan was paranoid about skin cancer, so she'd never bask in direct sunlight. I wasn't thinking about Morgan, only that I was so freaking cold. But now that it's on my mind, I can recall countless afternoons where I'd be in a bikini and tanning oil while Morgan hid under an umbrella with a sun hat, huge glasses, and SPF 75. I always thought that quirk was adorable and slightly glamorous, but it's kind of a pain in the ass now that I'm not allowed to act like my sleepy, sun-worshiping lizard self.

"I forgot. Could you get it please? My hat and sunglasses, too."

She gives me a look, like she thinks it's more likely that I'm possessed than I forgot my sun aversion. But then she does as I ask, leaving me to drop my head against the back of the lounger with an exhausted sigh. At least it's warm out here. *Damn, it's not easy being someone else, even if she's your best friend.*

I finish out the day with a cozy, if overly protected nap, then I go upstairs and destroy a helpless laptop. Since Frost Tech makes good gear, I drop it four times before it looks good and broken. An hour later I'm having a late dinner with Mr. Frost. Since I'm going to school in the morning, I can't really keep pleading that I need to eat in my room. Got to keep my story straight. So I ask questions that I hope don't set off any alarm bells.

"Developing anything new and exciting?"

Mr. Frosts grins. "You never get tired of trying to work me, do you?"

"You don't trust me?" I pretend to be hurt.

"I'm not exempt from the NDA."

What's an NDA? But I imagine Morgan would know, so I keep quiet and eat. During the next conversational lull I say, "I'm sorry, but . . . I broke my laptop earlier today."

He shows the first sign of impatience I've seen since leaving the hospital. "Dammit, did you get it wet again? No matter how good a product is, it will *never* be Snapple proof."

I know exactly how Morgan would reply to this. Leaning in, I give him a cajoling smile. "Can't you consider this part of quality control testing?"

He sighs. But I can tell he's not seriously mad. "What happened this time?"

Huh. I guess Morgan wasn't good at making her electronics last. That's something I didn't know, and it makes me feel closer to her, even though she's gone. It's so strange that I could miss her this much when I see her face every time I look in the mirror.

"I tried to take it downstairs but I guess I'm not as steady as I thought. I dropped it." That should explain the four times I threw it, right? I have no idea what a tech can tell from a broken computer but TV detective shows have taught me to be cautious.

"Down the *stairs*? Well, that's a new one." He sets his jaw like he's sucking back a spate of chastening words. "Okay. I'm just glad you didn't fall. I'll have one of the techs look at it and if it can't be fixed, I'll bring you a new one tomorrow night."

"Thanks."

"Try to make this one last a little longer, okay? It's only been three months since you Snappled the last one."

"I feel like you need to put that on Urban Dictionary. I'll invent a definition for Snappling, don't worry." When I smile, his face softens.

"I'm glad to see you're . . . coping," he says quietly. "I thought it would be months before I saw anything like that again."

He's right. I shouldn't be joking. Morgan wouldn't if I were dead; I'm the worst person in the world. I can't be happy when she's gone, and I don't know where she went, if she's all right—and all this while my family is mourning me. My face crumples. I tuck my lips in, and I can see Mr. Frost realize he shouldn't have said that—because he's reminded me that I'm a selfish asshole for not grieving every minute of the day. But he doesn't understand; this isn't survivor's guilt.

Or maybe it is, just not in the form he expects. I get up from the table and retreat upstairs.

As I head down the hall toward Morgan's bedroom, her cell

pings with a message. Since I expect it to be Clay, I try to ignore it. Not surprisingly, I can't.

Finally I take the phone out of my pocket, but Clay's picture hasn't popped up. Instead it's the baseline icon, the default for when you don't have the person in your contacts. Curious, I tap it open to find:

You look pretty today, sweetheart. But time's running out. $10K or I tell your dad.

8

To say I don't sleep much after the creepy text comes in? Massive understatement.

The phone gives me no clue about who sent the message or why they're trying to shake Morgan down. I scroll through her message history, but she seems to run a cleaner app that purges her messages regularly. *That's . . . weird, right?* It's not like I never delete anything; when Nathan sends me his sweaty abs pics, I ogle for a while and then remove. That's just sensible preventive measures in case of parental intrusion.

This is next level caution, possibly veering toward paranoia. Part of me wants to answer the text, but that might just make things worse. Eventually, I power the cell down, but I'm conscious of it, a heavy metallic weight on the table next to me. I swear, I watch the thing like it's a bomb about to go off.

Must've dozed at some point, and I wake up as it's getting light outside. Worry camps out in my head—so many problems for me to deal with, and I don't even know where to start.

There's a little voice in my head whining, *It's not fair.* I want to say, *Screw this* and go tell my parents everything.

I'm not Morgan. I can't do this. Those desperate thoughts haunt me as I walk to the bathroom. On Morgan's legs. I get in her shower and try not to cry.

Mrs. Rhodes brings breakfast while I'm in the bathroom, in and out like a ghost. Jesus, it's so quiet in this house. At home my parents would be yelling down the hall at us to hurry up, as my mom cooks and my dad sneaks the bacon while accusing random family members of stealing essays he was supposed to grade a week ago. We live close enough that I can walk to school, though Morgan sometimes picks me up. Nathan and I always said it was unfair that we had no wheels unless we doubled with Clay and Morgan.

Nathan.

My heart aches as I stand in front of her walk-in closet. Choosing an outfit seems bigger than what it is, somehow. Then I realize why. For the last three years, I've watched her the night before, planning the perfect look. Sometimes she asks my opinion but not always, as I'm not a fashion icon. Whatever I pick, the next day twenty girls will be scouring stores to find something close but not identical. For the first time I realize how daunting that is.

Trying to match Morgan's impeccable taste is impossible, and I only have ten minutes to get ready. Normally I'd just wear jeans and a cute top, nothing extravagant. But Morgan's wardrobe doesn't run to simplicity. Whatever, I'll do my best to be fashion forward.

Hair is easy, thankfully. It's her best feature, long and straight, easy to style. I pull off the long ponytail with the hair wrapped around it and then do light makeup, Morgan-style, not mine. She wears more eyeliner whereas I did lips. But Liv's mouth was better, I think.

Liv. Me.

My mouth was better.

"Are you almost ready?" Mr. Frost calls.

Grabbing phone and backpack, I head downstairs carefully. My incision still hurts, so I have pain meds in my bag, just in case. He's waiting at the bottom of the stairs in helicopter mode, not that I blame him. With a faint frown he eyes the shoes.

"Is that wise?"

The heel doesn't bother me right now, but maybe it's a bad idea. My side will probably hurt like hell if I wear these all day. But there's no way Morgan would yield on fashion without a fight. I try to cut a deal.

"Ask Wanda to get me a pair of flats from upstairs. I'll wear them to walk around later. Just please let me arrive in these."

Mr. Frost wavers. "Okay. But only because you said please."

He calls out the request and the housekeeper hurries upstairs to find some ballet slippers that should be easier on my various injuries. Five minutes later, he's driving me to school, despite my protests I'm well enough to take my own car. Morgan drives an adorable blue Beetle, the model that looks like a Barbie car. Here, he stands firm; as a dad he knows to pick his battles. Shoes? *No big deal.* Daughter who barely survived a fatal car accident? *Yeah, let's put a pin in driving, honey, at least until you're fully recovered.* Since that reasoning makes sense, I don't argue, and it's no hardship going to school in his town car.

On the way I get a message from Clay. *Good luck. I'll be thinking about you.*

Because he's a decent guy and I don't want to hurt him more than I have to, I send back, *Thanks* ☺. Which is less than I'd want to get in his shoes . . . but better than silence. Right?

Mr. Frost pulls right up to the front doors and I slip out with a wave. Already the eyes are on me. Maybe it would've been better if I could've come to my own funeral because people would've already seen my reaction then. But because it's Morgan, this moment is . . . intensified. Everything about her drives gossip at this school, but she's so cool about it that I never wondered how it feels.

Answer? It sucks.

These shoes do too. My side already hurts by the time I get to Morgan's locker. Thank God I've seen her spin the combination a thousand times. Otherwise I'd have to plead amnesia in the main office or go after the padlock with bolt cutters. Popping it open and seeing it empty excavates my stomach like a fresh grave. The school makes us clean them at the end of the year, though they give us the same one when we come back in the fall. I can understand why they wouldn't want food moldering for three months in this heat, but what harm could it do to let us keep plushies and pictures? As a result of their totalitarian sanitation regime, there's nothing here that was hers, only my memory of what was.

Sure, *I* can redecorate. I know more or less what she'd pin up. But it'll be a facsimile of Morgan, just like me. Quietly I lean my head against the inside of the locker door.

"You look like I feel," Nathan says.

Closing my eyes, I steel myself for a few seconds before turning. And it's worse than I expected. His face is thinner and he's growing an *I don't care* beard. He doesn't seem to be sleeping either, as his green-cast hazel eyes are deeply ringed, which gives him a tortured-artist vibe. Even his haphazard style goes with the theme, torn jeans and paint-stained hoodie.

"Did you sleep in those clothes?"

"Maybe," he mutters.

The irrational part of me can't stand that he doesn't recognize me. All that charming star-crossed bullshit, my soul will find yours? I want to burn all those romantic movies down. Because I'm right here and he can't see me; the eyes aren't mirrors to anything.

At this moment, I want to hold him. But Morgan isn't touchy-feely, and Nathan will likely shove me away so fast my head will spin. Yet maybe under these circumstances . . . I mean, we're both grieving. *It's bad, I'm awful, but . . . I have to try. Just look at him.*

"So . . . do you want a hug or something?" I ask with enough edge that I can claim I was joking if he reacts like it's weird.

Nathan huffs out a laugh. "From you? Not really."

That hurts more than I expected. "Screw trying to be nice, I guess. So you know, I'm not exactly okay, either."

As I shove past him, I stumble in these cute, stupid shoes and a shooting pain tears through my side. Nathan catches me, holds me; it's strange being on eye level with him, but it doesn't distract me from how good, how sweet and familiar it is when he touches me. And I swear, for a crazy second, he *feels* it. His gaze locks on mine, and I try to tell him silently.

It's me, I'm here. I didn't leave you.

9

Nathan lets go instead of pulling me in. I'm Morgan, his brother's girlfriend. I must've imagined that moment.

"Sorry. I know she was your best friend for way longer than I dated her."

"Yeah," I say huskily. Then I cut away from this conversation because it's like chewing glass. Somehow I manage to get to Morgan's first class.

After the encounter with Nathan, my hands are cold and shaky. As I settle at my desk, I remember the text from last night, and suddenly, the phone feels like it's burning a hole in my bag, but I don't take it out. I can't afford to let the teacher confiscate my electronics. It appears that Morgan had problems she didn't share with me . . . or anyone, maybe. As soon as I get back, I'm searching her room for clues.

The school is small enough that there's only one lunch, four classes before, and three after. We start at eight; lessons run for fifty minutes with a five-minute passing period between them. Morgan's schedule is way different from mine. Since I'm interested in genetic engineering, I've been taking hardcore science and math since freshman year. But now I have American Literature, Graphic Design 2, Visual Arts, Sociology, a break for lunch, then afterward French, World Government, and study hall, which will eventually turn into PE.

I'm so screwed. While I can memorize for Government and Sociology, Morgan is in her third year of French, and I don't know more than three phrases: *s'il vous plaît, omelet du fromage,* and *merci beaucoup.* So in France, I can politely order a cheese omelet, then thank the waiter afterward. That won't cut it in French 3. American Lit will be okay; that was the one class we would've had together. I'll probably crash and burn in Graphic Design and Visual Arts, too.

As predicted, I'm every bit as lost as I guessed in second and third period. First and fourth are okay, then I'm cut loose for lunch. Belatedly I recall that I can't eat anything here and that Morgan usually packed a lunch. I hover outside because I'm not sure where to sit, plus the prospect of watching people eat when I'm starving doesn't thrill me. Morgan and I ate together, but I never wondered what she did on my rare sick days. As Liv, I'd go sit with the science types, but that won't work now.

"Forgot your lunch?" Nathan's standing behind me, brow cocked.

I'm too conscious of him and that makes it hard to think. "Yeah."

"Did you bring your car? I'll go with you to the store, if you want."

Ruefully, I shake my head. "I'm on lockdown for a while. M-my dad is being overprotective." That was a close one; I almost said Mr. Frost.

"Then I guess you'll have to hold out until you get home." But he's making no move to go join his buddies.

Nathan hangs with the young GQ set, normally. By which I mean well-dressed, smart, academic overachievers who prefer clubs to athletics; they also masquerade as clean cut when in fact, they're the ones who throw the best parties. Nathan's on the swim team, too, but they don't have the same mentality as the football players. Confession: I've had his activity schedule memorized for way longer than we've been dating. Morgan used to tease me about how I'd position myself throughout the day, dropping into his line of sight until he started talking to me. Over the course of sophomore year, we progressed from casual greetings to banter, and eventually, as I was hoping, he asked me out.

Standing here with Nathan is keeping me from obsessing over that ominous text message, but he won't stay forever. Yet he tilts his head toward the side doors. "Want to go sit in the courtyard? I'm not hungry anyway."

"Sure." As we walk, I'm wondering if this is prudent.

I suspect he feels sorry for Morgan and that he regrets his attitude this morning. But it's not like there are tons of people clamoring to hang out. While people idolize Morgan, they don't feel comfortable offering sympathy or support. So while I've gotten a lot of concerned looks, nobody's approached. Morgan didn't go out of her way to dispel that mystique, either.

The sun is bright but it feels good. This space used to be wasted; the school is designed in a square O, and they recently greened it up to make use of this area. Which means a few picnic tables, benches, and plants have been added. It's an ongoing project for the agriculture students, actually, and a few of them are planting a tree as Nathan sprawls in the shade before a trellis where someone's trying to get jasmine to grow. There's a small flower garden and a patch of sweet-smelling herbs. Most students prefer air-con and safety from bee stings, so there are only five people out here, including the ones who are working.

"Better?" he asks.

"Yeah." *But why do you care?*

"Clay asked me to watch out for you," he says then, crushing my nascent dream that he senses who I am, what we meant to each other.

"You don't have to. I'm dealing." My tone is icy, pure Morgan. I've heard her deploy it when someone crosses the line.

"You're doing me a favor. The guys are so awkward, they don't know how to treat me. One asshole is talking about all the condolence pussy I'll get, like that's a bright spot."

"Seriously? Let me guess, Braden Wilkes."

Nathan flashes me a surprised look. "How'd you know?"

"It's the Young Republicans you have to watch out for. They seem so responsible and then they come out with the most revolting shit."

"True. But I didn't think you knew my friends that well."

"Liv and I did talk, you know. I paid attention." At least I hope that's true.

He flinches slightly when I say her name. My name. God, this sucks. He shakes it off, running a hand through dark hair that's already practically standing on end. With a sigh, he tries to smile, like I didn't see how much he's hurting. It only exacerbates how I feel.

"You don't have to pretend with me. Don't act like everything's okay."

"Thanks," he says softly. "That . . . helps."

For, like, ten minutes, we just sit there soaking up the sun, and I'm nearly asleep when he whispers, "You never told her, right?"

What the hell? Does this have anything to do with the text? And why does Nathan know, if I don't?

"What do you think?" That's not a great response, but it's the best I can do on the fly. I'm starting to wish I'd pretended to have amnesia. Then nobody would expect me to know anything.

"I'm guessing not. Liv wasn't the type to hide it if she was mad."

That answer doesn't clarify anything. This is going to drive me crazy. "I don't want to talk about it," I snap, pushing to my feet.

Great exit line, but I can't shake the questions this conversation has planted. Doubts spring up like weeds, and I already have more of those than I can handle.

10

The rest of the day, if I'm not worrying about that text, I'm wondering what Nathan was talking about. In study hall, some art kids surround me. For the most part I recognize their faces but I can't remember half of their names. The ringleader is Oscar Sanchez. He hasn't come out, but he's fabulous, all Goth glam style. With a full coif, black nail polish, eyeliner, and a spiked collar, he's clearly going for a particular vibe.

"You didn't even wait for us when you left Visual Arts," he complains. "And you vanished when I was looking for you at lunch."

So this is Morgan's social backup system?

"Sorry," I mumble.

"I figured you'd want to hang out more, now that your circumstances have changed." Oscar makes it sound like Liv has moved away and cut Morgan loose. At long last.

"Be nice," one of the girls chides. She's wearing a black latex dress, ripped fishnets, and combat boots.

"It's fine," I say with Morgan's inscrutable half smile.

"I didn't mean it *that* way," Oscar protests.

The teacher comes in and shushes us. I pass the period reading for American Lit, as little of my homework can be completed sitting at a desk. I have some research to do for Sociology, and two projects already assigned in my two art classes. I'd always thought art must be a blow-off specialty, but I'm already learning how badly I misjudged Morgan's workload.

After school, a Frost Tech employee is waiting for me out front in a logo-bearing hatchback. I've already been delegated. I don't know the man behind the wheel, but since he's waving, Morgan must. *Crap. He's not wearing a security badge.* Pretty soon I'll be reduced to saying things like, *Hello, name, how is your family and/or significant other?* Then when people give me that look, I'll tell them I'm practicing to be a robot for an avant-garde art show. I'm sure that'll work.

Somehow I choke down a semi-hysterical laugh. This is so dangerous. Since I don't know everyone Morgan would, a kidnapper would have the easiest time playing me. He'd just have to say that Mr. Frost sent him and I'd be afraid to question it, afraid if I do, it's a mistake, and I'll be found out.

Then . . . what? They'll perform an exorcism? Honest to God, I can't even conceive of how anyone would react if they *did* suspect. Maybe they'd write off any inconsistencies—*it's a result of stress or whatever, she'll be fine in time*—sort of thing.

The Frost Tech guy lowers his hand, crestfallen. "You don't remember me."

"Sorry," I say with a shrug and a smile.

"Well, your dad sent me. You can call to confirm if you want. He's in a meeting but he'll pick up for you."

I'd rather have Mr. Frost think I have a bad memory than get in a car with someone who might make me disappear, especially since I know Morgan's been keeping secrets and it seems like she's being blackmailed. Clay's words resonate with me: ". . . this will eat you alive, along with everything else." *Does he know what's going on?*

Without wasting any more time, I switch on my phone, half

expecting another sinister message. *Nothing new. Good.* I call Mr. Frost to check this guy's story. He picks up on the second ring. "You okay?"

I can hear a low hum of voices behind him. "Fine. Just making sure this tall blond guy is really my ride."

"Flint's driven you around before."

"You think I pay attention?" I manage a sweetly teasing laugh, not identical to Morgan's but close enough.

"True. You're always on your phone."

"See? But I'm being careful. Points for that?"

"Definitely." Mr. Frost doesn't even say bye before hanging up on me.

"All set?" Flint asks as I climb into the front seat.

"Yeah."

In the car, I try using reverse lookup, but the site only tells me that it's a mobile number, registered in Renton, and "low risk" for fraud or spam. I need to know who's after Morgan, but I have no idea how to find those answers. The scientist in me wants to come up with a hypothesis, but this is the kind of shit that's damn near impossible to corroborate.

I exist. I am Liv. I am not dead.

Yeah, I can't prove any of that.

Or figure out who's out to get Morgan. I curse beneath my breath.

Otherwise, I don't speak except to thank Flint as I climb out. My side hurts like hell, even in flats, so I pause in the kitchen to take some pain meds and scrounge up a snack. There's a note on the fridge letting me know that the housekeeper is at the market and I should text her if there's anything special I want her to pick up. *That means I'm alone here, nobody to interrupt or ask what I'm doing.* So I eat quickly, then head upstairs as fast as my wobbly legs will carry me.

It feels like burglary when I open Morgan's dresser drawers.

At first, I find only meticulous clothing. Like, I've never seen anything so neat and organized. The T-shirts are all folded into perfect squares and then, instead of lying flat, they're pressed upright vertically in two neat rows so you can tell at a glance what's there, by color, at least. I marvel at that before moving on to her desk, where I find about what you'd expect: old movie tickets, stubs of charcoal and pastels, ink pens and pencils, a few ragged-looking hair accessories, a handful of coins from various European countries. I dig deeper and find a birth control wheel, about half the pills missing.

This isn't exactly a surprise, though Morgan didn't tell me much about her sex life. I knew she wasn't a virgin, though. She did it for the first time when she was a freshman, some guy in Venice, she claimed, and said it was no big deal. I was still in junior high then, and she seemed so amazingly grown up. *That means Clay will probably expect you to sleep with him, sooner or later.*

Great, another problem.

I lift a tray full of paper clips and other office oddments to find an unmarked manila envelope. Since Morgan was prone to doodling, that seems noteworthy. I pull it out and dump the contents onto the desk. First I pick up some candid photos of Morgan and a guy I don't know. He seems older but these are black-and-white, taken in a strip of four at one of those stupid booths, so I can't be sure. These are not exactly high-res.

In the first pose, she's sitting on his lap while he nuzzles her neck. The second one shows them full-on kissing while the third is mutual sly smiles, and the last is her head on his shoulder. I flip the photos over and see that she's written *Step one* in Sharpie on the back. *What the hell?* From any normal teenage girl, you'd be more likely to find hearts and the guy's name. But Morgan is a law unto herself. And I'm only now realizing how much she kept hidden.

But where does this leave Clay? Maybe she dumped this other dude?

The next thing I find is a broken friendship bracelet; this thing is filthy and smells faintly of blood. When I pick it up, a wave of horror floods me, and I drop it on the desk. Yet to look at it, this is just frayed blue and green yarn woven together with plastic beads bearing faded letters that spell 4EVER. I don't touch it again, just nudge it aside with the envelope and go on digging through her stash of incomprehensible secrets. There are two receipts, one for a convenience store near the school, and one for a shop I've never been to, mostly since it's in Paris. I have no idea why these two things were important enough to save. There's also a Post-it with six numbers and a scrawled, *gate code*. I memorize that since it might come in handy.

Finally, I pick up a blue film. I stare at it for a few seconds, trying to process what I'm seeing. This is a freaking ultrasound. I immediately slap my hands over my stomach. Is Morgan . . . am I *pregnant*?

11

Reeling, I brace myself against the desk.

If so, who's the dad? Clay? Mystery photo guy? This might be what the blackmail text was about. I can't *believe* she didn't tell me.

Wait, but wouldn't the accident have caused problems? The doctors would've informed me if I'd lost a baby while I was in the hospital and they would've mentioned an existing pregnancy, too.

Searching Morgan's room hasn't helped at all, only raised more questions. Time to explore elsewhere.

The pain meds have kicked in, so I hurry downstairs, favoring my side. I find the study unlocked. My hands are shaking as I turn on Mr. Frost's computer. But he has a password, dammit. I should've thought of that. This is pretty much his forte, and I was dumb to think I could just wander into his home office and unearth his secrets, if he has any. His desk drawer is locked, too. Because of a childhood obsession with using my grandparents' RV as a secret fort, I have rudimentary lock-picking skills. I always wanted to take Morgan and hide out to get away from Jason, but Mom said it wasn't a place for us to play, so she'd never give us the keys. At nine, that didn't deter me, however. I read basic books about locks and I didn't stop until I could get into the camper without the key.

If I'd gathered some supplies first, I might have gotten inside, but I'm not exactly an expert, so I might scratch the metal on my way in. Disappointment spreads like spilled beer, so I turn. No point getting caught when there's nothing I can accomplish.

But as I head for the door, a picture on the far wall catches my eye. The man in the photo with Mr. Frost looks familiar. I take a couple of steps to verify, and holy shit. This is *totally* her make-out buddy from the candid strip upstairs. In this picture, full color, it's obvious that he's in his late thirties, old enough to know better. By the way he's shaking hands with Mr. Frost, it seems like he's Somebody, a politician or another CEO, maybe.

What were you doing, Morgan?

"I'm home," Mrs. Rhodes calls.

I scurry out of the study and close the door, then go to meet her. She seems surprised by this, another clue that Morgan wasn't gregarious at home. But before we can play another round of *Gosh, you're weird and not acting like yourself,* Clay calls.

You're always saving me lately. Relief fills me, and it's like sinking into a hot, sweet-scented bath. Consequently, my voice comes out warmer than I intend. "Hey, what's up?"

"Not much. I'm off today. Want to hang out?" He's tentative, remembering what I texted about needing some time.

Not a good idea. But I can't think how to backpedal from my bright greeting. "Sure."

"I'll be right over."

"I'd rather hang out at your place." Where I can see Nathan. *I'm horrible. But I'm doing this anyway.*

A long pause. "Really? But . . . you hate my house."

"Not today."

"Whatever you want," Clay says.

Ten minutes later, he's at the front gate, buzzing the intercom. I let him in and am waiting outside by the fountain when he pulls up. He's driving a small green hatchback, not the Corvair. I get in and after I fasten my seat belt, he touches my arm lightly.

"How much did school suck?" he asks.

"On a scale of one to ten? Six. Where did you get the car?"

He starts the engine. "The auto shop is loaning it to me while they check out my Corvair."

So the Corvair might not be beyond saving. I'm not sure I'll be able to ride in it again, though, considering that I died in it.

I'm quiet as we cover the six miles between Morgan's mansion and the Claymore house. They live, literally, on the wrong side of the tracks. Cliché, but Renton does have train tracks and if you live on the south side of them, well . . . I watch as the slightly seedy, trying-to-become-gentrified downtown yields to rusty chain-link fences, cars up on blocks, and living room furniture in the front yard.

I don't mind Nathan and Clay's place, though Morgan apparently did. We pull into a gravel alley shared with the house next door and he parks in back. The front yard is fenced, and it's cleaner than the neighbors' on either side. They live in a shotgun house, once painted orange for cheer, but now peeling badly. Cement blocks support the structure, and I know for a fact that stray cats sometimes have kittens under there; Nathan showed me a litter earlier this summer.

Sagging wood steps lead up to the front porch. I approve of the swing, having spent some sweet nights there with Nathan. Considering how rarely I've seen Mrs. Claymore around, the house is pretty clean, even if everything is ancient, worn, and faded. The appliances and carpet date to the seventies, I'm sure.

"Home sweet home," Clay says with enough edge that I know he's waiting for me to come out with something judgmental.

The sofa and armchair are covered with faded sheets, probably to hide the stains that can't be scrubbed off, but I can tell from the smell that they've been washed recently. The carpet is forest-green deep shag, and the walls are a dingy gray. There are posters up, none framed, and one of them is hiding a hole that Mrs. Claymore's asshole boyfriend added with a fist. The door that leads to the front bedroom is closed. Pressing one hand to my side, I sit down carefully. A sigh slides out. This isn't home, but it feels closer than Morgan's place. She preferred to hang out at my house and I completely understand why.

"Want something to drink? I have beer, water, and lemonade."

"Pass on the beer. I'm still on the good meds."

Clay seems to remember Morgan's allergies belatedly. "You can't have it anyway. Sorry, I forgot. Water?"

"Lemonade please."

"It has sugar," he reminds me.

"Oh. Yeah. Water, then." God, this diet sucks. I'm going to end up devouring chocolate bars in Morgan's walk-in closet.

When he comes back, he's got a beer and I accept the Mason jar with a half-smile, the best I can manage. I thought for sure Nathan would be home. It's not like I believed we'd really have a chance to talk, but seeing him would've been enough.

"Thanks."

"So . . . are you going to tell me what's going on?" He sinks down on the other end of the couch, a move that leaves me grateful.

"Excuse me?"

"I can tell something's bothering you," he says quietly. "Besides grief. It's cool if you don't want to tell me why you're worried, but don't think I'm oblivious."

Clearly there's more to Clay than I previously estimated, and . . . I'm so tired. There's a slim chance he may already know about this, plus I can't keep fighting alone. It's bad enough living in someone else's skin. Finding out the truth may prove impossible on my own. So . . . I decide to trust him.

Without comment, I pull up the text message and hand him the phone. He skims it, then his gaze snaps to mine. "What're they talking about?"

So much for the possibility that Morgan confided in him.

"I wish I knew," I mutter.

"You should tell your dad. Whatever it is, he'll be more pissed at whoever's shaking you down over it."

"That presumes me being able to confess only what I'm being blackmailed for," I say. "Because otherwise I have to dump my purse, so to speak."

He grins faintly. "The perils of being bad."

Ironic, because I wasn't as Liv, and I didn't know about Morgan's secret life, especially not the older guy from the picture. I mean, she told me when she did crazy shit in Europe, but those always just sounded like . . . stories to me. Maybe I didn't entirely believe her when she told me about having sex with a stranger on a train, or sneaking out to a club after her dad went to bed. *Seems like I should have paid more attention.*

"So what do I do?" I whisper.

"Good question." Clay puts a hand on my shoulder, and it's easier not to fight when he pulls me close. "I didn't think you'd go for this."

"What?"

His arms tighten on me slightly. "A little less frosty right now, huh?" That seems to be a joke, a pun on her last name and reputation. Since he's making fun of me, I try to pull away, but he doesn't let go. "Don't take it wrong, sweets. I like this side of you. It's kind of nice feeling like more than a warm body."

"Is that how I made you feel before?" The question slips out before I can stop it.

"I knew the score going in, so don't worry about it."

What does that mean? But I can't ask. It sounds like Morgan asked him out with the understanding that it was just physical.

Everything I learn about my best friend only confuses me more. But I feel a little better since showing Clay that text; he doesn't seem to think it's a huge deal.

"So . . . strategy ideas?" My head is on his chest where I can hear his heart and its rhythm is relaxing me.

Clay smells good, I decide, plain castile soap and cloves. He doesn't use cologne, but the clean smell of his skin is nice. It's layered with the fresh detergent smell of his worn black T-shirt. He's warm, solid, and with him holding me, it's easier to imagine that I'll find a way out of this impossible maze, maybe without being eaten by a Minotaur.

"For the text? I wouldn't stress. Just wait for this asshole to play his card and then deal with the fallout."

"That's not much of a plan," I point out.

"Are you the same person who was just bragging about having your dad wrapped around your little finger?"

I remember how Mr. Frost reacted to the news that I broke the laptop and decide maybe he's right. Yet it doesn't bode well that he's already asking that. Right now it's a joke, but as time wears on, I'll make more and more mistakes. Sighing, I manage a shrug. He's right; Morgan would probably aim a mental *screw you* at anyone who tried to blackmail her, so by flipping out over the message, I'm overreacting.

"Cozy," Nathan says from the doorway. "Sorry to interrupt."

I immediately straighten and sit away from Clay. He doesn't try to stop me; I realize why a few seconds later. Though it's early afternoon, the reek of liquor hits me like an uppercut. Nathan looked bad enough at school but in just a couple of hours, he's already downed half a fifth of whatever he's holding. Clay jumps to his feet.

"Give me the bottle."

"Screw you," Nathan mutters.

"You want to turn out like Mom?" The question is delivered

in a level tone, but the atmosphere thickens, making it hard to breathe.

"Second verse, same as the first."

I'm about to say, *Maybe I should go*, when Clay turns to me. "I hate to ask but could you keep an eye on him? I need to run to the store. We're out of coffee and pretty much everything else. I need to get some food in him, or he'll be sick as shit in the morning."

This isn't how I imagined my first visit with Nathan since the accident, and God, it hurts so bad, seeing him fall apart. "No problem."

As Clay leaves, he flicks a look over his swaying brother and adds, "I'll hurry."

12

Nathan lifts his bottle for another swallow. "Slumming, Morgan? You can get lost. I don't need a sitter."

"Seems like you do."

A muscle flexes in his jaw and then the bottle comes flying at me; it slams into the wall, spraying me in whiskey and glass shards. "I need Liv. I need not to have killed her. I need a *do-over*. But I'm not getting any of that, so why don't you piss off, rich girl?"

Jesus. I've never seen Nathan so drunk or mean. If anyone had told me he had this side, I wouldn't have believed it. I flick the glass off the couch and go find the broom. Silently I clean up the mess, though I'm a little dizzy now. I haven't eaten much today, just enough that I could take my pain meds without the pills chewing through my stomach lining. He watches me with a brooding stare, and then he's gone before I realize it.

Once I've scrubbed up the streaks on the walls and put the broken glass in the bin, I find Nathan sprawled on the back steps, leaning against the porch post. The sun's just starting to set, layering the sky in gold and amber with threads of pink. It won't be full dark for hours yet, as fall hasn't curtailed the sunshine yet. The air is muggy and still, and I have no idea what to say.

"You still here?" he mumbles.

"Clay asked me to take care of you."

"And you're so obedient, huh, Morgan? But you've never killed someone you love."

It feels like my heart is bleeding. If I ever wondered exactly how Nathan felt, here's the answer. Impulsively I touch the back of his hand.

"Stop. Liv wouldn't blame you."

It's true, I don't. The truck driver was lost, it was a dark country road, and I didn't have my seat belt on. None of that is Nathan's fault.

His fingers curl around mine with desperate need, and his eyes are like a green fire, ablaze in the scruffy pallor of his haunted face. "You shouldn't be so nice to me right now. It's not your style, and I'm . . . not safe to be around."

The Nathan I know is gentle, considerate, and thoughtful. "What're you talking about? You wouldn't—"

"I want other people to hurt," he cuts in. "I might feel better if I can make someone else bleed. Do you understand?"

"Not really."

In a sudden move, he yanks on our joined hands and I tumble against him. He smells like he's been drinking since he got home from school. Nathan grabs my shoulders as if he expects me to fight. In fact, I'm pretty sure that's what he's looking for; if I shove him back, then he becomes the villain, and he can keep beating himself up, adding to his list of imaginary crimes.

So instead I put my arms around him and give him the hug he refused earlier at school.

At first he goes rigid, his eyes narrowing. Then a shaky breath trickles out of him and he drops his head onto my shoulder, tucking his face against my neck. I imagine how Clay would feel if he walked in on this, but I can't stand seeing Nathan in pain. Gently I rub his back in slow circles. This much could be explained away, right?

"It's okay," I whisper. "You're not alone."

I can feel him relaxing against me, and it's heady, knowing I can affect him this way, even though he thinks I'm Morgan. But I have months of learning how to touch him behind me. As my mind skips through those lovely memories, my hands skim up his back. I work his shoulders like I used to after swim practice. He leans into me, recognizing the pressure on some level. Taking his response as an invitation, I rub the base of his skull. Nathan tips his head back like a cat; he always loved this.

"Don't stop." That husky tone is unmistakable.

And I don't know how I feel about that. Because these are Morgan's hands, and he's drunk, hurting. What I'm doing is probably wrong, definitely confusing.

"Better?" If I talk, it's not as intimate. I'm comforting him, that's all.

In answer he kisses me. It's not gentle, either; this is open-mouthed and hungry. His tongue tangles with mine, and I stop thinking. This reminds me of all the nights we spent, inching closer to sex. He pulls me onto his lap and I'm straddling him. We kiss until I can't breathe; he's moaning into my mouth. I nibble and tug on his lower lip. I don't consider that's *my* thing, something I used to do when I really wanted to drive him crazy.

"Liv," he groans.

And it's so right . . . but also completely wrong. Sick to my stomach, I shove him back. His face a study in shock and horror, Nathan falls off the porch. Shaking, I run back into the house to the sound of him throwing up. I'm in the bathroom, quietly banging my head on the wall, when Clay comes home. I can hear him talking to his brother while he puts away the groceries. Shame wraps me up to the point that I don't know how I can face the two of them.

I did not mean for that to happen. I didn't.

By the time I come out, Clay has coffee made and noodles boiling in a pot. Nathan's sprawled in a kitchen chair, eyes shadowed, but the look he gives me is pure poison. God, he hates me now, and I don't blame him. I mean, Nathan was never Morgan's biggest fan; in private he always talked about how spoiled she was. He must be wondering if he's gone nuts.

"You all right?" Clay asks.

Tell him, Nathan dares silently. *Make me the bad guy.*

But I can't be the girl who comes between brothers, and I kissed him back. So I say nothing and let it become a secret between Nathan and me. *That can't happen again. At least not until I find a way to fix things.* Each day that hope seems fainter. Logic asserts that there's just no way to come back as Liv, no matter how much people are hurting. No matter how much I want my old life back.

The brothers eat a silent meal of buttered pasta and mushrooms. It smells delicious, actually, and as Liv, I'd totally sprinkle some Parmesan cheese on and dig in. But Morgan can't have gluten, and I'm pretty sure it's not by choice. So I sip my water and wait for Clay to finish.

"Your girl took good care of me," Nathan says.

Clay's head comes up; he looks wary. "Yeah?"

"Definitely. Even after I chucked my bottle at her head."

I relax a little. That's not what I expected him to say, and Nathan knows it. His green eyes are equal measures mischievous and mean. Clay flattens a hand on the table as if he's restraining himself.

"I catch you drinking again, I'm reporting you."

"Yes, sir. I'll shape up, sir."

"I'm not kidding. You're better than this, and I'm not letting you screw your future."

"Over one dead girlfriend?" Nathan shoves away from the table and stalks into the bedroom they share.

For a long moment Clay stares at his plate. "Times like this, I wish my dad was here."

"I'm sorry." It's pitiful, not nearly enough.

"He misses our mom more than he lets on."

Huh? The way he's talking, this shouldn't be news to Morgan. But Nathan seldom mentions his mother, except in vague terms of contempt and in jokes about writing a "how not to raise children" manual. I know she isn't around a lot but that's all.

"Have you heard from her?" I ask.

Clay shakes his head. "Complete radio silence. It'll be two years in October."

That means . . . *holy shit.* Does that mean their mom's taken off for good? *Why didn't Nathan tell me?* I assumed, along with everyone else, that she was out drinking and/or shacking up, but that she came back periodically. Clay quit school early in his junior year, and now, now I think I know the real reason why.

I have to reevaluate everything about him.

"I probably never said so, but I admire you for stepping up like you did."

He lifts one shoulder, getting up to clear the table. "Someone had to, and Nathan's way more likely to make something of himself."

"Don't sell yourself short." I'm surprised to find I mean it.

Clay's smile is blinding.

13

I **get** back to the mansion in time for dinner.

Mr. Frost is already waiting for me, equal measures peeved and hungry. This is a man who isn't accustomed to being kept waiting, and to make matters worse, he has a guest. He's tall and lean with features too strong to be handsome, heavy at brow and chin, yet there's something striking about him as well. His medium-brown hair is cut meticulously, and his navy pin-striped suit looks expensive. Our visitor rocks a red power tie . . . and he's also the one Morgan's kissing in the photo upstairs.

I only know him as "Step One."

Shock leaves me struggling to breathe for a few seconds, and a swell of nausea makes me feel like I can't get through dinner. But Mr. Frost will probably overreact if I bail. I fix Morgan's cool smile in place and move toward Step One, extending a hand. To my astonishment, he takes it and pulls me in for a hug, and then kisses my cheek. In front of Mr. Frost. I glance over at him but he doesn't seem to read anything wrong about it. Strike Step One—he's Mr. Creepy from now on.

"You get prettier all the time," Mr. Creepy says.

"Thank you."

"How're you feeling, sweetheart?" The endearment makes my skin crawl, as he hasn't let go of my hand. "I visited you in the hospital but you hadn't woken up yet."

"That was nice," I say politely.

How many nights has Morgan calmly had dinner with her father and her secret boyfriend? My hands are shaking as I follow them into the dining room. The few meals I've eaten with Mr. Frost, we had in the breakfast nook, which is a deceptive phrase, as the space is still bigger than the kitchen at my old house. Thinking that gives me such a pang.

Mrs. Rhodes is setting hot dishes on the table, already laid with delicate, expensive china patterned with cherry blossoms. I sit to my father's right and Mr. Creepy takes the chair opposite mine. How can he be so cool about this? I wonder why he isn't worried that Morgan will tell her father everything.

"It looks delicious," Mr. Frost tells the housekeeper.

Her smile says she's not immune to his awkward charm, though she's probably fifteen years older. Mr. Creepy is watching me with a secretive glint in his eyes as Mr. Frost serves the food. They're having pot roast; I'm eating stir-fried vegetables and tofu. I never realized how lucky I was as Liv, able to eat pretty much whatever I wanted.

"Thanks, it looks good," I say to Mrs. Rhodes.

She gives me the *who are you and what have you done with Morgan* look before heading to the kitchen. As I eat, Mr. Frost talks to the creeper, but it's involved enough that I can't tell if they have contracts together or what exactly their connection is. It seems like they've been acquainted for a while, which makes it even worse that Mr. Creepy would get involved with his friend's daughter. And the *worst* thing about this situation is that the guy looks normal.

"Have you thought any more about my proposal?" he's saying.

"No business at the table." Mr. Frost glances at me in apology.

"I'm almost done. I can go if you need privacy."

Mr. Creepy says indulgently, "If you don't mind, Morgan, that would actually help a lot. I'm under time constraints here and I can't get your old man locked down."

"I've been a little busy." Mr. Frost sounds terse, as well he might, considering his daughter was in a coma.

But he doesn't invite me to stay.

I excuse myself from the table and leave the dining room but I don't withdraw completely. From this distance I can still hear their voices; a house this size has impressive acoustics. For a few moments the talk is general and then Mr. C says:

"She looks more like her mother every day." His tone bothers me, like, to the point of sending a cold chill down my spine.

Mr. Frost doesn't seem to register that note, whatever it is. "I know."

"Let's get down to it. Have you made a decision, Randall? I can't stall the investors indefinitely. You're the one who said this area could benefit from an influx of capital."

"Not like that," Mr. Frost says.

"That's a no, then." What an icy tone.

"I think you already knew that."

"Without you, this proposition is dead in the water. I need your support. What happened to the promise that you'd always be in my corner?"

"I'm not a member of your campaign team. This soft-soap emotional bullshit won't play here, though the old ladies love it on Sunday morning. And you should have lobbyists working on this. I'm disappointed, Jack, so any promises I made ceased to apply when *you* stopped keeping yours."

From there the conversation devolves into a hushed-voice argument. From what I can glean, Mr. Frost disagrees with his friend's policies. As I turn, I come face-to-face with Mrs. Rhodes. I'm tempted to apologize and flee, but Morgan would never react that way. I raise a brow, or I try to. I can't seem to do it, though Morgan could.

"Can I help you?"

Mrs. Rhodes shakes her head and brushes past me; the slight curl to her mouth tells me this is the sort of thing she expects. I wait until she's moved off down the hall and then I go upstairs quietly. In my room there's a new Frost Tech Pandemonium X, the latest model, still in the box. Mr. Frost didn't mention this at the table, so I'll have to thank him once Creepy Jack leaves.

I open the computer and do the setup. It takes me an hour to download the apps I want and reset Morgan's passwords. Fortunately she had most of her accounts linked to her phone, so the services text me a code and then let me change the logins. I've just gotten into her e-mail account when someone raps on my door.

"Come in."

Mr. Frost sticks his head in. "I see you found it."

"Thanks. This is perfect."

"Did you really say that word?" He smiles to show he's kidding but there's an undercurrent that makes me think he truly is startled. "Hope you weren't too surprised at dinner. Jack just showed up."

"I noticed some tension." Maybe I can pump him for information.

"Don't stress about it. I'm sure it'll blow over." No such luck, apparently.

We talk a little more and then he heads off to do some work in his study. I'm about to dig into the secrets of Morgan's inbox when a text comes in. I pick up the phone, tensed in preparation for another blackmail demand. But the message is from a contact called DL.

Come out, I'm waiting just beyond the gate.

I'm pretty sure I know who this is, and I don't want to go. But I need as much information as I can gather. My heart's pounding like a kettle drum as I sneak out the back, across the patio, and stay in the shadow of the trees. It takes me a little while to get down the drive, and I quickly hit the button so I can slip out. There's a car waiting. Clearly they've done this before as the system is down to a science. The idling vehicle is a sleek black BMW, the sporty model. I memorize the license plate number, though I'm not sure how much it'll help me if this weirdo takes off and doesn't come back. I'm not surprised at all to find Creepy Jack waiting for me with that off-kilter smile, though I have no idea why Morgan labeled him DL. My best guess is Down Low.

Something in his eyes sends my heart lurching into my throat. I know I'm being stupid as I climb into his car, but if I don't take this risk, I may never understand why I'm here in Morgan's body. In this moment I feel like I'm supposed to finish her work, and if I do, then we can *both* rest.

Not that I want to die. But I don't want to live her life either.

14

"I've been worried about you." Creepy Jack leans over; I avoid his kiss by buckling in.

His mouth slides over my cheek, and he sends a cold shudder through me by breathing deeply into my hair before easing back onto the driver's side. There isn't much space in the front seat and less in the back. This is the kind of car men buy when they start losing confidence in their ability to pull women in other ways. Close up, I can see the lines around his eyes that weren't evident in either picture, along with the receding hairline; he's older than the late thirties I initially guessed, and on his left hand, a golden ring glints on his fourth finger.

I feel like throwing up again.

He puts the car in gear and it lurches forward like a barely leashed beast. He's quiet until we put some distance between us and the house. The radio is playing some easy-listening station that underlines the massive gap between us. I don't want this; I'd rather be anywhere but here.

"Are you hurting?" he asks.

I nod. Because surely a painful, seeping incision will put him off. He rests a palm on my thigh, and the touch tells me everything about their relationship. We drive until I realize we're headed for the quarry. Earlier in the summer, I would've worried about being seen with him since a certain crowd comes here to party. But this is a school night and once September begins, it would be hard to find a more deserted locale.

For drowning a minor indiscretion.

I shudder.

"Is the air-con on too high? Before, you complained if I didn't set it to max."

"The accident took something out of me," I say.

"Sorry, sweetheart." The term sounds worse in the darkened privacy of the car, as if each letter has spider legs, tiny furry creeping things that are biting their way into my leg courtesy of the five fingers and a burning hot hand on my thigh. His fingers are stroking, stroking, stroking, like I'm a pet or something.

"It's been a while," I say softly.

That seems to make sense anyway since Morgan was in Europe and then a week after that, the accident. Since then, I've been in charge, and I definitely haven't hooked up with Creepy Jack. He nods, putting the car in park. It's so dark here. The place has been closed for thirty years. I've always secretly hated the quarry; it's a scar in the earth filled with dark water. Trees ring the place like they're standing guard over wicked things, drowned and buried deep.

"I know. The summer is too long."

Not nearly long enough.

He takes one of my hands between both of his, and the crawly, squiggly impression increases. "Don't feel neglected, but I'll be busy for a month or so."

"Okay," I say, though Morgan would probably protest, even if she's playing him.

She never liked being ignored.

"You weren't kidding. The crash stole all your vinegar. But that's fine, I like sugar better anyway." He nuzzles my ear, hot breath moist on my skin.

In another second, his mouth will be on my neck. Stir-fry

veggies and tofu heave into my throat. I clamp a hand over my mouth and hunch forward. "Uhm . . ."

The bastard lets go of me so fast, I might be on fire. He even nudges me toward the passenger door. "Don't throw up in here. Get out if you have to."

"Sorry," I whisper. "Can you take me back?"

I need to find out more about their relationship, but it won't be today. Between the scene with Nathan and this mess, it's just been an incredibly long day. In silence he starts the car and drives toward the Frost mansion. He doesn't touch my leg again.

"I'll give you some time to heal . . . and to miss me. You know I love you, right?"

I don't think Morgan would say it back, even if she was in love with this scary asshole. So I give an enigmatic smile. "I know."

"Don't tease me." In that moment he's more like a sixteen-year-old boy than a powerful politician, hungry for any scrap of affection.

"Isn't that what you like best?" I don't even have to think about what Morgan would say anymore; the words just slip out. "The fact that you can't be sure of me."

"Maybe. Here, I got this for you."

Creepy Jack hands me a black velvet box, and I open it to the unmistakable sparkle of jewelry. This is way over the top, a heart pendant studded with diamonds on a fine silver chain, could be platinum or white gold, too. Even I have heard of the shop it comes from, very expensive. He clasps it around my neck; the metal feels like ice against my skin.

"Thanks." Before he can reach for me, I add, "Give my regards to your family," as I slide out. I hurry toward the gate and input the passcode, unable to relax until the wrought-iron doors shut behind me.

I did it. I met with Morgan's sugar daddy and I didn't get abducted or molested. That shouldn't be the watermark for a successful day. More than anything, I want this asshole arrested. But without evidence, it's my word against his. One meeting, a hand on my leg, and a valuable present? If the news has taught me anything, a good lawyer will make Morgan look like a nympho with daddy issues trying to ruin a good man's life.

She must have had her reasons for doing this, and for the sake of my sanity, I have to unravel this tangle.

Mrs. Rhodes meets me on the back patio. Her eyes are guarded and watchful. "Your father was looking for you a few minutes ago. I told him you were resting."

Why did she cover for me?

"I appreciate it," I say.

"My monthly . . . bonus is overdue," she tells me, biting her lower lip. "I know you've been preoccupied but . . . I really need the money."

"I'll take care of it right now."

She seems relieved as I head upstairs so I guess I wasn't supposed to hand her a wad of cash. No wonder Morgan always seemed to get away with everything. Mrs. Rhodes is on standby, ready to provide an alibi. In the white room of doom, I take off the necklace and hide it in Morgan's jewelry box. But when I open the bottom drawer, I find two more pieces, a bracelet and earrings, both with the heart-and-diamond scheme.

So. Gross.

My best friend's e-mail account beckons, but first I have to see if there's a bank log-in. I'm ecstatic when I'm able to import her browser history and then I find the website. Since I don't know the password, I repeat the "forgot password, send me a code" routine I used earlier. There's also a security question, but I know the name of her first pet. I type *Trixie*, and the site tells me it recognizes my IP. Then I'm into her financial world, staring in astonishment.

I mean, I know she's well off. But Morgan has $102,191.82 in her checking account. In *checking.* There's roughly twice that in savings, plus CD and bond accounts with terms and benefits I'd have to google to understand. Yet I can do the math. In combined assets, Morgan Frost has over a million dollars already, and she's the sole heir to Frost Tech.

I feel sick to my stomach, like I set out to rob her or something.

Determined, I suppress the shock and nausea, perusing the account records. In history of bills paid, Morgan sends money to Wanda Rhodes on the twenty-eighth, but the amount varies. Best guess, the "bonus" depends on how helpful the housekeeper was. Amounts range between $250 and $1,000, so I average the payments and send $583 via e-transfer. For a little longer I study her spending habits and I'm astounded to see how much she bought in Europe.

Damn.

I shut that site down and do a search using the keywords "Jack," "politician," "Renton, GA," and "Randall Frost." Five seconds later, I have a picture of Jack Patterson, public assemblyman, smiling beside his wife and two young children, one boy, one girl. There are rumors that he might run for state senate in a few years.

Not if I have anything to say about it.

Next I get into e-mail. There isn't a whole lot since we keep in touch mostly via messaging. But I dig up a subscription to a cloud storage service and reset that password, too. I'm not sure what I expect but, given what I already know about Morgan, I'm braced for the worst. Still, it's surreal to open the folder labeled Photos and find my best friend in her underwear along with Creepy Jack not wearing much more than a smile.

This is evidence.

The photos aren't time or date stamped, but I remember that

haircut. Morgan was fifteen when these pictures were taken. *Fifteen*. That's not a lot older than my younger brother, and no matter what was going on in her head, no matter why she did this, it's *not okay*. That asshole needs to pay.

As I'm fuming, I open a folder marked Stuff. Something tells me that title is misleading, more important than anyone would guess. Inside there's a subfolder, called Read Me. At this point a random snooper would probably lose interest, as the most boring software instruction files in the world are called that.

I open it. And everything changes.

15

If you're reading this, I must be dead. I wonder if he killed me.

(Haha, I always wanted to type that.)

So I'm either dead, or my dad's hacked my account. Either way, I have to ask for a favor because I'm in no position to keep going. Can you help me out?

I pause, touching the screen, because this is so Morgan. The humor and arrogance don't conceal the warmth she was capable of. Though people didn't always understand her, nobody ever had a more loyal friend. I remember the time she staged a one-person protest because I was accused of cheating on a science test; the crib sheet belonged to someone else but the teacher found it on the floor near my desk. She picketed outside the principal's office until they called her dad, and when that didn't work, she went after the jerk who was letting me take the fall.

"Absolutely," I tell the message from beyond, and keep reading.

So, at this point, I'm assuming you said yes. If it's Liv, you definitely did. (I hope it's Liv.) Unless it's my dad reading this. In which case, sorry for disappointing you, but I guess you need to know that your buddy Jack is a pervert. I kinda hope I'm not around to deal with the fallout, is that wrong? Anyway. Here's some background in case it's not my dad because you don't know the deal, random stranger. Or Liv.

Actually, I'll just go forward with the belief it's you. Somehow I'm sure it will be; you're the only person who never let me down.

Oh, God. Tears spill over because I never knew she felt that way, and now I can't say that she was that person for me, too. It's too late; the door between us has closed, and Morgan's gone where I can't follow.

There are a lot of things I couldn't tell you, and I'm sorry about that. I didn't think you'd understand; I suspected you'd try to stop me. Even now, I can hear you saying, "What the hell are you thinking? Life isn't a Scooby Doo episode where teenagers catch villains who go to jail whimpering, 'And I would've gotten away with it if not for you meddling kids.' You're going to get hurt."

She's not wrong. The tears fall faster and I bow my head. She knew me so well.

But some things are worth the pain. You don't know this about me, but I dream sometimes. About my mother.

I'm getting ahead of myself, though.

My mother's name was Lucy Ellis. In high school and college, she worked as a model. There are old pictures in the document, examples of how pretty Lucy Ellis-Frost was, not that I need the illustration. I've seen their old family albums. Morgan gets her looks mostly from her mom, as Creepy Jack observed earlier. *I'm sure you didn't know this, but . . . she dated Jack Patterson first.* There's even a shot of them together, dressed in '80s formal wear.

"Wait, what?" I gape at the computer.

That adds another layer of awful to what he's doing with Morgan, gives it the flavor of obsession. Suddenly, the room is heavy with perfume, though I haven't sprayed anything. It's a bright smell, but a little cloying, too, citrus and flowers. Glancing around, I see the door is still shut. Why . . . ? After a minute, the scent fades, leaving me mystified.

She broke up with him her sophomore year of college, and within six months, she was engaged to my dad, who wasn't rich or well-known, then. But Jack kept hanging around. He made friends with Randall Frost. Don't you think that's weird?

"More than a little," I mutter.

Most people are eager to put a failed relationship behind them. Seeing the person who broke your heart all the time . . . how can you get over it?

I keep reading.

Me, too. And when I was little, I didn't question what happened. But the older I got, the more I wondered. I mean, it was a sunny day. There was no traffic. She had no drugs or alcohol in her system. So why the hell did my mother drive her car into a tree? Dad said she must've swerved to avoid an animal in the road because that's just how Mom was. She couldn't even kill spiders, so of course she wouldn't squish an adorable squirrel. Right?

But relatives whispered "she had a history of depression, so maybe . . ." and then my dad would rush them out of the room. I was old enough to realize they wondered if it was suicide. My dad got so angry. "It was just bad timing. An accident."

Nothing about it makes sense. So I started digging. I know for a fact that on the day my mother died, she met Jack Patterson. After so long, the restaurant owner barely remembered their faces, so I don't know what they talked about . . . and I'm aware that this isn't proof. But I know in my gut that he killed her. If he didn't, he's the reason she died.

But now my progress is halted. Or I've been stopped, I don't know. You'll say I should've left this job to people more qualified, right? But they'll just think I'm crazy, unable to accept that sometimes people just die and there's no good reason.

I can't stop crying, because Morgan is more on point than she could've imagined. She wanted answers about her mother's death, and there's an eerie sort of parallel here. Maybe I need to solve Morgan's mystery in order to understand why I got to live when she died.

Anyway, I'm begging you to complete my work. In the folder marked JP, you'll find everything I've uncovered about Jack Patterson. Please don't let him get away with it. (I swear to God, Liv, I will haunt you if you refuse. Every chill on your spine, every shadow in the corner of your eye, that'll be me.)

I laugh shakily because this situation is far beyond what Morgan could've predicted and she's trying to pressure me from beyond the grave. Sighing, I skim the last part:

You can trust Clay. Don't tell anyone else. Good luck, I'm counting on you.

That's it. Morgan seriously thinks that Creepy Jack murdered her mother? Or had her killed, maybe. And what did she mean by "You can trust Clay"? Maybe with this message, but . . . that would be in the case it's Liv reading this message. It doesn't make sense to go to Clay with a message I allegedly wrote. Picturing that conversation gives me a headache.

So Clay, I found this on my Cloud Drive. Odd, right? I know it seems like I wrote it but let me lay a little more difficult shit on you. I'm not Morgan.

My mind is whirling; there's no way I can process anything else tonight. Like a zombie I trudge to the en-suite bathroom and wash off my makeup. Sleep seems impossible but my body has other ideas.

In the morning I face another exciting round of Let's Pretend to be Morgan. Mr. Frost is long gone when I go downstairs and Flint is waiting to drive me to school. This is getting old. It makes me angry to be delegated like this, and he's not even my dad, so how did *Morgan* feel?

Flint is too polite to show impatience, but I've kept him waiting for fifteen minutes by the time I come outside. I'm starting to understand why Morgan liked being a pain in the ass. It feels like I'm the one in charge, even if I'm not. I mean, I'm not allowed to drive but I can decide when we leave.

"Morning," Flint says.

I look out the window. Intellectually I know my bad mood isn't his fault but shit just keeps piling up. How am I supposed to prove that something went terribly wrong ten years ago when the cops didn't detect foul play? Plus, today, I'll see Nathan at school, and I know him well enough to understand that it'll be awful at best. He now thinks I'm the kind of girl who'd cheat on her boyfriend with his own brother.

Flint doesn't speak again until I'm leaving. "Have a nice day."

"You too," I mumble because my actual mother is stirring in my conscience, waving a wooden spoon and intoning, *I didn't raise you to act this way, Olivia.*

On my way to Morgan's locker, I spot three different girls rocking some variation of the outfit I had on yesterday. I've changed gears, so today I have on a poppy print sundress and red sandals. I pretend not to notice the whispers.

"Look, she doesn't even seem upset."

"She's so cold," the other girl agrees. "I'm glad *you're* my best friend."

I'm bulletproof glass, I tell myself. The words bounce off. These assholes never knew Morgan, so they don't realize that when she cries, she does it alone. Poise is her armor, impenetrable as steel. And now I have to be the same.

16

I get my books and head to class.

Already I've failed to complete an assignment on time, but I don't let it rattle me. Morgan often turned in work late, but she had a knack for getting around the teachers. After class, I pause at the instructor's desk. "I'm sorry. It's been . . . rough. I'll turn in the assignment tomorrow."

Mrs. Flanagan gives me a soft smile. "I understand. To be honest, I'm a little surprised to find you back in school already, Morgan."

"It seemed like a good idea at the time," I murmur.

"Let me know if I can do anything. Any of us, really. I'm so sorry." She doesn't say "about Liv" but I can see it in her eyes, hear it in her voice.

"Thanks."

I have barely enough time to make it to my next class, where the art kids surround me. There's Oscar, and walking beside him, I spot Goth white girl Sarah Miller. Quickly I identify the other four. Tish Jones is a pretty, black artist who creates exquisite pen and ink sketches. Emma Lin is an aspiring musical actress of Filipina descent; she also threw the last party I attended as Liv. White farm boy Eric Mitchell, and Ben Patel, whose grandparents are from India, round out the group. Eric is in choir, and Ben kills it on the debate team, so it's unfair to dub them strictly art kids.

Whatever their classification, they're determined to annex me, it seems, so when lunch rolls around, I follow them into the cafeteria and eat at their table. Halfway through the period, I feel eyes on me and glance around. Nathan's staring at me from the double doors, practically daring me to confront the situation. I'm sure he expects a haughty chin lift and a silent pretense that it never happened.

But I'm Liv, not Morgan. That's the main reason I need to stay away from him, but we can't settle this through avoidance. *I can control myself, right?*

I nod and pack up what's left of my lunch. "Bathroom," I mutter, pushing to my feet.

The others are talking about some Lithuanian artist and Morgan would probably know why his work is so exciting whereas I'd only get so enthusiastic over the potential for advancement in stem cell research. Nathan has disappeared but I know he's waiting for me in the courtyard. That's where we sat before the kiss.

Sure enough, he's on a bench, leaning forward, hands between his knees. From the other side of the patio doors, I touch the glass between us, tracing the line of his slumped shoulders. What happened yesterday, that has to be the last time. Maybe I knew that on some level, and that's why I got so carried away. Dead girls don't usually get the chance to kiss their boyfriends good-bye.

I push through the door and join him in the warm, balmy air, perfumed with kitchen herbs and sweet-smelling flowers. He glances up as I sit down and smooth the white-and-red patterned cotton across my knees. Morgan's legs are long and graceful; I can't even fault him for staring when I cross them.

"I owe you an apology," he says.

Of all directions I thought this conversation would go, I never predicted that one. I expected blame or possibly a demand that I break up with Clay immediately. Maybe that's my own guilt talking. But Nathan's a good guy at the core. Maybe I should've seen this coming.

"Me too."

"No, it was my fault. You were just trying to be a decent human being. I wish I could blame the booze, but . . ." A long sigh shudders out of him. "Honest to God, I don't know what came over me. I must be losing my mind."

Why? I want to ask so bad, but I'm afraid he'll tell me that it's because I reminded him of Liv. Which is awful because that's exactly what I was trying to do. But now that I can see the damage, the confusion and pain . . . I have to accept that this is a closed door. I have to.

Even if it feels like I'm dying.

"You were drunk," I say. "And sometimes that's enough to make you do stupid things."

For the first time, Nathan meets my gaze, a half-smile curving his mouth. "Are you calling yourself a stupid thing?"

"Sometimes I am." It's impossible not to be honest.

"Me too," he mutters. "So . . . are you planning to tell Clay?"

"Do you want me to? I can. I don't want him to get hurt later."

"You think I'll get wasted again and brag about it?" Nathan stares at me, hard, like he isn't sure what to make of me.

"More like you'll be overcome with drunken remorse and want to make amends. But it'll be worse if he finds out that way, not from me."

"Then yeah. Tell him." He pauses, his gaze dropping to his hands. I don't make the mistake of touching him. Neither of us can handle it.

Nathan acts like a sandcastle while I'm the flamethrower

threatening to melt him into a sheet of glass. But I don't react to that either.

"I'll make sure he understands the circumstances. You weren't thinking of me." It hurts to add this part. "You were missing her."

"That's the weird part," he whispers. "When I'm with you, I don't. And that's why I need to stay away. If I start thinking of you as the only painkiller that works, it'll hurt the one person left who gives a shit about me."

He's not the only one.

But there's a limit to how much comfort I can or should offer as Morgan. If I keep hanging out with Nathan, it'll only confuse him more. Me too, for that matter. The girl he loves is dead, even if I remember being her.

"I have a question."

His brows go up. "Is this on topic?"

"Kind of. I'd like to check on Liv's family but I don't know . . ."

"If you'll make it better or worse." Nathan sighs. "I so know how you feel. It's like my life's been cut in two, you know? I used to spend half my time over there, eating dinner with her folks, and now I wonder if they'd even want to see me."

"So you don't know the answer either."

"We should check in," he decides eventually. "Have your fancy housekeeper bake something. If the vibe is weird, we can make a quick escape."

The atmosphere is better between us now, more normal. And though it wasn't my intention, I've gotten his mind off everything. It's impossible to obsess over your own issues when you're worried about someone else, and we both care about Mom, Dad, and Jason. I used to tease Nathan that half my appeal was my awesome family.

So much for my brief resolve to keep my distance. But this is different, right?

"Then . . . I get my stitches out next week. After that I'll be clear to drive, so I can pick you up. Should we call first?"

"Probably." He's looking more cheerful.

My chest eases a bit.

"Okay. I'll call Liv's mom next Tuesday. By Wednesday I'll be good to go."

"Wednesday won't work. I have swim practice and after that, I have a meeting." He doesn't tell me what kind, and Morgan probably wouldn't be curious.

"Thursday?"

"Yeah. I'll see you then." Nathan stands and heads out of the courtyard first.

When I get up, I find a cluster of girls watching us. One of them is frowning, like I'm not allowed to talk to my dead best friend's boyfriend. They glare as a unit.

". . . so wrong."

I'm supposed to hear that, but I pretend I don't and keep walking. Is this what it was like for Morgan? On the surface she has everything, but each step in her shoes is painful. A while back, I read this horror story about a demon that doesn't die. Instead it leaps from body to body, an ethereal parasite. The host is slowly strangled to silence while this thing takes over their life. It was fiction, but I wonder . . .

Do monsters always know what they are?

17

Saturday is the soonest I can go see Clay. He works late enough that it would be dickish to ambush him afterward. Not that it's any better before work on Saturday morning. But I ask Mrs. Rhodes to pack up some breakfast anyway. She makes the fanciest basket I've ever seen, full of rolled eggs, cut fruit, and fried potatoes. Then I pull Morgan's car keys off the peg and dare her to tell me I can't.

There's little traffic passing from the country to the small city limits, ten cars or so. I obey all the rules of the road, coming to a full stop before making the left once I drive through downtown. Clay's neighborhood is quiet as I park. His borrowed car is here, one hurdle overcome. That was a minimal risk, however, as it's only nine now.

Taking the basket from the passenger seat, I hop out and go up the stairs. It doesn't occur to me until I'm knocking that I didn't do Morgan makeup. Actually I'm not wearing any, no jewelry either, and I think these yoga pants are probably what she wore to work out in. Morgan wouldn't have gone out looking like this, but there's nothing I can do but roll with it now.

I knock a second time before I hear footsteps inside. Clay comes to the door wearing only a pair of faded jeans. The top button is unfastened, so the denim hangs low, revealing a strong chest, sculpted abs, the smooth indent of muscle on his hip, and astonishingly beautiful ink. A complex geometric pattern done in red and black frames his broad shoulders. For a moment I just stand in stunned silence because I honest to God had no idea he was this . . . breathtaking.

His skin holds a late summer bronze, and dark stubble shadows his cheeks and jaw. The guys at school look like little boys in comparison. His eyes glint with gold in the morning light. Lazily he stretches and I watch the interesting things that motion does to his tight, rolling muscles. It's obvious that he's just slid out of bed because his shaggy black hair stands on end, worsening when he tries to tame it.

"This is a surprise," he says, smiling.

The dimple pops in his left cheek, telling me he's happy to see me. That expression may not last when he finds out I kissed his brother. Suddenly my palms are wet around the handles of the basket because I truly don't want to hurt him. Though I don't know him too well, the fact that he's working full-time for Nathan says everything about what kind of person he is.

"I brought breakfast." Offering the food is a great distraction.

Clay cocks his head. "It's not my birthday."

"I know."

"Well, come in. Nathan's still asleep."

Good. It'll be better if I can get this done without seeing him. But the problem with their house is that you have to walk through the bedrooms to get to the kitchen unless you come in the back door. Clay decides that's the best option, so we close the front door and slip in that way. There's plenty of sunshine in the kitchen, and I get some plates while he quietly closes the bedroom door so his brother can sleep longer.

"How did you know where they were?" he asks.

Shit. As Liv, I spent a lot more time here than Morgan did. I also know they don't have a washer and dryer, and that

Nathan walks six blocks to the Laundromat when he runs out of clean clothes. But nobody else would. I have to watch myself.

Smiling, I shrug. "Common sense? Most people put plates near the fridge or the stove."

"Should I make some tea?"

Since Morgan loves it, I should say yes, but I'm tired of pretending. "It's too warm. Water is fine."

"Don't tell me you're already working out." Clay touches my shoulder. It sounds like he's gearing up to lecture me, which is oddly heartwarming.

"No, I'm not. Why, am I not formal enough?"

"You *know* you're beautiful," he says. "You don't need me to tell you."

Heat suffuses my cheeks, early warning that I'm blushing. No, this cannot happen. *Clay, put on a damn shirt.* Now I can't even look at him because he's propped against the counter and the sunlight's burnishing his skin, and he's like somebody out of a magazine. *Rugged guy in kitchen, take one.* I busy myself setting the food out, and he goes out onto the back porch. Through the screen door I can see some T-shirts drying on the railing. Great, now I'm imagining him washing them by hand, muscles flexing. He pulls a white one down and shrugs into it. By the time he comes back inside we're ready to eat.

"Did you make this?" he asks.

I laugh. "Seriously?"

"Didn't think so." He grins back. "But why are you being so nice to me?"

The question makes me go, *WTF?* Even if they're just bang buddies, why would Morgan need a reason to see her man? "Isn't that kind of our deal?"

"Nobody told me there was an amendment." He's smiling, so I can't tell if he's joking or not. The real Morgan would know.

"You've been great since the accident." Which is true. "So I figured . . ."

"The food is top-notch. Thank your housekeeper for me." Clay is wolfing it down like he hasn't eaten in days.

"I will." As I eat, I keep an eye on the door to the bedroom because I didn't bring enough for Nathan and I'll feel like an asshole if he wakes up before we finish.

"You seem to have something on your mind."

Okay, here we go.

"I do have something to tell you, yeah."

"Go for it." He leans back in his chair, folding his arms.

"So basically, Nathan was pretty drunk the other night. He forgot who I was for a few seconds . . . and kissed me. When he realized I wasn't Liv, he threw up next to the porch."

Once it's out, it doesn't sound as bad, though I've omitted how I responded. Clay doesn't need to know that. If I'm lucky, Nathan was hammered enough that he can't be sure what happened exactly, and he'll wonder if his memory is playing tricks on him.

But Clay . . . Clay is thunderstruck. I mean, he's staring at me like I'm the devil. Or no, that's not exactly right. He's just dead shocked. By what, I have no idea. Can't even guess.

The silence lengthens until I can't stand it. My gaze drops to my plate.

"Why are you telling me this?" he finally asks.

"To make sure you heard the story in context. Nathan would probably make it sound worse than it was. You know how he is."

"*I* do, yeah." The emphasis is delicate; something has changed in the way he regards me. His focus sharpens.

"And I wanted to make sure you didn't get hurt," I add. That's common courtesy, right? Even if you're not super serious, it's an asshole move to treat someone's feelings like nothing.

His reaction is still incomprehensible, but there's a subtle softening to his smile. "Okay. Let me know if he gets out of line again. The kid's struggling, I get it. But he can't chuck his future when he's so close to getting out of this town, you know?"

I nod. "Liv wouldn't want that."

"I'll take your word for it. She never liked me."

That makes me start guiltily. I had no idea Clay noticed, but I did judge him based on what other people said about him. Whenever he was home, I'd make an excuse and take off, dragging Nathan over to my place instead. Back then it was like I thought his bad reputation was contagious or something.

"She just didn't know you," I say.

"True." His gaze lingers on mine, then it drops slightly, and I feel a tingle in my lips, bare arms, shoulders.

This is . . . crazy.

To interrupt whatever's happening here, I stand and pick up our dishes. I'm at the sink washing them before it occurs to me that Morgan probably has never washed a plate in her life. But it's too late to back out of this, so I just finish up and stack everything in the dish drainer. Then I get a dish cloth and turn around because the table still needs wiping. Though I didn't hear Clay move, when I turn, he's right behind me. I back up against the counter, but he doesn't take the hint to give me more space.

Instead he steps forward, close enough that I can feel the warmth radiating from his skin. "What are you playing at, Morgan?"

"Excuse me?" There's nowhere for me to go.

"Are you trying to make me fall for you?"

Hasn't that happened already? But it's not the kind of question I can ask. I mean, you don't interrogate a guy about loving you. I manage a nervous smile and say nothing.

He cups my face in one hand, long fingers curving over my

jaw, and his thumb skims down slowly until he's almost touching my lower lip. My lashes tremble before I even realize I'm halfway to closing my eyes. Clay moves in until our bodies are flush, heat prompting more. He's so close that I can feel his heart against mine. With his other hand, he brushes the hair from my face in a move so gentle that I can't pull away.

This kiss isn't like the other one. He slides his right arm around my back, pulling me up against him, and his other hand tangles in my hair. Clay's mouth is firm, but it's like he's asking a question with every brush of his lips. With each flicker and turn of his head, the spark builds a little more, until I wrap my arms around him and dive deeper. His shoulders are incredibly strong, and I can't resist moving my hands, digging my fingers into his back. In response he lifts me onto the countertop and steps between my legs. I wrap them around him, not thinking about anything but his mouth on mine, the delicate way he breathes me in. He pulls back for a few seconds to stare at me with glazed, incredulous eyes and then comes back in for another round.

This time his mouth feels both softer and hotter, plus a thousand times hungrier, and I respond the same way. I've never felt like my bones were melting before. Clay trails his lips away to nuzzle my jaw, my throat, the curve of my shoulder. His hands rove over my back, just like I'm touching him, and I'm not thinking of anything else. I just *want* him.

But he backs off first, leaning his forehead against mine. His breath comes in quick, heaving gulps, but I sound about the same. I'm shivering a little, too. *Jesus.* My head drops onto his shoulder and he follows as if he doesn't want to lose that contact point.

"What the hell?" he breathes. "That was . . . it was . . ." But he can't find the words either.

I curl my fingers around the nape of his neck, holding on.

The way I feel, I might topple sideways if I don't. "Too much for post-breakfast action?"

Clay laughs softly and strokes the side of my cheek. "Probably. Now my morning shower has to be a cold one."

"Well, that's something I didn't expect to hear today." Nathan ambles out of the back bedroom in rumpled pajamas.

While he rummages in the cupboard, I hop down from the counter. Clay gives me a little space, but I sense him watching me as I maneuver to the other side of the kitchen. His brother grabs a box of Krispy Flakes and cuts me a look. I nod slightly.

Yeah, I told him.

But Clay intercepts the look and punches Nathan in the shoulder hard enough that his brother staggers back. "Touch her again and you'll get a beatdown."

"I know," Nathan mutters.

There's no way I can stay to watch him eat cereal, so I say, "I need to get going. I'm AWOL right now, and if my dad comes home before I get back, it'll get ugly."

Clay raises a brow because he knows this is bullshit. "I'll walk you out, sweets."

Guilt is creeping in, now that my hormones are cooling down. I can't meet his gaze as I move through the house toward the front door. Remorse, regret, they become an unsavory cocktail in the pit of my stomach. I can't believe I got so completely lost in someone I'm not even dating, except on a weird, after-death technicality.

But maybe it's not your fault. He implied that their deal was primarily physical, so maybe it's just . . . biochemistry. Morgan's body + Clay's body = insane, sexy flashfire. That reeks of highly unscientific rationalization, but it makes me feel a little better.

Until I think, *Nathan would be so wrecked if he knew.*

Clay lifts my chin with firm fingers before I can slip away.

For a long moment he studies my face and then shakes his head. "I thought I had a handle on things, but . . . you're totally throwing me lately. You know that, right?"

"What do you mean?" I suspect I know *exactly* what he's getting at.

He sighs slightly. "Never mind. Be careful going home."

"Don't work too hard."

Clay walks me to the car and kisses my temple before shutting the door. The warmth of his lips lingers long after I've driven away.

I'm operating on automatic, making turns according to a whisper or an impulse. I'm also smelling that weird perfume that flooded Morgan's bedroom as I was reading the letter she left. Gasping, I open the car window a crack and realize that I'm not headed for the Frost mansion, or my old house. In fact, I'm not even sure where the hell I am when I start paying attention to the road again. Glancing around doesn't yield much help. I'm out in the country where there are few signs posted and there are miles between houses.

But as I go over a small rise, I recognize the tree from a clipping that Morgan included in her file on Creepy Jack. *This is where her mother died.* Trembling, I pull over onto the dirt shoulder and walk across. The road has been paved over since then, repainted, so it's not like there's a crime scene for me to investigate. But the tree itself bears a scar. Is that normal? I mean, I think I read somewhere that trees don't heal, but I've seen telephone poles knocked down by the impact of a crash. Maybe it depends on the relative size of the tree versus the weight and velocity of the car. Physics isn't my thing, so I can't do the calculations in my head.

Nathan could. But I don't text him.

This is a really lonely spot, so out of the way that I can't imagine where Mrs. Frost was going when she passed by here.

It's possible a deer darted out in front of her car and she swerved, just like Morgan's dad said.

More to the point, it's beyond bizarre that I've found this spot without even trying. I circle the tree slowly and try to imagine what it was like on that day ten years ago. Mrs. Frost drove a little red sports car, and it was daytime. Not raining. Like a movie the scene comes to life in my head. She's speeding along, the radio is on. There are no other cars on the road, so she's going a little faster than she should. The wind whips through her hair, dark like Morgan's, and her sunglasses hide part of her face.

She's not smiling. Something is bothering her. I remember how Morgan's letter said she's positive that her mother met with Creepy Jack the day she died. *So what did they talk about?* The scene feels almost too real as she zooms closer to the spot where she dies. But just before I see what happened, the picture in my head cuts out. Now there's only black and screaming, the sound of crunching metal and then silence. I open my eyes. The summer morning feels cold as ice, and when I exhale I can see my breath.

Then I hear Morgan's voice, clear as a bell. *I told you. This wasn't an accident.*

But my mouth isn't moving, and there's no one else here.

18

On shaky feet, I stumble back to the car. The summer sunlight does little to dispel the icicles growing in my veins. I whisper, "Are you there?"

But this time no reply comes.

I manage to convince myself that I'm going crazy and start the VW. But I can't forget the scar on the tree and the way I felt standing in the shadow of its branches. In self-defense, I crank up the volume on the last song Morgan played, and it's oddly cheerful, upbeat even. When I get back to the Frost mansion, I find a note from Mrs. Rhodes informing me that there are plates in the fridge ready to be microwaved and that she'll see me Monday. She probably doesn't normally stick around on Saturdays but since I just got out of the hospital, Mr. Frost asked her to put in some overtime this morning. I suspect she figured that if I'm well enough to make her pack breakfast for my boyfriend, she can knock off work. That logic isn't inaccurate, either.

I head up to Morgan's room, sit down at her desk, and get out a notepad. Okay, I have several questions that demand answers, so I list them in no particular order.

1) What was Nathan talking about with, "You never told her, right?"

2) Who's trying to blackmail Morgan and why?!
3) What the hell am I supposed to do about Creepy Jack?
4) Did CJ really kill Morgan's mother?

Seeing the list in black ink makes everything feel more real. The weekend looms before me with no prospect of relief or entertainment. The walls close in, and I want nothing more than to grab the car keys off the hook in the kitchen and escape to my old life. But I imagine my parents reacting to Morgan pleading for asylum and let out a sigh.

Yet I can't resist dialing. It's okay for me to check in, right? Plus I need to ask about Nathan and me visiting on Thursday. On the third ring, my mom answers, sounding tired. Her voice is quiet and flat, a little husky, which makes me think she's been crying. Tears clog my own throat instantly.

It takes all my self-control to say, "Mrs. Burnham?"

"Morgan!" At least she seems pleased to hear from me.

"Yeah." But I can't push out the words; there's just no way. I know how stupid it is, so I can't frame the question, *How's everyone doing?* The answer is self-evident.

"You holding up okay, honey?" She shouldn't be asking *me* that, but it's indicative of how awesome my mom is. Even though she's hurting, she still cares about Morgan, who's been my best friend for so many years that she probably thinks of her as a second daughter.

"Not really," I whisper.

My mom sniffles. "Me either."

Oh, God, my chest hurts. Rubbing it doesn't make the ache go away, and I try to control my breathing so she can't hear me cry. The tears slip down my cheeks. She must pick it up from the silence, however, because her voice comes back soft and shaky.

"Did you need something?"

"I was just . . . checking in. Nathan and I were wondering if we could come by on Thursday, but we weren't sure—"

"Of course," Mom cuts in. "You two practically lived here, before."

That word is a shackle around my ankles and a weight dragging me down. I sniff, hoping she doesn't hear it.

She does. "You're welcome anytime, Morgan. Both you and Nathan. I'm sure you must've been wondering if it would hurt us to see you but it hurts more pretending Liv never existed. If you're up for it, I'll make her favorite dinner and we can go through the album."

I'm in hell. There's no other explanation.

"Okay," I whisper.

As soon as we disconnect, I tip over onto my side and curl into the fetal position. It pulls my stitches, so the pain lets me hold together for an extra thirty seconds before I dissolve into messy, hiccupping sobs. My head's aching by the time I cry myself into a damp, twitchy ball. The house is still quiet, nobody to disturb me grieving for myself.

Before I can think better of it, I pick up my phone and message Nathan. *We're on for Thursday at Liv's house. Meet you after school?*

God, it's weird writing about myself in third person.

He replies faster than I expect. *Did you talk to her parents?*

Yep. I hesitate before sending. Yet what else is there to say, really? I can't tell him to have a good weekend, and I shouldn't encourage him to text me. We're already on shaky ground because I can't stop thinking about how Nathan said the pain only stops when he's with me. I wish I could say the same, but it only reminds me how screwed up everything is. So I just add what Mom said, and I have another message a minute later.

Christ. Not sure I can handle a stroll down memory lane.

You have to go, I send back. *She's expecting us.*

This time it takes almost five minutes for Nathan to say, *Fine. Thursday after school. What're you doing anyway?*

I swear I lose my mind temporarily because I answer him just like I would've as Liv, with complete honesty. *Just finished crying my eyes out. Otherwise, not much. You?*

If there was any way to get that text back, I'd vaporize and beam through the atmosphere to suck the words back into my fingertips. But once the imp of impulse takes over, it's a free-for-all, and I'm locked on my screen waiting to see how Nathan will respond. Morgan never would've said anything like this to him, but death is a game changer, I suppose.

I'm no better. Come over, stop me from drinking.

I swallow hard. Just this morning, I was perched on the kitchen counter with Clay kissing me. It's beyond wrong to hang out with Nathan when his brother's not around, no matter how much I want to. Under no circumstances can I get between them, but I'm legit worried about Nathan. Maybe that sounds heartless, but Clay is bedrock solid, maybe because he doesn't realize what he's lost. I message Clay at work. It might kill me to friend-zone Nathan but I can't watch him self-destruct. I solicit permission for self-indulgence, swearing to myself that I can keep a lid on feelings that I'm not allowed to have anymore.

Just got an emergency flare of a text from your bro.

What's wrong with him? comes the immediate reply.

Hands trembling, I forward the text to Clay. If I'm not lying or sneaking around, then it's marginally less awful. Right? The speed of Clay's answering text humbles me. As I read, a fist closes around my heart.

Anything you can do, I'd appreciate it. It . . . means a lot to me that you're willing to help me keep what family I have left together.

Okay, I send back. *As a special favor to you.*

You're the best. I'll make it up to you, I promise.

No, I'm officially the worst.

I try not to think of this as a date as I put cold compresses on my eyes. Morgan's pale complexion shows the redness, and the swelling is bad enough that I can hardly see. Once I'm steady enough to drive, I leave a note for Mr. Frost, though there's no telling what time he'll be home. As Liv, I always thought Morgan was lucky; she could basically do whatever she wanted, any day of the week.

Now that I'm literally in her shoes, I realize how lonely that is.

19

As I drive past the Claymore house, I spot Nathan sprawled on the porch swing. My hurried steps crunch over the gravel up the alley, and as I come around the corner of the house, he cracks open a beer. Before he can drink it, I reach over his shoulder and dump it out.

His eyes widen. "Holy shit. You actually came."

I shrug. "I'm on a mission to make sure you don't ruin your life."

Nathan shifts, dropping his leg so there's room for me on the swing. The chains creak when I settle. "*Your* life must really suck if you're willing to babysit me."

"Poor little rich girl," I say with just enough edge to sound like Morgan.

"Let me guess, Clay asked you to check on me." He makes it sound like I've been sent to scout a radioactive bomb site.

I skirt that guess. "You have friends. Why aren't you with them?"

"Because I don't feel like partying." His tone contains a certain irony.

"Whereas drinking alone is fine."

He slams a palm into the external wall so hard that the clock on the other side topples onto the love seat; through the window I see it bounce. "What part of 'stay away from me' didn't you understand? Seeing you without Liv is like having my insides cut out with a rusty garden trowel."

"That one of your SAT vocab words? And *you* asked me to come over, remember?"

"Jesus, were you always this much of a pain in the ass, or did Clay rub off on you?" Nathan lurches off the swing, but I think his lack of balance comes from leaving a moving seat, not being shit-faced.

I follow him into the house before he can shut the door and lock me out. Maybe it's because of the role I'm forced to play, but right now, he seems *so* young. Technically, he's only a month behind me, November to October, and we're among the oldest in the junior class. Who knows, though? In his shoes I might refuse to get out of bed at all. This morning, I saw him eating cereal, but he probably hasn't had anything since. I sigh softly.

"If the Claymore villa isn't up to your standards, go home," he snaps.

That does it. I push past him, through their two bedrooms, and into the kitchen. Rummaging through the kitchen turns up a couple of half-empty fifths of whatever, whiskey probably. I dump that down the sink while Nathan grabs at the bottles from behind. One advantage of being Morgan is that he can't reach over my shoulders as easily. The fridge has milk, eggs, butter, various condiments, lunchmeat, some lettuce, tomatoes, half a loaf of bread, and beers. But there are only two left, not enough for him to get drunk. I leave those.

"Want a sandwich?"

Nathan levels a long look on me, and I can't read it. For the first time I realize I don't know him as well as I thought. The question echoes in the back of my mind: *You never told her, right?* Dammit, what secret do Nathan and Morgan share? The idea that my best friend and my boyfriend have been conspiring behind my back is enough to kill me a second time.

"Fine," he says at last.

Silently I build him a sandwich, adding lettuce and tomato, omitting the mayo for a thin layer of mustard and precisely six pickles on the bottom slice of bread. It's not until after I've put it all together that I realize Morgan wouldn't know his tastes so well. I should've checked first. Nathan stares at me so hard it feels like the top of my head might burst into flames.

I try to play it off. "Does it look okay?"

"It's perfect." His eyes are bottle green in the afternoon sunlight, sort of murky and opaque, too.

There's only one way to explain this. "I don't think you realize how much Liv talked about you. I know all kinds of things." That comes out sort of taunting when I didn't mean it that way, but his expression lightens.

"That doesn't explain why you remember, rich girl."

"Lately everything she told me seems more important," I murmur. "Even when it's about you."

"I can't decide if that's a compliment or not."

"Mostly not," I say, because Morgan would.

Yet the snark makes Nathan smile. He picks up the sandwich from the plate and takes a huge bite, studying me across the battered kitchen table. The sunlight is good to him, finding coppery lights in his dark hair and gilding his skin. He's finally shaved, too, and I remember all too clearly how it feels to skim my palms down his cheeks.

But I can't show Nathan how much I want him or how much he means to me. I get him a glass of water quietly and sit down across the table. He eats fast without offering me anything. There's nothing in the house I can have anyway. Ignoring me, he washes his plate and then comes back. I recognize this expression, though I didn't see it too often as Liv.

Regret.

"Sorry. I used you as a verbal punching bag again."

Morgan probably wouldn't forgive him easily, but I'm not her, and this is all I can offer. "Don't worry about it. If it helps to vent, I'm stronger than I look."

"I know," he says.

Before I've even made a conscious decision, I'm tiptoeing toward their secret. "Let me ask you something . . ."

"What?"

I can't meet his gaze or he might realize I'm shooting in the dark here. Which would make no sense at all. "Did you ever consider telling Liv?"

"About us?" Those words feel like they're launched on a barbed line that sinks into my chest and yanks my heart out in a bloody gush.

"Yeah." I can barely breathe.

Morgan and . . .

I can't even pair his name with hers in my mind. Nathan was mine. He was always, *always* mine. Right? Tears burn the back of my throat but Morgan wouldn't cry over this. This is idle curiosity, nothing more, so I examine my cuticles.

Nathan has no idea what he's doing to me, so he doesn't hesitate even for a second. "She never had a clue. And it doesn't matter now, does it?" He touches my hand, forcing me to look up. "It's not like we were a couple. It was just sex."

This . . . this is worse than I thought. My whole body locks, and I can barely move my mouth to respond. "True."

"Do you ever think about me when you're with Clay?" By his smirk, I know he's joking, but the knife twists slowly in my stomach.

"Heh, no." *I have to know.* When *did this happen?* I fake a yawn. "That was what, a thousand years ago?"

Something flashes in Nathan's green eyes. "Cruel. Don't people claim you never forget your first time?"

"Is that what I said?" Once, I fell off the jungle gym and got the wind knocked out of me. That's how I feel now, though I frame a smile, trying to cover that gut-punched reaction. "Maybe I lied. Maybe my first time was with a hot Italian guy."

He seems oddly serious, palms flattened on the counter, as if he's restraining the urge to reach for me. Or her. The uncertainty is excruciating. "Some things, you can't lie about. In some cases, it's pretty damn indisputable."

So . . . the summer before our freshman year, Morgan hooked up with Nathan. I don't know the circumstances and I can't ask, but . . . she *lied* to me. She claimed it was some guy in Venice. I remember the dispassionate way she talked about it. Fast, awkward, and messy . . . that was Nathan? Who claimed he was waiting. For me.

I don't know what's true anymore.

All I'm sure of is that the guy I thought loved me more than anyone in the world? He was Morgan's first. Shit, if she'd wanted to keep him, he probably wouldn't have even looked at me. Pain lances through me, so I have to curl my fingers around the edges of the table in discreet, white-knuckled anguish.

If Nathan was Morgan's first, does Clay know?

There's a limit to how much I can take. Before, I was so anxious about Nathan, but now I can't stand to look at him. My phone pings.

It would be awesome if it was Clay or even one of the art kids who want to annex me, but instead, it's from my favorite blackmailer. The message reads, *Tick-tock. Your father's getting an email tomorrow.* While Clay told me not to worry—that I can talk my way out of it—I'm not so sure anymore. The deeper I dig, the scarier my best friend's secrets become.

And the more painful.

"Who's it from?" Nathan asks.

"My dad." I lie without hesitation. "I have to get home. Sorry to cut this short." Morgan wouldn't ask if he's all right, and I don't. At the moment I don't particularly care.

Being careful has gotten me nowhere. As I pause outside the blue VW, I tap out a reply. *Don't be like that. Let's meet and talk about it.*

Just send the money.

No deal. I may be in for a shit-storm, but without seeing me, YOU don't get paid. This is more for your benefit than mine.

Maybe this scumbag has some answers.

An hour later, I'm on my way to the arranged meeting point and wishing like hell there was someone I trusted as backup.

20

I'm ten minutes early for the meeting.

The blackmailer will know Morgan on sight, but he or she hasn't given me anything to work with in terms of a description. I take a seat near the window. Georgette's Diner has delicious pancakes, decent patty melts, and mediocre iced tea. I order the latter since the first two are off the table. This place has a retro vibe with checkered flooring, red vinyl booths, and an actual jukebox at the back. This seems like an odd place to meet up for clandestine business, but I wouldn't have agreed to something like, "the quarry at midnight, come alone." Each time the bell jingles, I eye the door with chills crawling down my back.

A bearded guy in his forties seems a likely suspect, but he strolls past me, directly to the washrooms. Five minutes go by. Ten.

Now this asshole is late.

I check out the people who were here when I arrived. Two elderly couples are nursing coffee after dinner while other booths are occupied by people from my high school. With a wince I recognize Oscar Sanchez, but oddly, he's alone. He stares at me for a full five minutes, then he finally comes over and slides into my booth.

"I see you got my message." His face is dead serious, and I have *no* idea what's going on.

Trying to imagine how Morgan would react, I say, "If you need to borrow money, I can probably help you. Forcing me will get you nowhere. Go ahead, send my dad whatever."

His eyes ice over. Grabbing my glass, he swigs half of my tea like he's proving a point. The silence builds, until I can hardly stand it. What, exactly, does Oscar know? Somehow, we've started a staring contest, and neither of us is willing to look away.

Finally, he grins. "How far are you going to take this?"

Oh my God, is this a drama thing? An improv piece they were working on?

"You seemed pretty committed to the bit," I say coolly.

"Props for playing along. But if you wanted to hang out, you could've just said so. No need to be melodramatic."

I point out, "Drama is like cake to you."

Relief swirls through me. Finally my luck has broken the right way. Oscar might have a terrible sense of humor, but at least I'm not being blackmailed.

I wonder why Morgan purged Oscar's contact information, though. His name and picture should've come up if they messaged each other regularly.

Did she think someone was spying on her? Given what I've uncovered about her secret life, it's not the most outlandish theory.

"You make a good point. I know I'm not supposed to talk about the pictures, like ever, but I can't help wondering what happened with that old guy."

It clicks for me then. Since Morgan couldn't have taken the photos I found on the cloud, a third party had to be involved. I never would've guessed she'd be working with Oscar, yet photography *is* one of his hobbies. He's always popping up with a camera, and his specialty is unflattering candid shots. Hypothetically, if *Morgan* had gotten Oscar's text, she would've recognized the number and realized he was making an oblique reference to a secret they shared.

"It's kind of hard to explain," I mumble.

"Try." By his tone, I can tell he's let this slide before but curiosity must be getting the best of him. If I don't give him *something*, a blackmail prank could turn into the real thing.

I can't open the Pandora's Box of *I think he killed my mother, therefore I'm Humbert-Humberting him.* So I come up with a story that I think Oscar might believe. Adopting Morgan's faintly scornful expression, I say, "Have you seen any of his campaign ads? He promises family values and honesty yet you know how easy it was to get him to abandon those principles? I'm waiting for the next election and then I'll leak those photos. With some judicious face-blurring on my end, of course."

Oscar tilts his head, obviously unconvinced. "There are dishonest politicians all over the place, Morgan. What makes you so eager to bring this guy down?"

"He's giving my dad a hard time." That's kind of the truth, though it's more that he's pestering him about supporting . . . I'm not sure what; I just remember something about an influx of capital and that Mr. Frost isn't on board with the project.

Comprehension dawns. "I can see why you'd fight to keep some old bastard from chopping down your money tree."

It seems like Oscar thinks Creepy Jack is threatening Mr. Frost's business, and I roll with that assumption. "You'd do the same in my shoes."

"Maybe," he allows.

It's good that Oscar is appeased without knowing too much. There must be a reason why Morgan trusted him enough to ask him to take those photos. The fact that he hasn't posted them says volumes about how much *I* can trust him, even if he has a caustic personality and a twisted sense of humor.

"Want something to eat?" I ask. "It's on me."

"That's more like it." He grins and opens the menu.

Oscar orders a patty melt and a chocolate shake. The best thing about him is that he seems able to carry on a conversation with minimal input from me. He rambles about a project he's working on for Visual Arts and I make interested noises until his food arrives. Then I try not to drool while watching him eat.

"It's been a while," I say, hoping he'll fill in the blanks.

He nods. "Almost three months. We haven't hung out since school ended last spring."

"Sorry about that." Maybe Morgan wouldn't apologize but he seems to appreciate it, based on the smile I get in reaction.

"You've been busy with Claymore the Elder since you came back, I get it."

"Plus, I'm bad about keeping up with anyone during summer break."

Fortunately he takes the bait. "How was Europe?"

This is one area where I can shine, as I spent hours listening to Morgan recount her adventures. I muster some animation and repeat a couple of stories. He likes the one about the hot musician busking on the tube platform, and he cracks up over the pickpocket chase scene at Camden Market, too. This carries us through the meal at least.

"I need to get back," I say eventually. "My dad doesn't even know I took the car out, so there will probably be a reckoning."

If he knew Morgan as well as Clay did, Oscar would object to this, but he nods. "Call me when your old man cuts you loose."

"It should be better once the stitches are out. I really can't blame him for feeling overprotective right now." That's the most honest thing I've said in this conversation.

He sobers. "Yeah, about that . . . I'm sorry about Liv. I didn't know her well but she seemed like a cool person."

No matter how many times I hear that, it never gets easier. Not because my old life is gone but because I'm living a lie and nobody suspects a thing. It's heartbreaking for both of us—for Morgan, that I could slip right into her life and *nobody* can tell the difference—and for me, because not a single soul, no matter how much they loved me, senses that I'm still here.

It's like people are LEGOs, and everyone is replaceable.

21

Lately, I have all the privacy I could want and it's sort of hellish.

When Morgan's dad comes back, he seems exhausted and I regret some of my resentment over being delegated. I can't imagine what kind of problems would plague a CEO, so I should cut him some slack. It's not like I'm entitled to his time and attention.

I'm just . . . lonely. I miss my mom and dad. And Jason.

"Productive day?" I ask.

He stares at the meal I've laid out. "Is it a special occasion?"

"Huh?"

"Normally when I work late on the weekend you make me eat alone."

Maybe I'm too sensitive, but there seems to be a major rift between Morgan and her dad. "Oh. I guess I'm trying to be more understanding. How am I doing?"

"Great," he says, smiling, but his eyes are wary and watchful.

He doesn't say much as we eat but I can tell he's preoccupied. Asking doesn't yield any results, though. Mr. Frost only says, "I'll take care of it. You focus on feeling better, okay?"

"Sure," I mutter. "I'll just sit quietly and watch my flesh knit together."

That doesn't faze Mr. Frost. "On that note, you have an appointment Tuesday morning to get your stitches out. Flint will take you."

"I'm fine to drive myself. I'll take it easy, I promise."

Hesitating, he looks me over as I pick at my roasted vegetables and tofu. Since my lack of appetite might mess things up, I take a huge bite and smile. My head's still swirling from what I learned from Nathan, so it's an effort, but it seems to reassure Mr. Frost. I can tell his resolve to keep me like a caged bird is weakening, though.

I press the advantage. "Do you *want* me to develop a phobia of driving or something? The longer you keep me from getting behind the wheel—"

"They say you should get right back on the horse that threw you, right?"

I'm not sure that applies if the "horse" in question killed your best friend, but since I want the freedom Morgan flaunted, I don't object to his analogy.

"What time's my appointment?" I prompt.

He finally gives me the info and reminds me it's at the clinic where I had the checkup before, like I'm brain damaged in addition to being banged up. I swallow a cranky retort and promise to be there on schedule.

"You sure you don't want anyone with you? Wanda can—"

"No, I'm good. But I'll miss the first few periods of school. Don't forget to call that in."

"I'll e-mail the principal and the attendance secretary now." Mr. Frost gets out his phone and from that point on, it's like I'm not even there.

I don't want to sit with him. I don't want to eat. I just want to run. And I'm not even sure why. A haunting sweetness drifts to me on the air-con breeze, a familiar woman's perfume; I've smelled it twice before, but I still can't remember the name. My knee starts to jog.

Need to go, now. I mumble an excuse, but he doesn't look up from his screen as I hurry upstairs. Once the bedroom door shuts behind me, an odd sense of sanctuary steals over me. The tightness in my chest recedes and I let out a long, slow breath.

Is this how Morgan felt?

Sitting down at the desk, I get out the list I made and draw a line through the first question. Now I know what secret Nathan and Morgan shared, and I kind of wish I didn't. I also cross off the blackmail issue. It's a profound relief to realize that there isn't a sketchy individual about to send incriminating evidence to Mr. Frost. While I'm all for Jack Patterson being punished, I can't take action until I at least *try* to finish what Morgan started. Whatever my misgivings, however conflicted I feel, I owe her that much.

The rest of the weekend, I rest and work on projects I have no idea how to complete. With a miserable pang, I think about all the science and math I'm missing. Instead of studying what I want, I'll turn in substandard work and try to talk the teachers into going easy on me. From what I've seen, Morgan's good at that.

Monday, I avoid Nathan and hang out with the art kids.

In this clique nobody seems to be dating anyone else, which is what usually kills a group. First comes the hook-up, then the ugly dump, and then the circle takes sides, and pretty soon nobody is talking to anyone else. These guys have been hanging out since freshman year and I don't remember anything like that.

"When are you inviting us over?" Oscar asks, out of the blue.

I can't tell if he's joking. "I have a doctor's appointment tomorrow, so how about Wednesday?"

They all seem astonished for, like, ten seconds and then Eric says, "Are you serious? That would be amazing."

He's had a crush on Oscar's younger sister, Kendra, for, like, six months. Everyone knows about it but either Kendra hasn't gotten the memo or she's ignoring it. Maybe he's afraid to make a move because Oscar is one of his best friends. My throat tightens when I recall how Morgan and I watched Eric circling Kendra at Emma's party a few weeks back. Like a slightly evil sports announcer, she ran such hilarious commentary that I almost peed my pants laughing.

He's got a beer. Now he's chugging it. He's watching her from across the yard. Is this it, ladies and gents? Eric is heading for Kendra. He might speak, he might—oh, no, a last-minute choke and he's veering off.

Those moments are gone forever; I'm alone in Morgan's skin. The pain of it washes over me until I don't know why everyone at the table can't hear the screaming in my head. It's so loud, it practically deafens me, but they're excited, making plans to hang out at the mansion on Wednesday night. I let that wash over me, wishing I could escape like Morgan did. Then I cut that thought down to the quick because it seems like I think she did this to me on purpose. For all I know, it's something I did, this life I stole.

Thankfully lunch ends soon and I muddle through another day. Clay messages me as I exit my last class. *You have your car today?*

Yep, I send back.

After gathering my stuff, I head out the front doors into the sunshine. I'm astonished to see him shove off the bike rack and saunter toward me, offering a brilliant smile. "Thought so. If you didn't talk your dad around by now, well . . ." He answers my unspoken question next. "I bummed a ride. Since I'm off today, I figured we could do something."

"Like what?"

He steps into my space so smoothly that I don't recoil. Clay drops a soft kiss onto my mouth and then unloops my backpack from my shoulders. He doesn't seem self-conscious about carrying it, though it's definitely a feminine design. I lead the way to the VW and unlock it, still waiting for an answer as to what he wants to do.

"I'm more interested in what *you* want." Like he hasn't just dropped a massive bombshell on me, he opens the door and gets in.

It feels like forever since anyone's asked that. The fact that Clay is helming the question, that's messing with my head. I consider as I start the car.

"How about the mall in Anderson?"

"Is there something specific you need to buy?" he asks.

"Not really. I just want to get out of Renton. Walk around a little, maybe get a drink."

"Sounds good. I'm all yours today."

"Yeah?" I'm happier to hear that than I should be but I can't staunch the thought, *At least somebody is.*

"Definitely. Remember, I promised to make it up to you if you checked on Nathan on Saturday. And he seems to be doing better now."

"That was nothing." As we talk, I pull out of the parking lot and head for the highway.

He brushes the hair away from my face lightly, so gentle that I can hardly believe that he has a bad reputation. "It was something to me."

I find myself softening toward him, and before I know it, I'm saying, "You know, Nathan and I are having dinner at Liv's house on Thursday. It might be . . . bad. Do you think . . . could I stop by India Ink if I need to see you, afterward?"

His breath hitches, barely audible over the air-con vents

blowing chilly air. "When you put it like that, you could do pretty much anything you want, sweets."

"So that's a yes?"

He nods. "Close to closing, it's usually just me and Blue, and she won't say anything if you swing by."

"It's not against the rules?"

"Nah. You just never showed any interest before." The soft way he says it makes me think maybe he wishes otherwise. He studies my profile for a long moment before adding, "You're different somehow. Since the accident."

My heart skips a beat. "I am?"

"Yeah. I feel like an asshole for asking, but . . . have you changed your mind about us?"

"What do you mean?" There's a sinking sensation in my stomach.

"Don't mess with me," Clay says quietly. "It's not funny. You know damn well I'm wondering if you want a *real* relationship now."

22

What did we have before?

I swallow the question. He's waiting for an answer, and I don't know what to say. If I want to stop this—whatever it is—this is the perfect opening. Immediately I decide it's too soon and that Mr. Frost will be worried about the breakup. But if I'm honest with myself, that's an excuse. I just don't *want* to, because Clay's concern seems sincere and from what I can tell, he's always completely honest. No secrets, no shadows.

I'm not ready to lose that.

It could be desperation and loneliness talking but the only time I'm anywhere close to happy in my new skin is when Clay is nearby. There are tons of reasons why this is a bad idea, selfish, self-indulgent, and possibly codependent, but I don't have it in me to cut him loose. He shifts in the passenger seat, likely uncomfortable with the long silence; his long fingers tap out a staccato rhythm against his thigh.

"Would it be okay with you?" I ask finally.

"Is that what you're worried about?"

"Are we *this* dedicated to answering questions with questions?"

I sneak a look to find him smiling reluctantly. The dimple plays hide-and-seek in his left cheek. His jaw is shadowed, dark stubble against his summer tan. In profile he's beautiful, and . . .

I can't let myself be distracted. With effort, I focus on the highway.

"Fine, I'll show my hand first. If you want to take things to the next level, I'm game. But . . . if we date for real, I *have* to pay you back."

"Don't worry about it," I say automatically while my mind is whirling.

Every time I think I understand Morgan's life, another layer peels away, leaving me with onion tears pooling in my eyes. *What the hell is he talking about?* But I'm sure Morgan wouldn't care if Clay borrowed some money. Her spending habits suggest that she has no sense of scale and that fifty bucks, even a hundred, would be pocket change. The more baffling question is the phrase "if we date for real."

"You might be fine with it," he mutters, "but I'm not. I can't keep three grand if we're rewriting the agreement. I'm not a man-whore."

Agreement? Three thousand dollars? Holy shit. The only thing I can figure is that Morgan hired him as her fake boyfriend, though for what reason, I can't fathom. Does it have to do with her secret past with Nathan or is it intertwined with the investigation of Creepy Jack? Most frustrating, there is nobody I can ask. Unless . . .

I have to frame this just right.

With a quiet laugh, I murmur, "Didn't you think I was crazy for suggesting this?"

I'm banking on that. There's no way Clay would've gone to Morgan and asked for money in exchange for dating services. She's pretty and tons of guys were after her, so it's not like she had no other options. Logically speaking, she must've propositioned *him*.

"A little. But . . . I know how you feel about attachments."

"They only hurt you in the end." I'm quoting Morgan. This

is why she cultivated mystique at school and didn't let people close.

I'm one of the few who knew her at all, but I didn't realize she'd go this far to present a normal image. With this much context, I don't need Clay to explain. Morgan wanted a partner for dances and double-dates, so she could hang out with Nathan and me without feeling like a third wheel. Everything else was a front. And I bought it, even if I suspected it was a physical thing. Yet Clay seemed genuinely upset when I first woke up in Morgan's body; I remember the feel of his tears on my skin.

"It wasn't supposed to happen like this," he's saying. "But I can't spend six months with someone and keep it all business. I'm not wired that way. So . . . sue me, I care about you. Lately you're making me think it's not just me. But . . . it's up to you where we go from here."

I'm quiet too long, so he adds, "Look, I get it if you're not into someone like me."

"Someone . . . who quit school to take care of his family? Someone who works his ass off?" I'm a little pissed that Clay doesn't seem to think he's good enough for me.

Morgan.

Whatever.

"We've definitely got a princess-and-pauper vibe going."

"I don't care about that." It's not my money anyway.

"It's harder to dismiss on my end." He's trying to be cool but his jaw is clenched. "I'm not a charity case. Three thousand may be chump change to you, but it was enough to pay the back taxes on the shit box we call home, plus keep Nathan in shoes and shirts until graduation."

Oh man. I recall Clay saying that his mom has been gone for two years. I wonder how long it's been since the woman took care of their bills? No wonder he was willing to fake couple-up with Morgan. It had to seem like a miracle from above.

His pride is at stake, so I can't be insensitive. "Can you do installments? I get that you don't want to feel bought and paid for, though you have to know I don't feel that way."

Since I just found out about the money changing hands.

"No need. I sold the Corvair. Insurance paid out the total value of the car and then I found a collector willing to buy it on salvage title. So I have money now. If you want to be my girlfriend for real, you need to take what I owe you."

"Okay," I say. "Write me a check."

"Seriously? You don't have anything else to say?"

God. I'm so confused that I hardly know what's happening in my own head minute to minute. But he deserves something.

"I don't know what's going on with us," I tell him honestly. "But I'd like to find out. No deals, no rules. Let's just . . . be together and see how it feels."

"Okay." He settles a hand on my neck, sifting through the long hair until his warm palm rests on the nape of my neck and then he just . . . strokes. I didn't know I was knotted there until Clay started working out the kinks.

It's a real effort to keep my eyes open. Damn. I want to lean forward and stretch like a cat, have his hands all over me. As delicious tingles start, I nudge him away.

"Don't distract the driver. We'll be at the mall soon."

So maybe that's an overstatement. The needle noses upward on the speedometer, though I'm careful not to exceed the posted limit. Twenty minutes later, I pull into the parking lot and as soon as I park, Clay reaches over and touches my cheek.

"You sure? I mean, you told me before there was no point in starting with someone when you'll be off to Europe for university in a few months."

Damn. I haven't contemplated Morgan's future, mine now. I don't want to study art in Paris, which was *her* dream. My ideal school is Johns Hopkins, though my parents probably couldn't have afforded it. That's no longer an issue, but I don't have the academics I need on record anymore. While the knowledge is still in my head from those classes, like the rest of Liv's life, I have no way to prove it was real.

That I *was* somebody else.

"We have almost a year," I point out. "That's long enough to make some memories. And I won't let you break my heart."

"It's not you I'm worried about."

"Huh?"

"I'm the one who'll only be a shadow in your rearview mirror when you drive off."

If anyone had told me that Clay could be this vulnerable, I'd have said they were insane. But I take him seriously because his expression is unmistakable. "Then . . . are *you* sure?"

He laces our fingers together, lightly rubbing his thumb against my skin. "Are you crazy? Life's rarely offered me anything good without immediately following it with a kick in the face. You're the only beautiful thing that's ever been mine, free and clear."

My heart dips. *Not me.*

Morgan.

But he said *I've* been throwing him. And the way I act made him ask if I was trying to make him fall for me. So maybe it's Liv he likes; he just doesn't know it.

How could he?

I should tell him.

I can't tell him.

My pause makes him think I'm hesitating, so he adds, "If it wasn't clear, yeah, I'm sure."

Then he's kissing me, or I'm kissing him. Either way, it's the best way to make me stop caring about anything but Clay's mouth and Clay's hands. Clay, who never actually hooked up with Morgan. That means he's mine, not hers, and this is okay.

Right? His lips are hot, rough, and soft at the same time, and it's all brand new. He likes it when I sink my hands into his hair, and he tries to pull me into his lap, across the gear shift and emergency brake.

I whimper because I'm still sore and the angle is bad. Right away he realizes it's not a good noise and lets go. "Damn. Sorry."

"It's okay. The VW isn't made for this."

"That's probably why your old man bought it for you. Hard to get down and dirty in a Barbie car. In fact, I feel kind of wrong just picturing it."

"In a good way?" I tease.

Clay grins, and my heart does this flippy, clenching thing. Then he bounds out and races around the car to open my door for me. "No comment. Come on."

23

When Clay looks at me like that, I am butter, and he's the sun. Asking a sensible question is almost beyond me. "Where are we going?"

"To walk around. Wasn't that the point of driving over here?"

"Pretty much."

He takes my hand, threading our fingers together, and I'm conscious of each point of contact, almost giddy with it. The Anderson Mall is probably nothing compared to what Morgan saw abroad but it's fine by me, even if the anchor stores are Sears and JCPenney instead of Saks or Nordstrom. We window shop, joke around, and tease each other about trying on ridiculous outfits. Clay surprises me by walking into a shop that sells suits.

"Pick one out for me."

"Seriously?"

"I need something to wear to the dances this year, right? I mean, that's assuming you want me to take you."

To Homecoming, the Winter Formal, and prom.

"Of course," I say.

I've never selected clothes for a guy, so I'm excited as I follow him into the shop. The sales guy takes a look at us and goes back to his phone, freeing us to roam around. After five minutes of browsing, I settle on dove gray in fine fabric and offer him a white shirt and lilac tie to try on. I'm already planning my dress to match that dreamy purple.

Clay looks dubious but since he asked me to do this, he likely doesn't want to hurt my feelings. And when he comes out, he looks better than I imagined. Even the tousled curls and scruff add to the impression of sexy elegance. I give him two thumbs up while inviting him to spin around with a twirl of my fingers.

"Are you ogling me right now?"

"A little."

"Sweet. You sure I don't look like a jerk in this?"

"Are you kidding? You're completely pulling it off."

At my words, Clay takes another long look in the mirror, then nods. "Okay. I'll get everything and keep it nice for . . . October?"

"I'll check the school calendar online when I get a chance."

He takes everything off and changes back into his usual apparel. I can tell that the bulk of the clothing budget goes to Nathan because Nathan's stuff always looks brand new, whereas Clay has been working the same two pairs of jeans for years, and his tees are threadbare, cotton worn until it feels like whisper-thin velvet. I like the feel of how it curves over his chest and shoulders a little too much, which is why I'm pretending to brush some lint away.

"Want to get something to eat?" he asks.

At first I nod, but then I realize I have no idea what I can eat at the mall food court. He leads me to a Japanese stall that specializes in sushi, then he looks over the menu. "Can you make this without the shrimp?"

I look over his shoulder and see that leaves rice, cucumber, and avocado, all good as far as I know. The girl nods, and then he adds, "Make sure everything's gluten-free, okay?"

"No problem."

"Then . . . two orders of that . . . and I'll have a couple boxes of this."

Smoked salmon, cream cheese, cucumber . . . mmm, that sounds delicious. But Morgan is lactose intolerant and she might be allergic to fish. Definitely shellfish. I need to get a list of food allergies from Morgan's doctor ASAP. *Maybe tomorrow at the appointment . . .*

As we eat, I fight the feeling that I shouldn't be doing this. I mean, this is a step Morgan never would've taken but that makes me even more determined to continue. If I don't carve out a little space in her life, I'll go insane trying to investigate Creepy Jack. Plus, maybe Clay can help. Morgan even said I could trust him, which means she thought he was a solid guy, even if she wasn't *into* him.

I don't want to contemplate the downside, but the doubts creep in. *What if this isn't permanent? What happens when I finish what she started?* Instead of closure, could it be something else? There's no guarantee, as every minute I live as Morgan is a moment I'm not meant to have. The phrase "borrowed time" has never resonated so much.

The logical part of me says this is ridiculous; human bodies can't just vanish into sparks of light, so I won't cease to be after completing her mission. Yet I can't let go of the idea that she could come back and then I'll really be . . . gone. I mean, this is her life. Her body. What if she's just taking a break somewhere, letting me drive for a while?

"Want something else?" he asks.

I polish off my water and then reply, "I'm good."

Afterward, we walk around for a couple more hours, just . . . being, as I said before, and seeing how it feels. The answer is amazing. I had no clue how smart Clay is. Not about academics, but he knows about cars, music, and surprisingly, World War

II history. I'm listening to him dispel a commonly held American misconception.

"You know how they always make such a big deal about D-day?"

I nod. "What about it?"

"Well, it's bullshit. The actual turning point of the war was the Battle of Stalingrad. Americans talk about how we waded in and saved the day, liberated the French and kept England from being bombed to rubble, but if you look at it from this perspective . . ." He goes into lecture mode, correcting all of the biased history I've been taught.

It's kind of adorable.

"If the Soviet Union hadn't held out as long as they did, we'd be living in a *much* different world. And you know what made that possible?"

"Please tell me." I hope I don't sound amused because it's his enthusiasm that makes me want to smile, not disinterest in the subject.

"The T-34 tank." Clay expands on this war machine's merits, listing specs about the size of the ammo and sloped armor. Eventually he notices I'm not saying much. "Boring?"

"No . . . but what got you interested in World War II anyway?"

"Well, my dad was a fighter pilot buff. He collected memorabilia. Mom sold it after he died." That's the first time I've heard Clay sound bitter. "Then, in junior high, our history class did a unit on the Holocaust, and I was kind of . . . transfixed by it. What we learned was just so horrible, death camps and ovens, mass graves and genocide. I started digging into it and the more I learned, the more I realized that the teacher didn't have her facts straight."

"How did that go over?"

He gives me a crooked half smile. "Me putting the truth on

the test instead of what she was teaching? I got a D in history that grading period."

Before I know it, I'm checking my phone to find that it's eight already and we still have to drive back. Mrs. Rhodes has called twice and messaged me once. So far nothing from Mr. Frost. But as I'm looking, a message pings from DL. *He said he would be busy . . . but I guess he's thinking of Morgan right now.* Tempted to delete it entirely, I change that contact to CJ.

I've got the shakes, bad. Since Clay's got his arm around me, he feels it. "You okay?"

"Yeah. I should get back, though."

I don't want to. This feels like a magical interlude in between the awful that I don't want to deal with. But I can't just vanish with Clay. There are scary questions that demand answers. Plus, Nathan's still around, and he owns a permanent piece of my heart, even if I'm hurt and angry. I don't know how I'll feel about this move with Clay when I see his brother again. All at once, doubts and fears rush in like bat wings, fluttering about my face until I can't see or breathe.

"You look pale. Want me to drive?"

"Please."

I pass him my keys, though anyone can drive with the push button as long as the fob is in the car. We walk a little faster. He's spot-on about sensing the mood has changed, but he doesn't pester me with questions. Instead he just tucks me into the VW and heads for Renton. I don't speak until we're nearly to the freeway exit.

"You know you can tell me anything, right?" Clay's soft voice contains an unmistakable promise, husky with tenderness.

I want to kiss him again.

And I'm so tempted to spill everything.

But when he parks in front of his peeling orange house, I can see Nathan on the porch. The light is on overhead, creating a golden glow around him. He kicks out for a lazy, creaky swing and I can't whisper that crazy truth, not with Nathan fifteen feet away.

Just a little longer. Just until I'm sure.

After a toe-curling kiss, I drive off with an unsettled feeling. The silence I held and the words I bit back taste of bitter melon, the essence of white lies for someone else's good.

24

Mrs. Rhodes doesn't scold me when I get back, though I do receive a frown. But she only says, "Your father's on his way. Dinner will be on the table soon."

"Thanks."

Sitting down to wait, I swallow back the lump in my throat and open the message from DL. *Miss you. I can sneak an hour or so on Thursday. 8pm, as usual.*

This is so gross.

Thank God I already have plans. My fingers fly in typing the rejection. *Eating dinner at a friend's house. Sorry.* I can't physically make myself type that I miss him too; the closest I can come is a cryptic, *Waiting is the worst.* I hope wishful thinking will make him fill in the blanks.

Sure enough he comes back with, *I know. You're so beautiful, it makes me crazy.*

I ignore that message and delete the whole chain, though I know that the messages can be retrieved from the cell phone company. Did Morgan worry about that at all? Maybe I've seen too many crime shows, but I imagine them dredging up this sludge after this body is discovered naked in a field, after Creepy Jack finishes his devolution into an obsessed psycho.

Thanks to these texts and the snack at the mall, I'm not even hungry when Mr. Frost trudges in. The poor guy has coffee stains on his shirt and looks like he had a rotten day. I play with my food long enough to try to pretend I'm trying. Is this *normal* for them, only half an hour of daily chitchat? It must be, or Mr. Frost would comment on how reclusive I've become since the accident.

Memories come without my volition. I don't *want* to recall how warm and noisy it was at home. How the TV was always on and my dad drove my mom crazy surfing; she'd steal the remote and turn on music instead, and then they'd wrestle and sometimes end up kissing, until Jason or I groaned, "Gross," even though we secretly thought it was cool our parents still liked each other after twenty years. It was a . . . safe, solid kind of feeling.

Now I'm awash in longing for moments I didn't know enough to appreciate. I want to eat my mom's cooking and listen to my dad ramble about the Renaissance. Instead, I retreat to a huge bedroom with every possible luxury, and I feel like a captive princess in a tower.

But I have to save myself.

I pull out Morgan's hidden cache. I inspect the receipts a second time and I notice something. At the convenience store near school, she bought condoms. She's on birth control, which isn't protection enough for certain STDs and she wasn't hooking up with Clay. Does that mean she's done it with Creepy Jack? I'd certainly be worried about catching something from that pervert. Poor Morgan. That's too much, even to catch her mother's killer.

Part of me wishes that there's nothing to her suspicions. But as I'm turning the ultrasound over in my hands, some faded white lettering catches the light. It's partly scraped off from age, but judicious tilting lets me make it out. Lucy Ellis-Frost, dated ten years ago. Stunned, I drop it on the desk.

"Holy shit. Morgan's mom was *pregnant* when she died?"

If the family was whispering of suicide and the authorities didn't suspect foul play, there wouldn't have been an autopsy. Admittedly, I'm basing most of what I know about that stuff on TV shows, which might be a mess, procedurally, but I'm pretty sure the principle holds in this scenario. Which means Mr. Frost probably didn't know.

How did Morgan find out?

What I saw of her files online didn't mention this, but I haven't finished all her research on her mother's death. At the moment I'm tired and overwhelmed. Being Morgan on a daily basis is exhausting. I'm just grateful she didn't have a ton of clubs and activities, too. After basic hygiene, I fall into bed with a soft groan.

This can't be my life forever.

It can't.

But the alternative is dying.

I don't remember falling asleep; there's no demarcation between, no sense of being relaxed or drowsy, but I'm not in bed anymore. The tall grass is cool beneath my feet and damp with dew. Morgan's mansion is nowhere to be seen, and there's only this endless expanse of featureless ground, a field of stars overhead. I turn in a slow circle, puzzled, and then I spot Morgan coming toward me with the long, elegant stride that I still haven't mastered. She moves like a model, and for the first time I realize that I'm Liv again.

I'm *Liv.*

I'm dreaming.

Or is this reality, and everything else, a dream?

As I twist that question like a German pretzel, Morgan smiles at me. There's sorrow in her eyes and she's not all here, ephemeral and incandescent, like a ghost, a fairy, or possibly a pop-culture vampire with phase-shift powers. She's even got on a white flower-child dress, nothing she'd ever wear in life. I'm definitely asleep.

Right?

"Sorry I left you with my mess," she says.

"Why *did* you?" I realize that I desperately want to hear from her two lips that she doesn't blame me for this—that it's not my fault.

Even if she lied to me by omission and banged my boyfriend for her first time, not some Venetian guy, I still don't want to think of her hurting and alone, despising me.

"I was tired." Her voice holds a musical tremor, like wind chimes attached to a door. "That night I was so tired. And then it hurt, it hurt *so much*, and I couldn't hang on . . . but you were there. Dying, but you couldn't let go. And I . . . could."

In the darkness there's a ghostly fluttering of hands, a spark between them, not quite a memory but it feels . . . familiar. *Is this what happened?* I said yes to life and Morgan said no, and *this* happened? The way she's explaining, it sounds like we're equally responsible.

"Is it better where you are?"

She gives me an enigmatic smile without answering directly. "You can't imagine what the last year and a half has been like . . . the things I've done. Wondering if I ruined my life, my future, for nothing. If I'm crazy." Morgan stares at me. "Am I crazy, Liv?"

I don't know. Am I?

Sounding wistful, she goes on, "Maybe there's nothing weird about my mother's death. Maybe she had coffee with Jack and then ran off the road avoiding a squirrel. Maybe there's no mystery, just a stupid, twisted girl digging for truth where nothing is buried."

I have no answers yet, but I can't stand to see my friend hurting. Extending a hand, I can't touch her. My fingers pass through in a shimmer of light. "Sorry."

"Don't do that," she says, smirking.

That's the Morgan I knew. Somehow I muster a tremulous smile. "You were never stupid. Do you have any idea how hard this is? How much I miss you?"

There's so much to ask her, *so* many questions: her mother and Mr. Frost, Clay and Nathan, Oscar Sanchez, and the perv she called DL, whom I've renamed Creepy Jack.

But she holds up a hand. "Time's up, I'm not your spirit guide. My life is yours now. Live better than I did."

I wake up reaching for her. My fists are knotted in her bedcovers, so tight that it takes me a full minute by the tick of the clock to make them unclench. My fingers hurt and the room is cold again. Drawing my knees up, I wrap my arms around them and rock slowly. Intellectually I know this was just a dream, not Morgan, just my scientific mind attempting to provide a rational explanation for this inexplicable situation. In my heart, though, it feels real, as if I truly spoke to her, said good-bye, and got her blessing.

"It's not real," I whisper. "I'm the crazy one."

Even though the clock reads 4:14 a.m., I hop out of bed and open my laptop. A search about soul transference turns up a bunch of New Age junk about "walking in," what happens when one soul is ready to move on and another isn't. Apparently they come to an agreement and swap. The new resident is supposed to get the host's original memories but usually feels as if past events happened to someone else. This often leads to people randomly ending marriages, quitting jobs, and starting over, much to the chagrin and confusion of their loved ones. Sometimes if the switch is traumatic, the new soul takes over knowing *only* what they did as the other party. I stare for a few seconds in silence, wondering. When the article devolves into aliens, beings of light, and chakras, I sigh and close the page.

Maybe I should tell Mr. Frost and get treatment. I'm Morgan, who thinks I'm Liv. There are probably meds for this.

With a whimper, I put my face on the desk. There's no more sleep for me tonight.

At 5:35 I get in the shower, much earlier than I need to for an eight o'clock appointment, the earliest the clinic had available. I skip breakfast and leave before either Mrs. Rhodes or Mr. Frost is up. To keep them from freaking I leave a note about visiting Liv's grave.

Not a lie.

I need to see where they buried me.

25

Full daylight is a little over an hour away, so the sky is sewn with golden needles, pink fingers pulling at the threads. I stop at the convenience store and buy one of those pitiful, plastic-wrapped roses that sit in a dirty water bucket all day. This is a memorial gift I'd be ashamed to offer anyone else. The poor rose is blush pink, browning at the edges inside the cellophane; it crinkles as I carry it back to the car. Already the air is balmy, warm enough to make me think it'll be sweaty-hot later. I don't mind, but Morgan would.

Driving to the cemetery takes about ten minutes. I must be buried near my grandparents, so I cut through the ornate wrought-iron gates. The caretaker has already unlocked them, chain swinging free as I slip by. I see him in the distance getting his tools out of the shed. He waves to me and I lift my hand in turn, picking a careful path so I don't walk on anyone's grave. As I crest the hill to where most of the Burnhams in Monroe County are buried, my feet stop.

Because someone's already here.

From the shoulders to the shape of his back, I can tell it's Nathan, the last person I wanted to see, mostly because I planned to avoid him until I could make sense of that betrayal. Just thinking about his hands on Morgan's body—*this* body—fumbling, awkward, while they learned *everything* together? I nearly get sick.

Hopefully I'll be okay by Thursday, well enough to fake it. But despite the discomfort, there's also a warmth in my chest that feels like sunshine. No matter how complicated it is now, what we had was real; he misses me.

Even if it's done.

It *has* to be done.

Stepping closer, I can smell the booze. The cemetery is four miles from his house; did he stagger here in the dark? I can't decide if I'm touched or angry. A little of both, I guess.

He's sprawled against the headstone, one arm curved around it, head tilted to where my name is carved. Below it, my family has chosen an Emily Dickinson quote as my epitaph. It starts, *"Hope" is the thing with feathers* . . . There's one more line beneath that simply reads, *We'll meet again.*

Just barely, I swallow hysterical laughter. *Sooner than you think. Thursday, in fact.*

Nathan bangs his forehead against the stone, whispering, "Where are you? Nobody . . ." His voice hitches and breaks, then he cries quietly for a few seconds. ". . . told me that surviving is the shittiest thing."

Tell him. You have to tell him. You can stop this.

But that's a Pandora's Box. Once it's open, I can't close it. If Nathan believes me, he'll want to tell my parents. I can already imagine it spiraling, and then Mr. Frost will step in. He won't tamely accept me seceding from the family, especially since Morgan is all he has, apart from money. As long as I'm underage, it'll get complicated. Ugly. The road always leads back to a psychiatric unit, no matter what angle I take. Last but not least, I think of Clay and the life Morgan gave me—at least according to the crazy dream—which is mine but also . . . not mine. The pain in my chest is excruciating. My fingers clench on the rose stem, rustling the plastic.

Nathan raises his face with a bleary look. "Why is it you? Why are you the one who always finds me?"

"I wasn't looking. I came for her." But the question rattles me to my bones.

The idea of a soul mate is ridiculous. We're not magnets pulled together because we can't resist a predetermined charge. Yet here we are again, despite my best intentions.

What the hell, universe?

With a soft sigh, I sit down next to him and unwrap my spindly flower. From what I can see, Nathan only brought a bottle, now empty. But this visit can't be what I originally intended, some solitary vigil where I ponder my existence and make peace with the strange imploding star that is now my life.

He plucks the rose from my fingers and twirls it. "Sad. You can afford a decent bouquet."

"Hey, it was an impulse buy. At least I brought something besides self-pity." That sounds more like Morgan than me, as if I'm . . . fading.

"Harsh," he mumbles.

Taking in his wrecked expression, I soften. There's no way I can drop tough love on Nathan when he's grieving so hard for *me*. I settle my shoulder against his and lean back on my own grave marker. The ground is still damp, probably wrecking the back of my shorts. Morgan would've remembered to bring a change of clothes or a blanket, probably, but I can't keep up the pretense forever. Over time, people will notice small inconsistencies and it's better they get used to the new me, I guess.

"How often are you here?"

He shrugs. "First time this week."

"It's Tuesday. Are you doing homework at all? I can't believe your so-called friends are letting you melt down this way."

"You think Braden Wilkes ever stopped anybody from drinking?" His sneer is more than a little mean.

"Find better friends, people who care if you ruin your life."

"You sound exactly like my brother . . . which makes sense since you're banging him." Without looking at me, he adds, "I hate you, Morgan. I hate you for being here when she isn't."

That stings, but I don't show it. "Why don't you spout some shit about how you can't believe the earth still turns and the sun still rises? Then I'll sing some crappy folk song and we can both die of 'feelings.' "

The chuckle bursts out of him, strangled, but *out*. Nathan's expression becomes comically horrified. Like, I can practically see him thinking, *I'm laughing on Liv's grave.*

I rest my hand on his arm for a second and say, "Trust me, she wouldn't mind. Now get your ass up. If you think you're ditching school for no good reason, you're crazy."

He sighs, letting me help him up. "I suppose you're driving me yourself? They'll probably suspend me for showing up half-toasted."

I nudge him ahead of me so I can keep an eye on his balance. No letting Nathan fall and crack his head open on a tombstone. Some things are too morbid for life. I'm quiet until we get close to the looming gates.

"Not exactly," I say.

He half turns, looking irritated. "What, then?"

"I'm giving you a reason."

"Huh?"

"Wow, Honor Roll, booze really makes you stupid. Let me try again in smaller words. You're coming to the doctor with me, so you won't get in trouble. I'll even buy you some cruddy gas station coffee."

"Is this for Clay, too?" he asks through his teeth. Without

waiting for my response Nathan kicks a spray of gravel toward the VW, like it's responsible for his problems.

"No. It's for me. And Liv."

Some of the tension seeps out, leaving him limber. He must feel so alone right now, regardless of how many dude-bros he has. We were inseparable this summer. The urge to pull him into my arms is overwhelming, but things are too raw and agonizing between us for me to trust that I can stop at comfort. Last time was a mistake, and repeating that error would be cruel. Nathan's like a Jenga tower; one wrong move will topple him.

"I can live with that." He hops into the car and puts the seat back.

Which is when I realize Clay didn't yesterday, even though he's taller. That says something about both of them. Nathan doesn't hesitate to make his mark, even when he's hurting, whereas Clay hides his strength and sweetness like a turtle, intent on making a slow, quiet passage through the world. Life has made opposites of them, one brother stoic, the other assertive, and I can see all too clearly that they're both lovable.

I keep my promise, stopping again at the convenience store for stale pastries and fresh coffee. Nathan devours the sticky bun and licks the plastic while I drive to the clinic. I'm just as happy not talking. A sad song pops on the radio and my heart drops. Before, it was nothing special, a couple fighting. *Who is this again?* I remember asking that.

You're still here, but I can't touch you. Just a wall, just a wall between us, might as well be a thousand miles.

My eyes cut to Nathan and he's pale, *so* pale, sweaty. He reaches for me, blind with it. His fingers tangle with mine. And I'm shaking so hard that I have to pull over.

This. This is the song. That played while I was dying.

26

Nathan snaps the radio off with enough force that I wouldn't be surprised if the knob fell off. For another moment, we hold hands until the trembling subsides. I've seen the phrase "trigger warning" before, but I never understood what it was like to *be* triggered; it feels like someone's wired an emotional bomb inside me that could go off at any time.

Once I calm down some, I untangle my hand from his and merge into the sparse morning traffic.

"This sucks."

Since I can't disagree, I just pull into the clinic parking lot. The lobby doors have been unlocked but it's still twenty minutes before the actual office staff arrives, so I'll chill in the car for a bit. In close proximity it's really obvious that Nathan has been boozing it up. I decide to swing by his house after this and make him shower. That's older sister territory, something I never would've done as Liv.

If I was Liv, he wouldn't be drinking.

Nathan closes his eyes, tipping his head against the seat. His lashes are dark and thick, fanning against his cheeks. The stubble on his cheeks and jaw is only a day or two old, though the circles are just getting deeper. A few seconds later he's asleep. I watch in silence, which is a little creepy, so I deliberately turn my face away until another car pulls into the lot. A trim black woman in a blue suit unlocks the front doors, and I recognize Jeanette King, who works for Dr. Jackson. After giving it two more minutes, I follow her in.

No need to wake Nathan.

There are no forms to fill out, but I wait another ten minutes before the nurse shows up. The doctor comes fifteen minutes after that. Eventually Jeanette leads me to the exam room where the nurse checks everything and writes on my file, then Dr. Jackson makes his way in to look me over.

"How are you feeling?" he asks.

I decide to test the waters. "Okay. But . . . I was reading this book about a girl who thinks she's someone else. Does that . . . ever happen?"

Dr. Jackson tilts his head. "Is it a book about mental illness? That's a standard delusion, though root causes may vary."

"What do you mean?"

"It could be schizophrenia, bipolar disorder, or psychotic depression. I'm guessing you haven't gotten far enough in the story for the writer to explain?" He's smiling at me, chart in hand, and I make my face respond. "It's also possible there could be a physiological problem."

"Like what?"

"Some brain diseases result in psychosis. Parkinson's, dementia, or even a tumor might create the same issue."

"Interesting," I say. But I had an MRI before I left the hospital, so that's not it.

"Let me know how the story turns out."

"I wish I had a clue," I mutter.

"Enough procrastinating," he adds, like this whole conversation was a red herring to keep him from removing my stitches. "Lie down and turn onto your side."

If Morgan wasn't Randall Frost's daughter, I suspect the nurse might handle this, but instead Dr. Jackson does the honors. It doesn't hurt at all, more of a tickle-tug. I close my eyes through it, and five minutes later, Dr. Jackson finishes up.

"That's it, you're good to go. Give my regards to your father."

"Will do." Funny, how the human body can heal trauma in a matter of weeks whereas scars on the heart and mind can last for years. I straighten my shirt. "By the way, I need an official copy of all my allergies for travel reasons, can—"

"Ask the receptionist to print it for you on our letterhead. Are you going away to camp or something?"

"Or something," I agree.

At the front desk, I repeat the request and it takes all of five minutes for Ms. King to supply the information I need. It's good to know that I could choose to stop being a vegetarian as most proteins seem to be fine. Top of the list, Morgan needs to be gluten-free due to celiac disease. The strongest allergy is shell-fish, though apparently fish is all right. I'm also lactose intoler-ant and sensitive to strawberries. Surprisingly, I seem to be okay on peanuts.

Nathan is still asleep when I hop in the car.

He starts as I slam the door. "What time is it?"

"Just past nine."

I ignore his mumbled curse as I back out of the parking space and head for his place. Clay will be there, which means Nathan will start bitching as soon as he figures out what I have in mind. Sure enough, as I turn down Magnolia, he fixes a death stare on me.

"Stop the car," he demands.

"You can't go to school like that." I ignore his objection, driv-ing down the alley and parking behind his house.

Once I cut the car engine off, I can almost hear his teeth grinding, and I have to drag him out by the arm.

Nathan resists until I get him up on the porch, then his irritation melts into a nasty little smirk. "Are you going to scrub me down if I resist?"

"No, I will." Clay steps onto the back porch wearing a ferocious frown. "And I'll use the toilet brush. Jesus Christ, you reek."

He shoves his brother up the stairs and into the bathroom. I follow, mostly because Nathan needs a ride to school or he'll just skip today entirely. I'm wondering if Clay will be pissed at me for showing up with Nathan, like it's somehow shady—though this time it really isn't—but his expression is just . . . weary at the moment.

He steps up to me and rests his forehead against mine. It's early so his skin is deliciously warm, not sweaty, and I put my arms around his waist without thinking about it. He reacts a little slower, drawing me in with an inexorable sweetness that makes me feel like he has my heart on a line, only I don't resist being caught. Clay can pin me to the wall if he wants, though unhurried and tender is good, too.

"Wrangling that jackass is a full-time job," he mutters. "Where'd you find him?"

"Liv's grave. I got some food and coffee in him. Figured a shower might finish the job."

He sighs softly. "Thanks. I keep saying that, but I'm starting to feel like it's not enough."

"More than," I say.

Clay's big hands move on my back, skimming up until they're in my hair. In that moment I can't remember what his first name is. I mean, he's just been Clay forever. But now that I'm thinking about it, I'm pretty damn sure he wasn't named Clay Claymore. Clayton Claymore? No way. He's not a Clayton. Smirking, I rub my cheek a little against the soft cotton of his white T-shirt. With my fingertips I test the muscles of his back and he jerks as if it tickles.

"Cut it out."

But making him squirm is fun, so I don't quit, and then he whirls me, pinning me up against the kitchen counter. Hips against mine, his eyes are melting gold. Through the dirty window panes, the kitchen is gilded with light, crowning him, so it's all butter and cream and bright, bright lemon, like falling into the sun. My heart does a funny skip-hop, and I hate myself because I can't pull away. It's terrible and lovely, longing for someone you know will only break your heart.

Not Clay's fault. Mine. Morgan's? Mine.

"What's your name anyway?"

His thick brows shoot up. "That's what you're asking? Right now."

"Seems like something I should know. I'll have you fill out a survey later to be sure I can hold up my end as an informed girlfriend." The words come out with no hesitation at all.

I'm Clay's girl now. Not Nathan's. And it's a different kind of death, but for a second, that same pain flashes over me, flash flooding me, and I'm alone under a starry sky. I have grit under my fingernails. One of them is torn clean off and I taste the blood pooling in my throat. My pulse sounds in my ears, drumming until—

And I'm back, not dying, but *hurting*, because each step I take down Morgan's road is a step I never will as Liv.

27

Reaction sets in, and I can't breathe. I *can't*.

My chest is tight, my heart pounding so hard that it's an ocean in my ears. The pain climbs upward, my arms, my shoulders, until it feels like someone is choking me, and there's a sharp throbbing in my head. Everything is white, roaring, and I'm about to pass out.

"Please." I'm reaching for Clay, but I can't find him. My knees give.

The world swirls around me, so far away, but I can feel Clay's hands. Somehow, I'm on his lap in the middle of the kitchen floor. He's holding me and rubbing my back as that awful floodwater recedes. I've read about panic attacks. Studied them. Never understood how much like death it would feel, like a heart attack that might kill me. No wonder people who have never taken psych classes go to the ER.

"It's okay." He's stroking my hair without asking any awkward questions. "Better now?"

I manage a nod.

"Noah," he tells me eventually.

Breathing is easier, thank God, but my muscles feel quivery and I'm so dizzy. "Two by two, building a boat Noah?"

"Cute. Nobody but my dad ever called me that anyway."

"Clay sounds like a sports nickname." I'll shake this off, one heartbeat at a time.

He nods. "It stuck in peewee football."

"But you didn't play when you got older." It's strange how I could live my whole life in the same town with him and yet know so little. I love him for being so casual with this conversation; he's not freaked at all by what just happened.

"Nah. I was doing odd jobs by the time I was eleven to help pay the bills."

"Seriously?" I'm embarrassed that I've never even had a part-time job. I always told myself Morgan was the lucky one, but as Liv, I was privileged, too.

Breathing gets easier. I'm still unsteady, but the worst has passed.

"I mowed lawns, cleaned out garages and attics, walked dogs. Pretty much anything I could manage on my own."

"That's amazing," I say.

He rests his cheek on top of my head so I can't see his expression, but he must be feeling shy. On the surface, Clay is a badass with a serious reputation but I wonder now what's true and what's been told about him, telephone-style, until the truth is unrecognizable.

"Not really. At fifteen, I stopped contributing and decided work was for suckers."

Oh.

"But you'd been helping out for, like, four years by then. Anyone would be sick of it." I can only imagine how much I'd have bitched. I used to whine over having to watch Jason.

"Are you determined to defend me?" Clay asks, tipping my face up.

"Maybe."

"Don't bother. I was a dick, right up until my mom split. Then I *had* to man up."

"You really were a delinquent, just like they say?"

"The worst shit I did was never reported. I never got caught. And since I turned eighteen, my juvenile file was supposed to be wiped. Do you care?"

Morgan wouldn't, and I don't anymore. The truth is in the warmth of his arms, sheltering me. "Are you tough on Nathan because you don't want him to repeat your mistakes?"

"Basically. Not that he appreciates it. I hear that I'm a hypocritical asshole five times a day and 'you're not my father' twice that often."

"He just doesn't appreciate you," I say. "Sometimes you don't realize how important someone is until they're gone."

The words echo in my head, reminding me of Morgan. I'm just recovering from the panic attack, not braced for the wave of sadness that drenches me, pushing tears to my eyes.

"Hey." Clay drops a light kiss onto my mouth. He tastes like morning coffee and cream. "Don't look like that. My heart can't take it."

But my *missing-Morgan* train of thought is a Japanese bullet. Now that I'm on board, I can't get off early. Longing spirals through me, but there won't be any more late nights, no more texts, no more *anything*. I miss her. She must have been so lonely—the white room of doom, the housekeeper she pays for silence, the father who's never home, and the scary asshole who loved her mother. Neon flashing, the facts of her life excavate my skull like needles, scratching the meat from the bone. There was no one she could trust. *Not even me.* The realization dissects me until it feels as if my insides have been butterflied, neat fillets of my heart.

My expression must give away what I'm feeling because he cups my face in his hands. "Neither of us would be okay without you, Morgan."

The name breaks the bond between us as if it was made of

the spun sugar they put on top of fancy desserts, so pretty but fragile. Like my new life.

I extricate myself with a forced smile. "Now you're making me feel weird. I just happened to stop by the cemetery. Instead of letting him wallow, I made him go with me to the clinic and here we are."

That sounds heartless but I'm allowed to be, surely, about my own death. I step away as Nathan stumbles out of the bathroom. His hair is a mess but he's got on clean clothes and he doesn't look nearly so cranky. *Guess this was a good move.*

"Enjoy your day off," I say.

Clay kisses me good-bye and I head out the back door with his brother. Who says nothing until we're almost to school. Finally he mutters, "Thanks."

"For what?"

"Not giving up on me."

That makes it sound like I'm on a personal *save Nathan* crusade. Maybe I am. If I can't be with him anymore, then that's the least of what I owe him. He has to survive this shit and get out of Renton. Once he makes it to college, what we had will fade.

Damn. Enough.

"You're worth a little trouble." As I get out of the car, I toss the response, casual, and then I hurry into school without waiting for a reply.

I hand in my doctor's note at the office. Nathan comes in a few minutes later, probably so it doesn't look like we were ditching together. He takes the unexcused tardy. But Kendra Sanchez is in the hall with a pass as we come out together, ruining his careful effort. By her narrowed eyes, she disapproves of me spending time with my dead bestie's man.

The rumors I expect about me and Nathan are full-blown by the end of the day. Some people whisper that I spent the night with Clay and gave Nathan a ride to school after. Others are saying it was a threesome, and a third report has me cheating on both of them.

Morgan must've been used to this. For me, it kind of stings, when I'm trying so hard not to hurt anyone.

The next night, I have no idea what to expect. The art people are coming over in half an hour, so Mrs. Rhodes has made a boatload of snacks and I've got the lights on in the TV room, which is more of a VIP cinema with couches and lounge chairs, and the most massive screen imaginable. The stereo is top-notch, surround sound, all kinds of specs that make Oscar lose his mind as soon as he steps in.

"Wow, this place is the shit!" He's circling, admiring all the expensive gear while we wait for everyone else. "Do you mind if I move in?"

"Your parents might."

"Eh, it's a big family. They can spare me. Sorry about my sister, by the way."

"Whatever. She's trying to make her mark."

"By dragging you down? I don't approve."

I smile. "Thanks."

Before he can reply, the bell rings, and the rest of the group arrives in twos and threes. Mostly I'm quiet, letting them choose the movie. They opt to rent a movie online, a foreign film with subtitles. It's a Hungarian thing, indie, with lots of blurred shots and rainy windows. Morgan might have loved it, but I'm pretty bored.

Not by the company, they're nice enough. Maybe if I could be myself without worrying that they'll start asking awkward questions, we might even become real friends. But under current constraints, that's impossible. Like Nathan, I just have to hang on and wait for college. Once I'm accepted, I can go un-decided for a while and then switch majors. If I need to, I can even transfer schools and claim that time has changed my in-terests.

For now, however, I laugh when Ben Patel makes a joke that I only half understand. The night seems endless. My phone pings four times. I don't check. It seems rude to have guests and then spend the time texting someone else. The food is a huge hit, so there're only empty plates by the time the movie ends.

"I really think the dead cat was symbolic," Sarah says.

Oscar shakes his head. "You're reaching. It was just gross."

"Urban decay?" Ben offers.

"You're all missing the point," Tish cuts in. "Didn't you no-tice how it was foggy in *all* emotionally significant scenes? The whole movie is an allegory about life and death."

Actually that sounds right, though I was only half paying at-tention. Emma taps a nail, thoughtful, while Eric launches a counterargument for nihilism. That goes on for half an hour.

But finally, they start making departure noises, and I walk them to the front door. Their cars are parked by the fountain, and they're all pumped, thrilled that they finally got an invite to hang at Morgan Frost's place. I caught Sarah taking pictures of the downstairs bathroom; I expect them to be online in an hour.

"It was awesome, thanks for having us!" Ben calls.

I nod. In silence I watch my new friends get into their cars and drive away. When they hit the bottom of the hill, I open the gate for them via remote and close it behind them. With a house this size, I'm kind of surprised that there isn't a guard out-post at the halfway point or something.

"That was . . . different," Mrs. Rhodes says.

Shit. I didn't even hear her creep up on me. Her expression is weird in the artificial light, sort of scornful and knowing. But that's bizarre when she depends on Morgan supplementing her income. I can understand why a grown woman would resent waiting on a teenager, but . . . she's worked here for ten years.

On impulse, I ask, "What do you know about my mother and Mr. Patterson?"

It's a shot in the dark, so when she staggers, catching herself on the wall, I can only stare. Her face is pale when she manages to whisper, "Nothing."

She's off to the TV room like a hunted rabbit, like I'm the hound baying at her heels. Whatever happened ten years ago, the housekeeper knows something about it.

I owe it to Morgan to find out what Mrs. Rhodes is hiding. I just hope that finishing my friend's secret business doesn't mean the end of me.

28

Up in my room, I check messages.

The first one is from Nathan, confirming we're still on for dinner with my family. For a few seconds I close my eyes. *This won't be easy.* Then I send back, *Yep. See you after school.*

Next up, Emma has sent me a funny gif, and it's sort of hilarious that she did this *while* she was at my house. I find one of a dog dancing in a bow tie and send it back.

I'm happy to find a text from Clay. He's probably home by now, though I'm not sure how long it takes for him to finish cleaning. *What're you doing?* I've gotten this kind of text before, and usually it means your guy's thinking of you, but he doesn't want to be cheesy.

Not much, I send back. *Just getting my stuff together for tomorrow.*

Remember it's cool for you to come by if you need to.

With a half smile, I remember asking if it's okay to visit him at work. Maybe the dinner with Mom, Dad, and Jason won't be as bad as I think. But deep down I know it'll be worse because I can't let on.

Every moment is a struggle not to get in the car and tell them everything. If I could be sure they'd recognize me, I'd go. Right now. But I'm really scared of the aftermath, of the pitying looks, and the reasonable reaction that what I need is not to go home, but a mental health assessment. I'm afraid they won't hug me and say, "Welcome home." Instead they'll tell me I can get better with time and treatment.

I text a little more with Clay, just bits of nothing that leave me feeling more cheerful.

Then I remember there were *four* pings. Which means I have an unread message. The last one is from Creepy Jack. My skin crawls as I open it. *Busier than expected, don't be mad. I miss you.* Letting out a slow breath, I close my eyes on a drowning wave of relief. I mean, I already told him I have plans on Thursday, but I was afraid he might insist on getting together. Now that my stitches are out, my excuses will only go so far. The clock is ticking on Morgan's investigation, and I have to turn up some answers before Creepy Jack gets suspicious.

I'm tempted to ignore the text completely but that will probably piss him off. So I write, *I'll be waiting,* and then turn off my phone.

In the morning, as I pull out of the garage, I spot Mrs. Rhodes in the doorway, watching. Normally this would strike me as sweet, but given her reaction to my question last night, it's more like she's keeping tabs on me. *Shit. I already know she needs money. Would she report on me to Creepy Jack?* The scary goose bump answer is, *Yeah, probably.* This morning I can't get off the estate fast enough.

Last night's group is hanging out by the school's front doors when I stroll up. Oscar breaks away from the pack to fist bump me while the others keep talking about whatever's hot on the art scene. Eventually Sarah calls, "Thanks for having us over."

I don't think she means for her voice to carry like it does, but ten heads swivel in our direction and the whispering starts. Jesus Christ, I can't even have movie night without it being a thing? Wait. Morgan. Morgan can't. My knees go weak when I realize how I'm sinking into her life like I'm in quicksand. Will there come a point when I don't even *remember* being Liv? As I stumble back against the wall, I wonder if that would be such a bad thing.

"You okay?" Emma asks.

Tish comes over to inspect. "You're pale, even for you. Did you eat?"

"Yeah. I guess I'm still . . . adapting."

I'm surprised to get a sympathetic arm pat from Emma, then Sarah and Tish fall in beside me, as if they'll protect me from the buffeting crowd. Letting them do it—that's very un-Morgan—I take the escort while the guys follow. The rest of the day goes quicker than I want, probably because I'm so nervous about this family dinner.

Oscar's waiting for me outside my last class. "You busy?"

"Yeah, why?"

"I should've known you wouldn't hang out with us two days in a row." By his smirk, I know he's poking me about the mystique Morgan cultivated.

"I'm going over to the Burnham place," I say, before I think better of it.

He goes quiet. Nothing like a dead best friend to kill a conversation. Finally he mumbles, "Sorry. I think Ben's trying to flag me down. Catch you later."

I don't see Ben anywhere but I let Oscar make his escape and head for the front of the school, where Nathan is already waiting. Today he's actually clean, shaved, and dressed in normal clothes. Until now it didn't occur to me, but he might have shown up in torn jeans, a dirty hoodie, drunk off his ass. But at least he has enough common sense not to do that to my parents.

"Ready?" I ask.

"Yep."

"They aren't expecting us until five, so I'm going to the library to work for a couple of hours. I can take you home and pick you up later if you want." I like the quiet of the town library, plus it's open longer hours, the resources are better, and there's free Wi-Fi.

"No, it's fine. I'm behind in all my classes anyway." He finally sounds like the Nathan I dated for nine months.

Maybe he's done melting down over me.

I have mixed feelings. I mean, I want Nathan to be okay, but not this soon, maybe. It's not like sorrow has a kill switch.

But I don't say anything as I head out to the car. Nathan feels like a question mark walking beside me. There are so many things I want to ask, but I can't because Morgan would already know. While I drive, there's a movie running in my head, no soundtrack, just Morgan kissing him. God, why the hell was Nathan her first? Why did she lie? The fact that she didn't tell me before we started dating is driving me crazy.

Homework gives me the excuse not to talk to him, though. We pass from the sunny afternoon to the shady building with tables spread out among the shelves. I recognize the librarian as Miss Pat but Morgan probably wouldn't. I can't remember her ever coming here with me. Nathan greets her with a smile; he even pauses to chat while I pick out a spot near the computers at the back. My phone at hand means I probably won't need to use one of them, but it's better to be close, just in case.

I'm already reading for Lit class when Nathan sits down. Though it takes some effort, I don't look up. Morgan wouldn't let him distract her.

An hour and a half later, Nathan stretches. "That's it for me. I don't have anything left."

"You're already caught up?"

"You know I'm a genius, right?" Nathan's really proud of his 147 IQ.

"Whatever," I say, collecting my stuff. "Let's go."

The drive to my old house is quiet, painfully so. I'm aware each time Nathan shifts, each time he drums his fingertips on the door. Finally he says, "Did I piss you off somehow?"

"Excuse me?"

"You're acting weird, even for you, rich girl."

"I'm just nervous. Wondering how this will be."

At this excuse Nathan's perplexity evaporates. "I hear you."

The place looks exactly the same. Not surprising, as it's only been a few weeks. But I feast my eyes on the simple brick ranch house for a long moment while pretending to fortify my strength. By the time I climb out of the car, my mom has the door open. She looks a little better than she did at the hospital, though she's still pale and tired. I can tell she hasn't been sleeping.

Guilt nearly drowns me.

Before I take more than two steps, she rushes down from the small porch and swoops. As Morgan, I'm six inches taller but she somehow manages to mom-hug me. I hug back, awkward, as Morgan would be, but only because I'm fighting the urge to bury my head in her shoulder and sob my heart out. As Morgan never would. Thankfully Nathan nudges me aside to take his turn and then she leads the way into the house.

It's a mess, Jason's shoes everywhere. With a lump in my throat, I take in the cushy brown couch and the stained beige carpet. The wall art we purchased at various garage sales, so there's no real theme. On one wall it's boats and another one has a series of faux-Victorian portraits. The TV is on, some talk-show host chattering about the latest big issue.

My dad isn't home, so we follow Mom into the kitchen. She's making stuffed peppers, my favorite. Morgan's version will have soy, tofu cheese, and rice instead of ground beef. But it's sweet of my mom to remember Morgan's dietary issues when I, the crappy best friend, couldn't keep track.

"It's so good to see you two," she says, spooning the filling into a hollow green pepper.

"I miss you." Nathan perches on a stool at the island without waiting to be invited, and his eyes are so green and wistful, like a rainy spring afternoon.

"Me too, hon." Mom pats him on the shoulder, leaving a smear of tomato sauce. "You're awfully quiet, Morgan. Is it . . . strange?"

For a moment I can't believe she asked, but my mom's always been up front like that. So I nod. "Would it be okay if I went into her room, just for a sec?"

Her room. My room. This weird, hellish emotional limbo will wreck me.

29

My mom nods, and Nathan doesn't follow. Maybe he thinks this is a girlie good-bye that he can't share. He's not wrong, though he's not right in the way he imagines. I trudge down the hall to the end, where the last door is closed. It creaks when I open it, making me think nobody's been in there for a while, and I find things exactly as I left them. The bed's still unmade, even. My shoes are still where I threw them—in the corner near the closet, which is cracked open, showing the mess I promised to tidy up and never did. A thin coat of dust has settled, and *I know* the reason my mom's reluctant to clear it away is because once it's gone, *I* am gone. The dust is me, gross as that sounds, but it's my dust, my cells, my hair, and cleaning this room is the same as admitting that Liv Burnham is a memory.

Tears pool in my eyes as I stare in the mirror that tops my white dresser. There are tons of photos pinned up around the edges in the framework of my life: candids of Morgan and me, strip photos from goofy booths, and a pic collage that Morgan made for my one-month anniversary with Nathan. I didn't even realize she'd raided my phone, let alone had our selfies printed.

I kneel beside the bed and rest my cheek on the sheets. From my weeks at the Frost mansion, I can tell these have a much lower thread count, cheap even, but they feel better than the fanciest Egyptian cotton. My fingers curl into my blue plaid comforter, bunching it closer and closer, until I'm hugging it. A couple of stuffed animals tumble onto my head and land beside me on the floor.

Why can't I come home?

I want to go home.

The tears drip down my cheeks, off my chin, and dot the dark shirt I'm wearing. Though I didn't do it consciously, I've come to my old house in mourning, black on black. Eventually Nathan comes in search of me. He pauses in the doorway, and I watch the memories hit him, a beating he didn't expect.

"Pull yourself together," he orders. "It'll be worse for Mrs. B if you break down."

That's true.

I wipe my face with my sleeve and start to get up, only to find Nathan transfixed, blocking my exit. "That's *exactly* what Liv used to do when we were watching some tearjerker."

Though my heart skips, I try to play it off. All this time, I forgot about something crucial: body language. "I don't have a tissue or a handkerchief. What else can I do?"

Nathan can't seem to look away, struggling to put it into words. "It's not so much what you did as how you did it. That . . . Morgan, that was *eerie*."

"We were best friends for eight years. Is it so strange that I'd pick up some of her mannerisms?" Part of me wants him to guess, so I won't be alone with it.

If he loves me, if he really, really loves me, he'll know. That's unfair, I get it. But that's how I feel at this moment.

"I suppose not. But I never noticed before."

"Have you ever seen me cry?"

His expression finally clears and he steps aside. "Not that I can remember."

"Well, there you go." I pluck a T-shirt I borrowed from Morgan as Liv from the closet and add, "I need to wash my face."

Lingering in the bathroom, I manage to get myself together. By the time I head back to the kitchen, you can't tell that I melted down. Dinner is in the oven now; I can smell it. And Mom is cleaning up the kitchen. Though Morgan wouldn't think to offer to help, I can't just watch. So I nudge her aside and roll up my sleeves.

My mom looks seriously startled. "Are you sure?"

"I only *look* helpless," I assure her.

The ordeal gets easier when Jason smells the food and emerges from his lair. He's quieter than before, but he looks better than Mom. Dad is the last one home, as usual; he rolls in just as the food is coming out of the oven. I swallow the joke that he does this on purpose to avoid helping. Coming from Liv, that was funny; from Morgan, it would freak everyone out.

Dinner is fine, but my insides feel like they're on fire when my mom drags out the album and settles between Nathan and me on the couch. There are tons of Morgan-Liv photo ops over the years. I can remember when I fought so hard to keep her from showing Nathan the shot of the two of us in matching ruffled swimsuits, aged nine. This time I don't attempt to hide any of the pictures, and we listen to her reminisce for over an hour. These stories are all that's left.

She doesn't even seem to notice she's crying until I shut the book. "If it's okay, I'd like to push pause on this for now."

We didn't even get to junior high.

My mom sniffs, her chin trembling, and I lose the battle. While Morgan may not be demonstrative, I can't watch this anymore. I can't, I can't. I *won't*. I wrap my arms around her, tight, and hold on like I used to, before the accident, before everything was broken.

Before.

She surprises me by squeezing hard, rubbing my back like this is for me. And maybe it is.

"I know I can't take her place," I whisper, which is insane for so many reasons, "but what if . . . I mean, I lost my mom. And—"

"You're already like a daughter to me," she says. "I know what you're going to say. And yes, of course. You will always be welcome here. You're family."

It's not what I want, but it's all I can have. I nod. Then Nathan leans over, wrapping his arms around us both. The three of us lean and cry, until my dad clears his throat. At first I think it's because he wants us to stop, but when I glance over, there are tears in his eyes too. Jason turns up the volume on whatever game he's playing in his room.

"Me too?" Nathan asks.

"Definitely."

"We're not sending either of you to college," my dad mutters.

But that's how he's always been, acerbic when he gets emotional. I give a shaky laugh like I'm supposed to, and say, "Thanks for dinner, but we should probably get going."

"I want you here at least once a month," Mom says.

That's not enough, but it's more often than most dead people get to visit their families. At this point my soul is starving and I can't turn away crumbs.

"Sounds good."

Nathan thanks them again for dinner, then trails me out to the VW. But he pauses beside it, staring up at the half moon overhead. The stars are spangled bright, too.

Maybe I'm supposed to ask what he's thinking about, but I've had enough. I get in and wait for him to do the same.

"You okay?" he asks when he does.

"Yeah."

"I guess you could call that cathartic."

"Mm." It's shitty to ice him out like this, but I'm so breakable. Driving away feels impossible, the last thing I want to do.

When I go to start the car, he puts his hand over mine, forcing me to look at him. As Liv, I don't think I ever drove Nathan around, so the angle feels weird. He's definitely not thinking about our shared automotive past, however. A niggling worry makes me try to pull back. There will be *no more* accidental making out between us, especially not in my driveway.

"What are you doing?" I demand.

He turns my palm over and with silent, heartbreaking focus, inscribes *LIV* on my palm. When Nathan raises his gaze to mine, I'm pretty sure he's asking a question.

30

I pull my hand back, afraid to answer. But Nathan does that for me. "We should ask my brother for a discount and both of us get her name inked somewhere."

He doesn't know.

For a few seconds, I'm flooded with such a mix of relief and disappointment that I can't tell what feeling takes precedence. When the emotional waters subside, it's about equal. Starting the car, I nod.

"That would be nice. But wouldn't future girlfriends mind you having someone else's name stamped on your arm or whatever?"

"Liv will always be etched on me," he says. "The ink would just make it visible."

That's unexpectedly sweet. And permanent. I don't know what the future held for us before the accident, but things have taken a sharp left now. Now it can't happen, even if I'm the same person inside.

It hurts to reply, "We'll talk about it later."

The way I'm feeling, I'd agree to nearly anything. Dinner at my old house has pared me down to the bone. It's weird, though, because what I want most is to drop Nathan off so I can take a break from the grief and guilt associated with him. Not that long ago, the only solace I could imagine would be in his arms.

Yet when I pull up in front of his house, I don't stop him from hopping out. When I drive away, I don't look back in the rear-view mirror, either.

Now I'm faced with a different choice, only it's not a hard decision. Without much reflection I head for India Ink, which is in the small strip mall out toward the highway. At this hour, only the sandwich shop and the tattoo place are open. The dry cleaner and the discount shoe store both closed at six, and it's almost eight. After locking the car, I head into the shop, where Clay is manning the counter.

He glances up when the bell jingles, and his expression brightens when he spots me. "I'm glad you came by."

"You're a receptionist now?" I tease.

"I wish. It's a slow night, so she cut out early. I'm just watching the front for half an hour while Blue finishes up on a client in back."

The inside is different than I expected. I guess I had a middle-class bias because I was anticipating dark, punk, and possibly seedy. India Ink is bright and modern instead, very clean, with red vinyl chairs in the waiting area and pristine black-and-white tile like a purposefully retro diner. Light fixtures overhead are conical chrome, and the back wall is adorned with designs I presume must be available for tattoos.

"This is cool," I say, leaning my elbows on the counter.

He meets me halfway for a kiss, though I wasn't angling for that. At his touch, the emotional turmoil left from wading in the wreckage of Liv's life recedes like floodwater. Without meaning to, I curl my hands into the fabric of his uniform shirt and keep him from retreating. Clay deepens the kiss, making a little growl in his throat over the enforced distance between our bodies, and my stomach muscles tighten. I'm breathing fast when I step back.

I'd love to go around the counter and use him to forget *every-*

thing but that wouldn't be fair to either of us, even if he says Blue would be cool about it. He loves working here, so I can't be the reason he gets into trouble. I let go of his shirt and he covers my hands with his.

"How was it?"

"About what I expected."

At that he rounds the counter and pulls me in. When his arms lock around my back, I feel like I've become bulletproof. With careful hands he sifts through my hair, soothing strokes that make me want to close my eyes. I never would've imagined he could be this sweet or this gentle. The words older girls apply most often to Clay are "dirty" and "wicked."

I could stay like this for another hour, but movement and voices coming from down the hall prompt me to withdraw. Clay raises a brow, then he notices, too. I'm sitting in one of the red chairs by the time a slender, blue-haired woman comes out, trailed by an older lady wearing what I'd call a church lady ensemble—pink pantsuit, floral blouse, beige purse, and matching shoes. She even has the hairstyle, set in rollers once a week and protected the rest of the time.

Oh my God, this is Mrs. Marlow, the Presbyterian pastor's wife. I smile, pretending I don't recognize her as she pays for her tattoo. Once she's gone, the blue-haired girl smiles at me.

"You must be Clay's girlfriend. He mentioned you might stop by. I'm Blue."

"Did the hair or the name come first?" Curiosity overcomes my good manners.

"Hair first. I dyed it when I was fourteen and it suits me, so the nickname stuck." Her features are delicate and pretty, and I guess she's between twenty-five and thirty.

"I'll take it from here, if you want to head out," Clay says.

"Thanks. I have people waiting at my apartment. Nice meeting you," she adds.

As she leaves, Blue flips the sign to CLOSED and Clay locks the door behind her. I stand up and try to look like I know what I'm doing. "How can I help?"

He doesn't seem convinced. "Just wait for me, I won't be long."

"If I pitch in, you can leave faster. You should clean the equipment for sure, but I can do floors and counter. That doesn't require high expertise."

Clay thinks about it way longer than necessary, in my opinion. Finally he says, "Okay, wipe down everything out here. Counter, chairs, move the magazines and clean the tables, too. If you finish that before I'm done in back, you can do the floors." By his tone, he thinks that hell will freeze before this happens.

Morgan would not have wanted to do this, but she's gone, and the work settles me down as much as Clay's warmth. I hum as I clean, wishing I'd helped my mom more when I had the chance. All the little things about the life I lost seem magical now. Since I'm experienced at this, it takes me all of ten minutes to complete my task.

I call, "Where's the broom and mop? I'm ready for the floor."

Clay emerges from the back looking skeptical, but once he checks everything he gives me an approving smile. "You're surprising me all over the place. Let me get the bucket."

Sweeping is easy. I'm not sure if I'm supposed to move the furniture, so I just sweep under it and dump the dust and scraps of paper into the bin behind the counter. Mopping will be a little more challenging, as I've never used an actual janitorial bucket with the wringer attached, but I figure it out pretty fast. I'm finished before Clay is done sterilizing the equipment in back.

But I'm now trapped in the hallway; I can't walk on the wet floor without messing it up. So without being asked, I clean the bathroom and then mop my way down to the back room, where

Clay is finishing up. He glances up in surprise when I pause in the doorway.

"Washroom and corridor are done. Did you do the floor in here yet?"

He shakes his head, eyes wide. "Normally it takes me at least an hour to close."

"Told you it would be faster if I helped."

"Explain to me why you know how to do *any* of this." But his tone is all sweetness. It's not like he doubts that I'm Morgan; he just wants to get to know me better.

"I've helped my mom before," I say.

"You must've been really young. I can't believe you still remember."

"You don't forget the important stuff."

"That's true. I was just a kid when my dad showed me how to change the oil on a car but ten years later, and I can still do it."

"Exactly."

He's quiet as we wrap up in the back, then clean the supplies we used and store them in the janitor's cupboard. Clay sets the alarm and then we slip out the back so as not to mess anything up. The parking lot is pretty empty, however.

As I'm wondering, he says, "I bummed a ride here, hoping you'd stop by."

"I'm glad I did. Come on, I'm parked this way." I take his hand and he laces our fingers together, a little intimacy that shouldn't feel so profound. But I'm moved that he put his fate in my hands like this.

"You don't mind driving me home?"

"I just mopped floors for you," I point out.

Clay grins. "That's true. I'm starting to think you're *really* into me."

"Shut up and get in the car." But I'm smiling as I say it.

31

Clay no longer looks strange sitting beside me. Inch by inch, I'm letting go of my old life.

Morgan's life isn't a good fit either, so I'm in this weird 'tween place, not hers, not mine, either. These thoughts preoccupy me when I pull up outside the Claymore house. The lights are off in the front but when I pull around back, I see that Nathan's in the kitchen.

"He better be sober," Clay mutters.

"I'll let you check on him." I didn't intend to stick around, but Clay pauses with his hand on the door.

He turns to me with a searching look. "It's not that late even for a school night. You really have to take off right now?"

"Maybe not," I say.

"I'll get drinks and meet you on the porch."

I can read between the lines. Going to the kitchen is an excuse to make sure Nathan's okay. Then he can join me on the swing. Since that was my spot with Nathan, my misgivings increase. Yet I don't have the heart to refuse. Clay is gentler than I expected, despite a lifetime of being kicked around.

Ears straining for an argument, I perch on the porch swing; a creak and sway coaxes me to sit back. In five minutes he's back with two glasses of water. Since I didn't hear any raised voices, I figure Nathan isn't drinking. That's a step in the right direction.

To my surprise Clay takes my hands and holds them toward the light. "Are you looking for something?" I wonder aloud.

"Blisters. You aren't used to hard labor."

He's right; I wince when he runs his fingers over the tender, puffy skin. That didn't even occur to me. But he smiles as he massages my hands, smoothing his thumbs back and forth. By the time he wraps his arm around me, I'm too relaxed to react.

"This is nice."

"Better since I replaced the chains."

Come to think of it, that's right; the swing isn't squeaking as much as it did, and no rusty flecks are raining down on us. I remember threatening Nathan when I got orange smears all over one of my favorite T-shirts. But as Morgan I wouldn't know the difference.

I'm about to compliment his handiwork, however, when Clay shifts, drawing me across his leg, and suddenly he's all around me, arms about my shoulders, my back to his chest. The melting warmth contrasted to the pleasant chill of the evening air feels incredible. At first I'm not sure how to act, but it's inevitable that my elbows nestle into the pockets of his hips and so my hands end up on his thighs.

"This okay?" he asks.

"For me, yeah. What about you?" The question comes out more layered than I intended.

And from his pause, Clay's registering it too. "It's . . . good. Surprising, but good." To punctuate the statement, he brushes back my hair and kisses the soft spot behind my ear. "So much that I might be disinclined to let you go home later."

"My dad would call the state police," I say, though I'm not sure that's true.

Rather, I suspect Mrs. Rhodes would conspire to keep the absence from him, permitting me to spend the night wherever I want. The terrible pictures of Morgan and Creepy Jack certainly seem to imply as much. And that fast, I'm back in the morass of worry.

"Point taken. Let me know when you need to go."

The fact is, I don't really *want* to. And that worries me. I mean, I was with Nathan for nine months and sex never seemed right; the timing was always off, we were rushed or sneaking. Yet I'm already contemplating a night in Clay's bed. That seems way more Morgan than me, and it scares me, like little tendrils of her are weaving through my soul and I really *am* dying. I tremble hard enough for him to feel it, and his arms tighten around me.

"I'm okay," I say, because his next question will be *Are you cold?*

Clay kisses the top of my head. We sit for a while in silence while he kicks us into motion idly. The sway is soothing, as is his heat against my back. Such a restful moment, I could never have imagined it between him and me. But the peace is shattered when Nathan steps onto the front porch. I tense and try to jerk away before I even think about it. Clay doesn't let go so easily, however, so I'm pinned against his chest. Guilt seeps into the tranquility to the point that I can't even look at Nathan.

God, I'm a mess.

"Are you staying over?" he asks.

"Like that's your business." Clay isn't having whatever this is.

I can't get a read on Nathan because the kitchen light is behind him. It crowns his head in light but shadows his features. He taps one foot then sighs.

"Yeah, it is. Because our rooms are connected by a thin wall."

Yeah, that guarantees I'm not staying. Ironically, it's also why I never let Nathan talk me into it either. I peel Clay's hands away from me and stand up.

"It's fine, I need to take off anyway."

With a dark look for his brother, he follows me. I hear the front door slam as Nathan stalks back inside. I honestly can't figure out what's going on here. Nathan's almost acting like he's jealous, but that makes no sense, unless he's pissed off that Clay isn't alone. But that's small, too bitter for me to want to believe it. The romantic in me wants to imagine that he does sense it's me and it bothers him seeing me with Clay, but considering he's hooked up with Morgan, it could be that too.

For a moment, I *feel* her. It's like she's here and she's mad at me for such petty thoughts. I smell the perfume again, not Morgan's but familiar. Pain spikes through my left temple, making me stumble over the gravel. Clay catches me before I hit the ground, hands steadying on my shoulders. Once I'm stable, he lets go, tipping my chin up as if for a kiss. But instead of lowering his head, he studies my features for a long, intense moment.

"What?"

"I have the weirdest feeling about you," he says.

I still. "Excuse me?"

"Never mind. It's crazy. Be careful going home." But this time he doesn't call me Morgan or even "sweets," and he's still standing in the alley as I pull away.

Questions about Nathan and Clay are way more palatable than figuring out what to do about Creepy Jack or Morgan's mom, so I linger mentally over their words and expressions. This carries me through town, and I'm turning onto the country road that leads to the Frost estate when a pair of halogen beams on high flash up over the rise. I flick my headlights but the other car doesn't respond. *Shit, I can't see.* The road is only a blur before me; this feels like the night of the accident all over again. Somehow I stay within the lines until the other vehicle passes.

Only now there's a car angled across the road. It looks like the one Morgan's mom died in. I slam on the brakes, narrowly avoiding a collision. The VW skids right up to the passenger door, and I climb out. The driver must be sick or injured, so even if I feel shaky enough to throw up, I have to see what's wrong.

Two steps toward the car, I blink, and it's gone. *What the hell?* I did *not* imagine that. Did I? Now I'm the one blocking the road with more headlights bearing down. Quickly I scramble back into the Beetle and slam it into gear.

Dammit, Morgan. I'm doing the best I can here. That vision or hallucination, whatever, was a reminder from her to me—stay on task. Had to be, because the only alternative is that I really am losing my mind.

It takes all my composure to get to the gates that lead into the Frost estate, but there's no sanctuary for me here either. I find another car parked just outside, and while I wish this one was imaginary, it doesn't vanish, no matter how many times I close my eyes. I sense him watching from behind tinted glass, and my fingers tighten on the wheel.

The driver's-side door opens. Creepy Jack steps out.

32

At first, terror freezes my knuckles on the steering wheel.

The Creepy Jack steps toward the VW with an avid smile that sends awful chills, prickling my arms into goose bumps. I don't want to roll down the window; I don't want to acknowledge that a person this bent even exists. *You dated Morgan's mother, you sick bastard.* I lock the doors. When he taps the glass, I power down the window. Cold streams through me like my veins are filled with dry ice.

But I shake it off. Where the resolve comes from, I have no idea. In this moment I'm only sure that I can't go on pretending to be Morgan. I made a promise to help her but I won't continue with whatever the hell this is. In my dream, even she seemed to feel this was a huge mistake. And I'm done being afraid. This is *my* life now. Time to start living it.

"I need to get home," I say.

Maybe he can take a hint.

"Come with me for a little while first," he says with a smile that's supposed to be charming.

I've seen this look on his campaign posters; it makes my stomach churn. "Let me be crystal clear. We're done. And if you make it awkward, I'll tell my father."

He reacts like I've knifed him. The color drains from his face, leaving him haggard. His age is more apparent now, too, lines and hollows in sharp definition. For a few seconds his mouth moves but no sound comes out. Finally he whispers, "Don't do this, Lucy."

Bile surges up into my throat, so I can taste the acrid vomit. I choke it down. "My name is Morgan. And *you* are seriously disturbed."

My fingers are trembling when I hit the power button, closing the gap between us. He doesn't move away from the car, though, so I panic a little, afraid of what comes next. Somehow I manage to tap the opener so the gates swing open with excruciating slowness. Each second that ticks with me staring fixedly ahead, I'm waiting for his fist to pound through the glass. When that doesn't happen, I step on the gas and the Beetle lurches forward, depositing me on the grounds of the Frost estate.

Creepy Jack was standing close enough that I might have run over his toes in getting away, and I *so* don't care. Another touch and the gates close behind me. I settle down enough, somehow, to drive the rest of the way to the house. After I park in the garage, it takes another five minutes before I feel like my knees will hold my weight. Eventually I stumble out of the car and make it to the house, dark and cavernous. There is no food warming for me in the kitchen, which I'd mind if I hadn't eaten at home. No light in Mr. Frost's study either, so he must still be at the office.

That, or he has a secret girlfriend.

I can't believe that didn't occur to me before. Morgan would probably have thrown a shit fit if her dad brought another woman home. But it doesn't make sense for a man to live like a hermit for more than ten years. He must have someone, right? While he can claim that he's insanely busy due to some work stuff, I don't believe that he has to work every single night until past ten. And he goes in on weekends, too.

Unless he's seeing someone at Frost Tech?

Curiosity leads me to knock on the housekeeper's door. When she answers, she looks tired and not very pleased to see me. "What's up, Morgan?"

"How long has Dad been seeing her?"

The guilty flicker of her eyes tells me I'm right. But she tries to bluff. "Excuse me?"

"The girlfriend. How long?" Morgan's icy tone comes out naturally, I've heard it so often, and it has the desired result.

"Almost a year."

"She works at the company?"

Mrs. Rhodes nods, looking chastened. I'm sure she's worried about the fallout. But I'm not Morgan beneath the skin, so I don't have the same visceral reaction, and I have enough problems of my own. Deep down I'm afraid of what comes next; Creepy Jack doesn't seem the type to accept rejection politely. And that scares the shit out of me.

But there's no reason to trouble the housekeeper further. So I simply nod and retreat to my bedroom, turning this latest information over in my head. After the usual skin and oral hygiene ritual, I get in bed, but I can't relax. The white room of doom is quieter than ever. It seems like hours, though a glance at the bedside clock tells me I've only been rolling around for forty-five minutes. With a sigh I give up and grab my phone. Normally I'd find something to read, but for some reason I'm texting Clay.

You asleep?

A minute later, I have a ping back. *Not yet.*

I should've stayed at your place, I send. Even the prospect of Nathan listening to us doesn't bother me as much as it did. Plus, sleeping over doesn't automatically mean sex. I wish I was in Clay's bed, and I hate myself because Nathan is already fading. The longer I'm Morgan, the less I feel like Liv. I mean, I'm *not* Morgan, but I am, now. Which means Liv is gone. Each time I form that thought it hurts less.

Are you trying to keep me up all night? he sends back.

Before thinking better of it, I answer, *Maybe,* and put the phone down. Sleep comes quick after that, and the new determination sticks with me, even the next morning. I put on Morgan's simplest clothes and only do light makeup. I no longer care about maintaining the perfect masquerade. While I can't know if my second life is a bug or a feature, I have to make this life work for me. However long I have, I'm done faking it.

An hour later, I'm in the school office, using Morgan's considerable charm to persuade the secretary to adjust my schedule. So far it's not working.

"I understand," she says patiently. "But you can't just drop into advanced science courses. There are prereqs that you don't meet."

I smile. "According to the handbook, I have the option to test for class credit. Otherwise, you have no way to ascertain how much knowledge I may have gained independently."

She hides a smirk behind her hand. "You think you can test into an AP science class on a whim?"

"Who does it hurt to let me try?" If I have to, I'll threaten them with Mr. Frost. He's made several donations over the years, enough to give his wrath some weight.

Earlier, I wouldn't have dared try this. I was too afraid of getting caught, but . . . how can they prove I'm not Morgan? I suspect they'll attribute behavioral changes to the accident and any similarities to Liv, well, wouldn't they think Morgan is paying tribute in her own way? The truth is too crazy for anyone to stumble on. People change, right? I just have to take it slow and let everyone get used to the new me.

Luckily the principal steps out just then. "Can I help you, Morgan?"

I explain my request all over again, and Mr. Gallo doesn't seem opposed. "It's a little unusual, but we could use another girl in the science program. Talk to Mr. Finney. As long as he's willing to let you take the finals for the prereq courses, I have no objection."

"The time has passed for changing schedules," the secretary protests.

"We can make an exception for Miss Frost." His tone is final, so the woman gives me a resentful look but she fills out the request form, stamps it, and gives it to Gallo to sign.

The only issue with this plan is Morgan is a senior. Which means I have to test out of a class I haven't taken yet to get back on the science track. This . . . is a problem. The art kids will probably feel betrayed, too. I hope we can still hang out; it was pretty fun the night they came over, even if I didn't understand all of the foreign film references.

Thanks to Mr. Frost's generosity, Gallo gives me an open pass that lets me wander the halls with impunity. I'm supposed to head straight to the science department to get the ball rolling, but instead I dodge out into the courtyard. The sun is bright overhead and, for once, there are no students tending to the garden. For five blissful minutes I just bask.

Until someone flicks me in the back of the head. I open my eyes with a frown. "What?"

It's the one person I shouldn't see, the boy whose heart I'm breaking with my silence.

33

Leaning down, Nathan stares into my eyes with a disconcertingly intense expression. "The hell are you doing?"

"Some light sun worship, duh."

"You're terrified of skin cancer."

I shrug. "Not anymore. The accident put a lot of things in perspective."

"Such as?"

"Shouldn't you be in class?" Evading the question is better than continuing this conversation. Why won't he leave me alone? A phantom ache tightens my chest.

"I could say the same to you."

Lazily I wave my pass. "There are benefits to being me."

"Likewise." Nathan sits down beside me without waiting for an invitation. "The teachers are *so* sympathetic. If I make a noise in class, they send me to the bathroom for as long as I want. Dead girlfriend perk."

Without meaning to, I flinch. "Asshole."

"You're playing the dead bestie card to ditch. How am I worse?"

He'll find out sooner or later, so it's probably better to get it over with now. "Actually I'm switching my focus and changing my schedule. There's no point in attending classes that I won't have all semester."

"What are you dropping?" he asks.

"French, Graphic Design, and Visual Arts."

Nathan stares as if I've grown another head. "Those are your favorite classes. How will you get into—"

"I'm not going to school in Paris," I cut in.

"Don't tell me you're staying in Renton for my brother?" Mockery renders his tone sharp enough to cut glass. "Before, I thought you were just using him, but lately I wonder. Don't tell me you're developing a taste for white trash, rich girl."

My hand lashes out, delivering the slap before I process the intention. The sting of my palm and his reddening cheek, sunlight bright overhead, and the sweet smell of the still air stretches between us. His gaze locks onto mine, and I can see the wheels turning in his head. Morgan would never have done that, no matter how provoked she felt; she was far too controlled, and words were her weapon of choice.

My voice comes out soft. "You're hurting, I get it. But you owe him better than that. He's given up so much to make sure you have a future. If he's trash, what does that make you?"

He tips his head back, staring directly up at the heartbreak-blue sky. "Infinitely worse. You think I don't know that?"

The sheer anguish in his tone startles me. "Nathan—"

"Am I such a bastard that I want to steal from my brother? It's like I can't stand for him to be happy, even for a minute. Jesus, I look at you and I *ache*. Since the night we kissed, I can't stop thinking about you, and it's driving me insane."

The silence is so deep I can't break it. I want to run, but I want to touch him, too. Which is wrong. I can't, I can't, I can't. The girl he loves is dead.

Officially.

But there's a buoyant joy rising in me. Because on some level, he *does* know. Logic just won't permit him to make such a ridiculous leap.

Suddenly he grabs my hand and presses it to his chest. Beneath my palm he's warm even through his T-shirt and I can feel his heart racing. There's no reason I should open my fingers but I do because this is Nathan, and it's been so long since I touched him. He's a lifeline connecting me to my world before.

"What am I supposed to say?" I whisper.

"Hit me again. Say I'm crazy. Tell me you love my brother."

"This can't happen. You're grieving." I try to make my tone comforting, but my hands operate on their own, coming up to stroke his face.

Mixed messages much? This so isn't fair to him.

His eyes spark green and then he grabs my wrist, pulling me off the bench and through the quiet halls. I have no idea where we're going until he drags me to the maintenance stairs that lead to the roof. I've never been up here, though I know sometimes people sneak off to make out. The roof is flat, sticky in the heat, and it offers access to various heating and cooling elements. Otherwise there's nothing up here but privacy.

"Why didn't you stop me?" He steps closer and presses his palm over my heart. "Don't screw with me. Are you feeling this, too?"

"I just ran up all those stairs," I mumble.

Of course I feel it. Love doesn't disappear in a few weeks. I've buried it, but he's still in my heart, now thundering madly beneath his fingers. Nathan is and always will be my first love. But nothing is so simple anymore.

While I'm trying to figure out how to stop this without making it worse, he whispers, "Remember that summer?"

My whole body chills.

"You borrowed your dad's car, even though you didn't have a license. We drove out to the quarry, but you wouldn't get in the water until I covered every inch of you with sunblock."

I have a feeling I know where this story is going. My tongue cleaves to the roof of my mouth, and I can't find the words to stop him. There's also this awful, morbid curiosity. I've wondered how it happened, and Nathan seems to think he's seducing me with his memories.

"We might've gotten caught if we'd been in our pool."

He smiles. "That's what you said then."

The knot in my stomach gets bigger, but I don't pull away. He cups my shoulders in his hands, though the spark of longing I felt earlier has died to smoking ash. I can taste it as bitter sulfur on my palate, and he keeps talking.

"That day . . . I haven't forgotten."

Before, he said it was just sex. But it was also his first time. I guess that makes it special. Through some superhuman effort, I choke down the tears because now I have to wonder if he was thinking about Morgan every time we made out, if he was imagining her in my place. My breath hitches and he takes it for encouragement.

"You, too?"

I step back then, breaking his hold. "From what I remember, it was really fast, messy, and awkward. It wouldn't be in my top five."

He flinches, but doesn't let go of me. "Morgan, please. The only time I stop thinking about Liv is when I'm with you."

That helps a little. But . . . it's not enough. I wrench out of Nathan's hold.

He doesn't know who I am. If he did, if he saw Liv in Morgan's skin, I might have done something stupid. The disappointment stings from the inside out, and I hate that I almost fell into this pit again, after just crawling out of it. Without waiting, I yank open the door and race back down to the back hallway. The janitor almost catches me dodging out of the stairwell but I'm fast enough he can't be sure. I don't give Nathan a chance to catch up with me and book top speed for the science department.

Mr. Finney is first surprised to see me and then irritated as hell at my presumption. "You haven't had science since freshman year. Do you think my classes are a joke?"

"No, sir." I like this teacher a lot, and he was fond of me as Liv. Maybe he'll learn some respect for Morgan, too. "I'll take the Bio final first to prove I have the knowledge to take the next one."

"Well, it can't be today. I'll schedule it after school next week. Until then, attend your regular classes." His disapproving tone tells me he suspects this will be a colossal waste of time.

"Thank you, sir."

By now I've missed all of first period, and everyone is getting out of class, so the hallway fills with students, most of whom stare hard at me. I smile at the ones who make eye contact, startling them. The rest whisper to each other and don't acknowledge me otherwise.

Oscar breaks my isolation bubble, however, calling to me from down the corridor. "You're looking all-American today. What gives?"

"I got tired of trying," I tell him honestly.

"It's exhausting. Once I went without eyeliner and wore a polo shirt, and people legit did *not* recognize me for half the day."

Squinting, I try to imagine him without cosmetics and in preppy clothes, but I can't quite make the leap. I'm too used to his groomed coif, the black nails and J-pop eyeliner. Today he has on black jeans with lots of zippers, a vinyl jacket, and a mesh shirt underneath.

As he walks me to second period, he says in a musing tone, "You've never asked me, you know. Unlike pretty much everyone else in the school."

"Asked what?"

"If I'm gay. Aren't you curious?"

I shrug. "It's your business. It would only impact me if I was trying to hook up with you. Since we're friends and I'm not—"

"Thanks for that." His tone is unusually serious, his expression almost brooding.

"For what?"

He summons a smile, banishing the momentary darkness. "Your friendship. For not asking. I'm still figuring some things out, and it's tiresome being on everyone's to-do list."

I laugh. "Please tell me you're being ironic. Because I don't think I can handle that much conceit so early in the morning."

"Since you laughed, obviously that's what I was going for." Oscar shoots me another lazy grin and detaches to head into his classroom.

Trying not to think about Nathan, Creepy Jack, or the potential reality that Morgan's mother may have been murdered, I doze through the rest of the morning. At lunch I stop Isaiah Emerson, a science nerd I knew pretty well as Liv. He's a tall, thin black kid who's on track to be valedictorian with a scholarship to Cornell already locked down, and he has no patience for nonsense.

He frowns when he hears my request. "Don't waste my time."

"I know you have all your notes along with last year's syllabus. What does it hurt to let me borrow them?"

Thick brows shoot up; Isaiah stares, obviously surprised. "*Why* do you know that?"

"Liv told me."

His expression softens a little, maybe enough. "Oh."

There's an awkward pause with Isaiah studying me from behind wire-framed glasses. He dresses like he's already working for a company that permits business casual: khaki slacks and a striped blue button-up. No pocket protector, though. If you didn't know he's the top science student, you could mistake him for a Young Republican.

"Consider it a posthumous favor to Liv, if you want." That's true enough.

"Give me some collateral," he says finally.

Without hesitation, I pull off the platinum bracelet I'm wearing. "I know your notes are invaluable, but this should prove I'm in earnest.

Isaiah accepts the swap, beckoning me over to his locker. Inside it's impressively organized, so he finds the notes fast. "I want these back in a week."

That's about how long I have to study anyway. "No problem."

Isaiah brushes by with a final nod of farewell, freeing me to head to the library to review. I'm confident I can pass the freshman and sophomore exams but I haven't even taken the junior class yet, which is why I have this impeccable study guide.

But can I learn a year of material in seven days?

34

Right now I don't want to think of anything but science, where the formulas make sense and I can predict the result of an experiment. I might be wrong, but the process is never painful. Unlike encounters with Nathan.

Unlike visions from Morgan, her mother's secrets, Creepy Jack, and the fact that my family is in mourning.

At this point, I need a pause.

I don't care anymore if my sudden change in behavior sets off alarm bells. Genetically speaking, it is indisputable that I'm Morgan Frost, and as little time as Mr. Frost spends with his daughter, both before and after the shift, I doubt he could say if her interest in art and fashion was a fad or not. Plus, that's kind of the deal with growing up, isn't it?

I remember how desperately Morgan wanted to be an actress when she was thirteen, and nobody doubted she had the looks, but then she realized celebrities lose their privacy . . . and she switched gears. Morgan never explained herself to anyone, not even me. It's ludicrous to imagine she'd clarify any sudden changes. I can picture her icy, incredulous look, one brow arched. Now that I know how much pain her composure covered, I wish she *had* confided in me; her secrets were of the dark and destructive variety.

From here on out, I'll try to finish what she started while

shaping her life to fit. That firmly in mind, I head out after school determined to find out whatever Mrs. Rhodes knows about Morgan's mom and Creepy Jack. It's no surprise to find the housekeeper polishing the floors—that's her job, after all— but when she spots me, she tries to retreat.

"You're home early. I'll make you a snack."

"I'd rather chat," I say.

Her face pales. "About what?"

I don't have the patience to be gentle, so I lead with, "How do you think my dad would feel if he found out about our bonus program?"

She stumbles back a step, catching herself on the wall, but then she tries to bluff. "You wouldn't. If you tell him, you lose your precious freedom." From the way she spits the word "precious," I can tell she hates covering for Morgan and despises herself for the necessity.

My indifference is real. "I won't be living at home that much longer."

"What do you want?" she demands.

"Information. First, tell me everything you know about my mother and Jack Patterson. And then I want to hear about my father's girlfriend."

"Is that all?" Her expression tells me she expected something worse.

"It's not enough?"

"Come on." She props her mop against the wall and beckons me toward the kitchen. "I'll make tea while we talk."

"Sounds good."

Ten minutes later I'm sitting across from Mrs. Rhodes, who looks more tired than anything else. She stirs her drink exactly six times and then sets her spoon on the saucer. "I suppose you already know that Mr. Patterson is your mother's ex?"

I nod. "That's not news, I found some mementos after she died."

"What you probably don't know is that . . ." She hesitates, twin pleats forming between her brows. I can see that she's conflicted about sharing this. "Your mom and dad . . . things were rocky just before she passed. He's said some things when he was drinking I'm sure I wasn't meant to hear."

"So . . . ?"

"From what your father let slip, your mother was . . . seeing Mr. Patterson when she died."

The air gusts from my lungs in what feels like an asthma attack, except that's not a problem Morgan has. "What?"

At my expression she adds, "I don't know what he meant, exactly. That night, he wasn't what I'd call coherent."

"Why?"

"It was five years ago, the anniversary of your mother's death. I got the impression your father blames himself. If he'd paid more attention, spent more time with her, the accident wouldn't have happened."

Wow. This is a lot to process. Does this mean Morgan's mother was having an affair with Creepy Jack? That possibility sends a hot rush of bile to the back of my throat. It's like Morgan and her mom are interchangeable to that pervert.

"Did he know she was pregnant?" The question slips out before I can stop it, and judging by how Mrs. Rhodes reacts, she had no idea.

"Are they still gossiping about her?" She makes a tsking sound. "Whatever your mama may have done, there are some that should really learn to shut their mouths."

I shake my head. Now that I've gone this far, I might as well tell her the rest. We're already conspirators of a sort. "Hardly. Anytime the extended family is here, they stop talking about her whenever I come into the room. But among her things I found an ultrasound picture."

"Are you sure it wasn't from when she was pregnant with you?" The housekeeper sounds gentle, one of the few moments of peace I've had in this big, lonely house.

"Definitely not. It was dated six weeks before she died."

Mrs. Rhodes reaches for my hands and cups her rough ones over them, her gaze steady and concerned. "Morgan, nothing good will come from churning up the past. As far as I know, she never told your daddy, and if he found out now, wouldn't that just be something else for him to regret and . . . to question?"

The unspoken implication is clear. Mrs. Rhodes is wondering just like I am: Who did that baby belong to? I get the chills when I realize—depending on the answer, it changes the picture entirely. Would Jack Patterson murder his unborn child? And if Randall Frost found out his wife was cheating on him, what might he have done about it?

"I think someone killed her," I whisper. "How can I ignore that feeling?"

It's the first time I've said that out loud to anyone, but Mrs. Rhodes doesn't speak the immediate denial that I'm half expecting. Instead she lets out a slow breath and stares up at the ceiling. For a few seconds she drums on the table with her fingertips and when she meets my gaze again, she seems to have come to some fresh resolution.

"I won't lie, there was talk. But your father shut it all down."

"Because he didn't want to encourage the whispers of suicide." At least that's what Morgan always said, the few times she mentioned her mother at all.

But I don't have the same emotional bond with Randall Frost. It's easier for me to make the leap and entertain the notion that he may have used money and power to cover up a crime of passion. Of course, it's equally plausible that Creepy Jack did, too.

"Probably," she says, visibly relieved.

Yeah, I wouldn't want to chat with my boss's kid about his potential motive for murdering his unfaithful wife either, and she doesn't know if she can trust me with this information. For all she knows I'm milking her for gossip and then I'll run to Mr. Frost, saying just enough to get her fired.

It's unlikely that she knows more than this, though I'd give a lot to know exactly what she overheard five years ago. I can't picture Mr. Frost raving with drunken regret, but as I've learned the hard way, everyone has secrets that should never see the light of day. The main question is, how bad are Randall Frost's? But now's not the time to press.

I force my features into a friendly expression. "Next item on the agenda. What do you know about my dad's girlfriend? Have you met her?"

She shakes her head quickly. "I just heard him making plans with her . . . oh, it must be ten months back. It's not like he confides in me. But every now and then I catch his half of a conversation and it's not hard to put the pieces together."

"Oh. So you don't know more than the fact that he's seeing someone at Frost Tech?"

"Basically. She works in sales. That's all I know."

"Hm. Maybe I should visit my dad at work and check the situation out."

Mrs. Rhodes smiles, clearly relieved that the worst has passed. "I'm sure he wouldn't mind. He's always saying he wishes you were more interested in the company."

"Good to know." I sip a little more of my tea and then push to my feet. "Thanks for the chat. Sorry if I came on strong in the beginning. It's just frustrating, not being able to talk about my mother. I . . . miss her." Since my mother is alive and well, three miles down the road, the hitch in my voice is pure theater.

But it has the desired effect. The housekeeper's eyes widen, as if she's just thought of something. "Your mother's best friend lives in New York. She didn't come for the funeral, but she sent a lovely arrangement. I still remember the lilies . . . and oh, I packed away all the cards. I can probably find her address for you."

"Thank you. I'd love to get in touch with her, maybe hear some stories about what my mom was like in college, stuff my dad would never tell me."

Mrs. Rhodes hurries off and within five minutes, she hands me a white greeting card envelope, gone faintly yellow with age. But I can still make out the return address. Ten years is a long time, so maybe this won't help at all.

Or maybe it's the key that unlocks everything.

35

My heart's pounding like crazy as I run up to my room, clutching the sympathy note. Before checking out the address online, I study the handwriting, which is careful and elegant cursive. When my mom was alive, Aunt Tina came to see us twice a year, once on my mother's birthday, which was in July, and to ring in the New Year—

Wait. *How do I know that?*

Those are Morgan's memories, not mine. I can't remember being around for either of those visits, yet the fact sits in my skull indisputable as sunrise. I rub my knuckles across my brow. It seems like a memory that just won't come, a word hovering on the tip of my tongue. Somehow I feel as if I know Tina Goldsmith but I never met her, though Morgan must have.

My head aches, a throbbing drum in both temples, and as the pain sharpens, a mental image forms. She's a slender woman with rich brown skin, big eyes, and natural hair worn short, and she favors bright colors. I can see her in a yellow sundress complemented with black and white bangles. I'm on her lap, clacking them together in delight while she and my mom giggle over something I'm too small to understand.

That fast the images fade to white noise and I reel to the side. The bed catches me, so I only hit my side on the frame, my head landing on the mattress. Beside me the card flutters down to the floor, slower than it should. I don't want to touch it but I can't resist. It feels cold enough in here that I should be able to see my breath. I'm smelling that damn perfume again, and I can feel Morgan, close, like she's whispering but I can't quite make out the words.

My fingers tremble as I open the envelope to reveal a vase of lilies on the front, simple and innocent in death. When I unfold the card, an old photo tumbles out.

At first I just stare at it because this can't be real.

I blink once.

Twice.

But it's definitely Lucy Ellis-Frost and Tina Goldsmith, who's wearing the exact outfit I envisioned a few seconds ago, down to the bracelets. They're standing outside a bistro-style restaurant, arms around each other and beaming wildly at the photographer. Fighting nausea, I set the picture aside and read the message.

> *Dear Randall (and Morgan),*
>
> *Words can't express how sorry I am. I'm sending you a copy of this picture because it means the world to me and I hope seeing her smile so brightly will help when you miss her most. Morgan, I will always be your Aunt T, so if you ever need anything, I'll be there. I wish I lived closer and that I could do more, but I'm only a phone call away.*
>
> *All my love,*
> *Tina*

Before I can think better of it, I pick up my cell and dial. The whole time it's connecting, I hold my breath. The out of service message is rather anticlimactic, but I guess it's too much to hope that she would've kept the same number for ten years.

She didn't say if this was her home or cell, either. She may have disconnected her landline and gone mobile only.

"What the hell is going on?" I mumble.

Nothing makes sense anymore. Am I Morgan who remembers being Liv or Liv who almost remembers being Morgan? At what point do I accept that I'm not okay and ask for help? Misery sweeps over me, inch by inch, creeping over my ankles, chilling my knees, foreboding fingers clutching like cold bone. When my phone rings, I jump and nearly drop it. As I check the ID, I pray that it's not Creepy Jack, and relief streams through me when I recognize Clay's icon. My heart still hasn't settled when I answer.

"Hey, you."

Clay's smile comes across enough to thaw the block of ice my torso has become. "You've been quiet today, so I'm checking in. Everything okay?"

The automatic answer won't come. I'm beyond weary from carrying this alone. Today the baby steps I took with Mrs. Rhodes are the first of many down a road I never expected to travel. I might as well be the unnamed narrator in that "Road Not Taken" poem by Robert Frost. I'm staring in two directions, checking out my options, and neither path is rosy. Neither ends with me living at home, eating dinner with my family. My soul diverged in a wood—no, it was a field beneath an infinite starry sky—and that has made all the difference. Maybe I *am* insane.

Maybe I am.

At this moment I only know I can't handle this shit alone, and the person I choose to share my delusions with is Clay. I want to let him all the way in, carve my secrets between us in trust and truth. What happens next, I can't even speculate.

"No," I say softly. "It's really not."

"What's wrong?" he asks instantly.

"Nothing I can talk about on the phone. Can I pick you up?" I've kind of lost track of what day it is, but I *think* he should be off work by now.

"Are you okay to drive?"

The question puts a smile on my face, settling my nerves. It's amazing how steady Clay makes me feel. It's not that all my fears and uncertainties disappear, more like they're reduced by a factor of ten. A slow breath escapes me.

"Yeah, I'll be fine. See you in half an hour or so."

Normally I'd just leave without saying anything, but the talk I had with Mrs. Rhodes makes me want to be polite. She's spent ten years cleaning our house and cooking us food; this is the least I can do. So I call, "I'm going out with Clay. I won't be late."

She emerges from the kitchen with a startled look. "Thanks for letting me know."

We exchange tentative smiles, then I let myself out and head for the garage where I parked the VW. After dropping my phone in the cup holder between the seats, I back out and navigate the curves of the drive, pausing only for the gate to let me out. Half the drive passes without incident, but as I stop at the four-way intersection on the outskirts of town, the passenger door flies open and suddenly Creepy Jack is in my car. My heart lurches.

If he looked abnormal in some way, I'd feel better. But he's not scruffy or unshaven; his eyes aren't bloodshot. To anyone else I'm sure he's the picture of control and sanity. Yet here he is, a married man, chasing me like I'm his reason for living. His abrupt arrival means he's been stalking me.

"Get out," I order, hoping I don't sound as scared as I feel.

"Not before we talk." He's smiling, but the number of teeth he shows me—it doesn't feel safe or friendly, more like he wants to take a bite.

"There's nothing to say. I've outgrown our arrangement."

I'm torn on what to do next; I really want him out of my car, but there's a truck approaching in my rearview mirror. In the ideal world I could jump out and beg for help. That would expose Creepy Jack and open the door to criminal charges. But as I look at the dilapidated pickup truck and the grubby neckbeard driving it, I'm not convinced I can rely on the dude to do the right thing. I'm better off alone with CJ. I step on the gas and drive toward town, hoping he doesn't know the way to Clay's house.

Except a hard hand settles on the nape of my neck. "Turn around."

So far he hasn't produced a weapon but he outweighs me by eighty pounds. In a purely physical contest, I don't see how I can win. Fear coats my tongue, tasting of copper and bile, but I try to remain calm. My breathing gives me away, though, quick and staccato beneath the rush of the vents.

"I have plans." My voice doesn't shake at least.

"Change them. I don't think you realize how important this is. I'm not a man you can play with, precious." With an awful smile, he runs his knuckles down my cheek and my whole body clenches in revulsion.

The idea of him touching me anywhere else . . . it makes me want to die. I can't believe Morgan did this—for any reason. She wanted to learn the truth about her mother's death, but I recall the pictures she stored online and I stifle a whimper. Assholes would say I invited this, deserve it even.

This isn't my fault. Is it? In my head, I hear Morgan echoing the question, all heartbreak and hesitation.

36

Dammit, no. He's the criminal. This isn't my fault.

Or Morgan's.

Even so, I have a thousand regrets—that I wasn't more on guard after breaking it off—that I didn't report him to the police and turn over all my evidence . . . the list goes on forever.

"I'm not your property," I tell him. "If you keep on like this, the truth will come out."

"Will it?" His voice is silky with menace.

He jerks the wheel, driving the small car into a spin. I stomp the brake in reflex so we come rocking to a stop at the edge of the road, and my head snaps sideways, slamming into the window. It hurts like hell and I'm seeing stars for a few seconds, long enough for him to yank me out of the driver's seat and into his lap. The gear shift bites into my hip. I scream then, full on ear-splitting shrieks, and it makes him hesitate. Then I process what he's actually saying.

"My God, you're bleeding. Morgan, are you all right?"

He cradles me like I'm infinitely precious, just like the endearment he used, and it unsettles me to the point that I can't speak. What the hell is wrong with this man? I use his concern, relaxing enough to make him drop some tension in his arms. It's like he really thinks I'll snuggle against him. When he puts his face in my hair, I slam my skull back against his nose and lunge for the door handle.

Though I'm dizzy as shit, in ten seconds I'm running full tilt into the field. The corn is tall and dry, rustling, whipping my face as I shove through, deeper into the rows, so I can't see anything. This is a scene straight from a horror movie, and I should know better, except all my choices are bad and worse. There are no houses around, and for a few heartbeats, I can only think, *Is this how my mother died?* I imagine her being driven off the road, surviving the crash and running, running, aware of the tiny, helpless life inside her. Is this how she felt in her last moments? I smell Creepy Jack's blood in my hair, and in this moment, I feel only mad revulsion. If I could, I'd plunge into a river and wash myself clean, even if that ended with me floating like Ophelia with flowers in my damp and streaming hair.

He's shouting but I don't stop. I run and keep running as if my life depends on it. Maybe it does. I've lost the ability to tell. In the headlong rush I don't see the edge coming, plunge down a bank and tumble through a briar patch. Wild raspberries, half-eaten by birds, smear my skin with red, underscored by scratches deep enough to bleed. I don't have the breath or strength to run farther. Injuries from the accident throb from the fall, so I press myself into the damp earth, weeds tickling my bare cheeks, and I don't move.

Creepy Jack is frantic. I hear him nearby, searching, searching, beating at the dry corn stalks. "Morgan, please. Don't do this."

His scuffed leather dress shoes appear, no more than ten feet from where I'm hiding. From this angle I can see only up to the bottom of his pant legs. My breath strangles in my throat, and my heartbeat thunders so loud that I'm astonished he can't hear it. It seems like an eternity before he moves off in the other direction, still calling for me. I hide for countless moments more, shivering as if I have a fever. By the time I notice that it's getting dark, my body has stiffened to the point that it's agony to crawl out of the thicket. The thorns catch on my clothes like I'm a prize the bushes don't want to relinquish, and fresh scratches scrape down my spine, deep enough that I feel the hot trickle of blood.

Finally I stumble forward and land on hands and knees in the clay-rich dirt of the embankment. There are raspberries growing along an irrigation trench, and it takes all my remaining fortitude to dig my bloody fingers into the soil and haul myself onto flat ground. All around, the wind rustles through the dry corn husks. I've arrived in a nocturnal agrarian wasteland. The word *desolate* blooms in my mind, and I picture myself dying alone, as my mother did. There will be no one to ask hard questions about my passing, either.

Pure defiance forces me to my feet. Despite the stitch in my side, the pain in my ankle, and all the myriad minor wounds that are bleeding sluggishly, I stagger onward. Now that it's dark, I'm not altogether sure where I came from. The rows of corn seem like an endless Halloween maze, only instead of music and laughter, I hear only the wind and insects singing their night songs. Now that the sun's gone down, it's getting chilly, too. Not enough for me to die of exposure, but I'm not dressed for the weather, and my skin prickles with goose bumps.

Pulling down the plants around me helps a little. I spin in a slow circle and eventually identify the road. From this distance it's a dark swathe cutting through the fields. I limp in that direction, each step feeling like a thousand, but when I reach the pavement, my VW is gone. Staring in both directions, disbelief sweeps over me.

That asshole stole my car?

If I had the energy, I'd be furious. Just now I only have room for fear . . . because my cell phone is still in the car, I don't have any money on me, and the only person who knows I'm missing is Creepy Jack. He might be driving the Bug around even now, silently searching. That threat is almost enough to send me back into the cornfield.

No, I can't hide forever. Still, I don't walk right on the shoulder of the road. Instead I pick a careful path along the shallow ditch set slightly below it. This way, I may be able to scramble into the cornfield if Creepy Jack stops. I'm twitchy, heading for cover as cars pass, but then after I see their taillights I realize maybe I should've flagged them down. I'm afraid of getting in the wrong car, just like with grubby pickup-truck guy.

Walking three miles won't kill me. Other people might.

Between my sore ankle and the fact that I skipped lunch to study in the library, I'm soon light-headed. I can remember my mom lecturing me about bad life choices and ending up dead in a ditch, but I never would've imagined her cautions could be so accurate. Somehow I take a few more steps, but the stars above are blurry, streaking into bands of light. Tears leak from the corners of my eyes as my knees buckle. I kneel for a minute or two, but an inner core of steel won't let me quit.

Maybe it's the same reason I held on during the accident when Morgan let go.

Assuming that dream is true. And I'm not crazy.

Right now my mental state doesn't matter. I just have to get home. I've gone fifty yards when it occurs to me that I'm dead set on getting back to the Frost estate, which says something about my degree of acceptance. For me, home isn't the Burnham house any longer; I'm not wearing Morgan like a dress that doesn't fit.

Whoever, whatever I was before, I'm Morgan Frost now.

Mentally I repeat the words like a mantra—*I am Morgan Frost*—and for some reason it gives me strength, permitting me to pick up the pace. Even the boost of adrenaline doesn't accomplish miracles, however. There are still two miles to go. But as I round the bend, the glimmering lights of a farmhouse shine through the darkness. I have no idea who lives here, and I doubt Morgan did either. Her family didn't exactly make friends when they bought three failing farms and turned that land into a posh private estate. Still, even if the homeowners recognize me, they would have to be heartless to refuse to let me use the phone.

I angle toward the gravel drive as the roar of a car engine gains on me from behind. Terror sends me sprinting toward those squares of light and I don't look back; I don't stop either, not even when I hear the brakes, tires squealing on pavement. This is it. There's no fight left if Creepy Jack takes me for the second time.

Never in my life have I felt this helpless, not even when I lay in a field dying.

37

"Morgan, wait!"

Even if it's a trick, I'm willing to believe. Stumbling, I slow and spin to see Clay illuminated by the headlights of the beater that replaced his Corvair. He jogs toward me and before I can say anything, he sweeps me into his arms and carries me to the car. Instinctively, my arms go around his neck. His body is solid and steady, heartbeat better than a lullaby. With gentle hands he deposits me in the passenger seat and then vaults the hood of the car in a move that leaves me dazed with grateful appreciation.

Creepy Jack wasn't the only one who knew, I realize then. *I told Clay I'd be there in half an hour. When I didn't show, maybe he came looking.*

Though he didn't exactly save me, I'm so touched that it feels like my throat's clogged up with words and tears. Wordless, he hands me a bottle of water and I sip from it, conscious that I'm filthy. He doesn't speak even after we're on the road, heading back toward town. At this point his place feels like sanctuary because Creepy Jack won't dare approach me where there are witnesses who can testify to his crimes. I have no proof he's the reason I look this way, but I want *so bad* to call the cops as soon as we arrive at Clay's house and tell them everything. Maybe I can't prove he basically carjacked me and made me run for my life, but I still have the pictures Oscar took. Those are enough to mess up Patterson's life permanently.

And yours, a small, frightened voice whispers. My sigh comes out as a little moan.

"You're not asking." I'm not surprised how hoarse I sound.

"It's obvious something serious went down." His tone is calm, but his hands are white-knuckled on the wheel, like it's all he can do not to lose his shit.

But I appreciate his composure. It allows me to wrap up mine like a tattered ball gown I've been wearing for days in the forest. I can almost tug at the satin edges, threading myself together with will and grit; I'm an oyster with secrets layered beneath the pink of my flesh. Maybe if I hold them long enough I can produce a pearl for Clay to admire. Or maybe the constant scrape of it will leave me bleeding and raw.

"Yeah," I whisper.

"I was worried when you said you weren't okay . . . and when you didn't show up, I nearly lost my mind." Still conversational, but his concern reaches me like a hug, untangling the knots of anxiety from the constant terror of the last few hours.

"I'm really sorry."

"Did you do it on purpose?" he asks.

"What? No. Of *course* not." I'm genuinely startled by the question.

"Then there's no need to apologize. Just point me at the asshole that hurt you and I'll break him in two."

That's not a threat, I realize. It's a guarantee. My resolve to share everything falters. If I tell him all about Creepy Jack, he'll end up in jail. Patterson has power around here, money, influence, access to expensive lawyers. While I desperately need someone on my side, I don't want Clay immolated on the pyre of my screwed-up life. It doesn't help that these problems started before I took over as Morgan Frost. No matter what, I'm the one stuck dealing with the situation as it stands.

"Can it wait until we get to your place? I'll clarify as much as I can," I say finally.

"That explanation better include a name." He doesn't look away from the road, each turn bringing us closer to the moment of truth. "I protect what's mine. Before now, it hasn't been much, but I'm twice an asshole if I let anyone treat you like this. I don't care what it costs me."

"That's what I'm afraid of," I mutter.

Clay ignores that, or maybe it was too soft for him to catch. He touches my knee lightly, comfort, reassurance, or both. "Sorry, forget that. I always come on too strong when I'm scared. Right now I need to patch you up, not figure out who to kneecap."

The mental image of Clay ambushing Creepy Jack with a bat is satisfying. I enjoy that mental image for a while. Then I say, "I'm not badly hurt. You can relax."

"Easy for you to say. They *just* did a special report tonight on a college girl two counties over who went missing on her way home from church."

Only the good die young, pops into my head but I swallow the macabre joke. Dark humor doesn't help and it will only reveal my ragged nerves. "Really? Damn. I'm not sure what that has to do with me, though."

"You fit the general profile," he says.

For a few seconds I can't parse that. "Huh?"

"Dark hair, blue eyes, sixteen to twenty-two, between five seven and five nine. The girl who vanished isn't the first, apparently. There have been two more in the last six months. The anchors were talking about a possible taskforce or something."

"So that's why you were so panicked," I whisper.

Questions burn a hole in my mind, two sides of the same awful coin—am I in danger of being taken because I look like them . . . or is someone snatching them because they look like me?

38

By some unexpected blessing, Nathan isn't home when we slip in through the back door. The kitchen lights are on, though, and the dishes still on the table tell me that Clay left in a hurry. Quickly he deposits the plate and glass in the sink, then he gets his first good look at me in full light. He curses so colorfully that, despite the situation, I make mental notes.

"Sorry," he mutters. "I'll get the first-aid kit."

Light-headed, I collapse into the nearest chair, waiting for him to return. Eventually I put my head on the table and rouse only when a warm hand settles on my shoulder. I jolt upright; Clay steadies me, but he doesn't let go. Blearily I note that he's got a basin of warm water, a pile of hand towels, plus the kit he mentioned before. Somehow, the fact that he doesn't speak before he starts washing my wounds makes the moment more intimate. The silence builds with his eyes on mine, and it feels incredibly important that he's willing to take care of me before I answer any of his questions, of which there must be, like, a hundred.

Even the water stings; I brace as he cleanses, rinses, and goes again. He sucks in a sharp breath when he reaches my back. "Your shirt has to come off."

"I bet you say that to all the injured girls."

A half smile quirks the corner of his mouth. "That makes me sound like a predator."

In answer I shrug out of my torn tee. It's not a huge movement, but I'm so tired and hungry that it makes me dizzy. He frowns at whatever he sees in my expression, yet he still tilts me forward so he can clean the scratches on my back. The window behind me is open, and between my lack of clothes and low blood sugar, I'm freezing. First the goose pimples pop out, then I can't stop my teeth from chattering. It might also be reaction settling in, who knows?

"Are you almost d-done?"

"Are you scared?" he asks.

Quickly I shake my head. "Sorry. I'm just—"

"It's okay." His voice is so gentle, I could crawl into it like an afghan somebody's kindly grandma knitted.

Clay works fast, taping gauze over all the sore spots like he's done this before. If he's raised his brother half as much as I suspect, then he probably *is* an old pro at this. The rumor mill didn't make their mother sound particularly protective or maternal, even before she left for good. So I can imagine that he's the one who blew on Nathan's skinned knees and applied Bactine and Band-Aids as requested. Right now, his warm breath over a long scrape on my forearm is making me quiver in an entirely different way.

Finally, he finishes with the treatment and gets a shirt for me to put on. Like Clay, the hoodie smells of fresh air, sunshine, and simple detergent. Shrugging into it is like snuggling into his arms. But he's not paying attention to my goofy smile; instead he's boiling water on the stove, probably for a hot drink. As I watch, he makes black tea liberally laced with honey.

"I don't care how you feel about sugar right now," he tells me, setting the mug in front of me with an authoritative thunk.

I smile. "It's fine. Even I'm willing to admit I could use the glucose."

"You probably need to eat, too. But all I have is bean soup."

"Sounds good."

Clay stares as if I've grown a second head. "It's made with chicken bouillon and smoked ham hocks."

"I'm making a few dietary changes. Some things I have no choice to avoid. Allergies," I add with a shrug. "But other things I *could* eat, I've just chosen not to."

"Then I'll get you a bowl."

The soup is still warm, waiting in a covered pot on the back of the stove. I'm awed that Clay knows how to cook; it's not something I've ever had to worry about—in either life. As Liv, my mom only asked me to chop stuff for her, and more because she wanted the company than needed my help. And since I've been Morgan, Mrs. Rhodes is always on hand to fulfill my every whim. I feel really young compared to Clay, even if he's only a few years older, and that makes it even more difficult to say what I need to.

"This is delicious," I say.

It's a little saltier than I'm used to, but it has an excellent flavor, just a hint of heat. While he cleans up the kitchen, I devour the whole serving along with the tea. I feel better fast; even my wounds don't hurt as much as they did, and the throb of prior injuries dulls to a bearable ache. The clink of him depositing the soup pot in the fridge rouses me from a near food stupor.

"Come on, you." He wraps an arm around me, tugging me out of the chair.

I don't ask as Clay leads me through Nathan's bedroom into his own and shuts the door behind us. Then he locks both doors, the one from Nathan's room and the one that leads to the living room. Though I'm not exactly nervous—I don't think Clay will do anything tonight of all nights—I'm also locked in with him.

I distract myself by looking at the posters on his walls, abstract art instead of bikini girls. The space is sparsely furnished: full bed on a simple frame, brown-and-gold patterned sheets, a battered desk that has been painted multiple times so several assorted colors peep through, and a rickety side table with a rather industrial lamp on it. There are some books and magazines but no family pictures, no mementos of high school, like the awards that bedeck Nathan's walls.

But one shelf catches my eye. The items must be priceless to Clay, though I'm not sure what two of them mean. He's got a pair of laminated ticket stubs on the right, a broken watch on the left, and in the center, there's a framed certificate. Despite the ornate font I can read the top two words from here: GENERAL EQUIVALENCY.

"You already got your GED?"

His careless shrug says this is no big deal. "I took the test last year over at the technical college in Macon."

"That's *amazing.*"

"Yeah, well. It's unlikely I'll be offered an apprenticeship without it. I'm working on my portfolio now and I need to take a few art classes before I'll become an appealing prospect."

"Can I see it?"

"What?"

"Your portfolio."

"Are you seriously asking to see my etchings?" But he's smiling as he opens the lower desk drawer and pulls out a black folder. "There's nowhere to sit but the bed. Is that okay?"

In answer I crawl across carefully and prop myself against the wall with my legs stretched sideways across the mattress. Clay settles beside me and I don't even notice when he wraps an arm around my shoulders, settling me against him, because I'm too absorbed in his pen-and-ink designs. Most are simple, geometric, and his eye for patterns is exquisite and precise. He's also got a few images that seamlessly blend different mythologies, like a Celtic love chain entangled with an ouroboros. I imagine how lovely this would be tattooed around someone's biceps and glance up to find his face really close.

"You're super talented," I tell him.

"Thanks. But you've stalled long enough. I feel like I've been patient, now it's time for you to start talking."

He's right. But . . .

"What about Nathan?"

"He's out with Braden, so he'll sleep wherever he passes out. Pretty sure he won't be back tonight." His tone says he'd like to track his brother down and beat some sense into him but Nathan is intractable. "Even if he shows up, he'll sneak in the back and collapse in his room."

"Okay then."

Apparently, Clay can read my doubts because he kisses me softly. "Maybe this isn't the time to say it, but . . . no matter what you tell me, it won't change how I feel. In case you haven't noticed, I've fallen for you so hard and fast that it feels like there's no bottom."

39

Clay's confession is so like him—low-key but also completely fearless. There's no way I can offer less. I can't believe I'm about to do this, but one part of my resolve hasn't changed. While I can't reveal Creepy Jack's identity, I'm unloading the rest.

I start with dying in a field and waking up in the hospital . . . as Morgan. There's also some rambling about Morgan's secrets, the scary older-man lover, and how I'm so completely unequipped to deal with any of it. The whole recitation doesn't take as long as I expected, a little less than ten minutes. Clay's hand stills on my shoulder, and I'm afraid to look at him.

"This older guy, he's the one who hurt you tonight?" Trust Clay to focus on that. He's put a pin in the rest.

"Yeah. Well, I acquired the scrapes and scratches running away from him. But he definitely jumped in my car and scared me out of it. He stole it afterward, and—shit. He might have my phone, too." That's a problem I just registered, and now I'm freaking out. If he cracks my password, there's no limit to the damage he can do.

Clay reaches for his, currently charging on the side table and dials. I clench my teeth, half hoping Creepy Jack will answer. A few seconds later, I hear the voice mail message, so that proves nothing. I might be delusional, a girl who imagines monsters and hurts herself running from them. Or damn, there's even a syndrome about people who wound themselves for attention.

The silence grows until I can't stand it. I finally muster my courage and peer up at him, but he's staring blankly at the portfolio page. *It's too much. He doesn't believe me.*

"This is a lot to take in," he says quietly. "You have to admit, it sounds—"

"Crazy. I know. That's why I haven't said anything before."

"Why tell me?"

"You noticed a difference on your own, didn't you? That's part of it. But . . . I can't be with you unless you know everything. It's too big a lie for me to live with."

Clay cups my cheek in his hand and searches my gaze, though what he's looking for I have no idea, maybe some inner conviction or a febrile gleam in my eyes. I hold the look steadily, but my heart beats so hard it almost hurts. I'm dying for someone to believe me; this isn't a mental disorder, a grief-induced denial, or any other explicable psychiatric phenomenon.

"I know *you* believe what you're saying," he starts, but I can't deal with his tone.

It's the way you talk to a toddler who's about to jam a fork in the light socket. In reaction I scoot away and lean against the wall where the headboard would be, putting two feet between us. He doesn't follow.

Great. I'm no longer the girl he wants to make out with. Now he thinks I desperately need mental help. At this point he might not believe me about Creepy Jack either if I told him that the guy's a respected local politician with a wife and two kids. Though I predicted this outcome weeks ago, the disappointment still stings.

Quietly I rack my brain for something that might convince him, but before Liv's death—how weird to think of myself in third person—I didn't have that much to do with Clay. To me he was just Nathan's slightly scary older brother, who I didn't know at all, and I disapproved of him on principle, based on secondhand bullshit. Now I'm ashamed of how I misjudged him without understanding anything.

Then it occurs to me—an event that predates Nathan, small and random—nothing that I would've mentioned to Morgan. "One time early in my freshman year, you were out behind the Dumpsters with some people who were smoking. Later, when the garbage caught fire, they blamed you. But you definitely weren't one of the smokers, so I told the vice principal that it wasn't you."

Clay glances at me, his brows arcing. "What were you doing behind the school?"

I suspect he didn't notice me back then. When he was a junior, he hung out with the bad kids, the ones who probably wouldn't graduate and didn't care either. They didn't attend school functions or join clubs. Half of them ended up in juvie before they graduated, and another quarter dropped out, Clay among them.

"Morgan dared me."

It had seemed *so* audacious to circle the school as a freshman, spying on all the groups who would kick my ass if they caught me poking around. People always took me as Morgan's shadow, and I didn't fight that classification until I developed a giant crush on Nathan Claymore.

His lack of response indicates that this isn't compelling evidence.

But then he says, "I saw Liv that day. Tiny cut-offs, right? I remember because those were definitely not compliant with the school dress code."

My eyes widen as I fight a blush. "Yeah."

"You're saying Liv got me off the hook? Because you're right, they had me pegged for a three-day suspension until someone cleared me."

"Not Liv. *Me*. Why would I have told Morgan about it? More to the point, why would she remember years later if she wasn't personally involved?" Eager to establish credibility, I add, "Look, I can answer any question you ask that Liv would know the answer to. Try me."

"Most shit Liv knew, I wouldn't," Clay says tiredly.

By his expression, he doesn't want to play this game with me. He'd rather take me home and report me as mentally unsound to those better suited to look after me. Tears pool in my eyes and trickle out the corners because this was such a huge step and it required all my courage. I suspect this won't end until I'm taking heavy meds. Angrily I swipe away the evidence that he's hurt me and move to slide off the bed.

But he catches my wrist with a gentle hand. "One day I scared Liv while she was pouring lemonade. What glass did she break and when was it?"

Afraid to hope, I raise my gaze to his. "It was a glass a bit taller than a Mason jar, rim around the top, and it had sunflowers on it. As for when, it was, like, eight months ago." Wracking my brain, I still can't come up with the date. "Just before Christmas, I'm pretty sure."

I had stayed later than usual and Clay came home from work a little early, startling me when he popped in the back door. The glass hit the floor and shattered everywhere. I felt bad, too, because they had a matched set of four, and my mom had taken me to enough rummage sales collecting Depression glass that I knew value when I saw it. Maybe it wasn't fancy crystal, but certain patterns were rare these days.

"Nathan wasn't in the room," he says then. "Liv told you?"

I shake my head patiently. "No, I was *there*. I tried to clean it up but you said I'd just cut myself. Which I thought was churlish but in retrospect, I'm guessing you were genuinely worried." Perception makes all the difference in how words come across. What I took for curt annoyance back then probably *was* quiet concern.

Clay nods, his expression troubled. "This . . . this is weird."

"Tell me about it."

And I haven't even mentioned the late-breaking development, where I've started getting trickles of memories that I'm sure belong to Morgan. What I'm experiencing isn't like any kind of amnesia I've ever heard of—how can I possibly know so much about Liv and so little about the person whose body I'm occupying? Doubtless, mental health professionals could rationalize it somehow and give my condition a name. If there isn't one, maybe they'll name it after me: Frost-Burnham Syndrome.

"In February of this year, Nathan and I were fighting when you came over. What were we arguing about?"

"The cable bill. Nathan ordered four Pay-Per-View movies without telling you and you were pissed and he said it was only twenty bucks, so you should take the stick out of your ass and stop being such a cheapskate, and you said—"

"He can buy whatever the hell he wants when he's earning his own money." His face is pale, his eyes wide.

I spot the first glimmer of belief in his gold-green eyes and it heartens me. "Yes. Ask more. Any little thing that's happened here, the more trivial the better, the less likely I'd have mentioned it to Morgan. And I'll know, I know it all."

"Not because Liv told you," he grates out.

"Because I'm Liv. This is a lot to take in, I get that."

Clay opens his fingers and releases my wrist. At first I don't understand and I knee-walk toward him, so unbelievably relieved that someone is finally ready to accept my impossible truth. But he recoils and crosses the room, backing all the way up to his desk, and then he leans on it like he needs the support.

He won't look at me.

"What's wrong?"

"I damn well wish you were crazy. Because . . . if I accept this as truth and you are Liv, you don't get that *this*"—he gestures between us—"is impossible? Your grieving family aside, my brother is breaking his heart over you *right now*. Liv is . . . and always will be Nathan's girl. And you made me . . ." Here, Clay's voice breaks. "You made *me* want you, too."

"I'm sorry," I whisper.

"That was cruel, whoever you are. Instead of me, you should've told Nathan. You're the one girl in the whole world that I can't touch, no matter how I feel or what I want."

"But I chose *you*."

His eyes close as if my words hurt, each one carving deep like a blade. "Even if you never tell anyone else, *I'll* know. And I can't do that to him, you understand? He loves you."

I swallow hard, hardly able to get the protest out. "So do you. Before, you said nothing could change that."

Haunted eyes lock on mine for an endless moment; it's like he's memorizing me. Clay's pain is palpable, matching my own, so his reply doesn't surprise me. "Nothing but this."

40

"**You have** the right to change your mind." I slide off the bed and take two steps toward the door. "But I'm not a prize you can bestow on Nathan. Just because *you* don't want to be with me, it doesn't mean I'll go back to him."

"It's not about what *I* want, it almost never is." Bitterness rings like a poorly tuned piano in Clay's voice.

Though I've admired how he sacrificed for Nathan, it never occurred to me to wonder if he minded. But it's human nature to imagine how things might be different if you made other choices. Maybe he'd already be apprenticed somewhere if he wasn't tied to Renton, keeping a roof over Nathan's head.

"Can I ask one favor? Don't tell Nathan. If I wanted him to know, I would've told him."

Clay clenches his jaw, speaking through his teeth. "Not revealing something this major is almost as bad as keeping you for myself."

"If you could stop talking about me like I'm property, that'd be awesome." I pop my neck, trying to check my temper. Anger provides welcome relief from the pain and sadness tapping away at my fragile composure. "Can you promise or not?"

"Fine. That's all I can do for you now. Just understand, I think this is a mistake."

No, you leaving me is the mistake. More words bubble up, and

I'm so tempted to argue with him. Yet I understand why he feels this way and can't fault his loyalty to his brother. But then I remember how Nathan was on the roof. He didn't care that I was dating Clay; he just wanted what he wanted, and the pain feels like it'll split me in two because Clay is used to giving things up for Nathan, and I doubt he's ever gotten the same in return. In a moment of crystalline clarity, I realize that even if I did tell Nathan, it would just be me comforting him. He wouldn't help me solve this, which is what I was hoping I'd get with Clay. A partner.

But I can't ask him to go against his conscience, especially when this is hurting him—and that's *my* fault. Because I was so worried about being found out that I pretended my way into his heart, and he can't live with the reality. So I swallow my instinctive protests.

"Then there's nothing else to say. If you could give me a ride home, I would appreciate it." My tone is clipped, formal, but it's the only way to keep from crying.

Honesty doesn't matter. I marshaled my courage, and in the end, I'm still alone in this.

"What about your car? Your phone? You need to file a police report."

I choose my words carefully. "While I appreciate your concern, it's not your business. Just take me home, please."

"Don't be like this. I can't stop caring with the flick of a switch."

"I'm not your girlfriend, fake or otherwise, and I just want to get out of here before I break down in front of you. Is that okay?"

You got to tell me how you feel at least. I can't, it'll only make things worse.

In answer he unlocks the door leading to the front room. We go out that way, quietly, in case Nathan came home while we were talking. I definitely don't want to see him tonight. In fact,

I'm ready to strike both brothers from the ledger of my life. The drive seems endless with only pop music on the radio to fill the silence. Finally he parks across from the gate that leads to the Frost estate. Funny how I shift back and forth; sometimes it's home and sometimes it's Morgan's house, which perfectly encapsulates the bizarre betwixt feeling that currently defines my entire existence.

Clay looks like he wants to say something but I'm already opening the door. "Thanks for the ride."

I limp across the road to key in the code manually. The gates swing wide and I slip in, hitting the button on the other side to lock up. *Don't look back,* I order myself. And somehow I manage not to, despite glimpsing the bright sweep of his headlights in my peripheral vision.

This is for the best. I don't have the time or mental energy for a relationship anyway. Shit is already complicated enough.

This pep talk lasts for a hundred feet, but then I'm distracted by my blue Bug parked beside the winding driveway. I approach with my heart in my throat, half expecting Creepy Jack to be waiting, but that's a considerable risk even for him. How would he explain lurking in my car to my father? Still, I'm nervous as I open the door. I find the keys and my phone in the cup holder between the seats. The car starts with no trouble, though I'm wary as I drive up to the house. But there's no sign of Creepy Jack . . . and my dad's car is still missing from the garage.

Not surprising, I guess, if he's with his girlfriend. It's only half past ten. For me the day feels a lot longer. Slipping in the back lets me dodge into my room unnoticed, not exactly a tough feat since Mrs. Rhodes is the only other person in the house, and she must either be asleep or watching TV in her room by now.

Poor little rich girl. It's easier to mock myself than to acknowledge the profound and bone-chilling loneliness. I remind myself that there are millions of people with problems much worse than mine. I head into the sparkling private bath and slowly strip off all the gauze Clay taped in place. The primary reason is that I can't shower with the bandages on, but the deeper significance is voluntarily peeling off all connection with him. If I'm alone, then I am, and I don't need any reminders that he cared until he found out the truth.

After turning on the water to let it warm up, I strip and jump in, vowing not to think about it anymore. The hot water stings skin and scratches equally, so I'm in a bit of pain when I climb out ten minutes later. I still have some meds left since I went light on my prescription after the accident. The pill bottle is in the cabinet but I'm probably not in the right frame of mind to take any. Better to stay clearheaded and hurt a little.

Now the only things on my mind will be solving a decade-old mystery—no problem, she said ironically—and passing the advanced science courses I want to pursue. On the minus side, I have zero allies in this fight, but since that's where I was before I spilled everything to Clay, I shouldn't get depressed over it. Considering how many impossible things I've already survived, I won't be the girl who collapses over a boy.

I've dried off and put on pajamas when it hits me. *Crap, my phone.* Before, I was so worried about what Creepy Jack might do with it. The password works as before, but when the main screen appears, my background picture has been changed. It's now a picture of Jack Patterson's smiling face. *Shit. Oh shit.* I stare at my phone, loathing every pixel of Creepy Jack's face. I change that, too, and erase that photo like it's a personal statement.

But it gets worse. He's deleted every male contact from my phone—Oscar, Ben, Eric, Clay, and Nathan are all gone, along with every message they've ever sent me. He's also input his own info again. The only other dude in my phone now is my dad. Creepy Jack has also filled my phone with pictures of himself, like that's something I want. Hands shaking, I delete them one by one, though they're not obscene. They feel like a statement of ownership and he's completely disinterested or disconnected from how I feel. There are other modifications too: deletion of certain apps, like he's imposing control. That's easily remedied, but the phone numbers I'll have to ask for, unless the guys happen to text me. All of it leaves me feeling queasy.

And then it gets worse.

In my notes app I find a message from Creepy Jack.

Those pictures were a bad idea, precious. I'll leave you these to replace the ones I'm taking. And I've warned you before about talking to other men. Don't make me jealous. Don't make me delete those contacts again. PS Your mother's birthday isn't a secure password.

That's why Oscar's number didn't register as a known contact. This asshole has stolen Morgan's phone before. My hands tremble so bad that I can hardly open the cloud storage app, and I dig through the directory, looking, looking, only to find the whole folder gone. I hope to God he just deleted the collection, but now I'm terrified that Creepy Jack has all those pictures. It's a dumbass move for him to save them, as no site is fully secure, but he doesn't seem to be operating as intended. What if my proposed extortion scenario with Oscar just flipped?

CJ might think he can use the pictures to control me, but that's not on. I'm a minor in those shots, so no matter how bad the scandal, he'll suffer more. I can always leave the state and go to college somewhere else, though I don't relish carrying a shadow everywhere I go. *It's not even you in those pictures. Not really.* That justification reverberates in my head because it sounds like the kind of thing a survivor might tell herself to stay strong.

Am I mentally ill? The question comes back like a boomerang. What if the shit with Creepy Jack, lingering issues from my mom's death, and then the accident . . . what if everything broke me? There's no shame in it; if that's true, I really do need treatment, and there's probably no mystery to solve.

But . . . the scientist in me quibbles. That explanation doesn't cover my situation.

There's no way I should know as much as I do about Liv's life, especially if I'm Morgan suffering from a psychotic break. There's no concrete answer to how the human brain stores memories, though there is fascinating work being done in neuroscience. Short-term and long-term memories are stored differently, and secondary memories are not supposed to be subject to the same decay. I could compare the brain to a hard drive, but that's an imperfect metaphor, as neurons don't have binary off/on settings.

Theoretically, it may be possible to retrieve memories from a dead person's brain. If you extrapolate that there are two levels of consciousness, a spirit, a soul or whatever you want to call it, plus the biological matter that carries imprinted data, it could be argued that I'm half Morgan, half Liv. Instead of dying, I brought Liv's life experiences with me in the form of energy, akin to a wireless transmission. But I've installed them on Morgan's physical being. A reasonable analogy might be that I'm running Linux on a partitioned Windows computer, and while it's functional, there's bound to be some data corruption in the exchange, which is why I'm remembering things that Morgan knew.

Because it's imprinted in my brain. Whether or not it was mine to start with, it is now.

These hypotheses settle my nerves in a way that more creative pursuits never could, which reinforces my conviction that I'm not mentally disturbed. I'm also willing to accept the premise that I'm neither Liv nor Morgan, more of a hybrid—Miv or Lorgan, which are terrible smush names. But maybe the designation doesn't matter so much. I just need to make peace with my new life and figure out how to solve all of these problems, so I can move on.

I won't be in Renton that much longer anyway.

Part of me wonders if this would make a difference to Clay, but I won't ask. Even half of Liv is more than he wants. Which is ironic because he fell in *love* with enhanced Morgan, featuring special ingredient Liv.

I realize then; there's a way to test this, and I love seeing how my theories pan out.

As Liv, I had little talent for drawing, whereas Morgan was skilled at capturing everything but her own face. The portrait I did for her was clumsy in comparison and only earned her a C+. I remember the art teacher was puzzled, but like I told Morgan, a C+ is better than a zero since she couldn't finish the assignment. Crossing the room, I dig out one of her sketchbooks and flip through it. Most of these are clothing designs.

I close my eyes, trying to relax, and set the pencil to paper. My wrist is moving before I've even decided what to draw. The clean line of someone's jaw takes shape, and I'm *fascinated* because I don't remember learning how to shade this way. This is physical memory at work. It feels like someone else is creating this picture, though my hands are doing the work.

In the end, it's a lovely portrait of Morgan's mom, as she looked just before she died.

41

"Wow," I whisper. Maybe this sketch wouldn't hold up for anyone else, but to me, it stands as evidence supporting my fused identity theory.

I pin the picture on the bulletin board and study it. Sometimes when I'm focused like this, I can feel Morgan, like she's about to whisper in my ear. Today I only get a whiff of that haunting perfume. It happens whenever I think of Lucy Ellis-Frost, and since this isn't how Morgan smelled, it stands to reason that it could be her mother's signature scent. As Liv, I don't remember that, so this must be more Morgan-memory filtering through.

Or hell, maybe I've possessed Morgan and am haunted by her mother in retaliation.

Sighing, I open my laptop. With everything that's happened, I haven't followed up on Tina Goldsmith. A basic White Pages search online doesn't turn up anything, so I get out the credit card and input her basic data to one of those background search companies. It's crazy how much info you can get for $19.95. Five minutes later, I have a PDF including her credit rating, how many traffic tickets she's had, current residence and phone number, prior addresses, employment history, and more. The Internet has to be a stalker's best friend, as this package even includes her social media imprint. I immediately choose a popular site and send a friend request. It will probably be a while before she responds.

It's past midnight, but I'm not tired. Sighing, I wipe my phone entirely. I wouldn't put it past Creepy Jack to install GPS tracking or spyware apps, so he can watch my every move and read my texts. Tomorrow I'll ask a tech nerd to make sure the reset cleared any potential problems. If I can't get a definitive answer, I'll just chuck it and buy a new one. For now I shut the thing off after the wipe.

Sleep isn't coming any time soon, so I spend the rest of the night reviewing notes from Bio.

After a long, lonely weekend, concealer can't hide the fact that I didn't rest and I default to an oversized gray fuzzy sweater, black jeans, and ass-kicking boots to hide my minor injuries. Downstairs Mrs. Rhodes has a veggie frittata waiting for my breakfast, and I make sure to thank her. I'd like for this truce to last.

"Your father didn't come home last night," she whispers conspiratorially.

I smile. "Okay, I *definitely* need to swing by the office."

"It doesn't bother you?" Her cautious tone says she expects a tantrum of some sort.

"After ten years? Not so much. I'll be leaving next year anyway, so if they want to get married, at least he won't be alone."

She gives me a look. "Yes, completely alone."

"Sorry. You know what I mean. If you get a better job, you could move on anytime."

Mrs. Rhodes mumbles, "If I could, do you think I'd still be here?"

This makes me laugh as I down my food in a few gulps. With a wave, I'm off to school.

The halls are clogged with people before first period, and a few girls are trying to copy whatever I had on Friday. This year I must be driving them crazy because my fashion choices are erratic at best.

From what I remember the science crew will be in the lab screwing around before the bell, and that's who I need to see. In particular I'm looking for Noemi James, a biracial black girl who's legendary in what she can do with cell phones. Rooting, cracking, cloning . . . as Liv, she always impressed the hell out of me. But I've underestimated the weirdness of Morgan Frost entering the science room. Everyone goes quiet, staring at me wide-eyed.

"Hey, guys."

Isaiah Emerson glances up. "Did you give up? You can put my notes over there."

"Wait, what?" Noemi's curious.

If I want her help, I have to explain that I'm trying to test into the advanced science program, senior year. Now they're all gaping like an alien has taken over my body. Which is not the most implausible guess. There are so many memories that we shared when I was Liv that if I wanted to freak them out, I could pretty easily. But I want a new life, not for people to think I'm possessed by my dead best friend.

Half of my dead best friend?

Whatever.

A white Physics bro, Arden Fox, is laughing so hard, he can barely stand upright. "If you pass *any* of those tests, I'll come to school dressed as Goku from *Dragon Ball Z*."

I smile. "Challenge accepted."

The science club starts placing bets, and most of them are against me. I play it cool while Noemi checks my phone. "What's wrong with it?"

"My dad might have put some spyware or tracking apps on it. He's gotten really protective since the accident." Which was true for the first week, but now he's defaulted back to hardly knowing I'm alive. That's what Morgan was used to, based on what she said about how taxing it was to make the annual Europe trip with him.

I'm just not used to spending that much time with my dad, she'd said.

I didn't realize how true that was. All these years, most of her parenting has come from Liv's folks. That's probably why she spent so much time at my place. I can attest, the Frost mansion is depressing and lonely. You could move ten people in and hardly notice them.

"You did a factory reset?"

I nod.

"Okay, then let me check a few things. I should be able to tell you if it's clean."

A few minutes later, she hands the phone back. "There was one hidden tracker app that survived the reset, but I've deleted and scrubbed it using an app I wrote."

"Holy shit, you are *awesome.*" Which is what I'd have said before; it just sort of slips out.

"How much?"

Without hesitation, Noemi names the price and I slide her a couple of bills, more than worth it for peace of mind. "Come back if you get caught again."

Wincing, I shake my head. "I hope not."

"I'm starting to understand why Liv was friends with you," Noemi says.

Isaiah scrutinizes me and Arden seems like he might be worried now. My smirk widens, but I'm on a mission, so I can't linger. "Thanks. Let me know if I can ever help you out."

Next stop, the art department. I find Oscar encircled by the rest of the group. I wave to them from the doorway, and it looks like everyone might come over, so I make meaningful eye contact with Oscar and jerk my head in a way Morgan never would. Not subtle or cool.

He separates and threads the desks to draw me a little farther down the hall. "What's up?"

I take a deep breath and whisper, "First, do you still have those pictures?"

"You said you'd shave my head and leave me to die in the wilderness if I didn't delete them immediately."

"That's not an answer."

He grins. "Kidding, of course I saved them. You don't get dirt like that every day. I'd be an idiot to toss away so much leverage."

"Over me or him?"

Oscar makes an *either/or* face. "Whichever I need."

Since he's kept them secure, I can't even get mad. Plus, Morgan trusted him enough to make him her conspirator in the first place. "Thank God. I'm ready to pull the trigger."

He freezes. "Are you serious?"

"Deadly. I was hoping you'd send them two places for me. The gossip site that's all about catching politicians with their pants down . . . and the police."

Morgan was probably waiting to find out more about her mother's death, but *I* need Jack Patterson in too much trouble to bother me. Otherwise I won't have the breathing room to investigate. Every time I leave home I'll be worried that he's lurking. And logically, I can't think of any reason why the police investigating him for sexual misconduct could work against him later being accused of murder, if it comes to that. No, the more I consider the issue, the more I think that tarnishing his public image will make it more likely serious charges will stick later.

And if it turns out he didn't kill my mother, he still did this terrible shit to *Morgan*.

Either way, Creepy Jack needs to pay.

42

Somber now, Oscar leads me out of the hallway and around the corner, looking for a private place to talk. He chooses the girls' toilet, an interesting move, but it's probably cleaner than the guys'. I check all the stalls, and then he wedges the door closed with the chip of wood that's supposed to prop it open. For good measure I move the trash can, too.

"This is a huge deal, Morgan. You understand just how ugly this could get? I'll blur your face, but it's possible you still might be identified. Hell, that asshole's PR team might even drop your name to the media."

"He's already raised the stakes." I give Oscar an edited version of last night's events and show him the scrapes on my back.

"Shit, yeah. This is probably your best move. Make it too hot for him to screw with you."

"Figuratively or literally."

"As long as you're sure, I'll stop by the public library after school and complete the job. I'll include an outraged, *This girl was fifteen!* complaint in the e-mail."

"Thanks." Since anyone can walk in and use those ancient computers, it should be nearly impossible to tell who sent the message if Oscar opens an e-mail account for this purpose and never uses it again. "What about the cameras?"

"There's a blind spot in the back row," Oscar answers at once.

I'm curious how he knows that, but his smile says he doesn't plan to tell me. Right now I'm so relieved that I want to hug him, but that's not Morgan's style, and Oscar isn't the cuddly type, either. "I honest to God don't know what I'd have done if you didn't have backups."

"Please, who do you think you're talking to?"

"Yeah, you're awesome. I need to repay you for your help."

Just then, someone thumps on the door, and I hurriedly unblock it. Emma Lin bursts in, looking queasy, but she stops when she sees Oscar and me. He just grins and I try to imagine how Morgan would play this, as it's really far out of Liv territory. Before dying, I never skipped a class in my life.

Nervous, I go for a bored smile. "Feel free," I say. "We're done in here."

"You and Oscar . . . ?" Her dark eyes are too shiny, her voice tremulous.

Oh, shit. Does Emma like him? Lots of people do, but if he's had a hook-up, nobody in Renton knows about it. Plus, as I observed before, the art kids don't date their own.

"This was a business meeting." Oscar saunters out, leaving Emma to dodge into a stall and me to exit with somewhat less panache.

By this point, first period is a quarter over. I'm planning to skip and study my science notes, but I check that Oscar's okay first. "You won't have trouble getting back into class?"

"Nah. I'm good with teachers. I'll text you after it's done."

"Could you message me now? Remember, that asshole deleted all my contacts." *Again.*

"Oh right. No problem."

A few seconds later, my phone beeps with a message that just reads, *Hey.* I promptly save his info and snap a picture so I'll get his face with later texts instead of the generic avatar. Somehow I've walked him to class without meaning to. I could go in with him, but then people would talk. I suspect Emma won't say anything about our bathroom strategy session.

I review in the library until it's time for the classes I'll still be attending after the schedule change. More studying through lunch and soon the day is over. The art kids have all sent texts, probably because of Oscar, so I reply to all of them, but Emma's is the only one that really requires a decision.

Emma: *Do you want to hang out?*

This has to be because she wants to know more about what Oscar and I have going on, but . . . I'm lonely for female friends. When I had Morgan, I didn't *need* anyone else, and I miss every damn thing about her even as I *am* her. We were yin and yang, a complete circle. Now there's a hole in my life. It doesn't mean Emma is the one who can fill it, but she's . . . asking. Her party is where everything ended, so maybe this is exactly right.

Sure, I send back. *What did you have in mind?*

We could go to the mall.

I'm typing a response when I spot her waiting by the front doors and the idea of texting when I can *see* her makes me laugh. I put away my phone and quicken my steps. She lifts a hand to signal me. The whispers around me are kind of mean— "Morgan and Emma Lin?" "Oh, look, Morgan's chosen her new sidekick."

Ignoring that, I say, "I have my car here. I'll drive."

"Cool. I got a ride with my brother anyway."

"He's a senior, right?" Like Liv, Emma is a junior, so I can see why people might misunderstand, like I'm looking for a substitute.

But it's not about replacing Liv. It's about making different choices as Morgan. Sure, I could be an ice princess for another nine months and then leave Renton behind me in a cloud of dust, but that's not how I want to spend my last year in school. If other people have gotten the chance to reinvent themselves so completely, I don't know about it. And since I *can* choose what kind of person I'll be, going forward, maybe I can incorporate the best of Liv and Morgan.

"You know Jay?"

"Only in passing. I think we had a class or two together freshman year."

Emma smiles, obviously unsure if this is a good idea, so she must really be devoted to Oscar. "He had a huge crush on you then. Oh God, he'll kill me if he finds out I told you."

"Don't worry," I say. "The secret's safe with me."

You'd be surprised how much of a vault I am.

"So you're still dating Clay?" she asks as I unlock the car via remote and we hop inside.

I shake my head. "We broke up last night, actually."

There's no point in hiding the news. People will find out sooner or later, and it's not like the relationship failed in a way that embarrasses me. In fact it's about as sweet a rejection as anyone ever received. *He left because his brother loves me.* But I can't see Nathan like I did before; too much has happened, and there's no going back.

"Man, I really put my foot in it," she mutters.

I start the car and back out of the parking spot before responding. "It's not a big deal. Since I'm leaving next fall, it's not like we had some big future planned anyway."

Now that's something Morgan would say, for sure.

"As long as you're not sad or anything."

"I'm as good as anyone ever is afterward. No need for ice cream and tears."

We've driven halfway to the mall, and I remember how Clay brought me here. This shouldn't be my prevailing impression since I went with Nathan a lot more, and yet what I remember is holding Clay's hand and feeling for the first time like everything might be okay. Like the rock that never shifted beneath my feet, I thought he was the one constant in my life, only to find he had a fault line that ran deep as the San Andreas—fraternal loyalty.

Maybe I can't be with Clay, but I can't stop missing him, either.

43

Emma finally breaks the silence as we're pulling into the mall parking lot. "So . . . I'm really curious."

"Finally," I say.

"Excuse me?"

"You're dying to know about Oscar and me because you're not sure if he was playing with you in using the whole 'business meeting' excuse."

Her brown skin gets a little ruddier. "Busted."

"There's really nothing to tell. He was helping me with a personal problem, but I assure you, my breakup has nothing to do with him." I pause, figuring I have to make the offer. "If you don't really want to hang out, I can turn around."

"No, it should be fun." Her relief is obvious.

Actually, it is. We spend two hours picking out clothes and I buy a few things that Morgan would never wear. No, that's wrong because I am Morgan, so no matter what I put on, it's exactly right. Emma looks adorable in anything, but I can't find the perfect pair of jeans to save my life.

"They look good," she assures me.

But I don't like the way they fit, so I grumble and try again. It takes me fifteen minutes to figure out the problem. I need Tall sizes now because I'm not a pixie anymore. I'm five nine with lots of leg. Average-cut pants won't work. Now I feel stupid but fortunately Emma doesn't seem to realize this was the problem. Once I make the switch, I lock on to some pants that make my butt look amazing.

Totally buying these.

My wardrobe needs more casual clothes. I can't spend the rest of my life looking like I've just walked off a photo shoot. Morgan cultivated an aura of perfection but I don't mind if people realize that I'm human. That means I'll get dirty occasionally, have bad hair days, or fall down and rip my pants. Resisting those inevitable moments is just a waste of energy better put toward more important things.

I take Emma by the perfume counter, pretending I need to buy a gift, but really, I'm sleuthing. The lady at the counter asks me what I'm looking for, but I don't know, so I try to describe the scent. "It has mandarin, I think . . . citrus, and some flowers, maybe lilies . . . ?"

She sprays a few cards, and I keep shaking my head, while Emma is probably thinking I'm *so* specific. Finally, the assistant brings me a bottle and I *recognize* it, even before she mists the perfume. This is it, Clinique Happy, which is kind of ironic, considering how Lucy Ellis-Frost ended up. I buy the orange box out of a sense of obligation, relieved finally to be able to name the scent that haunts me.

We wrap up at the food court and I get sushi, sort of in memory of Clay, which is ridiculous because we broke up; he's *not* dead. But he's also not mine anymore, and it aches like a sore tooth, a low throb I can't shake, because I hardly had any chance to be with him for real. For me most of it was fake, until it wasn't anymore, and then it was too late.

"This was fun," Emma says. "We should do it again."

"Next time we'll invite Tish and Sarah if you think they'll come."

"Are you serious? Everyone wants to hang out with you, it's

just . . . you used to come off a little scary. No, that's not it. Aloof, like you were waiting for someone cool enough to approach you."

Now I can only speculate. "People probably don't realize that I'm a little shy."

At least she was in elementary school. I remember clearly how she held my hand like it was a lifeline and wouldn't let go at recess. Sometimes she cried when I got off the bus before her, and she always, always wanted to be where I was. Though, later, her physical beauty made Morgan outshine me, so others believed I was the moon to her sun; I think I was always a bit braver, more willing to take risks.

Emma goes on, "We all wondered why you liked Liv so much. Not that I'm speaking ill of the dead," she scrambles to add. "I mean, she seemed nice . . ."

That's what you say about someone who left a faint impression. It doesn't hurt anymore. I'm still here, still leaving my mark on the world.

Of everyone in the world, why did Morgan like me so much?

Though I can only guess, I say, "Because Liv didn't wait. She decided we should be best friends in grade school . . . because of a joke." Then I tell Emma about Ed Keller's obsession with comics, how he accidentally created the crime-fighting duo of Frost and Burn.

And for a moment, I sense Morgan nearby. It feels like she's smiling, one hand on my shoulder, and that she's totally okay with me passing this on, so I don't ever forget her—that nobody does, though, to the rest of the world, it's Liv who's gone.

I won't let them forget you. Us.

"Wow," she says softly, her eyes damp with sympathy. "I can't imagine what it would be like to lose your best friend."

"It's bad. There are no words."

I don't realize I'm about to cry until the tears spill over.

Mortified, I dive for a napkin and mop up as best I can. Thankfully, Emma doesn't say anything else, and we finish our food without additional waterworks. This has probably impacted her image of me and will shape the way she treats me going forward. Because I'm not an ice princess or a heartless socialite or whatever label they've slapped on me at school.

I'm just a girl with too many problems and too few friends. But if I'm brave, if I show a little faith, maybe I can change that.

"We should head out."

I clear the table and we leave the food court just as my phone delivers the message from Oscar: *Done.* Emma reads over my shoulder but she doesn't understand how scary or momentous this is. From today on, life will get much more difficult for Creepy Jack. But I couldn't wait to see what he'd do with the pictures, assuming he kept them. I'm tired of wondering how much worse things can get.

It's time to find out how this ends.

44

Just like that, Creepy Jack's life explodes.

The local news is running amok, though his campaign team does their best to lock the scandal down. According to various special reports, the police are investigating because they take allegations of criminal sexual misconduct seriously, at least that's what one of the big shots says on TV. Behind closed doors he may be colluding furiously with Creepy Jack to figure out how they can sweep this under the rug.

So far, apart from Oscar, me, and Creepy Jack himself, nobody seems to know who the mystery girl is. Reporters are asking "the victim" to come forward to clarify the story and set the record straight, but so far, I'm not making a move. This has accomplished what I needed and given me some breathing room.

In that time, I've passed both the freshman and sophomore Bio exams, allowing me to take the junior year test, which is a crazy amount of chemistry that I've never even been taught in a classroom. The day after, Arden Fox shows up in a Goku costume, which is far more interesting to Renton students than political outrage. I'm ridiculously relieved that so far, nobody has mentioned that the dark-haired girl looks like me when I was younger.

I'm basically waiting for the other shoe to drop.

And then it does.

Clay's waiting by my car when I get out of school. By his posture, he seems totally relaxed, propped against the passenger side. Emma nudges me. "I thought you broke up."

"I guess he wants to traipse down memory lane."

With a worried look, she jogs to catch her brother, Jay. I was going to give her a ride, but it looks as if life has made other plans. My nerves feel like a just-drilled tooth, so raw that even the air hurts when I breathe. It's hard to look at him; where Clay stands, everything gleams a little sharper—from the curve of the Beetle's hood to the way his knee bends—like the world's shifted to high-def. The sky is too blue overhead, and I smell cut grass, the exhaust from the cars pulling out of the parking lot.

Suddenly I'm aware that I haven't been sleeping well and that I didn't bother with makeup at all today. Before this week, I doubt the rest of the school could've imagined what that would look like but my hair's up in a messy twist, and I'm wearing the jeans I bought at the mall with Emma the other day, along with a T-shirt that Morgan used to sleep in. Closer inspection tells me that Clay must be struggling, too. His hazel-gold eyes are rimmed in shadows and he hasn't shaved since we split, I suspect, because he's working on a beard, and his faded jeans have a new hole in the knee.

"Need a ride?" I ask, because there's no way we're having this convo at school.

"Yeah."

I catch a few clusters of people watching us. Because I didn't tell Emma to keep our breakup a secret, I heard gossip making the rounds the next day. The stories were crazy, too—varied as me cheating with Nathan to me having a college guy on the side. None of the rumors are wild enough to match the truth, however. After we both get in, I start the car and drive, aimless since I don't know what he wants.

"The park near here is fine."

So I cut over four streets and park beneath the spreading branches of a crepe myrtle. This green space is small, just one set of swings, monkey bars, and a slide, but it's more than we had ten years ago, all part of the city gentrification program that Creepy Jack is taking credit for, though he should have larger business for the state of Georgia. From what I can see, he uses his power in all the wrong ways for all the wrong reasons.

Turning off the engine, I shift to look at Clay. "So . . ."

"You're the girl in the photos," he says.

I don't deny it. Between the blurred picture and what I told him about the older guy who was stalking me, Clay put the pieces together. Not surprising, it's not exactly a complicated puzzle. But from the way his mouth tightens, he was hoping I'd say no.

"What about it?" If my tone is cool, I can't help it. Technically this is none of his business, though I'm not collected enough to say so. I don't have that much experience breaking up with people. I mean, there was one guy I dumped before Nathan, and with Nathan, I didn't leave so much as . . . die.

Talk about extreme exit strategies.

For a few seconds he struggles for the right words. "I feel like shit . . . like I abandoned you in the middle of a tornado."

"It's fine. There's nothing you could do anyway." That's a huge lie because just knowing he's there when I need him would help.

"That asshole needs to die. Those pictures were taken a while ago, weren't they? Your hair's a lot longer now."

Which is one reason nobody's made the connection yet. Nobody is devoted to charting my hair-growth trajectory, and with my face blurred out, courtesy of Oscar, maybe I won't burn alongside Creepy Jack before I'm done. Of course we're starting to see fundie apologists on TV talking about how it's possible for a good man to make one mistake, and "Let he who is without sin cast the first stone." Then they say that the jezebel probably seduced him, and there's no proof Mr. Patterson had an affair with a young girl.

I'm the proof.

But I'm not ready to come forward. Already I can imagine the cameras flashing at me, the kind of questions I'd be asked. *Not yet. Soon. Before people stop caring.* I just need a little longer to investigate my mother's death, and then I'll make sure that asshole pays.

I'll be brave. I'll speak up.

"Just let this be the second secret you keep for me," I say then. "Thanks for not telling Nathan, by the way."

Clay leans his arm along the door frame, tilting his head slightly out the open window as if he needs the air. "You couldn't pay me to talk to that jackass lately."

"You two fighting?"

"No. He's just . . . Nathan." He hesitates. "I wasn't going to tell you this . . ."

"What?" Anything that could divert me from my precarious situation, even momentarily, seems like a welcome distraction.

"He brought a girl home last night." From his tone he expects this to destroy me.

And sure, there's a twinge because before, I thought Nathan and I had a soul-deep connection. Fact is, he's a little immature, a lot selfish, and I just never noticed. They say love is blind, but *I'd* say that infatuation is blind, and love is tolerant. When you really love someone, it's not that you can't see the flaws; you're just willing to forgive them.

Belatedly I realize he's expecting a reply. "I'm not surprised. Nathan is used to getting what he wants just like you're used to giving things up. Oh, I was going to ask him to drop this off, but since you're here . . ." I fish in my backpack for his hoodie.

Yes, I've been carrying it for, like, four days. First I hesitated to wash it, but I didn't want to be a sad girl who's still smelling her ex's clothes a month later. Then I didn't return it because that felt like final acceptance—superstitious, I know. Over is over, and random articles of clothing don't change anything.

"You didn't need to bother with that. I've had it forever."

"All the more reason for you to have it back," I say.

"Do you need to be this cool about everything?" he bursts out. "I know you have to be scared and hurt—"

"Yeah, I am, all those things. And yes, I have to be this way, or I can't function. Why are you even here anyway?" The pain and frustration cracks my voice, and I really wish I was anywhere else.

"Because I'm worried about you."

"Then stop. I accepted your decision, now respect mine. It'll be easier if I don't have to see you."

His jaw clenches, showing the force he's exerting to bite back whatever he wants to say. Finally he just takes his hoodie but he pauses with his hand on the door. "You know you can call me, right? Even if we're not together, I'd never let anyone hurt you. One call and I'm there."

My heart feels like it'll crack in two, but I'm resolute; I have to be. "I already deleted your number."

With that I turn away and I don't mean to look at him again, though I can't resist glancing in the rearview mirror. He's sprawled in the grass just beyond the curb cradling his hoodie like it's a warm memory. *I washed it*, I tell him silently. *It doesn't smell like me.*

My tears fall slowly, nonstop, all the way home.

45

In the white room of doom, I finally have a response from Tina Goldsmith. She's approved my friend request and responded to my preliminary message with apparent delight because she suggests we set up a time to video chat. Since I can't fly to New York right now, this is a great solution. I'm not sure what she knows, but they were best friends, so I suspect if my mom was having Creepy Jack's baby, Tina might've been looped in.

Luck finally seems to be with me, as she replies immediately. *Do you have time tonight?*

I quickly respond that I do, and we exchange our handles for the video-chat app. Now I just have to wait a couple of hours. To pass the time, I crack Isaiah's notes from Chemistry; this is the last hurdle I have to leap to get my life back on track. Everything is laid out here before me, however, and this is definitely my wheelhouse. The time evaporates while I'm immersed in the new material, so I'm startled when my alarm pings, reminding me of the chat.

It takes a few minutes to get ready, as I don't want this woman's first glimpse of me in over ten years to alarm her. At eight, I'm in front of my laptop and I don't think she'll be able to tell I've been crying. She initiates the call; I answer. Surprisingly, she doesn't look much older. She's still in her work clothes, a pretty blue suit with a blue-and-yellow patterned blouse.

"Look at you, where's the little girl I remember?"

I smile. "Time had its way with me."

"I'm so glad to hear from you, Morgan. I thought you forgot about me."

"To be honest, I did. Our housekeeper reminded me and showed me the card you sent when my mom died."

Her smile fades. "I know words don't help but I'm so sorry. You must miss her even more than I do."

I nod. "That's why I wanted to talk to you, actually."

"Oh?" Her curiosity is obviously piqued.

"I thought you might have some fun college stories that my dad doesn't know." Of course that implies that he ever talks about my mother, but that wall of silence is strangely impenetrable. It's like he deals with his grief by pretending she never existed. For all anyone knows, I might have popped out of his forehead like he was a Greek god.

"Definitely."

For the next half hour, Tina regales me with hilarious misadventures, most of which deal with guys or drinking or both. Some of it surprises me while the rest makes me laugh. She's just finished an anecdote and I'm still chuckling.

"Wow, I had no idea you two were so wild."

"Don't spread it around," she jokes.

The conversation hits a lull. If I don't ask my questions now, they'll have to wait for next time, and I don't know how long I have before someone figures out that I'm the mystery photo girl. I may not have the chance to talk to Tina again if my dad finds out about Creepy Jack. He'll probably send me to convent school.

It's now or never.

"I hesitate to ask this . . ." But my strategic pause catches Tina's interest.

As I hope, she encourages, "No, go ahead, please. I'll tell you anything you want to know about your mom."

Excellent.

"Okay, well, recently . . ." My tone is tentative. "I was looking through my mom's things, the ones the housekeeper packed up right after she died, trying to remember more about her. I was only seven."

"I know." Sympathy laces both her tone and expression.

That'll help.

"Anyway, I found some letters . . . and an ultrasound." I press my lips together, though it doesn't entirely block my nervous sigh. I'm not feigning; that's real.

"Shit." Tina's muffled exclamation indicates that I'm on the right track.

Lowering my voice, I continue, "So I was wondering if you knew anything about that. I promise I won't judge or think bad of her, no matter what you say. I just want to understand her." Mrs. Rhodes already confirmed an affair with Creepy Jack. Hopefully Tina knows more.

"Oh, honey." The older woman bites her lip, as if weighing the potential repercussions, then she says, "I think she'd want me to be honest with you."

"Thank you, Aunt T." That slips out because I remember that she loved it, as it sounded like "auntie" when I said it fast. For the briefest moment, I can feel the warmth of her arms around me. She always smelled of cinnamon and it was *so* fun bouncing on her knees. Aunt T would let me sit facing her so I could play with the beaded necklaces she often wore.

My head tingles. That was the strongest influx of Morgan that I've had since taking over her body. Though I'm discombobulated, I don't mind. *Feels like she's still here—in a way.*

"There's not a lot to the story. She fell in love with your father in college, and they married right after graduation. Pretty soon, he got obsessed with the tech boom, determined to establish his company as one of the giants . . . and consequently, your mother spent more and more time alone.

"I'm not sure if you know, but she dated Jack Patterson before your dad. He was always sort of hovering around, paying court, and by the time you were five, they were . . . back together. I don't think your father ever realized."

"Probably not. He doesn't spend a lot of time at home these days, either."

"He's still in love with Frost Tech?" Tina shakes her head. "That man will die alone in a pile of money and computer chips. Sorry, I shouldn't talk that way about your father."

"It's okay. I've lived with him this long." Then an awful thought occurs to me. "You're sure I was five when they got together? There's no way that . . ."

Please, no. He can't be Morgan's dad. Sickness roils in my stomach. If there's even a fraction of a chance—

She looks horrified. "Definitely not. Jack wasn't even in Georgia then, though I've always suspected he relocated to Renton because of your mother."

Thank you. Relief hits me so hard that I feel lightheaded. "What do you think of him?"

I have to be careful with these questions. It's unlikely that local gossip has made it onto national news, so Tina probably hasn't heard about the Patterson scandal.

Now I have to adjust my hypothesis slightly. I doubt Creepy Jack would kill his unborn baby, but maybe he didn't know my mom was pregnant? He might've wanted her to leave my dad and when she refused because of me . . . well, this is only speculation. There *must* be a way I can get more information, now that I've come this far.

Was she murdered? Or was it an accident?

Once I know the truth, I can move on. I no longer think

it'll end with me floating out of this body, however. It's just the last favor I can do for Morgan, giving her closure. Maybe then I won't feel so guilty about taking over her life.

"He was always obsessive," she says. "I admit, I didn't like him because he was just so . . . omnipresent, one of those boyfriends who doesn't like Girls' Night, won't let you out of his sight for five minutes. Once, I caught him tailing us when Lucy and I went barhopping, like he was afraid someone would steal her, like luggage at an airport, if he left her unattended."

"Jesus."

Yeah, I can confirm all of that. Time has not *mellowed him.* It's not evidence of violent crime per se, but he's undeniably a sexual predator, and the kind of obsessive shit Jack Patterson pulls can easily lead an unbalanced person down the darkest road. Remembering the ominous message he left in my notes app nauseates me all over again.

My expression must worry Tina because she adds, "He never hurt Lucy that I knew of, but I never liked him. Patterson *or* your daddy, to be honest. Your mama had terrible taste in men."

From my perspective, there's no arguing that. Creepy Jack is the worst of deviants and my father is so distant that he might be a stranger. "One last thing . . . Do you happen to know anything about the accident?"

"Like what?" she asks.

I shrug. "Anything, period. Nobody will talk about it. They whisper about suicide—"

"No," she cuts in at once. "There's no way Lucy would've done that. I talked to her two days before, and she was excited about the baby."

"Wow. That's a huge relief. Did she tell you who . . . ?" I can't make myself ask Tina about the father, but she can tell what I'm wondering.

"I did ask her because I like to meddle, but Lucy wasn't sure, either."

Well, damn. She's my last hope for definitive answers, so this secret goes with my—Morgan's—mother to her grave.

"Then I guess . . . any little detail might help me understand how the accident happened. I just want to know why I lost her, that's all." That's the perfect tactic, I think.

"Hm . . . I wasn't even there, but . . . oh, I talked to your father on the phone the day after, as soon as I heard. He was so rattled, he just kept rambling—" She imitates his voice, fairly well. " 'Lucy loved these flowers, so I ordered a thousand of them, and I sent her car to Mueller's Body Shop . . .' " Here, she resumes her own tone. "Like any of *that* mattered. But maybe someone there examined the car and could tell you a little more?"

Perfect.

"Thanks so much, this meant a lot to me," I say warmly.

After a little more chat and a promise to talk soon, we disconnect. I doubt anyone at Mueller's will take my questions seriously, and it's been more than ten years, so this is a long shot.

Regardless, looks like I'm breaking into a body shop tonight.

46

The fact that it's past ten doesn't deter me. In fact, that's even better.

Before I go, I pack up a few supplies and stop by Mrs. Rhodes's room. Since she doesn't know I broke up with Clay, I tell her I'm going over to his place and probably won't be home tonight. There's no reason not to use this mutually beneficial arrangement; she agrees to cover for me. If my father asks, she'll say I'm spending the night at Emma's house.

"Who's Emma, by the way?" she asks as I'm about to leave.

"A friend from school." Sort of. The closest I've got anyway.

"You have friends?" It's both playful and snarky, much more informal than Mrs. Rhodes would've acted before our talk.

"I'm working on it."

After exchanging a smile, I slip out the back and jog to the garage. My scrapes are healing and there's only residual soreness from the old wounds I aggravated in the fall, nothing that should slow me down tonight. I don't know what I'll do if the body shop has some elaborate security system, because it's not like I have *Mission: Impossible* level equipment and skills.

I make my getaway before my dad reaches the gate, but I'm pretty sure I pass him on the way to town. At least the headlights look right and it resembles him in the brief flash as we speed by in the dark. That feels like a metaphor for our family.

It seems weird how concerned he was, only until it became obvious that I'd survive. Once I proved I wasn't dying, he went back to ignoring me, like near death is the required search criteria, and otherwise, I don't qualify as worthy of time or attention.

When I get to Mueller's, I don't park in the lot; instead I leave my car a few streets over and go in on foot. I walk past to check the place out, and a ferocious dog bark shatters the silence. *Damn.* So I keep moving, strolling down to the convenience store on the corner. A bell tinkles as I come in, and the guy at the counter looks up from the tabloid he's reading. I get a chin jerk, then he goes back to the gossip magazine.

My options are limited. In movies they always give the guard dog a drugged steak, but I'm not giving roofies to somebody's pet. Finally I pick out one turkey sandwich and one roast beef, then take my items to the register.

The cashier rings the stuff up. "Did you know there's a nest of chupacabras in the Louisiana bayou?"

"I did not." I pay in cash because I don't want my card on file in this neighborhood, especially tonight.

"Here's your change."

Renton is fairly safe overall, so there are no security cameras outside, and inside they use those concave reflective mirrors to watch potential shoplifters. With this guy on duty, though, I'm pretty sure I could've put a six-pack in my panties. As I leave, he's reading an article about how the royal family in England are probably vampires.

Now I'm ready to make my approach. I circle from the back of the auto body shop, staying alert for the dog, but now that I'm closer, he seems to be inside with the cars they're currently repairing or restoring. I'm not interested in stealing cars; I just want the information in the office. The lock on the door is high quality, though, with more tumblers than I can manage. *Dammit.*

There's a window above the door, strictly for ventilation, but I'm pretty sure I'm thin enough to wriggle through. I take a running leap and, thanks to an exceptional fitness level, I use the wall nearby to kick off, then I latch on to the frame. My biceps tremble as I haul myself up and then swing through. I have to suck in my stomach as far as it'll go and my breasts get squished in the slide. I land smoothly, thanks to a gymnastic past.

The office is dark, full of junky desks and dusty papers, a rusted filing cabinet and a computer that's at least five years old. But before I can decide where to start, a low growl comes from the open doorway. From the shadows beyond I can just make out the gleam of angry eyes. *Of course the garage connects to the office. Of course it does.* I don't move and try to pretend I'm not scared. Even in the faint light I can tell this dog is huge.

"Good boy," I whisper.

The sandwiches are crammed in my jacket pocket, so I pull one out and break off a piece. "Good boy. Who's a good boy? Who wants to eat a sandwich instead of me?"

The low, threatening growl cuts off for a little sniffing; I take that as a good sign and throw part of the sandwich. Some guard dogs are taught not to take food from strangers, but from the sounds I'm hearing, that's not the case here. I keep whispering and feeding him until the whole sandwich is gone. Now the room is quiet, but I still don't dare move around.

"You want more?"

The dog makes a slurping sound, which I'm taking as a yes. I feed him the second sandwich slowly, still working on making friends. Before he finishes it, I take a step toward him, ready to run if he growls again, but he seems to accept that I have good intentions. By the time he eats all the food I brought, he's letting me pet him and I've even got his tail wagging. Up close, I can see he's a German shepherd mix and quite friendly, once he's sure of me.

He pads into the room as I flip on the computer. Unfortunately, it requires a login *and* it doesn't use any operating system I've ever seen. So that won't help. *Filing cabinet it is.* I open the first drawer and figure out that other than the current year, which is filed by month, everything else is organized by year. I locate the right folder, which is huge, and bring it to the ripped-up sofa. I don't dare turn on any lights, so I'm using my phone.

My heart hammers like crazy, so loud it echoes in my ears, now that I'm so close to finding some actual information. Each invoice is filed by date, so that helps me, too. There's no way I could forget the day my mother died. I locate her page about halfway through the stack and am dismayed by how sparse it is. Make of car. Model. Year. License plate number. They've filled in all of that, plus some basic notes:

Observed damage: Minor scrape on passenger side, traces of silver paint, ding on rear bumper. Windshield broken. Engine block cracked, frame bent. Radiator smashed. Estimated repair cost exceeds bluebook. Car totaled, per owner's request, sold to Gabe's for scrap.

And that's it.

God, I feel stupid. Was I *really* expecting to find *Brake lines were cut, this was no accident?* In retrospect, I should've known better. I mean, even if they were cut and the owner took a bribe to keep quiet, he'd hardly write it on the invoice. I put everything back as I found it. Since I'm not stealing anything and the dog is fine, nobody should know about my visit.

This door looks like it will lock behind me, and I don't see any alarm lights or power lines that indicate it's wired, so I slip out.

And nearly run into an old guy with a flashlight. Quickly I duck my head so he can't get a good look at my face, dodge away from his lunge, and sprint full speed toward the street. This is reckless because there's a car coming but I can't stop. Pushing harder, I zip past and I hear brakes screeching, and two men are yelling now, but I'm putting distance between us.

Can't stop, can't look back.

47

The direct route toward my car is through other people's yards, so I don't deviate. As I race by, dogs go insane and lights pop on. Once I get caught between a furious beagle and a fence. I make for the kiddie trampoline in the corner of the yard and hope I'm still aerodynamic enough to execute this vault. With one hard bounce I go airborne and land on the other side in someone's vegetable patch. Tomatoes explode all over me, turning the soil to a pulpy mess. Filthy, I scramble to my feet. More lights come on but I'm already running again.

By the time I slide into my car and take off, I can barely breathe. I drive like a mile and a half and finally have to pull over because I'm shaking so hard. As it turns out, being intrepid is terrifying. I have the funds to pay someone to investigate, but since I didn't grow up wealthy, I'm uneasy about trusting others with my secrets. I mean, if they're willing to do shady stuff for hire, wouldn't they spill my secrets to anyone who offered *more* money?

Common sense dictates that since tonight was such a colossal failure, I should go home immediately. With my luck, this would be the one night that my dad wants to bond with me. If he's already been informed that I'm staying at Emma's, he won't expect me home. That means my arrival will herald a problem, like I argued with my friend, and so he'll want to talk about it over hot cups of tea, specifically why I look like marinara-spattered hell.

Though I hate myself for coming to this conclusion, there's only one safe place for me to go. I'm not crazy enough to sleep in my car. While Renton's relatively safe, there's also some drugs and crime, and I can't drive all night. My mind made up, I head over to Clay's. Funny, it used to be Nathan's house to me, but now, in my heart, he's the extra.

When I pull down the alley, I spot Clay on the swing with one leg propped up and the other lazily kicking off. I park out back and circle to the front. If Nathan's in bed, I don't want to bother him, or more accurately, I prefer to avoid him. The swing stops moving as I climb the front steps to the porch.

"What're you—oh *shit*. Is that blood? Did that—"

"No, it's tomato juice. And he's too busy to bother me. But I do need a favor."

"Name it," he says.

"First, I'd like to borrow your shower. I also need a place to crash. Please don't ask why, I won't tell you."

A long sigh escapes him as he surveys me. "Are you okay?"

"More or less." It's not a comprehensive answer, as I'm tired, sore, and dispirited.

"You're trying to drive me nuts, aren't you?"

"Excuse me?"

"You don't tell me anything, then you show up looking like this and that just jolts my imagination into overdrive."

Like 90 percent of me is absurdly glad that he's worried. I know it's petty, but I'm happy he cares, even if he doesn't want to be with me. It's not even that I resent that decision. Clay's love for his brother is what defines him, and I couldn't be happy if he felt guilty about our relationship. That's why I told him the truth in the first place; he needed to understand my . . . unique situation and make an informed choice.

I offer a tired half smile. "Yes, that's my whole master plan. I ran half a mile and fell in a veggie patch just so you'd wonder what the hell is up with me."

This startles a laugh out of him, and by moonlight that's so beautiful, my heart aches. *How the hell did I fall for Clay? When . . . ?* I can't even put a finger on the exact moment it happened, and that bothers me. I draw in an unsteady breath and then he reaches for me.

"We're not getting back together," he whispers. "This is . . . first aid. Because I feel like I might die if I don't get to be close to you for a minute."

His arms envelop me, and I push on his chest at first, not because of our *it's complicated* relationship status, but because I'll get him dirty. He ignores my feeble protest and I stop because I don't really want him to let go. His cheek rests on my hair, rubbing tenderly back and forth. The heat of him scorches me from head to toe. At first, he offered security in a world that made no sense, but now he's like my sun and stars combined.

"First aid can save your life." My voice is muffled by his chest.

I hate that I'm not allowed to love him, now that I have a better idea what that means. Though I'm only a few months older, I feel like I've matured enough for a couple of years. Slowly I slip my arms around his waist and close my eyes, just letting the warmth soak in. The pain of failure recedes, making me regret my own stupidity a little less.

At least I didn't get caught. It could've been worse.

"You can't let me kiss you," he says then.

"Am I the gatekeeper?" Since my toes curled at the low, husky way he said that, I'm probably not the best person for the job.

"It can't be me. I'm not thinking straight right now."

"Why not?" I manage to ask.

"Because you're so close." But he doesn't let go. In fact, his hands glide down my back in a hungry stroke that tells me he knows exactly how good it feels.

As much as I don't want him to regret this, I also don't want to stop. Just being close to Clay sets off all kinds of fireworks inside me; my nerves are blazing like a zillion Roman candles, all sparks and incandescent yearning. I tip my head back just enough, and my mouth is so close to his chin. He just needs to dip his head a little—

And he does.

Oh, God, he's kissing me, but we can't, and it's so good. My fingers dig into his back, his shoulders, as his mouth works on mine. The hot press of his lips, the rough scrape of his jaw against my cheek. He tastes like tea and lemon and hope, so much sweetness that I think I might die when he finally pulls his mouth away and sets it on my throat. I don't know if he's trying to stop or if he wants to drive me crazy. Then he bites, just a little.

"You didn't stop me."

I can't breathe, let alone respond, and then he's pulling me on top of him in the swing. I straddle him like I did once before, and we're kissing more, deeper, longer. His hands frame my hips, holding me just so, and it feels so good I can't stop moving. It doesn't matter that I'm dirty or that we're out in public, more or less. I don't even care. He kisses my throat, my jaw, my ears, as I fall into him completely, grinding until all I can think about is—

"Yes," he whispers.

And I unravel. It's happened before, but I was alone then, tentative and fumbling. Afterward, I snuggle in his arms, unable to speak.

Where do we go from here?

48

"Shower," I gasp, not waiting to hear what Clay will say.

My knees barely hold me as I leap off him and practically sprint around the corner of the house. To use the bathroom I'll go in through the kitchen and hopefully if Nathan's home, I won't bother him. By the time Clay catches up, I've already locked the door. This room is tiny and dated; I'd never seen a blue enamel tub until the first time I visited the Claymore house. However, the tiles are meticulous and I can see a couple of spots where the walls have been repaired, probably by Clay.

The water runs rusty for a minute after I turn on the shower, and I make it quick, using the generic herbal shampoo on the window ledge. Five minutes later, I snag the towel on the closest hook. It's worn and stiff, a result of drying in the sun, yet it smells fresh, invigorating my skin like a loofah. I wrap up in it, frowning at my filthy clothes.

Just then, a knock sounds at the door. "I'm leaving shorts and a shirt outside."

"Thanks." I reach an arm out and feel around until I claim the soft cotton.

Pulling my haul into the bathroom, I find clothes small enough to fit me, or pretty close. I put my sports bra and underwear back on, then scramble into the gym shorts and T-shirt. The satiny red fabric dangles down to my knees and the 5K Run

T-shirt is baggy. Sheepish, I step out, still drying my hair. No point in delaying the inevitable. We have to talk about what happened; I just don't *want* to.

Clay smirks when he sees me. "My junior high clothes look better on you."

"Why do you still have these?"

"Nathan wore them last and he never throws anything out."

"Lucky me."

But he's watching me intently, only half listening. "With all that hair, you have to do a better job or you'll catch cold."

"I'm pretty sure that has more to do with viruses than wet hair," I say.

Clay ignores that, urging me toward a kitchen chair, and then he plucks the towel from my hands. "I'll do it."

"You're really sending mixed messages," I mumble.

I can't remember the last time anyone took care of me like this. The towel covers my whole head and the way he rubs, it feels like he's massaging my head. My eyes close. Tension flows out of muscles I didn't even realize were knotted. While he tends to me, I half doze through it, though I make some little sounds when he's combing my hair.

At the end, I feel like a lax rubber band when he scoops me into his arms. Clay carries me out the back door and around the front. *So Nathan's probably home.* But it's only a fleeting thought, nothing that mars my euphoria. I snuggle closer, arms around his neck. Maybe we don't have to talk tonight.

I snap alert when he takes me to his room, however. The last time I was in here, it didn't end well. "I can sleep on the couch, don't give me your bed."

"I'm not."

"Huh?"

The light clicks off.

Then he provides the nonverbal answer by depositing us

both on the bed. Yet he still doesn't let go of me. I've never been held this way, but it feels really good. Probably I should ask some clarifying questions or tell him I'm not sleeping with someone who isn't my boyfriend, but really, I don't give two shits about labels. He's still the person I love. Quietly, I reach for the rumpled covers with my free arm and pull them up.

"No arguments?"

"That would be stupid. This is where I want to be."

"You're killing me," he whispers.

Clay takes my hand and presses it over his heart, so I can feel how hard and fast it's beating. The tempo is so out of control, I'm a little worried about him.

"Does it hurt?"

"In the best possible way." He draws me even closer, so I can't see his face anymore, not even the lines and shadows. Gentle hands stroke my back. "I shouldn't say this. I shouldn't even think it. But . . ."

"Tell me. I proved before that I can share anything with you. Show me you can too."

"All my life, I heard from my dad . . . 'You're the oldest, Clay. Be a good example. Watch out for your little brother.' Seemed like that was all he ever said to me. And I did, I did my best, until I was just so sick of it."

"I remember you mentioning your rebellious phase."

His laugh sounds bitter. "Even then, I was still taking the blame for shit Nathan did. I mean, I raised my own hell but when he started to follow in my footsteps, I had to cover for him. Because I had nothing to lose and he had everything. He's always been the good Claymore, so unlike the rest of his family."

Until now I never knew how much this hurt Clay. "That's not true. You're—"

"No, let me get this out. Because it's ugly and it's chewing at me. You know how happy I was when you picked me? You've been with both of us, and you picked *me*. First time in my life that's ever happened. I want to be with you so bad, not just because I love you, but also because it feels like taking from him. But I *can't* treat you that way. You understand now?"

"Like a trophy?" I distinctly recall telling him not to treat me like property.

"Exactly. And it's all tangled up in my head—you, me, Nathan. I don't know what the hell's wrong with me."

"You've been carrying your family since you were nine," I say softly. "In one way or another. So it makes sense that you want someone on your side, somebody who sees you."

"It's not that simple."

"I think it is. You don't have to be strong with me. I can take care of you, too." To emphasize my words, I move my arm from around his waist so I can rub his back.

"Please don't," he murmurs into my hair. "It'll just make it that much harder to let you go in the morning."

"You're operating on a catch-and-release system?" Keeping my tone light, I smooth my palm upward until I can knead his neck.

A low groan escapes him. "Maybe not."

"Well, I'm not trying to weaken your resolve."

"What *are* you trying to do?"

"Make you feel half as special as you do me. Even when we were faking it, you were a better boyfriend than most guys."

He laughs softly. "Please, you thought we were together for real when you woke up. Which explains a lot, actually."

He sounds much more relaxed, so I keep rubbing his neck until he lets out another soft moan. Surely I'm not the first girl to do this for Clay, but he reacts like it's new. I work his neck and shoulders until he's practically purring. His breath tickles my ear, making me shiver.

"Are you sleepy?" I whisper.

"Not even remotely," comes the surprising answer.

"Really? I thought I was helping you unwind."

Clay laughs. "Baby, you got off on my lap, then you got naked in my shower. Now you're wearing my clothes, putting your hands all over me. Do you know *anything* about guys?"

Then he shifts so I can feel how turned on he is.

"Holy crap."

"It'll go down eventually. Just stop teasing me."

"I didn't mean to." My voice comes out fluttery, sexier than I've sounded before.

Apparently Clay agrees. "Okay, that didn't help."

Deep down I don't really want him to power through it. I want to touch him, just because. Not because he'll get blue balls or to even the score, just . . . for me. It doesn't matter if this is the only night we're together. This once, I'm longing to know what it's like to touch him. In a way, the idea makes me feel powerful since he's not asking for anything.

"Will this?" I pull away enough to slip a hand between us and run it down his chest.

He catches my fingers as they brush his hip. "What're you doing?"

"You, if you let me. Your choice, though."

49

The silence builds. I'm trying to be cool, but inside I'm all tingles and anticipation.

Clay laughs quietly. "Are you kidding? I didn't even have the willpower to keep from kissing you."

That seems like permission. He even shifts onto his back, settling onto the pillows. Moonlight shines through the window, and now that my eyes have adjusted to the dark, I can make out the muted hunger in his expression. But Clay doesn't *do* anything. Instead he leaves it all up to me. And that's really hot. I've never had a guy give himself to me as a present before.

"Shirt," I say, tugging at the bottom of it.

His fingers tighten on my hand, stilling it for a moment, and he puts his face close enough for me to see his eyes. "I don't know if I can make any promises. Maybe tonight, that's all there is. No matter what, he's still my brother. So I understand if you'd rather not. I still want you in my arms tonight."

"That's fine." I can't seem to stop smiling. Even though he's viciously turned on, I'm calling the shots.

If anything, that makes me more eager to be with him. After all, a good memory is better than nothing, and I'll never regret a choice made freely. Even I'm not sure how far I'll go. Morgan's not a virgin; Liv is. Which puts body and mind at odds.

In answer Clay shrugs out of his shirt. His chest is smooth

and defined; I can't resist touching him. He moves and moans, telling me without words what feels best. Soon he raises his hips, silently asking for my hands.

Breathless, I go for it. It doesn't take long before he's panting, whispering that it's so good, and he finishes clutching my head to his shoulder, like he doesn't want me to see. Afterward, he cleans up and comes back to bed to hold me.

"Sleepy now?" I tease.

"Shut up." But he truly does sound blissfully content.

We fall asleep tangled together, and it's late by the time I wake up. Blinking at his clock, I think, *Shit. I missed two classes already*. Clay rouses slower and he doesn't want to let go of me, which is bad since I need to pee. His arms tighten as I try to squirm away.

"Don't go," he mumbles.

My heart turns over. "I'll be back."

"Promise?"

"Promise."

Finally he lets go and he's asleep again when I pass through Nathan's room to go to the bathroom. Since I'm skipping, I'm especially glad that asshole went to school. The morning after, it would be awkward as hell to have breakfast with him. While I'm at it, I also wash up a little and brush my teeth with my finger. I *do* look like I got some last night, though. Before, I always thought it was an exaggeration, but my cheeks seem a little pinker today.

Clay is in the kitchen when I come out, scrambling eggs. This scene is so domestic that it makes my toes curl. Since he doesn't turn around, I hug him from behind.

"I could burn myself with distractions like that." But he's smiling when he turns to kiss me. "Morning."

It's almost ten, but yeah. "Sleep well?"

"God, yes. Do you want to go somewhere with me today?"

"Don't you have to work?"

"Not today," he says. "I always have October third off, no matter what day it falls on."

Now I'm intrigued. "Sure. I'll ditch. I'm sure Mrs. Rhodes will write me a note."

"People will say I'm a bad influence."

"I can live with that."

We eat breakfast quickly, and I leave the house wearing his clothes. It's not worse than what I've seen other girls wearing, but for Morgan Frost, it's a fashion faux pas of astronomical proportions. Smiling, I shrug it away as I climb in Clay's beater. To my surprise, he stops at the convenience store for pork rinds and beer.

"Well, that took a surprising turn," I murmur.

He smiles so the sun catches the gold in his eyes, and honest to God, he's so handsome I can't breathe. Some of the scruff is gone, and he's in jeans with a white T-shirt that accentuates both his awesome arms and the warmth of his summer tan. I could stare at him forever, but after a while, looking isn't enough so I run my fingers through the shaggy softness of his hair.

"Trying to drive here."

"Don't let me stop you."

"It's your fault if I put us in the ditch."

"I'm that distracting? *Really?*" My tone is skeptical.

"Not sure if I've mentioned this, but I'm pretty crazy about you." The gentle tone takes my breath away.

And I just can't believe it—this is the same boy that people whispered about. *He steals cars. He sells drugs. Older women give him presents for services rendered.* Now if I heard someone talking shit about Clay, I might punch them in the face.

"Likewise," I manage to say. "So where are we going?"

"It's a surprise."

He's not kidding. When he takes me to the cemetery outside town, I'm half afraid he thinks it'll be funny to make out on my grave. But his steps angle away from where Olivia Burnham was laid to rest. Taking my hand, he leads me up a small hill to where a crab apple tree spreads its branches. The headstones aren't large up here, just small markers.

He stops before a very unimpressive one and says, "This is my dad."

Kneeling so I can read, I see there's only the name and date, no space for sentiment. It registers then—this is the anniversary of his father's death. Clay joins me, taking the beer and pork rinds out of the plastic bag. He's also got some wipes, which he uses to clean off the stone and then he plucks the weeds that have sprung up over the summer.

"You come every year?" I guess.

"It's kind of a tradition. At least my dad's always where I can find him." The joke falls flat because I can see how much Clay still misses his father.

"Do you talk to him?"

"Sometimes. Mostly I drink a beer and eat some of these pork rinds because those were two of my dad's favorite things. I remember him saying, 'Here's the key to happiness, son. Well, that and baseball,' and he'd turn on the game. God, he loved the Braves."

"He would be so proud of you."

"You think?" The shy, hopeful light in Clay's eyes just scoops my heart out of my chest.

"Definitely. Let's drink to him."

While I drink a soda, he downs part of a beer and munches the pork rinds. Then Clay crumbles some up and empties the rest of his beer like he's making an offering. I've never known anyone to do that, but it feels right. Sometimes I think I feel Morgan nearby but this time it's definitely his dad. The sunlight on our shoulders might be his hands and the breeze could well be him ruffling our hair in passing. You'd think this would be a depressing way to spend the day, but I feel oddly peaceful when we finally prepare to leave. It's been hours, and that half beer is long gone.

"I've never brought anyone with me before," Clay says, offering his hand.

Afraid to hope, I wonder what this means. I take it, letting him pull me to my feet. "Not even Nathan?"

"Nah. He thinks this is macabre, at best."

That makes me bristle. "The human body is sustained by energy, right? And energy can never be destroyed, only transferred. So maybe death is more of a transition, so our loved ones never really leave us. They've just taken on a different form."

"Are you trying to science death?" he asks, amused.

"Maybe," I mumble.

"You're definitely Liv." But it doesn't sound like he minds anymore. In fact, after saying so, he takes my hand.

"I was. But I'm not all her anymore."

Since he brought it up, I explain my theory about the dual components that comprise human identity and then end by postulating that I'm now a hybrid individual. Brow cocked, he listens with evident interest to all my pseudoscientific rambling.

"Is this supposed to make me feel only half as guilty?"

"You *could* interpret it that way."

By this time, we've reached his car. He opens the passenger door for me, then says, "I can't quiet my conscience with a theory, but . . . it's cool that you're logical about this. If I woke up in Nathan's body, I'd just go insane."

I'm happy that he's thinking about us again—really thinking—instead of the knee-jerk *You're the one girl in the world I can't touch* I heard before. And if he decides it can't work, I'll accept it without being sorry about last night. Clay vaults the hood, which is kind of his thing, and I find it ridiculously hot. Then he climbs into the driver's side.

"Your car's still at my place. I guess you need to pick it up?"

Checking the time, I mumble a cuss word. "Could you drop me off at school instead? I have an exam scheduled . . . in twenty minutes."

God only knows how that'll play out—ditching regular classes and only showing up for my Chem test. But Mr. Finney won't give me another shot if I blow this one. Clay's already driving, thank God, as he seems to sense my urgency.

"Don't worry," he assures me. "Everything will be fine."

And in this moment with the sky so blue and the sun so bright, with Clay's hand on mine, I choose to believe that.

50

"I'm worried about you, Morgan." Mr. Finney frowns at me, taking in my ensemble and my general dishevelment. "You've changed so much in a short time."

"Change isn't always a bad thing. Sometimes a traumatic life event makes us reevaluate our priorities." I'm quoting a self-help book now, God help me.

"And your priority is skipping school?"

"I was sick. If you don't believe me, ask our housekeeper." I'm betting on Mrs. Rhodes being savvy enough to confirm any story I tell. She likes her monthly bonus. "I was so dizzy this morning, but then I remembered scheduling this test, so I threw on the first outfit I found and came to keep my promise, so I didn't waste your time."

The teacher sighs like he's only half convinced by my bullshit, which makes sense. Teenagers have been lying to him for close to twenty years. Yet he finally points at the first lab table. "Since you're here, go ahead and take the final. You'll also be performing a random experiment of my choice."

An hour and a half later, I'm mixing chemicals and hoping for the best. I'm relieved when nothing explodes and I manage to get the reaction I'm going for. Mr. Finney is visibly puzzled; likely he has no idea why Morgan Frost knows this much about science. Her transcript gives no indication that I could tell an alkali from a base. As I hold my breath, he marks my test.

68.

It's the worst score I've ever gotten in science in my life, but considering I learned a year of material in seven days, I'll take it. Because that's a passing mark, though barely, and I won't be going into advanced chem. I'm aiming for physics, so I have the complete gamut of science credits by the time I graduate.

"I didn't see this coming," he says, rubbing his jaw.

Happiness goes off in my chest like fireworks. "Does this mean you'll let me in your physics class?"

"That was the deal. I won't give you any breaks," he warns. "You've already missed the first month, so it may be tough."

"I'm prepared for that. Thank you, sir." Afterward, I realize I've spoken to him just as Liv did in the old days.

His chin jerks up and he studies me for a long moment, before finally giving an infinitesimal shake of his head. "See you tomorrow, Miss Frost."

Though I told Clay he didn't have to hang around, I know I'll find him waiting. Sure enough, he's playing a game of pickup basketball on the outdoor court. He's shirtless and glistening, going all out against the guy guarding him. I admire his speed and strength for a few minutes, and it's like he senses me watching him. He turns, scanning for me, which results in him taking a pass to the head, but he shakes it off. With a wave, Clay jogs toward me.

But I can see the moment he remembers that I used to be his brother's girl and he's not supposed to want me. The eagerness drains from his stride until his feet are practically dragging. The fact that he doesn't meet my gaze offers a hint of what's to come, and I try to brace for it, I do. But no matter how hard you try, getting kicked in the face emotionally always hurts.

Always.

"How'd it go?" He shrugs into his shirt as we walk to the car. *You'd never know he loves me, looking at him now.*

"I passed. I'll be able to change my schedule now."

"Congrats. I know how important this was to you." His tone seems ominous, like our relationship is a clock he's choosing not to wind, so each tick of time brings us closer to that moment when the gears stop forever.

"Thanks for waiting." That's not what I want to say.

"It was no trouble. Get in." He opens the door for me and I hop in the passenger side, knowing this is just a ride to my car.

Lost in thought, he drums the wheel as he drives. I don't ask what's on his mind. Though he doesn't have to work tonight, Clay won't ask me to stay. I tell myself this is not a big deal, and that I'm not hurt, even when he bags my dirty clothes and gives them to me with a polite smile. The gray plastic crinkles in my hands and I offer a jerky nod of thanks.

Spinning, I nearly run into Nathan, who's coming in the back. *Great, this is all I need today.* He stares at me, mouth agape. Finally he says, "I'm pretty sure those clothes are mine."

"Thanks for letting me borrow them."

"I don't remember doing that."

"You were drunk," I say, which is both bitchy and probable, given the way Nathan has been acting lately.

Behind me, Clay stifles a laugh. That only pisses Nathan off more, though. He narrows his eyes and grabs the hem of the shirt. "I want this back. Now."

"Don't be a dick." I jerk away and try to step around him. "I'll return everything after I wash it."

"Some things don't rinse clean, rich girl." Before I can guess what he's thinking, Nathan turns to his brother with an awful grin. "How are those sloppy seconds working out, bro?"

That's when the smell hits me. Despite it being five in the afternoon, Nathan is already hammered. But that doesn't eradicate the horror of what he's about to do. I lunge for him, trying to shut his mouth, but with drunken limberness, he dodges away, slamming into the opposite counter. Clay glances between us, a frown pleating his brows.

"Guess that means you haven't told him. Weird, you were so worried about that kiss, but it doesn't bother you *at all* to bang my brother after hooking up with me."

Clay freezes, his face instantly a study in anguish, and then it's all gone, locked away in some private vault. "You think hurting me will make you feel better? Give it a shot."

Suddenly I know exactly what to say because I *know* what Nathan was to Morgan, however he feels about her. "I wish you weren't like this," I snap. "Because you were *convenient*, Nathan. I wanted to punch my V-card, I was about to go to Europe for the summer, and I didn't want to be an awkward American virgin anymore.

"I chose you to be my first because you were there and I wanted to get it over with. If you weren't trying to use five minutes of bad sex to hurt your brother, I never would've brought it up. For the record, I haven't banged Clay yet because *he matters* and if he's willing, he'll get a hell of a lot more than five minutes." By the time I finish, I'm shaking because it feels like I've married Morgan's icy wrath with my own temper and the result is a sort of snow-white rage.

Both Nathan and Clay are staring at me. Then Nathan bolts and I get a furious glare from Clay, who chases after him.

I wait for a minute, ridiculously disappointed. Still, I watch the door; he doesn't come back. I'm not sure what I expected, but in my heart, maybe I'm hoping that Clay will realize he loves me more than life itself. Why I still have these romantic fantasies, I have no idea. By now I should understand that life doesn't work that way. It's often complicated, sad, and inexplicably painful. Sometimes you see old couples holding hands on a park bench but it's probably not because they still love each other madly after sixty years. Instead, one of them likely has Alzheimer's and the other is too tired to go looking for a lost spouse again.

That's the world I live in, where Clay chooses Nathan. Again. Of course he minds that I've hurt and humiliated his little bro, even if said brother is kind of a douche. Blood is thicker than water, they say, but the actual quote is, "The blood of the covenant is thicker than the water of the womb."

Loving me should mean something; it should matter to Clay, and it's breaking my heart that this is a battle I probably can't win.

51

Mrs. Rhodes is practically climbing the walls when I get in. "Are you all right? I played along when your teacher rang but your father . . ." She babbles so fast that I lose track.

"Wait, slow down. Did he call Emma?"

"I didn't know her last name and he blew a gasket. Honestly, Morgan, I've never seen him like that. He stormed around the house, smashed a brandy tumbler, and threatened to fire me if I don't keep better track of you. He must've called you forty times."

Wincing, I turn on my phone, which I'd switched off before my burglary run last night. Sure enough, there are forty-three missed calls and twenty texts. The messages start out normal, but by the end, they're kind of . . . out there. I guess he was crazy worried.

"Did he actually report me missing?" I ask, skimming the seventeenth message.

The housekeeper shakes her head. "He did call the sheriff and ask him to have his deputies keep an eye out for your car, which I told him was ridiculous."

Jesus. Now I'm imagining how badly shit could've gone wrong last night if they'd spotted my car in Clay's driveway. My father doesn't exactly approve of this relationship, more like he tolerates it, but he'd be happier if I was dating one of the preps instead. Finding me in Clay's bed wouldn't have improved the situation.

"Would you make some food that packs well? I'm going to shower, change, and take my dad dinner at the office. I've been wanting to poke around there anyway. Maybe if I go apologize he won't send me to a Siberian convent school."

"It's in Austria," Mrs. Rhodes says.

I freeze. "What?"

"There's a pamphlet in his office for an Austrian boarding school. I'm probably not supposed to tell you, but at this point, you pay me almost as much as he does."

For an infinite, appalling moment, I think, *He wants to get rid of me. Is it the new girlfriend? Maybe she doesn't want to be a stepmother.*

"Thanks for the heads-up," I mutter.

"No problem. I suspect my hours would be cut if you weren't around." Though her motives may be self-serving, her loyalty cheers me up somewhat. "You go get ready, I'll fix the food and pack it up for you."

"I appreciate it. Fingers crossed that it'll cool his wrath."

Taking the stairs two at a time, I lay out some power clothes, then rush to the bathroom. Somehow I manage to pull myself together in half an hour, including hair and makeup, though I cheated and used one of those French twist guides that I only need to wrap my hair around and pin. I look good in black and this suit lends me an air of somber elegance. In fact, I could pass for my early twenties dressed like this.

And I often did.

That's not my thought, more of an echo, but I know it's true, just like what I said to Nathan. The walls between Morgan and me are coming down in an avalanche of thought-stones. As time goes on, maybe I won't even be able to tell us apart anymore. I wonder if I'll forget that I was ever Liv. That prospect scares me a little, but not enough to keep me from moving forward.

Mrs. Rhodes meets me at the door and I take the basket with a murmur of thanks. "Wish me luck. If this doesn't work, I'll need your help packing."

Though I'm joking, after my failure at the garage and the scene in the Claymore kitchen, I ask myself if going to Austria is such a terrible idea. Maybe I need a fresh start. It will be better for me *not* to be in the country when someone recognizes me as the girl in the photos currently making Creepy Jack's life hell. His silence comes as a welcome relief, but I suspect it's a result of increased household surveillance. I mean, his wife's probably inspecting his phone daily, if she hasn't left already. From what I've seen of that circle, her reaction will depend on whether she married the politician or the man.

I can't decide if I should text my father or surprise him, but as I get in the car, I decide on the latter. Apologies always carry more weight in person. There's no risk I'll miss him because, to my knowledge, he hasn't left the office before eight in months. Before, I feared there was some problem in the company he couldn't tell me about, but now I'm thinking he must be with his girlfriend. That's better than a cash-flow problem, right?

Somehow that pep talk doesn't help much.

I drive the fifteen miles to Frost Tech, which is on the other side of Renton. We built some distance away because my dad wanted a short commute to decompress, or so he said. My mother also really loved the view; the house made her feel like a princess in a castle, though maybe toward the end, it's more like she was imprisoned in the tower. *Still can't see Creepy Jack as a viable alternative.* But loneliness makes people do weird, inexplicable things. Maybe it wasn't about Jack as much as about trying to recapture an earlier period in her life, when she was young, happy, and free.

The Frost Tech campus is impressive as hell. At the gate, the guard recognizes me and waves me through. Security guards zoom around on Segways, scouring the premises for trespassers. I navigate around them and park in the VIP spot reserved for me, though I'm almost never here. This probably pisses off the actual employees. I swing out of the Bug, dinner basket in hand, and click my way to the front desk. The receptionist must be new because she doesn't scramble to her feet when she spots me. In fact, she gives me a shitty look.

"Can I help you?" She's just about to pack up her stuff and leave.

"I'm fine, thanks."

"Wait, you have to sign in!" she yells.

I ignore her and use the code to call the executive elevator. Morgan knew this, not me, but my fingers press the numbers like it's second nature. This building only has ten floors, but the complex itself has eight buildings, housing various departments. My dad occupies the penthouse all by himself and this gives me a nonstop lift. There's no hallway; the elevator doors open directly into his office.

And that's kind of horrifying because he's got a woman on his desk. They're not quite going at it, but from the grabbing and moaning, if I had come ten minutes later, this would be a full-on case of coitus interruptus. The smart thing would be to get the hell out before they notice me, but it's just so awful and awkward that I start laughing.

My father shoots upright and tries frantically to finger comb his hair. He shields the woman with his body so she can fix whatever damage he did to her clothes, but neither one of them looks particularly reputable, even when they move away from the sex desk. I can't face either of them; somehow I choke off the inappropriate giggles, as I'm *not* twelve, but my eyes are watering to the point that I can't see.

"Hi, Dad. Going over this week's sales figures?"

"You should have called." From his tone, he's both embarrassed and enraged.

"Sorry, I wanted to surprise you." I look everywhere but at him, hefting the basket in my hands. "Mission accomplished, I guess?"

"You think I'm remotely amused?" He's speaking through clenched teeth, and that tone doesn't sound like anything I've ever heard before, it's almost . . . scary.

"I'm sorry. That's why I came. To apologize. I heard you were worried last night because I didn't give Mrs. Rhodes enough information about my school friend. So . . . I wanted to make it up to you. I didn't know you would be busy." I lower my head, studying my designer shoes.

For some reason I want to cry. It's like there's nobody in the world who's happy to see me. Tears spring up, but I choke them down. I'm not a little kid; I refuse to cry in front of my dad's girlfriend. *What kind of first impression am I making?*

"It's not a big deal," the woman says then. "I wanted to meet Morgan, and actually, it *is* kind of funny. I'm sure we'll laugh about this later."

Raising my head, I offer a tentative smile, but my face freezes. She's my mother replicated in miniature. While my mom was tall and lithe, this woman is petite, all cornflower-blue eyes, dark curls, and so, *so* young. I look again. Okay, on second inspection, their features don't look *that* much alike, and yet they're definitely of a type: skin, hair, eyes, and smile.

Suddenly . . . this isn't funny at all.

52

The next day, my father is still in the house so I eat breakfast with him before heading to school. In the main office, I enjoy the *hell* out of making the secretary change my schedule. Now I have classes I can be excited about, and maybe if I push, I can still get into a school with a decent science department. After all the weird shit that's happened, I kind of want to study neurology now instead of bioengineering.

All things considered, my mood is bright as I step into the hall. The silence hits me first, and then I notice how everyone is parting like the Red Sea. Men in uniform make their way toward me, each step measured like they're moving to the unheard strains of a funeral march. My phone pings, but as I check it, I already know.

I know.

The message from Oscar is succinct. *They found out it's you.*

Part of me wonders how they put it together or if Creepy Jack confessed. Either way it doesn't matter. I don't move, just wait, until the policemen surround me as if I'm a flight risk. But when the oldest one speaks, it's in a gentle voice. "We need you to come with us, Miss Frost. We have some questions."

In my heart I know nothing about this will be gentle, so his approach feels like a lie. It would be better if they slapped me up front and gave me the scarlet letter now. Only it wouldn't be an A; in our world, it would be an S for slut. Good girls don't mess around like that, good girls don't get hurt.

"I wonder what she did," someone whispers.

Soon it'll probably be "She deserved it" or "She was asking for it." They'll dissect my behavior and the clothes I wear, like anything can be classified that way. The world is more complicated than that. Most of all, I hate that some of them will think Morgan is a victim. She would despise that, even if it's true.

Quietly I follow them out to the waiting car. They put me in back, but they're careful to explain, "You're not in any trouble. Don't be frightened."

I'm not. I'm numb instead. Since I asked Oscar to turn in the pictures, I've been waiting for the other shoe to drop. Now I finally get to see how bad this gets. A phrase pops into my head: *For the guilty to be punished, the innocent must be hurt.*

The officers talk quietly in the front seat, as if they know I must be handled with kid gloves or my father will sue them down to skin and bones. That's probably true, but I think he will care more about the shame-stains this affair leaves behind than any real damage to me. Sometimes I think he sees me as property, like a car or a lamp. It reminds me of a movie I saw, where the women were literally owned, but they rebelled and wrote WE ARE NOT THINGS on the wall.

I'm writing it over and over in my mind as they take me to the station. The silver-haired one says, "We tried to get in touch with your father but his secretary said he's in an important meeting and took a message. But don't worry, I'm sure he'll come soon."

Story of my life.

We shake hands like this is a social occasion. The older one is Officer Danby. His partner is Officer Gutierrez. Neither one can meet my gaze without twitching away. They see me as a pathetic, damaged girl, and the weight of their discomfort makes everything worse. I'm pretty sure their victim-sensitivity trainer didn't mean for them to treat me like a broken vase.

After seating me in an interview room, they offer tea and stale pastries. I decline. They're clearly stalling. Because they don't know what to do with a quiet girl who understands that her father is not coming. The cops haven't figured this out yet because that's what parents do; they drop everything and run. They run with arms open for hugs and they whisper, "It'll be okay." At least that's what Liv's parents would've done. There would've been yelling, too, and some angry words and tears and more hugging, anything but silence.

Silence is death.

My chest hurts. I won't cry. I won't. I told Oscar I understood how bad it could get and this is only the beginning. If this is public knowledge now, school will be a nightmare. I breathe out, in, out again, studying the specks on the table. Randall Frost's behavior is puzzling.

But it's not like he's my father.

Not really.

Maybe he's honestly *in a meeting.*

An hour ticks away and finally Officer Danby says, "What would you like to do, Miss Frost? We can wait for your father. We can go pick him up. We can—"

"Can we just get this over with?" I'm aware that since I'm only seventeen and a half, I'm probably supposed to have a guardian with me for this interview, but the idea of going over the details with Randall Frost in the room makes me want to throw up.

"All right, we'll do what we can to expedite." The older cop hurries out.

I check my phone. There are four local gossip sites already running the headline "Frost Tech Heiress Unveiled . . ." or some variant IDing me as Creepy Jack's lover. My heart pounds so loud and hard it feels like it's coming from my throat. As I'm about to shut my cell off, it pings.

Clay: *You okay?*

I guess he's heard.

But before I can reply, a woman in a wrinkled suit comes in with the older cop. She has *social worker* written all over her. She must be my parental stand-in to make sure I'm not abused by the system. The recorder comes out, along with pens and pencils. And the questions, they are endless. Invasive. Sometimes insulting, even if they don't mean to be.

"Yes, I was fifteen. Yes, it was consensual."

As it turns out, Morgan wasn't old enough to consent. Even if she said yes, it doesn't count. The two cops talk in hushed tones, supposedly out of my earshot, about statutory rape and child enticement charges. Since I agree that Creepy Jack needs to be punished, I let the words wash over me like vindication. If I suffer, so will he.

More questions follow. I answer everything. I can't always give them dates but sometimes I can. This is normal, the social worker says. She tries to show empathy with a kind expression, but the throbbing between my eyes makes it impossible for me to appreciate her efforts. We break for lunch, which I can't eat for an encyclopedia of reasons, then they resume the interrogation.

"Are you willing to testify?" Officer Gutierrez finally asks.

"It may be difficult," the social worker adds.

I nod.

Whatever Morgan intended initially, this is what I'm doing with her plan. She was too tired to see this through, so I'll carry it for her and for every girl who ever got her head screwed up by a distant father and then went looking for some man, any man, to fill the silence.

Everything passes. I can do this.

"That's all we need for now, Miss Frost." Officer Gutierrez tells me a bunch of legal stuff about how the case will proceed and what I can expect next, but I just want to leave.

"We'll take you home now."

I take that as my cue and stand. "My car's still at school. If you could drive me there, that would be great."

It's so late that there shouldn't be anyone around. Even the extracurricular activities will be over. The cops agree to do that, but they want to escort me home. I'm not sure why, maybe to protect me in case Creepy Jack tries something or maybe if the paparazzi descends on Renton. This *is* a pretty juicy scandal, since I'm underage. I don't argue; it's taking all my energy to stay calm and to pretend I don't feel violated by all those questions. I saw judgment in their faces as I admitted to motel meetings and sneaking out late at night.

My daughter would never, they're thinking. *She's a good girl. Shit like this doesn't happen to good girls.*

Except it does, and they don't want us to talk about it. We're supposed to sweep it under the rug and take prescription medication and make eye contact with people who silently, secretly hurt us. How many dinners have I eaten with my father and Jack Patterson? How many? Nobody ever looks directly at the woman sobbing hysterically on the sidewalk, right? People circle wide and pretend it's not happening.

I can do this. One breath at a time.

53

I ride in silence back to my car. The cops don't talk either. They may be worried about going up against Jack Patterson, who's associated with the most powerful people in the state, but maybe his connections will desert him now that the shit has hit the fan. Maybe he's sweating alone in his office because nobody will take his calls. Then I think of his wife and children and now I truly *am* ashamed because they didn't do anything, but they must be suffering, too.

My phone shows me more awful. A conservative pundit is calling me the Lolita Peach who tempted a good man to his downfall and his chorus is gaining support online. On the site, they've posted shots of me in a short skirt, revealing long legs and smooth skin. I don't even know where this picture came from, but it makes me look like sex on a stick.

What red-blooded man would refuse her? Pyro99 asks.

I'd bone her, TedHead adds.

Way to go, JP! If there's grass on the field, play ball. From Anonymouse.

Okay, I'm done with the Internet. I switch my phone off. Part of me hoped there would be something from my dad, but his silence is . . . ominous, like I'm being silently disinherited. Of course, even if that's true, I have enough in my accounts to pay for college, which is way more than most people have when they're kicked out.

It will be okay.

When the police car pulls into the school lot, my blue Bug looks lonely. My heart thaws a little when I see Clay propped against the hood. The officers cut me nervous looks as I climb out of the back, once the older one opens the door.

"Do you know him?" Gutierrez asks.

Clay takes two steps forward. "I'm her boyfriend."

The joy rocket takes flight, dulling my headache. But maybe he's just saying that because otherwise our relationship is impossible to explain.

"Will you make sure she gets home all right?" Danby, this time.

"Of course." Clay takes the keys from my nerveless hands and tucks me into the passenger side.

"We'll be in touch."

I shut the door, forestalling whatever else they might have said. For now I've given all I can to law and order. Clay starts the car and drives, but not toward my house.

"Your place?" I ask.

"When I saw the news and you didn't answer me, I drove by your house. It's insane out there. Like, four deputies are on scene trying to keep reporters away from the gate."

"We'll probably have to contract some private security," I say.

But maybe not. There's always that school in Austria. If I'm gone, I doubt the reporters will bother my dad. They want more shots of the Lolita Peach, not a middle-aged man. Or maybe they want my side of the story, so they can cut and paste the most salacious bits.

"I don't care what you did," he says. "Or why you did it. Just know, you don't deserve any of this."

Those words feel like balm on a sunburn that was about to

cook me alive. I take my first deep breath all day and let them sink in. But I still feel different than I did yesterday, as if strangers are gnawing at pieces of me, leaving . . . less, somehow. As if sensing I need a distraction, Clay touches my cheek.

I glance over at him. "What you said back there . . . did you mean it? Or was that just so I could get away?"

He hesitates a fraction too long. "Right now you need me more than Nathan."

"Screw that," I growl. "And you. I'm not a bird with a broken wing. Let me be crystal clear—if you're here because you feel *sorry* for me, then stop the car and get out."

He doesn't. Ignoring me, he drives all the way to his house. But that only makes me madder. I want to fight with him, and that's probably not fair because I know damn well that I have a day of feeling powerless to work off; Clay is just here.

He's the only one who is.

That deflates me as he pulls down the alley and parks by the back porch. Then he unfolds the tarp he used to coddle his Corvair with and covers my VW. I realize he's worried about someone spotting the car. Even after I yelled at him, he's still trying to protect me.

"I'm sorry," I whisper.

He smiles then. "It would be weird if you were all sunshine today."

I understand then why he was hesitant to define things between us. Not because of pity or whatever, but . . . this just isn't the time. Things are messed up, both because of Nathan and Creepy Jack, and my emotions won't let me think straight.

"Let's go inside." Maybe I'm paranoid, but standing between the two small houses in Renton's low-rent district is making me feel exposed. My entire body is a raw nerve.

"I'll make you something to eat."

"Thanks."

He fixes scrambled eggs and beans, more than I've had all day. I love that my allergies are second nature to him now; he never offers me stuff I can't eat. The shakes subside as I devour the food. Processing the proteins takes longer but I'll feel better than if I'd just slammed some candy instead.

"No problem."

"Shouldn't you be at work?" I realize aloud.

"I called in. The shop can manage without me for a day." Clay piles my plate and cup in the sink and then leads me to his room. Due to the shotgun design, there's only one window and he draws the curtain. "Better?"

"For now. I'm trying not to think of tomorrow or the day after. Or the trial. When I turned over the photos, I said I knew what I was in for . . . but maybe I didn't. Maybe you can't really understand until you're swinging on the meat hook."

What I love most about Clay is that his eyes are still steady. He doesn't veer away from my face, and he reaches out to touch me like he's sure it's still okay, and I won't come apart in his hands like a china doll that broke in shipping. I'm not all glass dust and shards of regret; I'm hurting, but I'm not *ruined*. Things get ruined, not people.

"Sometimes shit is worse than we expect. Sometimes it's better. And sometimes when you're trekking through a muddy field, you find wildflowers." From the sweetness of his smile, I get that's a metaphor for his life . . . and meeting me.

I've never been anyone's sudden, secret beauty before. The barbed wire in my chest relaxes, so I can breathe a little better. When he pulls me into his lap, I know this isn't a sex moment. This is simple human contact, and I've never needed it more. No matter what happens from here on out, I will always, always treasure the fact that Clay loved me even for a minute.

He kisses my temples, my brows, my chin. I don't offer my mouth, but it's impossible not to snuggle closer. Our bodies were

made for this. I touch him like my license for it is about to ex-
pire, tracing the lines of his jaw, cheekbones, feathering across
his forehead. Clay closes his eyes, but the peace doesn't last long
enough.

Nathan breaks the silence with a scornful laugh. "Oh look,
it's the Lolita Peach. How much do you think they'd pay for my
personal encounter?"

Clay is on his feet in an instant, one arm around me protec-
tively. "Nathan." The name sounds like shots fired.

I step away because I'm not doing this. Whatever's eating Nathan, I no longer care, nor do I have the energy to fight with
him or plead for mercy, which might be what he wants, especially after the shit I said about our hook-up.

"Do what you want," I say, turning to Clay. "Thanks for being there for me."

For me, there's no escape from Morgan's life. Randall Frost
will *not* discuss my scandal in a police station; it will happen
behind closed doors. Considering what surely awaits, I don't
want to leave, but I can't put it off forever.

It's time to go home.

54

When I arrive, the estate entrance is miraculously free of reporters. I wonder if the deputies threatened to write them all tickets for blocking the public road or maybe my father used his connections to get them removed. It wouldn't surprise me if he could mobilize the National Guard. Quaking, I press a button and the iron gates swing open. Part of me suspected they might already be reprogrammed.

As usual, I drive up slowly and park in the garage but nothing about this homecoming feels normal. All the cars are present, so I know my father is home. My unease grows. The strangeness is only exacerbated when I step into the dark house and call out, but nobody answers. Usually Mrs. Rhodes comes looking for me, and dinner should be cooking by now. It's past six.

Exploring the downstairs, I feel like an intruder. Each room is pristine, but all the lights are off. Finally I tap on the door to the study and receive a quiet, "Come in."

Shit. He's in here.

After a steadying breath, I open the door. No lamps have been switched on, so the room is all shadows. With the last glimmers of the sunset shining through the windows, I can make out my father at his desk. His laptop is closed, however, and he doesn't seem to be working. It's probably not a good sign that he's just sitting in the dark.

What am I even supposed to say?

"I'm sorry," is what comes out.

Though if he asked me, I couldn't say for what. For shaming him, making bad choices, or sullying my own good name? For at least a minute, though it seems like ten times longer, he nurses the silence like a strong drink.

"I gave Wanda the night off," he tells me.

Really, it feels more like a warning. *No one will be coming to save you.*

"Oh." The silence is deep and wide, a chasm I can't cross, even with climbing equipment.

"You. And Jack," he finally grits out.

His teeth are metal gears and his mouth is a machine that wants to grind my flesh to meat and my bones to splinters and dust. There are no words for the anger and disappointment and downright revulsion that slam into me. From head to toe, I tremble because I think I knew this was coming. Morgan had *so* many secrets, and she hugged them to her chest like body armor.

Why didn't you tell me?

He should care if I'm all right. Why doesn't he?

But he's staring at me like I'm something he found on the bottom of his shoe. No, that's not quite right. There's also raw anguish and confusion, but I can't understand that expression. This is . . . I don't know. I can't make sense of it. If he comes toward me, I'll run. This doesn't feel right. Everything about it echoes with wrongness.

"Anyone but him," he says in a monotone. "It could be anyone but him. Even that worthless Claymore boy. I tolerated him, didn't I? So why Jack?" But it's a rhetorical question, I can see he doesn't want an answer. "It's always Jack. Just like your mother."

My mother is dead.

Randall Frost should be angry at Patterson for betraying their friendship and taking advantage of me. He should be *shocked*. But there never was a bond between them; I see that now. Their association was more a matter of "keep your friends close and your enemies closer."

"It was a mistake," I whisper.

But that doesn't appease him. "He's a *monster*. I tried so hard to keep this from you, but I suppose it doesn't matter now."

"Why doesn't it?"

You should run now. Morgan's voice echoes in my head. *Run.*

Perfume fills the room, that overwhelming scent of citrus and flowers, and by the wild look in his eyes, he smells it too. "Get out," he snarls, but I don't know if he's talking to me, or the ghosts. I'm afraid to find out.

The mansion is huge, so maybe I can hide long enough for help to arrive. The conviction rises that there will be terrible consequences for the way I've dishonored the family name, some attempt to cleanse the stain I've become. Any moment he'll say, *I'd rather not have a daughter like you.* I need to call the nice officers, who would be so surprised that the greatest threat to me is already inside the house.

"She was leaving us," he tells me in a broken voice. "Running to Jack . . . because of the baby. I begged her to stay. I said I'd do anything. I offered to acknowledge the child as mine, if she only promised not to see him again."

Oh shit. He knew. About the affair, about the baby that wasn't his.

All of my calculations tip over, spread sideways like spilled wine. My heart hammers so loud I can hear the tympanic echo in my eardrums. It nearly deafens me, though not enough to drown out what he's saying. His voice is relentless.

"But she still packed a bag. She said I didn't know how to love—that all I cared about was the company and my image. I didn't mean to hurt her." His voice drops to a whisper, tempting me to move closer.

But I don't. I can't. Fear has frozen my feet to the marble tiles. Hearing his final confession probably doesn't promise me a bright future. But he doesn't need me to contribute to this conversation; he's been waiting ten years to tell someone.

"I only wanted to stop her from leaving. That's all. My car scraped hers and she veered off the road. Morgan, when she realized I wouldn't let her go, she *sped up*. She chose death over staying with me. With us."

"Ten years ago, you were driving a silver BMW," I whisper.

He doesn't acknowledge that, but I remember the damage note from the body shop. I *did* find evidence, but I didn't realize it. And maybe what he's saying is true, or she panicked when the tree came hurtling at her, hitting the gas instead of the brake. Or possibly, he's twisted everything in his head so he's not responsible for her death. I'll never be sure what happened on that deserted road, if he murdered her or if it was an accident.

I only know he did his best to cover it up all these years. That doesn't speak of innocence.

"I could've lived with anything else," he says. "But not you and Jack. Not Jack and *my daughter*."

Once more I'm reduced to property. Jack's lover. Randall's daughter. It's like it doesn't even occur to him that I'm a person.

As he stares at me, something crystalizes in his gaze and then he unlocks the drawer I failed to get into when I searched his office. Out comes a small box. He opens it and produces a gun. I don't know what kind because it's dark and weapons aren't my thing. I turn to run then, but the click of the safety being removed stops me in my tracks.

I'm afraid to face him. So I don't see what happens next.

I only hear him whisper, "Don't tell, Morgan. You can never tell."

The gun goes off.

I scream then, and life floods back into my locked arms and legs. I stumble toward the desk and find my father slumped over. There's not as much blood as the movies lead you to believe when a man shoots himself in the head with a small-caliber pistol. Before I touch him, I know he's dead.

My knees collapse, dumping me on the floor nearby. There are pictures in my head now, things I didn't want to remember. Morgan sensed how her father found it hard to look at her after her mother died. There were no hugs, no tenderness. Despite what I read, I'm sure—the situation with Creepy Jack wasn't how she tried to frame it. That wasn't her plan, only what *happened* to her. Lonely girl, disturbed man, plus the slow, awful seduction of it, and her love-hate relationship with him, the sense of never being able to fill her mother's shoes—I understand why she couldn't hold on, why it was too much. Her whole life was an open wound, wrapped in red cellophane so nobody could ever see her bleed.

Not even me.

She was so, so alone. And I failed her. That message from beyond I found on her computer? It was a sign she was thinking about the end, and that she wanted people to hate instead of pity her if they read how cold she was in her own words. But she wasn't.

The tears fall in a heaving rush; I sob until I can't breathe.

It's over, everything is over.

55

Eventually, I dial for help because I can't stay on the floor forever. While this feels like the end of the world, it isn't. I have to go on.

The police come half an hour later. People ask me questions and they take pictures.

Hours later, county officials take my father's body away and ask if there's anyone I can call. Normally they'd probably send a social worker, but the police have already notified my father's next of kin—obnoxious cousins, who live an hour away and arrive sooner than I want. It's one in the morning and family is still pouring in, people I haven't seen since I was twelve.

The women hug and pat me too much and say things like, "Of course we don't mind packing up to take care of you. Just say the word and we'll stay as long as you need."

But in their eyes I can see them appraising the value of the house, the land, the furniture. They have no interest in me; they just want to live here. I'm the mistress of this place, but I don't want that either. Once the technical work is done and the authorities leave, I retreat to my room and lock the door. None of this seems real. But I pinch myself and it hurts, so I'm not dreaming. *He's really gone.*

I think about his girlfriend and how she'll feel when news reaches her. But she can't know, she can't possibly know that she's a substitute—like Creepy Jack, my father was obsessed with a dead woman for more than ten years. Maybe now Lucy Ellis-Frost can finally rest in peace.

Someone taps at my door, but I ignore it. Finally one of the cousins says, "I'll just leave this macaroni and cheese outside. Have it when you're hungry."

Dumbass. I can't eat that. Plus, it's two in the morning. These are the people who want to take care of me. Probably they're hoping that I'll die of grief, then they can start legal proceedings on the estate. I doubt any of these relations figure in the will; they're just vultures hoping for a chance to chew some tender meat off this carcass.

Sitting on my bed, numb, it occurs to me that Morgan finally got the answers she wanted. If it wasn't for her involvement with Creepy Jack, her father probably wouldn't have cracked. It was like she found the perfect lever for his psyche without even realizing it. I wonder if she would've pushed forward, though, if she'd known how it would end.

Maybe for her, it feels like poetic justice.

Me? I'm just exhausted and confused.

Eventually I pass out in my clothes and wake up at eleven the next morning. School is a distant dream. Between the Lolita Peach thing and my father's suicide, the administrators probably expect me to take some time off.

Showering takes all my energy the next day. Mrs. Rhodes lets herself in with a key, and God, I'm glad to see her. Even if she's only here because I pay her, I'll gladly double it if she can clear the idiots out of my house. She perches on my bed and puts a hand on my arm.

"I won't ask if you're okay." Her common sense feels like pure oxygen after breathing carbon monoxide until I nearly died of it. "What can I do?"

"Get rid of everyone."

"Already did. One of your awful cousins was already fingering the china."

It's good to know I'm not the only one repulsed by my distant relations. My mom had a brother but he died young and my dad was an only child, so I've only got great aunts and uncles, plus their offspring. I'm so relieved that Mrs. Rhodes shooed them out. At this point I should probably think of her as Wanda, but it seems more respectful this way.

"Thanks."

"I made your favorite this morning . . . oatcakes and honey, Silk yogurt, fresh fruit."

"That sounds really good. I'll get dressed and come down."

"Is there anything else I can do?"

"Not really. I just have to ride it out."

This will add fuel to the flames, making the story even juicier. I can see the headlines now: "Tech Magnate Driven to Suicide by Sex Scandal." But there's no way any reporter could ever discover what I know. My father told me, only me, before shooting himself in the head. I hear the gunshot again and it makes me flinch. Soon, the numbness and shock will wear off, and then . . . I don't know how I'll feel.

I was a little surprised to wake up this morning, still alive, still remembering what it was like to be Liv, but remembering more of Morgan's life, too. The scientist in me wanted concrete answers, but I don't think there are any, at least nothing provable.

Mrs. Rhodes is watching me, worry creasing her brow. "Morgan?"

"I'll be down soon."

"All right, I'll set the table."

Breakfast is a quiet meal, but it would be worse if she filled the kitchen with nervous chatter. Finally I say, "You must be wondering about your job."

"A little," she admits.

"I don't know what provisions my father made in his will. After ten years, I hope he left you something."

She shrugs like that's not her immediate concern. "I can always find work. Do you have any idea who he picked as your guardian?"

I shake my head. "He didn't talk to me about it. I just hope it's not any of the cousins."

"You'll find out soon enough, I suppose. The lawyer called. He'll be reading the will tomorrow. And I notified the same funeral home who handled your mother's services, I hope that's all right. They're taking care of things, but they may have questions about your preferences."

"Whatever we did for my mom is fine," I say, because I just can't deal with this.

I want to run away.

This can't be my new reality; it can't.

As I'm finishing breakfast, someone rings the bell from the front gate. I peer at the intercom screen and see a cluster of reporters banging at a familiar car. Liv's mom is yelling at the camera crew blocking her way while several deputies fail to wrangle the crowd. I definitely want *her*, but I don't understand why she's here.

"She saw the news," Mrs. Rhodes explains. "And she called earlier. I said she was welcome. She's like a second mother to you, right? Or . . . am I wrong?"

Bless you, Wanda Rhodes.

My eyes tear up. "No, that's exactly right. Thank you."

"You're saying that a lot lately." But she smiles at me, more kindness than I've ever had in this house.

I watch the screen as my mother inches her car forward until we can shut the gate behind her. The reporters shout in frustration, but she's already driving toward the house. Before I can stop myself, I run to meet her like she's the one coming home after a long absence.

"Morgan," she says, climbing out of the car.

Spoken with such tenderness, the name turns my heart over like a key in a lock, and the tears I've been collecting stream down my cheeks. She's not even as tall as I am now, but her arms still feel perfectly right when she pulls me into them. For endless moments we stand before the fountain and she just rocks me without asking anything at all.

Eventually I stop crying and she shepherds me back inside. I'm not sure what I expect, but when I sit down, she takes both my hands. "This may come as a shock, but a few years back, your father had us sign some documents. He was worried about you if something happened to him and he thought you'd be happiest with Liv." Her smile dims a little. "Nobody could've imagined it would happen like *this*."

"Are you saying that you agreed to be my guardians?"

She nods. "It's one of those events you plan for, just in case."

For a moment, I'm so bright and hopeful. Does this mean I can live with Mom, Dad, and Jason? It won't be exactly the same but we can be a family again. Sort of. But something in her expression tells me it won't be that simple.

"But . . ." I prompt.

"We're not equipped to look after you, given the current situation. There are no gates at our house to protect you from the media, and after everything you've been through in the last few months, I don't think you can continue without help. It's not reasonable."

I still. "What do you mean by 'help'?"

As she produces a brochure for a posh, private facility, she registers my resistance. "Morgan, honey, it's not a judgment. There's no shame in therapy. But you need to talk to someone about how you feel . . . and you should do it in a place where they can keep you safe."

56

At last I come to the place I've been running from all along.

I've been at Riverglen for a week—since the day after the funeral—and this place is nothing like I feared. Here, they specialize in discreet treatment for the rich and famous. My roommate, Alison, is an heiress from New Hampshire who can't stop pulling out her own hair. She also cries in her sleep.

They took away my phone so I can focus on healing and dealing with my trauma, so I don't know what's going on in the world. Today, they're allowing me fifteen minutes on the Internet, filtered and supervised, of course. I take a seat at the computer in the lounge while the aide smiles at me. Nobody is harsh; in fact, it's peaceful. My room is basically like a dorm.

I think about e-mailing Clay, but what would I even say? So instead I skim gossip sites. They're still writing about the Lolita Peach, now sequestered at a "rehab facility," so people probably think I have an addiction problem. Public opinion has turned against me, hard, as people seem to be blaming me for my father's suicide.

Don't tell, Morgan. You can never tell.

I've added it to the list of my many secrets, the things I can't disclose to the therapists. While it's pleasant here, this is also exhausting because I have to say just enough, express the precise amount of shock and grief. I need the right notes in my file when

I go. I have to swallow all the wrong words, all the confidences that I'm half tempted to dump on kind-eyed strangers.

I have some e-mails from Oscar and the art kids, but I don't have the time to reply properly, so I just send them all emojis and hope knowing I'm alive is enough. Just as I'm about to shut down the browser, a linked article catches my eye, of the "if you liked this, you may be interested in . . ." variety. I click and bring up a story about Jack Patterson. *New Charges Filed as Other Victims Come Forward. Amber Nelson, 18, alleges that her affair with the assemblyman began when she was just fourteen, engaged to look after his two small children.* The case is no longer just about him and me.

"Time's up," a cheerful voice tells me.

Head reeling, I step away from the computer and wander to a chair near the window. The grounds are lush and green. I can go out during free time, but at the moment, my legs might not hold me. Though I've heard "there's never only one victim," I always thought Creepy Jack was interested in me because of my mother, which made him a special kind of pervert, and I don't know if it makes it better or worse that he just likes young girls.

Another week passes in group sessions, art therapy, one-on-one counseling. My lead therapist is a thirtysomething woman with sun-damaged skin and red hair that comes from a bottle. I'm supposed to call her Samantha but she's Dr. Lasky in my head. Aloud I don't call her anything, and she's frustrated by my indifference in our sessions.

"You're repressing," she tells me. "It's okay to cry."

But I don't want to do that in here—in her office with the reference books perfectly organized and the knickknacks on her desk that speak to her interest in native art. The chairs are comfortable and the air smells like vanilla. Normal people might be able to unburden themselves to her and go back to their rooms feeling light as air, but I've only ever been able to do that with one person.

I miss Clay.

"I know. I'm sorry." I talk about my mother and how much I miss her. That wins me the most points. And then I end with how my father never seemed to get over her death and that even his latest girlfriend looked like my mom. "Why did he . . . ? I'm not enough?"

That's the trigger question that gets me all kinds of reassuring language. It's not my fault, Dr. Lasky says. My father was clinically depressed or he never would've done that, especially in front of me. She talks about how he was probably overwhelmed with guilt over failing to protect me, and that sometimes people make choices that don't accurately reflect their true feelings while they're dealing with heavy issues.

I muster a smile and let myself be comforted. "Thank you."

Dr. Lasky recommends some books I should read that are shelved in the library. Then she makes a note on her chart as our session ends. "See you tomorrow."

It's time for my fifteen minutes on the computer again. I have an in-box full of emojis this time, not just from the art kids, but some of the science club kids, too. Even Arden Fox, who dressed up as Goku because of me, sends one. I sense Oscar's instigation here, but I don't mind. Maybe the fact that they sent these means the whole school doesn't hate me. That's more than I expected out of this mess.

There are also two messages that surprise me, one I hoped for and another I didn't. The e-mail from Clay has the subject line *It'll be okay* and a single word for the body: *Promise.* I'm frankly astonished that Nathan sent anything after the way we left it, but his reads *I'm an asshole* as the subject and then, *Clay made me understand some things. I'm really sorry, I had no idea what you were dealing with.*

You still don't.

Nobody does, except Clay. And I trust him not to tell. This is the last hurdle I have to leap on the way to a normal life. I reply with random smileys to the art and science groups; it takes longer for Clay and Nathan. But I don't have a ton of time, so I simply say what's true. *I miss you.* With Nathan, I just accept his apology and add, *We're cool.*

With five minutes left on my computer time, I check the headlines. Since I'm in Riverglen, the police haven't updated me. I'm floored to read, "Plea Bargain Results in Two-Year Sentence for Former Assemblyman." It looks like Creepy Jack confessed, cut a deal, and got his sentence reduced. It's not *nearly* long enough for what he's done, and there will be no trial. Part of me is so relieved it hurts; I didn't really want to take the stand and answer those relentless questions and have the defense rip my psyche to shreds. This also means the media will settle down sooner instead of later.

This time I don't read the comments and just close the browser before the aide can pertly advise me to move along. I celebrate by heading out to the courtyard where a few other patients are basking in the sun. I stroll among the flowers that are supposed to soothe me. A lot of them have already died, though. Soon winter frost will leave the grounds bare.

Eventually I have to go back inside for group and I talk about my mixed feelings when it's my turn to share. "I feel bad that I'm relieved, you know? Because he might have been punished harder at the trial and I know there were other girls . . ."

"Or he might've gotten off entirely," Alison says. "At least this way he's registered as a sex offender, he's done in politics, and he has to face what he did."

Dr. Lasky is nodding. "You can't torture yourself with 'what if,' Morgan. You were brave and you did exactly enough. It's time to let go."

That's the best advice I've gotten here. The next day in my private session, I tell her that I'm ready to go home. She nods and agrees to process the paperwork. Surely I've been here long enough for people to believe I'm okay. And it *has* helped. The isolation was good for me, allowing me time to decompress and stop obsessing over what strangers think of me.

In the end, none of that matters. It only matters how *I* feel.

57

Two days later, the whole Burnham family picks me up at Riverglen. *This is so strange.* As I climb into the backseat of my other dad's Prius, I glance over at Jason, who has earbuds in, playing something on his Nintendo. I'm tempted to flick the back of his head like Liv would've but I'm wary of startling him.

"We cleaned Liv's room out for you," Mom says.

"Thanks. And sorry. You probably weren't ready."

"No, it gave me the push I needed." She's smiling, trying to be cheerful, but I can see that this is hard. They probably never imagined that the papers they signed out of goodwill would end with them responsible for someone else's kid.

But I'll be off to college in less than a year. *Ten months.* For me it feels like a reprieve, a chance to say an extended farewell to my family before I go.

"Welcome to the Burnham Group," my dad says. "There are no housekeepers where you're headed so you'd better get used to chores."

"Grant," Mom chides.

Their familiar banter makes me smile. "It's fine. It's not like I never visited you guys before. I know the drill."

Jason still hasn't said a word to me, but he didn't talk that much to Liv either, unless she forcibly removed his electronics and put her face right next to his. He doesn't know me well enough for that, yet. Maybe one day he'll look on me as a foster sister.

Maybe. And maybe someday my parents will look on me affectionately, like I'm almost a replacement for the daughter they lost. That hope is enough to keep me going.

The drive takes three hours and they don't pester me to chat. No reporters ambush us as we pull into the driveway. A rush of homesickness hits me in a drowning wave; I know every inch of this house, every smell, every stain. I can't wait to go inside.

"I hope you'll be happy here," Dad says gruffly.

"I'm sure I will be."

My clothes are already in the closet when I get to my old room, courtesy of Mrs. Rhodes. My mom explains, "We're leaving the housekeeper at the estate for now . . . as a caretaker. As your guardian, I attended the reading of your father's will, and he left almost everything to you. Stocks, bonds, controlling interest in Frost Tech—"

"Just tell me how much you need for room and board." Offering to pay for my keep is the least I can do, but she reacts like I slapped her.

"Morgan, no. Liv would want us to take care of you. I'll leave you to get settled. In case you forgot, dinner is at six, and I'll need you to set the table."

"No problem. But . . . what should I call you?"

"Jeannie is fine," she says with a tentative smile.

I wave as she heads down the hall toward the kitchen. Closing the door, I take in the changes to my old room. They've repainted so it's pale cream and there are new curtains, new bedding in abstract silver-and-gray patterns. Jeannie left all the mementos of my friendship with Liv, though really it's a monument to the time before—before two became one. As for the décor, Morgan would've liked it, I think. Since the gun went off, I haven't sensed her at all or smelled her mother's perfume.

The unopened bottle of Clinique Happy is on my dresser like a reminder.

Was it enough? I finished what you started.

More or less.

I plug in my laptop, marveling at small freedoms I took for granted before Riverglen. Now I can waste as much time as I want on the Internet. My phone is back in my possession, too, but I've gotten used to the silence. Online, there are more updates on Creepy Jack's prison sentence and other officials he may have implicated. The charges are piling up.

Clicking another link, I find updates on another mystery. They're finding bodies now, the girls who went missing, the ones who look like me or maybe more accurately, my mother. No new disappearances have been registered since my father died. I remember the bloody friendship bracelet in Morgan's room and try not to imagine where and how she found it. There are questions unanswered and I wonder now how much time he spent with his girlfriend and what might have happened to her if she eventually disappointed him?

I'm better off without these answers. Morgan only meant to find out what happened to her mother; she couldn't have imagined how deep the secret river ran. As for me, I'm done poking around in dark corners. Any debt between Morgan and me, it's discharged.

The world is wide open with the sun shining overhead. It's time for me to stretch, look around, and appreciate the fact that I'm still alive. I completed the mission, and I'm still here. My second shot at life is a gift, not a glitch.

For long moments, I stare at my phone before deciding to turn it on. I'm inundated with missed calls, voice-mail messages, and old texts. No, I'm not interested in selling my story. No, I don't want to be featured on that daytime talk show or help a ghostwriter put together a screenplay. Most of it is awful, so I

delete the rest without reading or listening. But this is starting
to feel like a gauntlet that will eventually end. I've seen the shelf
life of other scandals, and it's not like Creepy Jack was a presi-
dential candidate.

This, too, shall pass.

Once I've cleaned out the junk, I can focus on messages from
people I know. There are a few from Oscar and company; the
science club doesn't have my number. My heart turns over when
I see how many I have from Clay. He must've known I couldn't
reply, and yet as I scroll back, I see he's sent me a message for
every single day I was away.

I'm thinking of you.

I miss you.

I'm waiting for you.

There are eighteen of these texts and I read them like they're
Pulitzer Prize material. By the time I get to the end, today's mes-
sage, my hands are shaking. I'm crying, and I don't know why.
This is what I couldn't do with Dr. Lasky.

Despite tear-blurred eyes, I send back, *I'm home.*

He's probably at work, so I won't hear back for a while. I plug
my phone in and go set the table. That night I spend enough
time with the family in the living room that they won't think
I'm isolating myself in a worrisome way, but inwardly I'm dying
to get back to my cell.

"Are you going to school tomorrow?" Jeannie asks.

"Unless you're planning to homeschool me." It's a joke, but
she's not sure until I smile.

She laughs nervously. "You'll do fine. I think the storm has
passed. There's a state senator who's been caught with a prosti-
tute, so most of the reporters are on that story now."

"Really? That's both awful and reassuring."

At nine, I shower, then head for my bedroom. Jason comes
out to take his turn in the bathroom, and he's not wearing

headphones. He looks at me for a minute and says, "I don't hate that you're here, but don't touch my stuff," before shutting the door in my face.

I'll take it.

Somehow I make myself get dressed and towel off my hair without touching my phone. That fast, I'm thinking of Clay again, and how he took care of me. I'm not as alone as I was back then, but I still want him. Eventually compulsion wins out and I check messages.

To my surprise, I've got five from him.

Text 1: *Can I see you?*

Text 2: *Where are you?*

Text 3: *Mrs. Rhodes said you're not home, is she screwing with me?*

Text 4: *At least tell me if you're okay.*

The last one just reads, *Please,* and it's time-stamped forty-three minutes ago. *Holy shit, seems like he's frantic.* Hurriedly, I type a reply. *Sorry, I'm fine. Really. I'm staying at Liv's house. It's too late tonight, but I'll be in school tomorrow.*

Checking the calendar, I see that it will be Monday. To be honest, I didn't even realize what day it was. Riverglen had basically the same routine, regardless. But that means Clay will be off work.

He sends, *I'll pick you up in the morning.*

Jeannie and Grant may not approve of this, but they're aware Morgan has been dating Clay for a while. They don't know him as well as Nathan, but they'll have to get used to him if he wants to be with me. There's no way to be sure until we talk, of course, but I'm hopeful.

In bed I close my eyes and imagine family dinners with Clay at the table. He's starved of such warmth, more than anyone would believe. In time, maybe we can invite both Clay and Nathan, though I don't want to push since I'm finding my place all over again.

This new beginning doesn't terrify me at all. Rather, it's like a walk down a familiar lane after a long absence, admiring how well the trees have grown.

58

In the morning, I pay more attention than usual to my style. Not original Morgan levels of gorgeous, but more than Liv. And I suppose that basically represents the median I've reached in my new life as a whole. Breakfast is loud and cheerful, just like it was before. Morgan was here enough before that they're not awkward like I feared.

In time, I hope to fill the hole in their hearts. Maybe subconsciously they'll realize that Liv's not entirely gone. My purpose isn't to crack old wounds open. I just want to hollow out a space of my own. True family doesn't need blood ties; at the end of the day, they are the people who love you best, who laugh and cry with you, and who are always watching out the window when you come home.

Jason leaves first to catch the bus and Grant asks me, "Do you need a ride?"

I shake my head. "Clay is picking me up. If it's okay, I'll stop by the estate to get my car after school."

"We don't mind," Jeannie says. "It's not like you can't afford gas and insurance."

I smile. "Thanks for breakfast."

Her answering smile melts into a concerned frown. "Are you sure you want to stay in Renton? Though things have quieted, I can't imagine it'll be easy. There are some great boarding school options. Mrs. Rhodes sent over a packet that your father had put together, before."

There is some charm to the prospect of a fresh start. But I fought so long and so hard to get back here, I *can't* pack my things straight off. "Let's see how it goes. Maybe, if it's awful, as a last resort . . ."

Jeannie nods, obviously reassured. "That's all we can do, take it one day at a time. But let me know if it's too much and I'll help you with the paperwork."

"Deal. See you this afternoon."

To my surprise, she hugs me and kisses my cheek. Bittersweet delight floods me as I step out the front door to find Clay already waiting. He doesn't wait for me to reach him; instead he closes the distance between us at a run and hauls me into his arms, so tight I can hardly breathe. But I don't mind the intensity. His heartbeat hammers into mine like a promise.

"I was wrong," he whispers into my hair. "I don't care who you are. When you left and everything went quiet between us, it felt like dying."

"I'm glad you got your priorities straight. And all I had to do was spend a few weeks in a mental-health facility," I joke.

His grim look says he doesn't find this amusing. "I'm sorry for what I put you through. It's just that . . . giving things up for Nathan is kind of second nature at this point. I'm not doing that anymore."

"Glad to hear it." But a flicker of curtain tells me that Jeannie is watching us; it's kind of nice to have that worry again. It means somebody cares what I'm doing. "But we should find a better place to continue this conversation."

"Right," he says, sheepish, glancing over my shoulder.

Waving in the general direction of the kitchen window, I get in the car and wait for Clay to decide where we're going. He drives to the park near Renton High, an excellent choice as

there aren't many people at this hour, just the occasional jog-
ger or dog walker. We park beneath the spreading branches of
a stately live oak, the shadows granting considerable privacy.

"You were saying . . . ?" I prompt.

"No more yielding to Nathan, disregarding what I want. Plus,
it *is* up to you. And if I'm the lucky bastard, it'd be dumb as hell
to walk away." He takes my hand and flattens it on his heart,
like he did before. "I can't promise you a lot, except that I'll be
around until you don't want me anymore. And I know full well
that you'll be leaving this town before me."

No question I'm going to university. Johns Hopkins is still
an attainable dream, if I play my cards right this year. Yet I can't
resist messing with him a little. "Well, yeah. There's a boarding
school in Austria with my name on it."

His breath hitches, and he closes his eyes as if it hurts to look
at me. "When . . . when are you going?"

"I'm not sure yet. A few things are still up in the air."

"Like what?" he asks hoarsely.

"Whether my boyfriend asks me to stay."

"Huh?" From his expression, he might've just been punched
in the gut. "I'll never be an anchor tying you here when you
don't want to be. I won't ever be the reason your life is small."

I sigh. "You can be such an idiot sometimes."

Comprehension dawns, and he starts to smile when he realizes I'm teasing him. "Oh. Can I change my answer?"

"Please do."

"Then stay. I want to wear that gray suit and dance with you
under a dumb disco ball. I'll see you off to college with a smile
and visit as often as I can. Once Nathan graduates, he's on his
own, and I'll be hot on your heels. No matter where you go, I'll
follow . . . and I'll find a way to chase my dreams wherever you
are."

That may not be realistic but I don't care. Right now it's

exactly what I want to hear. "Remember, your girlfriend is absurdly well-off. I'm sure I can grease the wheels."

As I knew he would, Clay makes a face at this offer. "It's enough to be with you."

"I love you," I whisper, forcing him to lean in to catch the words.

When he does, I kiss him because I'm not the sort of girl who waits around. This morning he tastes of mint and his lips are so hot on mine. His tongue does things that make me squirm, and we kiss for ages, like I don't have to be at school. I run my lips over his jaw, across to his ear, and muss his hair wildly. Nipping gently, I can't control the desire to put my mark on him, this beautiful misunderstood boy with such a strong, lovely heart.

"Okay, that's enough," he finally pants, breathing hard.

"For now." I grin at his lack of composure, reveling in it. For me this is both familiar and brand new.

"Let's get you to school or I'll be tempted to take you home with me. I have the day off and some dirty inclinations."

"Any other day, I might go for that. But I can't get away with skipping. Jeannie will be watching me like a hawk for a while."

"Is that what you call your mom?"

"Yeah."

"You don't plan to tell them . . . and prove it like you did with me?"

I shake my head. "Not yet. I'll play it by ear, see if they notice. Even if they don't, it's all right. I'm in a good place now."

At Riverglen, they would say that I have an undiagnosed mental illness—that I am not Liv and never was. They would say that I've always been Morgan Frost, and I built this elaborate self-delusion to cushion myself from an awful reality and layers of trauma.

But I know who I am and who I used to be. I can't explain

it, but this is what I know to be true: For the first sixteen years, I was Liv Burnham, and she is dead. I will live the remainder of my life as Morgan Frost. Maybe there will come a time when I don't remember with such clarity. Years will blur my recollections until even I think I must've been mistaken . . . or ill.

That doesn't matter either. They say perception is reality, and reality is whatever we can bring ourselves to accept at the time. So reality is relative, just like Einstein's theory.

Clay kisses me once more and starts the car. "You'll be cutting it close."

"I always do."

In a way I wish we'd arrived earlier, but maybe it's better to run the gauntlet from the jump. People will stare and talk; this is inescapable. But I won't be the most interesting aspect of school forever. Everything passes; this is both a comfort and a subtle threat. Spring blossoms turn into ripe fruit that hang heavy and drop, half-rotten, for the birds to eat. Life is an endless cycle, and I am only a small player on a gigantic stage.

Being philosophical helps a little.

"I'll pick you up after school," Clay says, smiling. "I have a surprise planned."

"Looking forward to it."

Bracing myself, I square my shoulders and climb out of Clay's car. This is my first public appearance since my father killed himself.

59

No question people are watching me, whispering, but nobody approaches. The bubble created by Liv's death has widened, like I'm walking in a sphere of mortality.

"Can't believe she came back," someone says, loud enough for me to hear.

"I missed you." Oscar strides toward me, completely magnificent in black. His hair is coifed to perfection, and he's proving that he doesn't give a shit about the rumors. When he gets close, he gives me an actual hug, which is awesome since he's not like that.

But this is theater; he's proving a point.

Soon I'm surrounded by the rest of the group: Emma, Tish, Sarah, Ben, and Eric. They all hug me and form a perimeter. And we're *not* friends because I have a huge house. That was unfair, and I was an asshole for thinking it. As we get closer to the school, I can hardly speak for the gratitude choking me. None of them asks any awkward questions, though I'll talk later, as much as I can.

It seems like the worst is over, when reporters surge at us. A man's holding a video camera and a woman shoves a microphone at me. But before she can get going, more people appear, women who wouldn't be out of place at a church social. They're holding signs in support of poor Jack Patterson and condemning my lack of Christian morals.

The oldest protester screams, "You knew he was married, you *knew!*" and she hauls her arm back. Eric moves faster than I've ever seen him, putting himself between us, and he's the one who gets splattered with whatever she has in that bucket. It smells disgusting, like a combination of mulch and compost.

It's true, I did know. But he knew, too.

From the commentary, I figure the camera is rolling, catching the drama, but I don't feed it. Emma pauses long enough to say, "You people are disgusting," and then she herds me into the school. Security has been notified and they sweep the fundamentalists and the media off the property. They might be waiting when class is over, but I already knew this wouldn't be easy. I might not be the top Internet search anymore, but the world is full of crazy people who have nothing but time and plenty of hate.

After I apologize to Eric, he takes off to use the showers and change into sweats that he keeps for gym. Oscar is watching me like a hawk, as if he expects me to break down. But I'm stronger than that. While I might be scarred, I'm not broken. I'm not ruined. And there's no shame in knowing I made bad choices. Everyone does. There's no such thing as "perfect" in this world, only people who are pretending.

"I'm okay," I tell him. And it's mostly true.

The day isn't easy. There are cruel words and whispers. Some people act like I have a contagious disease, and one guy calls me a slut when I refuse to acknowledge him.

On the bright side, this is the first time I've gotten to attend my new classes, and they're fascinating. I'm really behind, though, thanks to my mental health break. I leave at the end of the day with a huge pile of assignments and a long reading list. I'm looking forward to the normalcy of studying, dates with my boyfriend, and having a curfew. These are small wonders that I will never take for granted again.

After school, I hunt for Isaiah Emerson and apologize for taking so long with his notes.

"It's cool," he says. "You were . . . busy."

Understatement. I don't ask for my bracelet back since I broke our agreement.

Oscar sends Eric out to check the parking lot and he reports that the coast is clear. I promise to invite them over soon. "But I'm at the Burnham house now, so our options are a little more limited."

"It was never your house we liked," Ben tells me.

"I know," I say, smiling.

Though it's completely unnecessary, they walk me out to Clay's car like a guard detachment. Only once Oscar's sure I'm safe does he jog off to catch a ride with Emma's brother. For the small effort I've put in, I have better friends than I deserve. And maybe that's all you need to go on, even when it's tough—that for every asshole who calls you names, there's someone willing to take a slop bucket for you.

Looking bemused, Clay kisses me. "Rough day?"

"A little. They're protective." I glance past him, startled to see Nathan already in the backseat. "That's . . . unexpected."

"He's part of the surprise."

"I'm game." But since I didn't mention this to Jeannie, I call after I buckle up. "Before picking up my car, I'm hanging out with Clay and Nathan. I'll be home by dinnertime."

"Have fun," she says.

So normal. So awesome.

On the way to wherever we're going, I pester the guys for hints, but neither one will tell me anything. I'm grumpy when we pull into the strip mall where Clay works. He glances back at Nathan, who's smiling. I also notice that he's sober, so maybe he's finally dealing with his shit instead of acting like a toddler.

"We're getting tattoos?" I guess, remembering what Nathan said that day in the car.

"It'll be the first design of mine that'll be done in ink," Clay mumbles.

My interest sharpens. "Can I see it?"

"Let's go inside first. Blue is expecting us." I'd swear he's blushing as he helps me out of the car, not that I need it. But it seems like he wants an excuse to touch me.

The shop is just as clean as it was last time. A girl working the front desk smiles a little too brightly at Clay, and I take his hand. Nathan watches this with a faint smirk, but there's no malice in it. Maybe he's immature and more selfish than I realized but he's not awful at the bone.

Oblivious to this microdrama, Clay gets out his sketchbook and shows me what he's created. I fall in love instantly, both because it's beautiful, and because it's a gift from him that I can emblazon on my skin. The design is fairly simple, black ink, stylized letters that read LIV(E), both my name and a reminder of how to greet each day, framed by two black lines that form half a heart around the word.

"Do you like it?" he asks.

"It's perfect."

Clay fills out the forms, occasionally asking a few questions about medical history and immunization. Once that's taken care of, Nathan goes first, choosing to get the tattoo over his heart. Though we're not together, it's impossible to feel nothing. Once it's done, I give him a sideways hug, so as not to irritate his chest. He pats my back.

"Don't get mushy on me, rich girl. This is . . . closure. Before, I guess I just didn't want to accept that she was gone."

I offer a lopsided smile as Clay takes his turn. "You're so sad. If I catch you drinking again, I'll send your ass to rehab."

"Yeah, yeah." But he's smiling.

Twenty minutes later, Clay emerges from the back room with his wrist bandaged. Though we didn't discuss it beforehand, that's where I'm having mine done, too. Blue beckons to me and I head back for my virgin ink. She goes over what I can expect as I relax into the chair. There are three rooms, two of which are occupied, and I can hear the gun already buzzing.

"Are you scared?" she asks.

"Not of this."

"You have a decent pain tolerance?"

I think of dying in that field and nod. "I'd say so."

"Okay, then this shouldn't be a problem. Where do you want this?"

In response I offer my left wrist. She takes care of all the hygiene procedures: cleaning her hands, surgical gloves, mask, sterilizing my wrists. It's all pretty relaxing until she actually gets to work on the design. It hurts more than I expected but with each prick of the needle, it's like she's perforating a boundary. *Before and after—in memory of Liv.*

I close my eyes and ride it out. Eventually the machine stops and I examine her handiwork. Lovely, just like what Clay showed me from his portfolio. Blue cleans the site, takes a photo, and then bandages me up.

"You handled that like a champ," she says with a smile.

"Thanks."

She goes over the after-care instructions and gives me an information sheet, though she must be sure Clay will keep an eye on my wrist, too. I stare at the bandage, thinking, *This is the real grave marker, not the stone my parents put down, and I'll carry it on my skin.*

"He loves you a lot, you know."

I glance up in surprise. "It's mutual."

"I'd take it as a personal favor if you didn't break that boy's heart," she says.

"That's the last thing in the world I'll ever do." It's a promise.

I get a nod. That's the end as far as she's concerned. Blue starts cleaning her equipment as I head out to the waiting area. Clay is pacing, like he thought I'd pass out or something. He stills when I appear. When he wraps an arm around me, it feels possessive . . . but in a good way, like he's saying, *This girl is mine*, to the rest of the world.

And I am his, because I choose to be.

Nathan is already gone, probably to give us some privacy. I give him full credit for knowing what's up as I reach up to kiss Clay. He doesn't let go of me as we stroll out to the car. It's past five, shadows lengthening on the ground.

"I've been thinking . . ." I start.

"About what?"

He pauses beside the car, so different from the Corvair that gave him half of his wild reputation. Clay probably understands better than most how it feels to have strangers talk like they know you. In this world it's rare to find a heart with matching wounds.

"I'm not Liv anymore, but I'm not Morgan either. And I've noticed you don't know what to call me."

"Sorry," he mutters, like this is a fault.

"My middle name is Ellis," I go on. "My mom's maiden name. When I go away to school, I'll probably ask people to call me Elle. If you want, you could start early."

Most people don't get to pick their names. But most aren't reborn into someone else's body. Elle is perfect because it belonged to Morgan but it carries two Ls at its heart to represent Liv, allowing me to be myself, a hybrid of who I am and who

I've been. In a sense, maybe that's true of everyone as they learn and grow and regret things they did before they knew better.

There's a light in his eyes; he likes having a secret name for me. "Okay. Elle."

For that bit of sweetness, I kiss him. That distracts us for ten minutes, until he's breathing hard and I'm glowing. "I was right, wasn't I?"

"About what?" I ask.

"Everything being okay."

I smile. "Better than, actually."

Life is strange, marvelous, and inexplicable. In this moment I feel brand new, like anything is possible. When Clay pulls me close, I believe that maybe—just *maybe*—it is.

After all, I was Liv, then Morgan, and now I'm Elle . . . and against the odds, I have come home.

ACKNOWLEDGMENTS

First, thanks to Whitney Ross for falling in love with this book. She is truly the perfect champion for the work, and she just *gets* me. The entire Tor Teen team has been fantastic and enthusiastic, and I couldn't be more thrilled to see this project come to fruition. Many thanks for all the hard work and dedication!

The idea sprang from a fragment of a dream—four teens joyriding on a summer night—and a Pablo Neruda poem, the one referenced in the epigram. "You Will Remember" is so visceral and evocative that I became obsessed with those four teens, the joyride, and how it changed everything. From that inspiration came the story of forbidden love and a heroine who is torn between brothers.

Next, I need to thank Kate Elliott for her encouragement. She made me believe I could succeed with this story. Her response to an early draft was so lovely and moving that I had a hard time believing she could be talking about *my* book.

I'm also indebted to my writing partner (in other projects), Rachel Caine. Her wisdom and expertise are invaluable, and she gives the *best* advice.

I want to thank the friends and colleagues who keep me strong, including but not limited to: Bree Bridges, Melissa Blue, Nafiza Azad, Elizabeth May, Lish McBride, Allison Pang, Justina Ireland, Annie Bellet, Karuna Riazi, Lilith Saintcrow, Cindy Pon,

Suleikha Snyder, Piper J. Drake, Silvia Moreno-Garcia, Lori M. Lee, and Courtney Milan. If I've forgotten anyone, it's because I'm absentminded, not that your care has gone unnoticed.

My beta readers need a special mention, though I've dedicated this book to two of them. Karen Alderman, Fedora Chen, and Pamela Webb-Elliott cheer me on when I need it most and give great feedback so I can consistently create quality stories.

I also thank my family for putting up with me. I must give special mention to my son, Alek, who often helps me think my way out of thorny plot problems.

Last but never least, I offer my heart to my readers, who've kept the door open for me for more than ten years. Thank you for your faith.